"PEOPLE [...]
WE ARE [...]
FURTHERANCE OF PEACE IN CENTRAL
AMERICA. WHAT YOU ARE SEEING IS
A FAITHFUL TAPED RECORD OF THE
EVENTS THAT TOOK PLACE AT LOGAN
AIRPORT. WE REGRET THAT INNOCENT
PARTIES HAD TO DIE, BUT WE ARE
PREPARED TO DO IT AGAIN, IF
NECESSARY. WE ARE CONTACTING
YOUR PRESIDENT TO INFORM HIM OF
THE SPECIFIC STEPS THAT MUST BE
TAKEN IMMEDIATELY IF THERE IS TO
BE NO REPETITION. ON BEHALF OF
US ALL, LET THERE BE PEACE."

Who had produced this prime-time terror show
on nationwide TV? Whose hand was on the
trigger of the deadliest weapon ever to be
aimed point-blank at America? In a panicked
nation where a President's grip on the reins of
power faltered and a Vice-President trembled
before his testing . . . in a quickening whirlpool
of savage violence and sexual treachery . . .
the search for answers was a race against time
that was running out in a stream of victims'
blood. . . .

STINGER

STINGER

DOUG HORNIG

A SIGNET BOOK

SIGNET
Published by the Penguin Group
Penguin Books USA Inc., 375 Hudson Street,
New York, New York 10014, U.S.A.
Penguin Books Ltd, 27 Wrights Lane,
London W8 5TZ, England
Penguin Books Australia Ltd, Ringwood,
Victoria, Australia
Penguin Books Canada Ltd, 2801 John Street,
Markham, Ontario, Canada L3R 1B4
Penguin Books (N.Z.) Ltd, 182-190 Wairau Road,
Auckland 10, New Zealand

Penguin Books Ltd, Registered Offices:
Harmondsworth, Middlesex, England

First published by Signet, an imprint of Penguin Books USA Inc.

First Printing, June, 1990
10 9 8 7 6 5 4 3 2 1

 REGISTERED TRADEMARK—MARCA REGISTRADA

Printed in the United States of America

PUBLISHER'S NOTE
This is a work of fiction. Names, characters, places, and incidents
either are the product of the author's imagintion or are used ficti-
tiously, and any resemblance to actual persons, living or dead,
events, or locales is entirely coincidental.

This book—and all those to come—
are dedicated to Nancy

1950–1989

May we be worthy of having known her.

ACKNOWLEDGMENTS

First and foremost, I'd like to thank George Pipkin, who supplied the seed idea for this novel with a single prophetic sentence over dinner one night, and who thereafter diligently researched most of the technical details. I couldn't have done without him. Other important data was provided by Dana Hornig, Doug, Sr., and Bernard Haxel. And thanks, too, to those who asked not to be mentioned by name.

PROLOGUE

THE
RECENT PAST

There were only four people at the gravesite. Two were workmen, dressed in dirt-stained bib overalls. The third, the Right Reverend, wore a lightweight dark gray suit with a clerical collar, and was sweating profusely in the August heat.

The fourth man was in his mid-thirties, and he was wearing jeans, a white T-shirt with a tear just under the left shoulder, and blue nylon running shoes. Though not a large man, the well-defined muscles of his torso were visible through the tight-fitting shirt, and his jeans stretched taut over his thighs.

As the man stared at the small, freshly dug hole in the ground, his gray-blue eyes had misted slightly, but otherwise his face gave no hint of the grief that lay like lead in the pit of his stomach.

A breeze swirled up, ruffling the man's hair. The color of white gold and as fine as silk thread, it rested on his head almost tentatively, as if the wind might lift it gently off and carry it a hundred miles before it settled slowly back to earth.

The breeze died and the man looked up from the hole.

He said, "Make it brief, Reverend."

The Right Reverend nodded, secretly grateful. "Man's life on earth is fleeting," he said, "and the ways of the Lord mysterious. Never more so than when His creatures are cut down before their time. We may ask why and not be answered. That is His counsel alone to keep.

"All that we may be given to know is that for His own divine reasons He has seen fit to call this woman Susanna Carson and this child Scott to His bosom. As we commit their bodies to the earth, so we commit their immortal souls to You, Lord. May they rest in peace. Amen."

As the Right Reverend bowed his head and the two

11

workmen leaned on their shovels, the man with the white gold hair stepped forward. In one hand he had a single lily. He threw the flower into the freshly dug hole. It turned end-over-end and settled lightly on the simple wooden box that contained the cremated remains of the dead. In the other hand the man held a brown paper bag. Inside were a number of documents: driver's license, birth certificate, MasterCard, passport, Social Security card, all identifying the bearer as Steve Carson.

The man paused as he looked at the bag, as if trying in some way to fix its image in his mind. Then he sighed. It was a sound that seemed to come from a place as deep as the grave itself. "Carson," he mumbled to himself.

With a jerky motion Steven Kirk threw the bag into the hole. It landed with a crisp rustle of paper and lay on top of the lily. Now Carson was as dead as Scott Craik, the identity Kirk had been using when he met Susanna and after whom his son had been named.

"I'm sorry, Susanna," he said softly to the hole. And then, more softly still, "Scottie." His expressionless mask threatened to crack, but he held onto his control as his final words came out in a hoarse whisper. "Never again."

He nodded to the workmen, and they immediately began shoveling methodically. The first clods of earth made a hollow thud when they hit the box. Then there was only the sound of dirt on dirt.

Without another word Kirk turned and left the cemetery. After passing through a set of arched, ornate wrought-iron gates, he got into a dark blue Buick Skylark and started the engine.

Just down the street, another man was watching. This man had a smoothly shaven, boyish face, an Ollie North haircut and steel-rimmed glasses. He was dressed in a blue seersucker suit. He'd been sitting in his gray Ford for half an hour, with the engine off and the window rolled down. He was not perspiring at all.

The Skylark pulled away from the curb, and the man in the gray Ford nodded once to himself. He had a small notebook in his lap. Underneath the date and the time he wrote: "Kirk buries the wife and child."

That was all Mr. Smith would need to know.

PART I

VEGA

And he doeth great wonders, so that he maketh fire come down from heaven on the earth in the sight of men.

—*Revelation* 13:13

1

Not until the second try did the two answering flashes of light prick the darkness.

When they did, Javier Vega allowed himself a brief moment of relaxation. The plan was going to work, he could feel it. The weapons had been transferred to the boat without problem, and now they were about to be off-loaded to the island. After that, there was only the plane.

He looked over at the two men who stood at the rail with him, and with whom he'd been cooped up on the foul-smelling shrimper during the trip down from Texas. Vega had thick black hair, a bristly mustache, three days' growth of beard, and black eyes that always seemed as impassive as camera lenses.

He smiled. It was not a companionable smile, Shake Ruland thought. It was the smile of someone who finds the behavior of his inferiors mildly amusing from time to time.

"Missed by a quarter of a mile," he said to the fishermen. "Pretty close. Okay, let's run her in."

Ruland glanced at his partner, Adam Ritt. Neither of them returned Vega's smile.

Though the *Celeste* was their boat, when Vega commanded something they obeyed. Fifty thousand dollars was more money than either man had ever come close to seeing. And that was *apiece*; half tonight, half when they got home. With so much at stake they were willing, this one time, to follow someone else's orders.

Ruland shrugged, pushed himself away from the rail, and went into the pilothouse.

A few moments later, the twin diesels rumbled and the shrimper shifted position, running parallel to the shadowy shoreline until it was directly opposite the flashes of light. As Ritt dropped anchor, Vega flashed twice more, and this time the answering signal came immediately.

The *Celeste* drifted on its anchor line, its port side facing the north coast of Roatan, largest of the Honduran Bay islands. When the boat had stabilized, Ritt hung two small lights over that side. They would be invisible except from land. Between the lights he dropped a Jacob's ladder.

Then the hold was opened and the three men went to work. It didn't take them long; there were only eight crates in all. Each of them was just over sixty inches long by eighteen inches square and weighed a hundred twenty-five pounds. In a few minutes the entire lot had been hoisted up on deck.

Since neither Ritt nor Ruland knew the contents of the crates, they had no idea of the value of their cargo. But their passenger did. It added up to two and a half million dollars, based on the retail price of each crate to the Defense Department of the United States.

Black market markup would be at least two hundred percent.

The intrinsic military worth of the crates' contents, though, was not easily translated into dollars and cents. They were as valuable as the functions they could perform. They could take lives and save lives. They could influence the outcome of a battle, perhaps of a war. How to place a price on that?

Finally, there was the weapons' potential, in the threat of their use, rather than the use itself. No one knew for sure what that potential might be. But those formulating strategy figured at least a half-billion dollars. Plus fringe benefits.

The sound of outboard motors could be heard over the *Celeste*'s idling diesels and, shortly, two rubber dinghies pulled alongside and tied up to the shrimper.

The dinghies' two pilots were both black, English-speaking Hondurans who, like the majority of Roatan's inhabitants, were descended from British-held slaves and lived in quiet isolation, maintaining little contact with the Spanish/Indian population of the mainland.

The transaction at the *Celeste* involved no speaking in either English or Spanish. The crates—with the words FARM MACHINERY stenciled in black on their sides—

were quickly transferred from the shrimper to the dinghies. Five were off-loaded to one, three to the other. The second would also take Vega.

When the transfer was complete, Vega went below. He returned carrying a duffel bag over one shoulder and a satchel in either hand, and stood in the pilothouse door. He beckoned to Ruland.

The two men went inside the pilothouse, where Vega opened one of the satchels. Neat, banded packets of money were stacked inside.

"It's all there," Vega said. His cultured voice had only a trace of an accent; fixing his nationality would require a keen ear. "I think you know our mutual friends well enough to realize that we wouldn't cheat you. I'd prefer if we didn't waste the time it will take to count it."

Ruland ruffled a couple of the top-layer packets. He paused, looked at Vega, then nodded. "All right," he said, "I believe you." He snapped the satchel closed and set it on the bench along the pilothouse wall.

"And the other fifty is waiting if you complete things satisfactorily. Otherwise . . ."

Ruland bristled at the casual way that Vega threatened him. His right fist clenched reflexively and he had to consciously relax it. Though muscular, Vega was a hundred and eighty, tops, versus two-twenty-five for Ruland. Ordinarily the man would have been dog meat.

Remember the money, Ruland told himself. Yet even as he did so, he knew in his heart it wasn't just the money stopping him. It was Vega's eyes, the pitiless black eyes that clearly warned him that a forty-five-pound weight difference didn't mean jack shit.

"Get off my boat, you sonofabitch," Ruland said with more conviction than he felt.

Vega calmly observed the other man for a moment, then turned and walked back out on deck. Ruland followed him after a slight hesitation. Ritt looked at his partner questioningly and Ruland nodded that yeah, everything was okay.

Vega tossed his duffel bag and the second satchel down to the dinghy pilot. Without another word he climbed over the side.

The first dinghy had already started back to the island. Vega untied the second, then settled himself on a narrow slat that served as a seat. He faced aft, toward the pilot. He didn't so much as glance up at the *Celeste* as the dinghy peeled away.

"Good riddance," Ritt muttered.

"Yeah," Ruland said. "Let's get the hell out of here."

They wasted no time. In just a couple of minutes they had pulled the anchor, goosed the diesels up to speed, and were heading back the way they had come.

Ruland finally felt free. "Yeee-hah!" he yelled almost into his partner's ear. "We're rich now! God damn me if we ain't!"

While the *Celeste* steamed steadily eastward, the dinghies sped toward shore, their pilots steering by instinct in the dark. The choppy open sea gave way to the rip marking one of the many breaks in Roatan's fringing reef that had been cut by fresh-water runoff. That, in turn, yielded to the calm lagoon known as Second Bight.

Vega rested his back against the crates stacked behind him and draped his arm over the side of the dinghy. He let his hand trail in the water. It was very warm. "Same temperature as the air," he said to the pilot. "It must be odd going into the water."

"I don' go in the water," the pilot said.

He kept his eyes on the shore. Though there was a scattering of stilted houses around Second Bight, no lights showed anywhere. The pilot was looking for a light where there shouldn't have been one.

"You don't swim?" Vega asked him.

"No."

"Surrounded by water, and you don't know how to swim."

"I fish," the pilot said. "I don' need to swim."

Vega nodded slowly to himself and said, "After tonight you won't have to fish for a while."

The pilot grinned, his teeth ghostly against the background of dark face and dark night sky. "That what I know," he said. "My fahmly need the money."

"More than we do, I'm sure," Vega said. "We're glad to be able to help. And you're doing us quite a service. You have children?"

"One boy, two girls. I buy my boy a boat with the money. Then he can hahve his own fahmly."

Vega nodded. "I'm sure he'll appreciate that," he said. "Every boy should have his own boat."

The dinghies made for the west side of the bight, slowing their engines to run more quietly. Soon the first dinghy cut its engine entirely. It coasted to the end of a long wooden dock, where its pilot tied it up. By the time he finished, his companion had arrived. Vega tied up the second boat.

The pilot of the first dinghy clambered up a rickety ladder onto the dock, and the other two men wrestled crates up to him. Then they switched, and the first pilot hoisted up his hundred and twenty-five pound weights, as if they were mere strings of fish.

Each of the men then shouldered a crate and trudged the length of the dock. It was sixty feet long and ended at a rock breakwater, where the men took an overgrown path that wound for fifty yards through the encroaching jungle, and ended in a clearing. There was an abandoned house, its roof caved in, vines pulling down its porch supports, its windows lonely blank holes. A black van was parked on a circular patch of sand in front.

One of the dinghy pilots opened the van and the men loaded their crates inside. Then they returned for three more. In three trips the job was done.

"I take boats back now," one pilot said to the other. "I meet you later."

"No," Vega said.

He had pulled out a silenced Tokarev TT30 7.62-mm pistol and was holding it steadily. The two Hondurans froze.

"Lie down there," Vega said, indicating the sand. "Do as I say and I won't hurt you. Facedown. Clasp your hands behind your heads."

The two men did as they were told. Vega stood over them.

"Don' shoot us," one said. "We don' say nothing. We have fahmlies. . . ."

Vega bent over one of the men and placed the pistol just short of the base of his skull. He pulled the trigger. There was very little sound. The man's body jerked once and then was still.

The other man quickly slipped his arms beneath him and tried to push himself up, but he didn't get far before the Tokarev delivered a single bullet to his temple. He pinwheeled and flopped onto his back and he too was still. Blood slowly stained the sand around his head. There wasn't that much of it.

Vega moved swiftly. He slipped the pistol back under his shirt, hoisted his one satchel and duffel bag into the front seat of the van. One at a time, he dragged the islanders' bodies to the edge of the jungle and rolled them into the dense undergrowth. Then he started the van and drove away.

2

The road that Vega followed, like most on Roatan, was dirt, this one just a single rutted track. On both sides the jungle was closing in, a solid green mass in the cone of light from the headlamps. It was like driving through a tunnel whose walls breathed in and out to the rhythm of some sleeping giant.

The one-lane track led to the two-lane road that served as Roatan's circumferential highway, and Vega turned west on it. The road ran down past French Harbour and then across the island to the north coast and the airport. It was a distance of less than ten miles, but because of the condition of the roads the trip took forty-five minutes.

Roatan's airport consists of a dilapidated wooden structure that serves as a terminal building and a narrow runway only recently graduated from gravel. Other than the odd military aircraft or occasional private plane carrying wealthy scuba diving enthusiasts from the States, the only traffic is a DC-3 that makes a twice-daily trip from Roatan to La Ceiba on the Honduran mainland. There are no landing lights, so every night at dark the airport shuts down.

When Vega arrived at the airport, it had been closed

for hours. The lone sentry posted at the entrance waved
the van on through.

The van's headlights picked out a small airplane parked
near the terminal. It was a squat, two-engine Skytrader
SCOUT-STOL utility transport, painted in camouflage
brown and green. With its long, pointed nose and double
forty-five-degree cantilevered tail, the plane looked like
it was kicking its own insides out its front.

The SCOUT had become the plane of choice for light
military ops, if you could get one. It required takeoff and
landing runs of only four hundred feet. It could carry
sixteen men or three hundred and thirty-five cubic feet of
cargo. Powered by twin four-hundred-horsepower Lycom-
ing engines, it could cruise at two hundred fifty miles an
hour, with a range of over two thousand miles. It could
be fitted with air-to-air missiles and .50-caliber machine
guns, though this particular one was unarmed.

There were three men waiting for Vega when he got
out of the van. Two wore Honduran army uniforms; one
was a foot soldier and the other a high-ranking officer.
The third was young, light-complexioned, with pale blond
hair, little more than a boy. He was wearing olive-drab
fatigues with no identification of any kind.

"Señor Vargas?" the officer said, holding out his hand.

Vega took the other man's hand briefly, then said in
Spanish, "Let's get the plane loaded, Colonel."

"Yes, of course."

The crates were quickly transferred from the van to the
airplane. The colonel watched while the other three men
worked.

"You ready to go?" Vega asked the American when
they'd finished.

The boy was chewing spearmint gum. "Piece of cake,"
he said between chews. "She's a good plane, damn good."

"How much fuel?"

"Full up, less what it took to get here. Why, you
worried?"

Ignoring him, Vega fetched the duffel bag and small
satchel from the van, handed the duffel bag to the blond
boy and said, "Behind my seat." Then he walked over to
the military men, who had been waiting discreetly next to
their car.

"Colonel," he said, handing the officer the satchel.

The colonel grinned and thanked him. "Of course," he said, "you realize I do this for my country. And for yours as well. The communists must be defeated."

"Yes," Vega said. "You want to count it?"

"That will not be necessary. The Americans pay their debts."

"Good. Now I think we had better get airborne. You know what to do with the van?"

"Of course," the colonel said, taking the keys. He passed them to his companion. "None of this ever happened. You paid off the boatmen?"

"In full."

"Good. They are simple people. A small amount of money buys their silence forever. I think you can be assured that they will not talk."

"No, I don't believe they will."

"Go with God, then." The colonel crossed himself. "I see your country soon delivered from those of no faith and returned to you."

"We appreciate your support," Vega said. "We are all working for a free Nicaragua. Now if you don't mind . . ."

The colonel bowed slightly, and Vega turned and walked to the plane. The pilot was already in his seat. Vega climbed up and strapped himself in.

The pilot turned over the engines, which caught immediately. He revved them, ran quickly over his preflight checklist. The instrument panel glowed softly. If necessary, its light could be reduced to almost nothing, for use with night-vision goggles.

"Hey, where do we file the flight plan?" The pilot laughed.

Vega watched the colonel drive the black car to the airport entrance, while his aide followed in the van. They stopped there, and the third soldier took the driver's seat of the car. The colonel stood beside his vehicle, watching the plane taxi out the runway.

"What's your name, son?" Vega asked the pilot.

"Charlie," the boy said.

"You got a lot of experience, Charlie?"

"Uh-huh. Been in six years now. Been down here for two. I've flown a lot of . . . specials. I like the SCOUT for that."

"Okay. Hold on a minute."

Vega turned in his seat and zipped open the duffel bag behind him. He took out a small metal box with a single button on its face and an antenna that telescoped out.

"Uh, what's that?" Charlie asked.

Vega faced forward. With his other hand he took the Tokarev from under his shirt and aimed it at the pilot.

"Just follow directions, son," he said.

Charlie swallowed his gum.

Vega looked at the car and the van, parked about a hundred yards away. The colonel was still standing next to the car. Vega pointed the metal box in that direction and pressed the button.

The van exploded in a huge ball of flame. It engulfed the car next to it. There was a secondary explosion as the car's fuel blew. The concussion from the blasts rocked the plane.

"Let's go, Charlie," Vega said.

The boy was staring open-mouthed at the burning vehicles.

"Now," Vega said, poking the Tokarev into his ribs.

The pilot's body jerked, but he snapped his head around to face forward. He wound the engines up until they screamed. Then he released the brake, and the small plane headed down the runway. Behind them the burning vehicles sent billows of heavy black smoke into the night sky.

The plane left the runway with plenty of room to spare. It climbed rapidly and within moments was out over the stretch of sea between Roatan and the mainland. Charlie banked and headed them southeast, toward the border.

He started to speak, but his voice cracked. He cleared his throat. "Ah, look," he said, "we're not actually going inside Nicaragua, are we? They told me that we weren't."

"There's been a change of plan," Vega said.

"Look," Charlie said nervously, "I'm just a Georgia farm boy. I don't know shit about politics, but I figure we're on the same side, right? Just tell me what you want, we'll do it."

"That's the trouble with Americans," Vega said. "You *don't* know anything about politics. You don't know anything about anything. You think only of what is best for you, and the rest of the world should follow. That is also going to change."

In one motion he put the Tokarev to Charlie's head and pulled the trigger.

With practiced efficiency, Vega took over control of the plane. He pushed Charlie's body out the pilot's side door. The body fell three hundred feet to the surface of the Caribbean. Almost immediately it began to attract interest from the creatures cruising below.

Vega wheeled the plane around and aimed it north, toward the United States.

The *Celeste* was running at full throttle. Two and a half hours had passed since they had left Roatan, but Adam Ritt was still standing rigid at the wheel, as if glued to it. Now at last he began to relax.

"By God, we made it, Shake," he said. "We're gonna be rich. Come *on*, let's count the sonofabitch!"

"Let's do," Ruland said, walking toward the satchel. "See what that money *feels* like."

In the bottom of the satchel was a small gray metal box with an ON/OFF switch on its side and a peg on top. The box was a battery-powered omnidirectional transmitter with a range of one hundred yards. The peg was spring-loaded. When depressed it kept an electrical circuit open.

As Ruland pulled out the stacks of bills, he released the pressure on the peg. The spring inside popped it up, closing the circuit and activating the transmitter. It in turn sent a signal to a detonator that had been wired into a mass of plastic explosive packed around the fuel tanks.

Neither Ritt nor Ruland had even a momentary awareness of what followed. The explosion sent a fireball racing through the boat and hurled scraps of wood and metal two hundred feet into the air. The concussion from the blast split the hull in two, as though it had been merely a brittle twig.

What remained of the *Celeste* sank in less than a minute. Former pieces of it continued to splat into the sea even after the boat had vanished.

Then there was only the smoke, which slowly dissipated in the steady breeze over the surface of the oil-filmed sea.

* * *

Vega couldn't have seen the explosion even if he'd been looking for it. By then he was flying at max cruising speed over the state of Campeche in southern Mexico, heading steadily northwest.

Beforehand, he had pored over the details of his route, committing them to memory. He'd studied a mockup of the SCOUT's instrument panel until it was as if he'd been flying the unfamiliar plane all his life. Then he'd scrutinized topographical maps and meteorological data, both general conditions for the season and the forecast for this particular night. And then he'd flown the route over and over in his mind.

Still, it was a long night flight over very rugged terrain. There was always the unexpected, and that was why Vega himself was at the controls. Included among his skills were those of a superb navigator and light aircraft pilot.

After Campeche, Vega's course took him across the Gulf, with landfall made prudently south of Tampico. Then he went west, crossed the Sierra Madre Oriental, and turned north. He passed between Monterrey and Torreon. From there the vast, barren desert of Coahuila stretched all the way to the border.

Here there was the remote possibility of encountering aircraft running drugs in from Mexico or a government spotter plane looking for such smugglers; this had been accepted as an unavoidable risk.

And, as the border got closer, there was American radar. Anyone detected in the area was immediately suspect. However, the only alternative would have been to head for Florida or elsewhere on the Gulf Coast, and then the approach would be over water. With the plane thus exposed, radar detection was a near certainty.

In southwestern Texas there was cover.

Vega dropped the SCOUT as low as he dared and, screened by the Chisos and Christmas and Chalk Mountains, entered American airspace.

Though contour flying in the dark is next of kin to suicide, Vega barely broke a sweat. He'd taken two amphetamines an hour earlier, enhancing his extraordinary natural powers of concentration. He followed State Highway 118 as if it were marked with phosphorescent paint.

The highway had not been chosen at random. It went, basically, from nowhere to nowhere, and in the early morning hours traffic was close to nonexistent.

Nevertheless, the men on the ground had prepared the landing strip with care. It was a half-mile stretch of fairly level road, running along a narrow saddle between two mountains. There was a steep drop on either side and a small parking area designated as a scenic overlook. The overlook was deserted except for a van and two cars that had arrived thirty minutes earlier. The van had a logo emblazoned on its side, proclaiming it an official vehicle of the CEDAR RAPIDS SENIOR MOUNTAINEERS. In none of the vehicles was there more than one person.

At points two miles north and south of the saddle, the "mountaineers" had erected roadblocks, striped with orange-and-white reflective tape, which read DANGER—ROAD CLOSED. From neither point could the landing strip be seen.

They closed the road at four forty-five. At five-fifteen they lined up the vehicles, started their engines, and turned on their headlights and several portable spots. At five-thirty the Scout came over the southern peak and touched down as smoothly as if it were making a routine landing at La Guardia.

The rest went off without a hitch. First the crates were transferred to the van. Then Vega got back into the SCOUT, started it rolling toward the eastern drop-off, and jumped out. The plane pitched over the side. It somersaulted once, bounced into the air, fell a hundred feet, struck a ledge, and exploded. The wings were torn off. The main body of it dropped end-over-end down the steep slope in flames, until it came to rest in a dry creek bed far below. On the thinly vegetated desert mountainside the fire soon burned itself out.

But no one was watching. The vehicles were pulling away from the scenic overlook. One car went south, to remove the roadblock there. The other headed north, followed by the van, and did the same. No civilian traffic had been stopped by either roadblock.

The van continued on, sticking to the speed limit, while the car sped off into the darkness. Inside the van were the driver, the passenger, and the eight wooden crates. A few minutes later the van stopped for a comfort break. When it started up again it had only a single man inside.

At the intersection of US 90 in Alpine, Vega turned the van east, then north on US 67. His immediate goal was the airport at Midland, Texas.

By evening, if all continued to go smoothly, he would be in Boston. The target.

3

Sleep was supposed to be the natural healer. It was simple: you went to sleep with a headache, the body worked its unconscious wonders while you were out, and you woke up feeling fine.

It didn't work for Steven Kirk, and it hadn't for six months. Not since the deaths of Susanna and Scottie, the shedding of the Steve Carson identity, the resumption of use of his real name.

In fact, it was often the other way around. He'd go to bed feeling okay and wake up in such pain that he could barely focus his eyes. It was as if the car bomb that had killed his wife and child was continuing to explode inside his head, day after day.

A bottle of Fiorinal with codeine was next to the bed, along with a glass of water that was always half full. When morning arrived, the pills were the first thing Kirk reached for. He knew he was semi-addicted to the drugs, but he didn't care. They worked, and he was able to maintain a steady, legal supply. He'd told a sympathetic Namvet doctor that he'd been caught in a vicious firefight during the invasion of Grenada and had had the headaches ever since. The doctor understood and wrote him scrip whenever asked.

Kirk didn't tell the doctor about the bodies of the only two people he cared about being burned beyond recognition. He didn't tell anyone about that. He lived with the memory in his head, and when it hurt too much he took the painkillers.

He chased one of the blue-and-yellow caps with some of the bedside water, then lay back on the pillow. Judging from the quality of the light he'd glimpsed through his squint, he figured it was around nine o'clock. Late for work again.

Claire would be long gone. She hadn't bothered to wake him. She never did anymore, not since the morning he'd mistaken her for some dream enemy and nearly broken her arm.

He hadn't meant to hurt her, but coming unexpectedly awake like that, he'd been unable to control the self-protective instinct that had once been so important to his life and work.

Kirk lay still for a while, willing the drugs to work more quickly. It didn't matter if he was an hour late, or two. His tardiness would be added to his previous sins, and one day the total would exceed some unspecified limit. He'd be fired. Then he'd either get another job or he wouldn't.

It wasn't working with Claire, he thought as he studied the insides of his eyelids. And it wasn't going to.

"I wish you wouldn't take so many of those pills," she'd said. "They space you out. And they make you . . . not so hot in bed."

It had been a courageous thing for her to say. She'd been brought up to believe that a woman never criticized her man about anything.

She was right, though. He *wasn't* satisfying her sexually. Yet he couldn't explain to her that he needed sex a lot less than the comfort and reassurance of a warm body lying next to him at night. He couldn't explain it to himself, either.

Claire didn't deserve him. She was a patient, decent person who lived with a man she didn't know very well, a man who suffered from some "combat experience" that he never talked about.

Tears trickled from the corners of his closed eyes.

He'd moved in with Claire, not knowing what it was going to feel like. Now he knew. He couldn't open up to her about the vibrant dark-haired woman who'd been his wife and their pudgy baby boy. He couldn't tell her of the things he'd once done for his government in the naive belief that that government would never abuse his trust in it. He'd tried to talk, but no words had come.

Worse still, he couldn't deny that he might well be taking unfair risks with Claire's life. He had no idea who'd murdered his wife and child. The possibilities were numerous. But beyond question the car bomb had really been meant for him.

Whoever had rigged it might try again.

This time Claire might be with him. She was no more innocent than Susanna and Scottie had been, but Susanna at least had known whom she was getting involved with. Claire didn't, and wouldn't. Yet, unknowingly, she was probably putting her life on the line and would continue to do so until Kirk found out who was behind the bombing and settled the issue, whatever it was.

And right now the thought of hunting them down sickened him.

He was thus condemned to live alone. Trying to make it with Claire had slowly taught him that.

With a sigh he pushed himself onto the edge of the bed. He looked down at his body. Amazingly, his pectoral muscles had remained taut and there was only a slight wrinkle to indicate that his stomach might not be as flat as ever. True, he was still several years short of forty, but he hadn't seriously worked out for months. And he hadn't been overly selective about the kinds of things he'd been asking his system to accept on faith.

He got up and went mechanically through the motions of a reliable employee preparing to report to his place of work. Shaving and showering and such were supposed to invigorate, cut through the fog of lingering sleep, not be mere rituals marking the line between one day and the next. Some fine morning he would neglect to perform them, and that would be that.

Was this a fine morning? He couldn't tell. It was still cool inside the small stucco bungalow, but the thick block walls were good at keeping the heat at bay before noon. It was an older house, and had been constructed before the coming of central air, when people were more aware that they were throwing up homes in a desert.

Kirk started to make himself some breakfast, but stopped in the middle of buttering the toast. It no longer looked like food. His head was beginning to do the slow-motion somersaults that the drugs brought on. The pain was receding, and eating was unimportant.

He got out a pencil and a note pad and began an affectionate note to Claire. But all he could think of were various forms of apology. He gave it up.

Outside, the harsh sunlight filtered down through the yellowish brown haze that was now perpetually suspended over the city. A whole generation was reaching adulthood without having experienced blue sky.

Kirk put on his sunglasses and climbed into the aged Chevy Caprice he'd bought after getting rid of Steve Carson's Skylark. All the old Caprices ended up here, where they could eke out a few more years in the desiccated air.

As Kirk turned the key, he visualized the circuit he might be closing and the fiery explosion that might follow. But there was none. There was only the slow grinding of the starter motor, the sputtering cough of the engine as it caught, and then the steady, rattling vibration of the Caprice as it strove to give its owner one last ride for his money.

It was a dreary, mile-long drive to the store, down streets populated by people who inhabited that fuzzy world between a low-level decent living and the real poverty of the barrios, and then through a district of warehouses filled with things that there was no great demand for.

Kirk's destination was a huge, corrugated steel Quonset hut that was both warehouse and wholesale/retail outlet. TRI-STATE AUTO PARTS was printed in fading white paint over its front door.

When he went inside, the smell of oil hit him particularly hard, threatening to instantly rekindle the pain in his head. He knew that he'd better take another pill as a precautionary measure.

He was at the time clock ready to punch in at 10:17, when he glanced in the direction of the store manager's office. Carillo was standing there, looking back at him. His expression was not friendly.

Kirk held his time card poised over the slot for a long moment. Then the burly Mexican gave a slight shake of his head, and Kirk replaced the card in the rack. Carillo motioned him over and the two men went into the manager's office.

Carillo put two shot glasses on his scarred desk and filled them with José Cuervo. The men drank.

Then Carillo said, "Steven," making the first syllable three times longer than the second. "What I'm going to do with you? I give you every chance."

"I don't know." Kirk shrugged. "When I'm asleep, I don't have the pain. I don't like to wake up."

Carillo looked at his employee. His dark brown face was seamed like a recently plowed cornfield and there was a gnarl of tissue where his left ear should have been. There was a bottomless sadness in his eyes.

The Mexican sighed and said, "Steven, I was in the war, too. I give you a chance because I was in the war and those who don't fight don't understand. I must wash the blood from my hands every morning. But . . ."

"You're a kind man, Leo," Kirk said.

"I am a businessman. A lady comes in and she needs a water pump for her Toyota Corolla. I have to find it myself because my Corolla man doesn't want to wake up."

"I'm sorry."

"No, I am sorry, my friend. It is truly so."

Carillo slid a white envelope across the desk. "There is some extra," he said. "I hope that it will be enough."

Kirk nodded and stood up. "Thanks for everything, Leo," he said. "I appreciate it." He took the envelope, stood up, and headed for the door.

"Steven," Carillo said, "you must find the answer inside yourself, man."

Kirk was back in the Caprice, turning the key, before he fully realized that he hadn't the vaguest idea where he wanted to go.

4

Smith sat behind the mahogany desk in his office in the agency's Directorate of Operations.

The office was of modest size and had plush white carpeting that exactly matched in hue the walls and ceiling. Lighting came from a recessed area where walls and ceiling joined; the actual lights were out of sight. Visitors' chairs were chrome and black leather.

On Smith's desk blotter lay a single manila file folder.

Smith stared down at the folder. He was somewhere around middle age, though exactly where it would be hard to say with certainty. Nothing about him attracted attention. His moon-shaped face was clean shaven and without distinguishing features. His hair was a neutral brown, thinning slightly and combed with a traditional part along the right side. He wore glasses with unobtrusive plastic frames.

He was of medium height with a medium build. His frame was fleshed out in such a way that he would be remembered as neither stout nor lean, in neither particularly good nor bad shape. He wore a dark gray suit, with a dark striped tie. The suit was tailored so that it fit him perfectly without seeming to.

In conversation his mouth moved only minimally; his voice was emotionless and devoid of any regional accent. When he smiled, which was seldom, he showed no teeth.

Despite being as near invisible as a human being can be, Smith managed to gather about him the air of authority. It was something you had in Operations, or you didn't survive.

Now it was going to be tested.

The center of the folder in front of him bore a heavy black ink stamp. In large block letters were the words NO

32

UNAUTHORIZED EYES over a fascimile of the Director's signature.

Smith opened it and once again leafed through the documents inside. Each was headed with the word SUNFLOWER. Though sensitive in the extreme, none of them carried any further classification stamp. The one on the cover was a sufficient deterrent to all but the most reckless. Anyone caught violating it was out of a job and subject to prosecution for a breach of national security.

Smith owned a high-ranking pair of authorized eyes. He was checking the file carefully, and not in order to refresh his memory. He knew exactly what was there or, rather, exactly what he *ought* to find there.

When a wheel came loose, especially during a black operation, the set procedure to be followed could be equally as important as getting the wheel lugged. Step number one was to make sure all of the documentation was where it should be. If anything was missing, step number two was to get it back. And step number three was, of course, to stay within reach of the shredder.

Smith eventually nodded as if satisfied with what he'd seen. He looked up from the folder and off into space.

Things looked manageable. Deniability was good, at least from here in the hierarchy upward. No one was going to get "ollied," the slang expression for the consequences of failure to properly clear confidential messages from the in-house computer. There was a decent probability of achieving the mission's objectives.

He would, however, have to get the retrieval process underway immediately. The network would have to be backtracked, cutouts contacted, an intensive search quietly begun.

But unless the absolute worst happened . . .

He dialed his secretary and said, "Miss Pritchard, please make me a nil with the Director for"—he thought about how much time he was likely to need—"for two this afternoon, will you?"

Then he went to work.

"We have a serious problem," Smith said.

The Director nodded. "I assumed that when you requested a nil."

Nil meetings were a common agency occurrence. For

all practical purposes, they were events which had never taken place. Participants' appointment books recorded something entirely different for that time period; secretaries and assistants cooperated if they valued their jobs. Nil meetings carefully preserved future deniability and had been especially popular since the blunders of the late Reagan years.

Smith smiled, but only to himself. Inside his jacket's inner pocket, the spools of the micro-corder were turning silently. The flip side of nil meetings was that any hard information about them could be invaluable in next week's transactions. Leverage was the primary fuel on which government ran, and the power to override deniability often constituted the greatest leverage.

"So," the Director continued, "how much do I need to know?"

That was the first question a director asked when a wheel came loose. And in most cases he wanted to know as little as possible.

In the wake of the Iran/Contra, South African, and other foreign policy debacles, the director had become primarily a liaison between the White House and the intelligence community. It was he who set policy, in the broad sense, through conveying the President's wishes to those under his nominal direction. After that, he could best serve his boss by getting out of the way.

Actual agency decisions involving the most sensitive covert operations were made at the level of Deputy Director or below, sometimes in cooperation with the National Security Council, sometimes not. Quite often the Director had no clear idea of how policy was being applied out in the field, and he could truthfully deny to Congress any knowledge of these ops.

Thus, when Smith said, "I believe you need to know everything," the Director winced.

A handsome, white-haired man of sixty, he leaned back in his chair. He tamped down the tobacco in the pipe he'd been holding in his hand. Then he stuck the stem between his teeth and set the mixture afire. The pipe gurgled as he sucked at it. Nicotine-rich water droplets rolled down into his mouth.

"All right," he said finally. "Give me the details, and

go slowly. I'll stop you if we get into a no-knowledge area."

"The downside is manageable, even if you know it all," Smith said casually. "It's after the fact, so there's not that much potential for harm to you."

The Director sighed. Smith was the master of this little game, and the Director knew it. Without saying anything openly provocative, Smith had decisively taken control of the meeting. He'd managed to convey a sense of urgency, assert his importance, and drop just enough hint of a threat, all in the space of two seemingly innocent sentences.

"A wheel's come loose in Central America," Smith said.

"Sunflower?" Smith nodded. "In the black?" Smith nodded again. The Director steeled himself and asked, "How bad is it?"

"We don't know yet. Some Stingers were ticketed for the freedom fighters and the delivery was aborted."

"I see," the Director said with an outward calm that didn't match his heartbeat. "It would have to be a major sanction item, wouldn't it?"

"Yes, I'm afraid so."

Nicaragua had been a thorn in the nation's side ever since the CIA invented the Contras and Reagan announced that they were the moral equivalent of Washington and Jefferson. Since then, there had been a wild potpourri of U. S. involvements in the country, including the economic embargo, harbor minings, funding of the anti-Communist opposition that swung between official and covert, and finally, the massive infusion of campaign money that helped bring about the Sandinistas' stunning defeat at the polls.

The 1990 election, of course, provided only a brief respite from conflict, and the army-inspired FSLN's voiding of the election and forcible retaking of power seemed, in retrospect, little short of inevitable. After spending ten years defending their revolution from military attack, the Sandinistas were certainly not going to let it slip away at the ballot box. And they were, by their reasoning, only reacting appropriately to the inadequacies of the elected opposition.

With the second coming of the FSLN came the war again.

The Contras, never entirely trustful of their Sandinista counterparts, had hung on to their weapons and were readily reassembled. Their numbers swelled by thousands of disaffected youths, militia defectors, and a contingent of anti-Communist Cuban/American mercenaries, they went back into the field, determined this time to physically destroy their sworn enemy.

The new American president completely supported the pro-democracy forces, but as it had been in the past, weapons resupply was a big problem. Congress, ever skittish about the specter of direct military intervention, had approved only nonlethal aid. This necessitated such nominally humanitarian operations as *Sunflower,* whose black side eventually had to confront the need for anti-aircraft weaponry. There was just no way to effectively counter helicopter gunships without a reliable shoulder-fired missile.

While everyone involved in strategy planning for Central America knew this, there remained the hard facts of political life. The President wasn't going to put his signature to any documents, or issue any direct orders, that contravened congressional intent. Yet his wishes were well understood, which left it up to those who implemented policy to determine how best to serve the boss.

So *Sunflower's* black arm had grown longer.

"How many?" the Director asked wearily.

"Eight pods," Smith said. "Twenty-four missiles. But the number of Stingers missing is not the bad part."

"The bad part is that we don't know where they are."

"Yes, exactly. The cargo was scheduled for shipment from Texas to Roatan by boat. There it was to be transferred to light plane and delivered to an insurgent base just this side of the border. Cutouts were employed at every point, which makes backchecking somewhat difficult."

"And what's overdue, the plane or the boat?"

"The plane." Out of habit rather than need, Smith looked at his watch. "By approximately twelve hours," he said.

"Do we know that in fact it took off?" the Director asked.

"Not for certain. But there was an explosion at the Roatan airport last night, around midnight. A car and a van went up. They found three bodies.

"The Hondurans are having a fit. They're a little sensitive about the extent of our presence to begin with, and their people getting torched at a covert rendezvous isn't sitting well. I think we've got to assume that they'll be able to tie the bodies to the resupply eventually."

"The plane wasn't there, though," the Director said.

"No," Smith said. "Which means that the most likely scenario is that the plane took off with the cargo after the intermediaries on the ground were tweaked." Smith used one of the current agency euphemisms for "terminated."

"No evidence that the plane might have crashed?"

"Not yet. I've got a recon chopper running along the flight path from Roatan to base, but personally, I'd be very surprised if we come up with anything."

"I suppose," the Director said. "What about the pilot?"

"One of our best," Smith said without hesitation. "Young, but dedicated. Plenty of experience. He could have been doubled, of course, and we're looking into the possibility. But I strongly doubt it."

"So the operative assumption is that we've got a hijack."

"That would be my assumption, yes."

"And the pilot . . ."

"Dead, in all probability."

"Shit. I *knew* it was a bad idea to be—"

The Director stopped when he saw the way Smith was looking at him. "All right," he said. "I suppose it's not very productive to pretend in front of you that I didn't know what was going on."

Smith cleared his throat. "Don't worry, I'll see to it that your public deniability is preserved. And the President's," he said. He paused, then added, "Sir."

The two men were silent for a while. The Director collected his thoughts and puffed at his pipe; Smith looked discreetly away. He focused on a photo of the Director, smiling and shaking hands with Mrs. Thatcher. Both of them had been a good bit younger then.

Finally, Smith said, "If you're worried, the rest of the agency is blanked. Sunflower doesn't have a black side and it never did. All of the paper is shred-ready. I've got my finger on every possible leak."

"It isn't just that," the Director said. "The situation is going to be a bitch, but I'm talking about real damage control. Any guess as to who might have grabbed them?"

"Not at the moment."

"What about the plane? What can we figure from that?"

"We use the SCOUT whenever possible," Smith said. "Which is unfortunate. Fully fueled, it has a range of two thousand miles."

"How does that work out?"

"Anyplace in Mexico, Central America, or the Caribbean. Peru, Colombia, or Venezuela. And a big part of the U.S., inside a circle drawn through Albuquerque, Detroit, and New York City."

The Director whistled softly. "My God. So we could be talking about Castro, or the Shining Path, or the Puerto Rican separatists, or drug-runners from Bogota, or American anti-nuke radicals, or you name it, almost any other goddamn thing."

"Yes," Smith said. "Or agents for someone outside the plane's range, of course. Iraq, Iran, Libya, the PLO. I think what we'd prefer is that it was some off-the-course foreign government, or one of their opponents. Iran or Iraq, Burkina, even the leftists in Salvador. Then the missiles get used up in a bottom-end war nobody cares about and we stonewall the whole thing."

"Alternatively?"

"Castro or the Sandies are more likely, of course. If one of them did it, they could embarrass us. We'd get some bad press and some screams from the Hill, but we'd come out all right."

"Agreed," the Director said. "So what we really have to worry about is the worst-case scenario."

"Yes. The worst case is why you had to know everything. There is a fair possibility that the Stingers are on their way back to this country, or here already. If they are, they could be in the hands of any of the hostile foreign factions, or even one of our own crazies, from anti-Castro Cubans to a militant bunch of survivalists up in the mountains of northern California."

"Organized crime?"

"Could be. The missiles would be useful to protect drugs coming in. The scenario doesn't have that feel to it, though."

"What's the net, then?" the Director asked.

"Well," Smith said, "two dozen Stingers in the hands of someone who knew how to use them, and civil aviation could be crippled in this country. The public would panic. The press would jump on the President's back. He'd be under tremendous pressure to give the hijackers whatever they asked for."

Again there was a pause, then the Director said, "We should assume the worst."

"Yes, we should," Smith said. "I've started a backtrack. It'll take time, but eventually we should be able to establish the chain of events. Maybe even find out who they are before they do whatever they're going to do."

"FBI?"

"If that's your choice. Though once the FBI gets involved, we're never going to be able to contain."

"I don't like using our people domestic. The President will have my ass if he finds out."

"I know that, Mr. Director, but I don't think we have any choice in this instance. There's a good chance that if it leaks, he'll have all our asses."

The Director thought for a moment, then said, "All right. I'll give you deniable approval. But use cutouts wherever you can."

Smith nodded. "I believe at this point we also need to consider a satellite search," he said.

"Under whose aegis?"

"The NSC would be best. The White House is going to have to know about this, and the sooner the better, in my opinion. If someone ends up having to take a fall, the President can always sacrifice some of *them*. Let me work through the CAT and I can be sure to keep both you and the President clean."

CAT was the common term for Central American Interagency Task Force. It was a low-profile link between the National Security Council, the agency, the State Department, and the military, for the purpose of supervising covert operations. It was the successor to the Restricted Interagency Group (RIG), which had been disbanded when its kingpin, Oliver North, had taken his nose dive.

It was also an essential part of the foreign policy apparatus. Somehow or other, there always had to be a RIG or a CAT. If there weren't, then the covert field would be taken over by any lone wolf with a hankering to run his own operation. There would be chaos.

"I appreciate your efforts," the Director conceded.

"Is that a 'go' on the satellite search?"

"A reluctant one. Do we need to tell the whole CAT?"

"No, if you'd prefer not."

"I'd prefer not. I want to limit the need-to-know."

"All right," Smith said. "That might be wise. I'll meet alone with Seamus Croaghan, and he can order the search with the NSC stamp. He can make the request sound like a presidential spot check of system efficiency. That'll give the *Urgent* tag plausibility."

"Fine. You want to let him decide when to involve the President?"

"I would. Let him buck it up to McBain."

"Okay," the Director said, "keep me informed." He paused, then added sincerely, "And let's just pray to God we don't have worst case here."

5

Seamus Croaghan was red in the face. But then, Seamus Croaghan was always red in the face.

"All right, Smith," he said impatiently, "what's so damned secret that we can't involve the rest of the CAT?"

The two men were in a windowless, soundproofed room in the basement of the White House that was used occasionally for impromptu CAT meetings. The CAT had no official offices. In fact, it barely had official existence.

But it, or some variation on the theme, would always be there. Over the years, presidential administrations came and went. The covert action groups changed names, and the players changed groups, but the game remained the same. As did the meeting place. When it came to cutting deals in the misty realm of executive privilege, the White House basement still played host.

"Seamus, you're going to have to stay calm," Smith said. "It looks as though a wheel's come loose."

Only the most careful of observers would have noticed any change in Croaghan's expression.

His was a florid Irishman's face, deeply pitted by acne over its entire surface. When he was a teenager, his parents had taken him from doctor to doctor, trying this miracle treatment and that. He'd been lanced and radiated; megadosed with Vitamin A, which resulted in a constant headache and the temporary loss of much of his wavy, reddish-brown hair; hypnotized and acupunctured and forced to apply a cream with a hydrochloric acid base that scarred what healthy skin he had left.

The condition had its advantages. For one thing, it meant that he had a permanent look of either impatience or anger or both. Nothing else. This made his thoughts extremely difficult to read. For another thing, he was undeniably ugly. And ugly people are, consciously or unconsciously, thought of as insensitive, boring, witless, and just plain stupid.

Despite this, Croaghan was one of the National Security Council's rising stars. Blessed by nature with a keen analytical mind, a John Riggins body, and a deep bass voice that encouraged deference, he had added a broad-based knowledge of computers and the ability to speak Spanish, Portugese, and half a dozen Amerindian languages, and entrenched himself as the administration's leading expert on Central and South American affairs.

Of course, it didn't hurt that he'd also been a friend of the incumbent National Security Adviser since childhood.

"It's Sunflower," Smith said neutrally. "We've lost a shipment of Stingers."

Croaghan smashed his fist down on the cheap metal desk, leaving a dent in its top. He got up, turning his back to Smith, and faced the wall. His shoulders rose and fell dramatically, until it seemed certain that he would hyperventilate.

When he turned to face Smith again, his face was redder than ever. "You've been shipping *Stingers* out of *Sunflower*?" he shouted.

"This was a private-sector delivery," Smith said.

"Yeah, sure. With the agency politely looking the other way. And us too by implicaton. Shit." Croaghan glared at the other man for a moment, then sighed and sat down. "How many?" he asked.

"Eight pods."

His face expressionless, Smith recounted everything he'd learned about the disappearance of the Stingers, giving away nothing that could be used to hold him accountable. He ended with an edited version of his meeting with the Director.

"That was two hours ago," he continued. "Since then I've been able to fill in a little more of the picture. The shrimp boat owners were working blind, both to cargo and deliveryman, who was a cutout named Ernesto Vargas. A very good man. Nicaraguan forced out by the Sandies. Completely trustworthy, in our judgment.

"Two days ago, a Juan Doe was found by the Corpus Christi police, dumped in a drainage ditch with his throat cut. I got a quick transmit on his prints this afternoon, and it was Vargas. Somebody who knew all the details of the op took his place."

"Son of a *bitch*," Croaghan said. "It's a hijack."

"I would think so," Smith said. "Whoever's behind it is good. He's got brains and timing and no compunction about killing. And I'm afraid it's impossible to even guess at his affiliation yet."

Croaghan pushed up the sleeves of his brown corduroy suit coat and rested his elbows on the arms of his chair. He interlaced his fingers, looking angry even in a posture that approached repose. "So what do we do now?" he said.

"Well, I think it would be counterproductive to search for the fishermen. I doubt they're still alive. I'm going to continue to have our people try to backtrack the operation. And—"

"Damn it, Smith! The President's going to be very pissed if he finds out you're using agency people for domestic."

"It's not strictly domestic," Smith said. "There's a strong possibility the hijackers are international. And if they aren't, the hijacking itself was. Precedent's been established for our involvement in cases like that.

"In any event, the President will be protected at all times. What you have to do is decide, now or soon, exactly who has a need-to-know on this. We can always muddy the water at our end. But depending on what these people intend to do with the missiles, you may not have, ah, the same range of options."

"You bastard," Croaghan said. "What are you telling me, that you're not going to take a fall over this, but that we'd better be prepared to? Even though we didn't know dick about it?"

Smith didn't say anything.

"If one of us hangs," Croaghan said, "we all hang." He pointed a thick forefinger at Smith.

Smith shrugged. He still didn't say anything.

"You sonofabitch! This is the office of the President!"

"I know what this is," Smith said quietly. "I'm merely saying that if we can't contain it, I believe the President will appreciate as much advance warning as possible. He'll want to have some answers prepared."

"You really don't have any feelings, do you?"

Smith looked the other man in the eye and said calmly, "I don't allow my feelings to interfere with my work."

Croaghan paused, considered what this conversation was really about, then said, "What's your opinion on dissemination?"

"Well," Smith said, "there's the rest of the CAT to consider. But they're all potential leaks. Personally, if I were you, I'd bottle it in the NSC for the time being, maybe just between you and McBain." McBain was National Security Adviser. "And then of course you have to decide when McBain breaks the news to the President."

"How long to establish the sequence of events?" Croaghan asked.

"It shouldn't take more than twenty-four hours. But we still won't know where the Stingers have gone. We won't know that until we hear from the hijackers. Or . . . we could do a satellite search. In my opinion, it's worth the risk of exposure."

"The pods had transponders in place?"

Smith nodded and Croaghan leaned back in his chair. Among the things he had made it a point to learn were the hardware specifics of as many different kinds of armaments as he possibly could. Few of the President's other advisers had bothered to commit so many details to memory. It was a potential edge.

He knew, for example, the configuration of a Stinger shipment. Stingers were transported in pods, or crates. Each pod contained three missiles in their disposable launch tubes; a reusable grip-stock for launching; and an

IFF (Identification: Friend or Foe) antenna, used to help determine the nature of the target in a potential firing situation.

In addition, a pod could be fitted with a simple tracking device—a battery-powered transponder programmed to be activated upon receipt of a uniquely coded transmission. Such transponders were routinely included if the Stingers' ultimate destination was a particularly unstable part of the world.

They could be activated by one of the low-flying military satellites that continuously circle the earth. The appropriate transponder would receive the signal and retransmit it. The transponder's reply would be very weak, but the satellite—with its powerful signal-gathering equipment—would be able to pick it up with ease.

The satellite could then continuously relay the missile pod's coordinates to a ground receiving station. Those coordinates would be accurate to within a mile or so. From there, mobile receivers could lock on to the transponder and find their way right to the crate itself.

The system was very efficient if you knew roughly where to look for the missiles to begin with. If you didn't, it could be a time-consuming process.

"They've got a sixteen-hour jump on us," Croaghan said. "Depending on what kind of transportation network they have, we could wind up scanning a pretty big chunk of the world."

"I know that," Smith said. "I still think it's worth it."

"Not to mention that they might have uncrated the missiles right off. All the transponders could be lying in a pile in the Honduran boonies somewhere. We'll look pretty stupid if we attack some jungle dump."

Smith nodded. "Still . . ." he said. "Limit the search to the U.S. if you want. They're only going to cause us a real problem if they're back here."

"Okay. I'm gonna have to run it through Fort Meade though."

"Tell them it's a practice search."

Croaghan examined the agency man as if looking for flaws. "You've thought this out, haven't you?" he said.

"Yes," Smith said. "And I'd advise you to do the same. If we don't proceed in some systematic manner, we're all liable to get burned."

Smith produced a small scrap of paper.

"I've set up a hot line," he said. "This is the number. Someone will be manning it around the clock. You'll need one too. And if the rest of the CAT does get pulled in, we'll need a conference link. But get yours to me as soon as possible."

"All right."

"And I'd assume," Smith said without a hint of urgency in his expression, "that we may be hearing from these people any minute."

10:15 P.M.

When the phone rang, Diane McBain was in the female superior position and riding hard. Derek Trane, the man beneath her, was gasping for breath.

It was not like this at home, with his wife.

Diane was sliding up and down on him, and at the same time twisting her body from side to side, causing the tips of her breasts to brush continuously across his face. His lips puckered reflexively, reaching for the stubby nipples each time they passed by. The warm, rhythmic caress returned him to infancy, but with all of his adult sensations intact.

There was also something happening deep within her as she ground herself against him on the downstroke— something that she did with her pubococcygeus muscles— that felt as if *she* were reaching into *him* in order to pull him inside out.

Trane had buried the fingers of one hand in the tawny blond hair that hung six inches below her shoulders. Without thinking about it, he slipped his other hand between her legs. The pleasure circuit hard-wired into her brain immediately began thrumming. She threw her head back, closing her eyes and letting her jaw go slack.

A sound with no name formed in her throat. The current in the circuit began to melt the wires through which it was flowing. Her scalp tingled.

And the telephone rang.

Diane McBain had three separate phones, each with its own distinctive ring. The one now sounding had a high, shrill tone that would penetrate even the deepest of sleep.

It belonged to the most private of her lines, a number known only to a select few.

Without a word she disengaged Trane's fingers, detached herself from her companion, and dropped off the bed.

He was in mid-gasp. He caught his breath, yelled "Hey—"

She didn't turn around. She walked naked to the small, soundproofed office adjacent to the bedroom. She closed the door after her and locked it.

Trane laced his fingers behind his head. His hairy body was damp with sweat and he was still breathing hard.

"Son of a *bitch*!" he said to the ceiling.

After the fourth ring, McBain's answering machine switched on. Her soft, uninflected voice said, "Hello. I'm not in right now, but if you'll leave a message after the beep I'll get back to you as soon as I can."

The machine beeped and a deep male voice said, "It's Seamus, Diane. We need to meet *toot sweet*."

The voice paused, and she immediately lifted the receiver, since Croaghan's final phrase had signified "highest priority" in their personal code.

"What is it, Seamus?" she said.

"The sunflower's lost some petals," he said. "We have to talk."

She paused to let the ramifications of what he had said sink in. "Give me fifteen minutes," she said.

She hung up and sat perfectly still for two of the fifteen.

Diane McBain was the first female to hold the post of Special Presidential Assistant for National Security Affairs, popularly known as the National Security Adviser. At thirty-seven, she was also one of the youngest. It was, however, a job for which she was highly qualified. Her Ph.D. thesis had been a detailed consideration of "defense" posturing between the United States and the Soviet Union since World War II. It had become *the* textbook in the field.

For the five years preceding her appointment to her current job, she had been an executive vice-president of the prestigious Stratech Corporation, preparing analyses of the interaction of emerging technology with American global political strategy, and providing them to conservative and liberal administrations alike.

When the new President had assumed office, he had taken a nearly unprecedented step. Never mind the question of gender. Rather than falling back on some longtime crony who didn't know Minsk from Manchuria, he had actually gone ahead and named a person who was ideally suited to direct his National Security Council.

McBain finished her two-minute meditation. She got up, unlocked the door, and walked back into the bedroom. Trane gawked at her nude body, his expression a parody of sexual desire.

"Sorry, Derek," she said as she went to the dresser. "Put your clothes on. You're leaving."

"Diaaaane!" he said.

She turned to face him. "Derek," she said as if to a petulant child, "sex is what we do for fun, but Washington is where we live. Get dressed and get the hell out of here. Now."

Trane, grumbling to himself, got out of bed and began to comply. After giving her instructions, she had turned her back to him. She stood in front of the mirror, adjusting her half-slip.

The National Security Adviser was not, by conventional standards, a beautiful woman. Halfway between fashionably slim and slightly plump, she did have the tawny blond hair and high cheekbones but she deliberately de-emphasized her physical attributes, dressing and applying makeup in such a way as to deflect attention from herself. The more a woman in public service played up her looks, the more media attention she got. And the more the press built her up, the more it would hunger to take her down.

None of this altered the fact that Diane McBain, because of her position, was a powerful sexual magnet, and her taste in partners tended to run along highly predictable lines.

Derek Trane, for example, was a young Deputy Undersecretary of State in the Latin American section, and was widely considered a comer. An ambitious would-be diplomat, he had a home in Chevy Chase, three very bright and adorable children, and a lovely, faithful wife who had no idea that he was committing adultery on a regular basis.

By the time he had dragged on his pants and laced his

shoes, McBain was holding the door for him. She had dressed in a plain gray wool skirt and cream-colored silk blouse. After giving him a kiss that held promise of things to come and patting him affectionately on the rear end, she followed him down the stairs, fetched his coat for him, and saw him out the front door of the undistinguished white brick row house.

He paused on the landing. "I really am crazy about you, you know," he said.

"Sure," she said. "Go see your lawyer. Divorce your wife. Abandon your kids. Wait for the administration to come to its appointed end. Get moving, Trane."

He looked at her questioningly, but she merely leaned a little more heavily on his arm. So he gave her a quick kiss and turned away. Five iron stairs took him to Georgetown street level. He went down the brick walkway and through the front gate, turned left. The sidewalks were slick from the fine, misty rain that had been slowly settling on them.

McBain watched him go. It was probably inevitable that a Deputy Undersecretary of State would think there was political hay to be made out of a liaison with the National Security Adviser. It was an understandable mistake. Only the most politically astute of the young and upwardly mobile are able to grasp that such temporary alignments are invariably more valuable to the person on the higher ground. The old hands know better. They realize that politics is the ability to effectively use other people. And it's a hell of a lot easier to use someone of lesser rank than vice versa.

When he was out of sight, she shook her head, then closed the front door.

Ten minutes later she was seated in the downstairs office in her house with Seamus Croaghan.

He wasted no time socializing and uncharacteristically refused his boss's offer of a cold Guinness. "Some asshole decided to ship a bunch of Stingers to the Connies," he said.

She gave him a cold, hard stare.

"Don't give me that look, Diane," Croaghan said. "You know damn well we've made covert shipments to the Contras. The President wants that. He gave his private nod and you authorized them."

"I never authorized—"

"Forget it. You're in a position for official denials and so is the President and that's fine. Come out of it smelling like a perfumed toilet seat. But there's a wheel loose here and if we don't get our act ready, then you can kiss your present job good-bye, and somehow I like the story much better where it comes out that you get to be Chief of Staff and I move into your spot. We clear?"

"We're not allowed to give missiles to the Contras," McBain said, her voice flat and businesslike.

Croaghan rolled his eyes upward.

"And we're not *allowed* to spit on the goddamn sidewalk," he said. "Fine, Diane, you're squeaky clean. Now here's the problem."

He told her as much of the story as he knew, along with the steps he and Smith had agreed should be taken.

"You went ahead and initiated the satellite sweep?" she said.

"Yes. Four hours ago."

"And why, may I ask, am I just hearing about all of this now?"

"Come on, Diane. I did the same thing you would have done. I waited to see if we were dealing with an agency screw-up. A dollar for every time they've lost sight of this or that and I'm a rich man." McBain allowed herself the trace of a smile. "The CAT has to deal with this kind of thing all the time. So I gave them a few hours to backtrack the resupply route."

She thought for a moment, then said, "You're working with Smith on this, huh?"

"Yeah. He's a prick, but I think he's as competent as they get over there. He's moved fast on this one."

"I don't trust him."

"Don't worry, I won't either."

The two officials looked at each other, then McBain asked, "What if we get a satellite fix and the damn things are in this country? What then?"

Croaghan shrugged. "Crunch time," he said. "Though we do have some choices. We could send in the FBI."

"Negative."

He smiled. "Then there's the local law, an option I don't much care for." She shook her head in agreement. "Which leaves us with either the military or the agency.

They're the only ones with the resources to get the job done."

"Great choice," she said.

"Yeah. One's illegal, the other's so bureaucratic we could be dealing with two dozen rusty missiles before all the papers got signed."

She gave him a sour look and said, "When will you have the first results from the satellite sweep?"

"I think we better figure eight hours, even with the *Urgent* tag on it. I'm having everything from Meade patched through to me at my place until six-thirty. I should be back in my office after that."

"All right," she muttered. "Go on, Seamus. Get some sleep."

After he had left the office, she reread her notes several times, thinking through the various potential scenarios. Then she picked up her phone and punched a special two-button combination.

"It's McBain," she said. "Yes I know it's late, but I need the President's schedule for the morning." She listened. "Okay, put me in the ten o'clock slot. . . . You'll have to bump them. . . . You're damn right it's important. Don't argue with me, just do it!"

6

March 15 4:40 A.M.

Javier Vega descended the weathered wooden ladder to the deck of the small motor launch moored in Charlestown harbor. Because the deck was slick from the early morning mist, Vega slipped, but immediately caught his balance. He steadied himself against the gentle rocking from the wavelets in the harbor and looked around, checking the docks for the least sign that something had gone wrong. His breath steamed in the cold, moist air. A foghorn sounded hollowly somewhere in the distance.

Both boat and mooring were sterile. The boat had

been purchased two months earlier through a dummy corporation, and the mooring's rent had been paid from a non-traceable account. Three times since the boat had first been docked, dummy trips had been made. A man had come in the early morning hours, taken the boat out, and returned in the late afternoon. Chances were no one would notice Vega's predawn departure.

In fact, on this morning there was only a single fishing boat, putt-putting slowly toward the bay. All those on board were gathered inside the pilothouse, drinking cup after cup of scalding coffee against the long day ahead.

Satisfied, Vega looked up again. His companion, the cameraman, handed down the long, skinny parcel, and Vega stowed it safely under the foredeck. Then the cameraman joined him in the boat.

Vega should have been tired. It had been a grueling twenty-four hours, and he'd only catnapped here and there along the way. Now he was preparing to go out on the water, little more than a day after the hijack.

But there would be time to sleep. This was the time to act, as quickly as possible, before the Americans quite realized what had happened to them.

Boston had been the logical choice for the first strike, for two simple reasons. First, it was a northern city, still chilly at this time of year. The missile's infrared lock-on device—the seeker—functioned better in a low-temperature environment. The colder the air, the more vividly the heat of the target would stand out and the easier for the seeker to get a positive lock.

Second, Logan Airport was particularly vulnerable to attack, since it was surrounded by water. That meant the runways could be closely approached with safety, and there would be an unimpeded line of sight to the target. Getaway problems would also be minimized.

It was close to an ideal situation.

The time of day had also been chosen with care. Again, there was a higher chance of success at night because of generally cooler temperatures and the absence of infrared interference from the sun. But, on the other hand, it was necessary to have sufficient light for the filming.

So the compromise had been made. The strike would take place just before sunrise.

Vega and the cameraman were in the small cabin beneath the boat's foredeck. The cameraman had just a Canon VM-E2 8-mm Camcorder, picked for its superior performance in low-light conditions, and a couple of pre-tested cassettes. There was no point in carrying a lot of backup cassettes; if the one in the camera somehow failed, there'd be no opportunity for a retake.

The cameraman ran a final check on the loaded cassette by filming Vega and then playing the result back through the Canon's viewfinder. Both camera and tape worked perfectly.

Vega was carefully unpacking the missile.

It had been transferred, within its disposable launch tube, from the original aluminum cylinder to an unobtrusive box that had been especially made for the purpose. Into the box had also gone the reusable grip-stock. They had left behind the optional IFF antenna that attached to the stock. In this instance, no distinction needed to be made between friend and foe. Every aircraft was the enemy.

Vega attached the grip-stock to the launch tube, hefted the apparatus onto his shoulder and balanced it. The tube was just over five feet long and the entire package weighed a scant thirty pounds. That was one of the beauties of the thing. Any normal adult was capable of hoisting a Stinger into firing position.

It was the finest portable ground-to-air missile in the world.

He nodded his approval. He placed the missile launcher on a cushioned bench and sat next to it, resting a hand on it as if to make sure it didn't get away. The cameraman played the tape for him. In the viewfinder Vega watched a tiny version of himself preparing the weapon for use. He smiled.

The cameraman looked at his watch. "One hour to sunrise," he said. Today the sun would rise over the city of Boston at five fifty-seven. The tide would also be near crest, another plus. The boat would sit that much higher with reference to the runway.

"Twenty-five minutes," Vega said, "and we go." Like the cameraman, he spoke in Spanish.

He raised his right thumb and the cameraman returned the gesture.

4:55 A.M.

Aer Lingus Flight 206—from Logan to Shannon in Ireland, with a continuation to London Heathrow—was seven and a half hours behind schedule, the result of a violent late-winter storm that had stalled over the North Atlantic.

The crowd in the Aer Lingus departure lounge was quiet. Many had leaned back in their chairs or stretched out on the carpet and nodded off. At midnight, when the delay had been three hours, the atmosphere had been one of near mutiny. But that had passed. After an eight-hour delay anger loses its ability to sustain itself, especially at this time of morning.

Among those who couldn't or didn't want to sleep, there were the desultory conversations of the weary. Crossword puzzles were filled in, magazines read from cover to cover. Inevitably, some relationships of the moment had sprung up.

Off by themselves under a window, a boy and a girl in their early twenties snuggled together. Strangers the day before, they giggled when not speaking in low, confidential tones. They'd just made a quick trip to the observation deck to finish the boy's last marijuana cigarette.

An elderly woman in a wheelchair was talking to her niece, a stout middle-aged woman in a wool suit who sat with her back straight and her knees pressed tightly together. They had been playing variations on the same theme for hours.

"No, Margaret," the elderly woman would say. "I am not coming back. I am going home to die. I want to die in Ireland."

And her niece would say, "Stop that talk, Auntie Grace. That's silly talk and I won't have it."

Two professors of literature had discovered one another and whiled away the time in gentle argument. Dr. Callahan, Ireland's leading authority on W. B. Yeats, had defended his belief that Yeats was the language's greatest visionary poet. The American, Dr. Armstrong, had taken the position that Yeats was second-rate when compared with someone like mad Billy Blake.

Glion Walsh had found that the seat next to him on the plane was going to be occupied by Father Dermot

Croaghan. He'd also found that Father Croaghan slept little in the best of times and never in airport holding pens. He himself might have slept if his six-year-old daughter Jennifer had not been curled up in his lap.

And so the two men talked. Or, rather, Walsh talked. For the most part, Croaghan listened. He was good at it, as a priest should be.

Walsh had explained how he was taking his daughter to see her grandmother, his mother, in County Clare. How his wife was terrified of flying and had refused to go. How he wasn't going to let that keep Jennifer from her roots.

The two men were hunting for possible mutual friends in Clare when a young woman with auburn hair and a green uniform made her way to the area behind the check-in counter. After a few moments of shuffling papers around, she picked up a microphone.

"Top of the morning, ladies and gentlemen," she said with a sheepish smile.

People began stirring. Heads popped up. Bleary eyes were turned toward the woman in green.

"Aer Lingus regrets the weather delay in the departure of Flight 206," the young woman continued, "but we Irish have learned to be patient when it comes to the wind and the rain. I'm pleased to announce that we have now been cleared to issue our pre-boarding call to those requiring special assistance."

The announcement triggered more purposeful movement. Several couples draped sleeping children over their shoulders, struggled with their carry-on bags full of toys and diapers and formula bottles. Margaret pushed her Aunt Grace's wheelchair to the entry door. The boarding began.

5:15 A.M.

Captain John McMillen and First Officer Brett Doone, the pilot and copilot, left flight dispatch after having been thoroughly briefed on the unstable weather patterns along their route to Ireland. Both men realized that they would likely have little to do during the next seven hours. Nearly every aspect of long-distance flying was now controlled by computers. Except in an emergency, the crew's function was primarily to monitor the machines.

On the other hand, Flight 206 could prove more challenging. There was a major storm out there, and who was to say what course it might suddenly choose to take?

The two went down the boarding ramp and up to the flight deck of the 747, where Captain McMillen saluted his Second Officer, Flight Engineer Thomas Braine, who reciprocated. Saluting was a habit the captain had carried over from his days in the RAF. His crew found the ritual a little silly but harmless.

McMillen and Doone took their places in the cockpit. The captain compared his figures for on-board fuel and gross weight with the flight engineer's. The figures were in agreement. He then informed Braine of everything that had been decided during the briefing at flight dispatch. After he had done that, all three men were capable of piloting Flight 206.

"The INS's are programmed?" McMillan asked Braine next.

"Yes," Braine said. "No errors."

McMillen nodded. Still, he doublechecked his Inertial Navigation System against those of the other crew members. As Braine had said, there were no errors.

"All right," he said to Second Officer Doone. "You can load the flight plan."

While Doone performed this task, McMillen conferred with the Flight Director about conditions that he would be expected to encounter during the flight. Afterward, the captain cross-checked Doone's flight plan and made sure INS units were in agreement.

Navigationally, the 747 was now ready to fly.

The Captain and First Officer ran through the preflight checklist, then McMillen said, "Everything looks good. And presto, here's the tractor."

Two minutes later, the tractor operator had pulled the 747 back from the gate. He spoke directly to the captain.

"You're 'go' to fire up," he said.

"Roger," McMillen said to the tractor operator.

The 747 taxied slowly toward the line of aircraft awaiting takeoff. It was cleared for sixth in the queue, and pilot and co-pilot ran through their after-start checklist.

"I don't think we have any problems," Doone said

finally. "I'm showing an outside temp of thirty-four, wind speed ten knots out of the southwest. No observable icing."

"Roger," McMillen said.

The plane came to a halt as it arrived at its position in the queue. Flight 206 was on schedule for its projected takeoff time of five fifty-five.

5:40 A.M.

The cameraman maneuvered the small launch slowly through the sheltered waters around Logan Airport. The overcast sky was pale gray with the coming of dawn. There was very little boat traffic at this hour.

Vega remained in the cabin under the foredeck, wanting to stay out of sight for as long as possible. He was also protecting the missile's delicate seeker from the potential fouling effects of the salt spray above.

Wind was out of the southwest, which meant that the planes would be taking off down Runway 22-Right in a northeast-to-southwest direction. Vega would have preferred it if the wind had been from the northeast, but he would adapt to conditions as they were. What they dictated was that the boat must come around to the north end of the airport, so that he was facing the engines' exhaust as the plane took off. It wasn't a big problem. There was an escape route mapped out for either end of the peninsula on which the airport lay.

No specific target had been selected, however. It didn't matter. Whatever plane was on the runway just before dawn would be the one taken.

A 747 would be a hell of a challenge, Vega thought. The Stinger was designed to be used against helicopters and small combat aircraft. It was a tiny missile, really, just three inches in diameter, and carried only a couple of pounds of warhead. High-explosive, to be sure, but it had little chance of seriously damaging a gigantic commercial jet unless . . . the person firing it was highly skilled. And lucky. The placement of the shot was crucial, as was the sequence of events following detonation of the payload. If everything went perfectly, then . . .

Vega felt a rush of anticipation. He was no Afghan

camel jockey five years out of the Stone Age. He was an educated man with a natural aptitude for weapons use, and he'd practiced to the point of mastery. He *wanted* one of the big jets.

The boat slowed and came to a stop, its motor idling. Vega went out on deck and looked at his watch: five minutes before dawn. Perfect timing.

Logan Airport lay just off to starboard. Jets were plodding to the head of the queue, each crew deep into the intricate ritual that leads to a successful takeoff. Beyond the clouds the rising sun was inching toward the horizon. And out on Runway 22-Right, a 727 was just taxiing into pre-takeoff position. Another plane, a 747, followed close behind. It bore the Aer Lingus shamrock.

Vega was smiling as he looked at his watch again.

"Get the camera ready," he said.

5:45 A.M.

Glion Walsh grinned at his daughter, as did Father Croaghan. She was by the window, straining at her seat belt in order to see even more of the concrete world below the wing.

"She's going to be a real beauty, that one," Croaghan said. "And lively as a Killarney trout. You've a fine Irish girl for certain."

Walsh beamed as the cabin attendants ran through the preflight briefing: how to use the seat belt, where the life preservers were, the location of the emergency exits. They lied about what would happen if the cabin became depressurized, how oxygen masks would drop down and that would make everything A-OK. For obvious reasons they didn't mention that sudden decompression had been known to cause a collapse of the cabin floor and that passengers in that unlucky instance had been sucked into the resultant hole and blown out the fuselage.

Then the captain came on over the intercom. He informed the passengers that there might be some rough spots during the flight, due to the storm over the northeast Atlantic. The storm, however, was moving steadily away from the plane's flight path, and nothing serious should be encountered. So, he said, other than the possible minor turbulence problems, a routine flight was expected.

"Relax," he counseled, "enjoy yourselves, and don't hesitate to call on our attendants for anything you might need."

At the back of the smoking section, the stoned boy and girl took to heart the captain's invitation to enjoy. They snuggled together under a blanket, conducting some preliminary explorations.

"You know," the girl said, "this is going to be a very far-out flight."

Professors Callahan and Armstrong settled comfortably in their seats, neither betraying any outward sign of nervousness.

"I've always wondered what goes on in the cockpit at a time like this," Armstrong said. "What do they talk about? What do they do?"

"One hopes that they are dealing with their machines and not with a friendly stewardess," Callahan said, and Armstrong laughed.

5:55 A.M.

The Aer Lingus 747 moved to first position in the queue. It paused, ready for takeoff down 22-Right. The pilot had determined that the plane's gross weight didn't warrant interrupting traffic flow—as 747's were allowed to—in order to use the longer Runway 22-Left, normally reserved for landings.

"Takeoff briefing?" copilot Doone asked.

"Nothing special. It's a milk run," the captain said. He briefly switched on the cabin intercom. "Ladies and gentlemen, we have been cleared for takeoff. Flight attendants please be seated."

They had just completed final checks when tower control announced, "Aer Lingus 206, you are cleared for takeoff. No delay if you please, Cap. We've still got a bit of a backup."

"Roger," McMillen said, then to his first officer, "gentlemen, start your engines."

It was always the last flight instruction the captain gave. It wasn't funny, but Doone chuckled dutifully.

"Okay," Doone said. "Spool up."

The four massive Rolls-Royce engines whined unmercifully as their turbines revved to takeoff level.

"Let's go," the pilot said.

The 747's brakes were released and it started down the runway.

"Vee-One," McMillen said as the aircraft's velocity passed the point of no return.

"Looking good," Doone confirmed.

"And . . . and . . . Vee-Two," the Captain said. Velocity required for lift-off was attained. "Got it. Nose up."

Aer Lingus Flight 206 raised its head. It shuddered a little as the Rolls jets strained to pull its five hundred thousand pounds away from the earth.

Javier Vega could not have been more pleased. It was dawn and there she was, a 747 ready to be taken. He had the launcher in position on his shoulder and a good view around the edge of the wooden fence at the end of the runway. The boat was riding fairly steady in the light chop. If he'd learned his lessons at all well, and had just a bit of luck, this one was a cinch.

He adjusted the earphones clamped to his head. They were set to receive a signal from the Stinger's delicate infrared/ultraviolet seeker mechanism. When the seeker had locked on, a steady tone would play through the earphones. If the seeker lost its lock, the tone would stop.

The seeker seldom lost lock-on.

Just to the southwest of the boat, the 747 had begun spool-up. When its engines reached maximum thrust, it headed down the runway. It required a little under two miles to attain takeoff velocity.

The range of the Stinger was listed as three miles. In reality, it could perform capably up to five.

Vega watched as the plane picked up speed. Timing was all important now. The farther away the aircraft, the smaller the target. But the optimum moment for a hit was that critical juncture before the 747 had leveled off, when it was bent at an angle to the ground and still needed full thrust from its four engines to prevent a stall.

In even the best of circumstances, a flameout at that point meant the risk of a crash.

Vega steadied the launcher, following the plane's progress through the optical gunsight. He was zeroed in on the outside engine, starboard side.

Twenty seconds after the 747 had started rolling, Vega flipped the first switch in the firing sequence. This released the argon stored in a small capsule in the grip-stock. The argon further cooled the seeker, for maximum sensitivity. Vega then activated the seeker itself. The tone coming through his earphones told him that he'd done a good job of visually tracking the jet. The seeker had gotten an immediate positive lock.

He waited another five seconds, carefully holding the lock, then he pulled the trigger. That was it. The Stinger is a true fire-and-forget weapon. Once the seeker gets a lock and the firing sequence is initiated, there is nothing further for the operator to do. The computerized internal guidance system assumes complete responsibility for delivering the missile to its target.

The Stinger popped out of its launch tube, propelled by the secondary motor which ejects it to a safe distance from the gunner prior to ignition of the primary rocket engine. Then the rocket kicked in.

The missile quickly attained its strike velocity of 1,760 feet per second. The plane that it was chasing had nosed up from the runway at takeoff speed of 176 feet per second. At the moment of launch, about twelve thousand feet separated the two.

The Stinger closed the gap in just over eight seconds.

It homed on the outside engine, starboard side.

Its seeker performed flawlessly.

When it reached its target, at an altitude of one hundred fifty feet, it flew straight into the engine and smashed through the rear compressor blades. Its small, high-explosive warhead detonated.

In the cabin, the explosion was perceived as a muffled *thump*. It was audible over the sound of the engines, but just barely. It did not suggest a serious problem.

Except to a man sitting just aft of the starboard wing. He heard the thump and saw the accompanying flash of light in the vicinity of the engine. The man screamed.

In the cockpit, First Officer Doone said calmly, "Captain, confirm that engine number one is dead. We've had a flameout."

"Close fuel line to number one," Captain McMillen said.

"Yes, sir."

"Steady," the captain said. "Let's just level her off and bring her back down."

In a normally functioning turbofan engine, air is drawn in the front through a set of compressor blades. A second set of blades, at the rear, vents exhaust and also serves to drive the front set. This system keeps air flowing steadily through the engine even in the event of a flameout. Thus there is almost always time to shut off the fuel feed to the afflicted engine.

Doone had no way of knowing that he didn't have a prayer of isolating engine number one.

When the Stinger had slammed into Aer Lingus Flight 206, it had both caused a flameout and jammed the rear compressor blades. The detonation of its payload had torn a small hole in the engine housing and had also ruptured the fuel line.

Fuel sprayed into the engine. With the exhaust system crippled, pressure built up rapidly. Air was drawn in through the hole in the housing. In a matter of seconds the mixture of fuel and hot, unvented gases passed the critical point.

The decision to close the fuel line had, through no fault of the flight crew, come a moment too late. There was a massive secondary explosion, far more violent than the original one.

Engine number one turned into a fireball. The man who had screamed stared in horror, completely paralyzed. Other passengers began to scream, for the sound of the second explosion had reverberated throughout the aircraft. It could not have been ignored. Nor could the sound of flying metal tearing into the 747's fuselage. Nor could the sight of the flames which now leapt high above the cabin windows.

The fire spread with sickening speed. It raced along the fuel line, melting electrical wires, rupturing hydraulics.

Captain McMillen was fighting to keep the plane's nose up. If he failed to get it leveled off at cruising velocity, then the 747 could go into a stall. The only way out of a stall is to dive, in order to pick up the required speed. And you can only dive when you have adequate altitude.

Flight 206 was way too low.

"What's going on?" the captain yelled.

"I don't know!" his first officer yelled back. "Something happened after the flameout. An explosion." Sweat had beaded on Doone's upper lip and was running from his hairline down his temples. He was desperately throwing switches back and forth. "I can't get the fuel line closed! Electrical's completely screwed up!"

"Come on, baby," McMillen said. "Just a little higher." He caressed the control column, but it had begun to shake in his hands, the warning of an impending stall.

The plane was tilting to starboard, in the direction of the loss of power.

"Come on."

"Sir," Doone said, "we're losing everything!"

"Shut down engine four!" McMillen commanded, hoping that would compensate for the flameout of engine one and begin to correct the tilt. "Switch to APU!"

The Auxiliary Power Unit is an independent backup which will operate the aircraft's electrical and hydraulic systems even if all four engines have been lost.

The pylon which held engine number one had been sheared by the force of the second blast. It flapped back and forth in the wind. Then it snapped. The engine plummeted into the sea.

"Sir!" Flight Engineer Braine shouted from the starboard window. "Engine one's gone! It blew off the pylon! The whole wing's on fire!"

The physical loss of engine one had lightened the wing to which it had been attached. This caused a further imbalance, and the plane listed even more to starboard.

In the cabin, flight attendants were hurrying up and down the tilted aisles, trying to calm the most hysterical of the passengers. They were inhumanly cool in the face of an obvious catastrophe, counseling people to stay in their seats, reassuring the frightened that everything was under control, yet giving detailed instructions about what to do in the event of an emergency landing.

Margaret was crossing herself furiously, but her Aunt

Grace was just staring straight ahead, a peaceful smile on her face.

When the pylon snapped, the boy and girl at the back of the smoking section came up for air after a deep, tongue-probing kiss.

"Something's happening," the boy said.

"Something's always happening," his new love replied as she pulled him toward her again.

"Ahhhh," Javier Vega said after the second explosion. "You get that with the zoom?"

"Of course," his cameraman said. "Of course. Perfect."

"I can't get any response, John," Doone said. "All our hydraulics are out. There's something wrong with the APU. It won't come on."

The control column was now shaking violently in the captain's hands.

"We're gonna stall," the pilot said. "Brett, can we go to manual?"

When all else fails, there are cranks and levers which give manual access to all control surfaces of the aircraft. First Officer Doone left his seat and frantically tried to work them, tried to level the 747 out so that they could make some sort of glide landing somewhere, anywhere, but preferably the water.

It was too late. The plane had heeled over into an unrecoverable Dutch roll. It stalled.

"We're going down," McMillen said.

Thomas Braine was staring out the window in horror. "Oh my God," he said hoarsely.

For the first time Captain McMillen saw what his flight engineer was staring at.

"Oh my God!" he repeated.

Standard operating procedure after a 22-Right Logan takeoff is for the aircraft to turn from the two-hundred-and-twenty-degree compass heading along which the runway is laid out. For purposes of noise abatement a course of one hundred forty degrees is taken. This leads the plane away from an overflight of the heavily populated areas below it and sends it out over the Atlantic. From there it adjusts its bearing according to the flight plan.

Aer Lingus 206 had not had time before the flameout to initiate the turn to the east. Moreover, the roll caused by the loss of engine number one, and subsequent damage to the starboard wing, had pushed its course even farther to the west. It was headed directly over Columbia Point.

There was another explosion as one of the fuel tanks blew. The plane continued to tip to starboard, until its wings were angled more than forty-five degrees from their normal position. Its nose had come down and it was heading back to the ground, picking up speed all the while. It was apparent to everyone aboard that the aircraft was going to crash.

Some screamed and some cursed and some wept.

Some, accepting their fate, had twisted themselves so they could hold hands and gaze with love into each other's eyes.

Flight attendants, and passengers who in their panic had unbuckled seat belts, were tossed from one side of the cabin to the other. Bodies became entangled. Punches were thrown as those on the bottom of the pile struggled to see what was happening.

Glion Walsh crushed his daughter's young body to his own as if to squeeze the life from her, as though it might be more merciful if she died there in his arms.

Father Dermot Croaghan had begun commending the spirits of all those present unto the Lord.

"Brett!" McMillen shouted. "The storage tanks! You've got to move us! We can't hit the tanks!"

Doone had braced himself against the tilt and was working the manual crank that controlled the rudder. The sweat was dripping from his face. He couldn't see what the captain and flight engineer were seeing, but he had already guessed. Though he knew the plane was going down, he fought hard to prevent an even greater catastrophe.

Below them, next to the Southeast Expressway, stood two huge LNG storage tanks used by Boston Gas.

Liquefied natural gas is one of the most dangerous explosives on the planet. It is a gas in its natural state, but in order to make storage of it economically practical, it is converted into a liquid by putting it under intense pressure. One cubic foot of the liquid expands to six hundred times that volume when it is returned to its gaseous form.

The huge Dorchester storage tanks each had the potential for holding 1.4 billion cubic feet of LNG. If the two tanks exploded simultaneously, and if each contained its maximum volume of the fuel, they would unleash a firestorm with a radius of over one hundred miles, turning the entire Boston metropolitan area into an inferno. Only a large thermonuclear device could cause comparable destruction.

Javier Vega and his cameraman could not see the final result of their strike, though the cameraman kept the videotape running even after the plane dropped out of his line of sight. There was no telling how dramatic the explosion was going to be. Some portion of it might be visible.

Inside the aircraft, Doone strained against the manual rudder as his two fellow officers exhorted him on. The whole plane shook as the rudder moved, inch by inch, making a succession of small adjustments to the 747's trajectory.

Out on the Southeast Expressway, a few early morning motorists had stopped their cars and were standing on the road's shoulder, unable to avert their eyes from the scene unfolding before them.

The flaming wreck that had been Aer Lingus Flight 206 was returning to earth carrying a pilot, copilot, flight engineer, flight director, purser, assistant purser, eleven flight attendants, and two hundred eighty-five passengers. When it finally crashed, the point of impact—due solely to the heroic efforts of First Officer Brett Doone—was in Dorchester Bay, three and a half miles southwest of Logan Airport and four hundred feet northeast of the Boston Gas storage tanks.

The final explosions buffeted the tanks, but did not rupture them.

PART II

BRUDERDAM

How could we dare spill
The blood that unites us?
Where is joy in
The killing of kinsmen?
                    —*The Bhagavad-Gita*

7

Steven Kirk had just popped his seventh Fiorinal of the
day. Everything was a bit dreamy, which was the way he
wanted it. The pain in his head was just a blip beyond the
far horizon. The inside of the stucco bungalow seemed
like alien territory, and not only because it was Claire's
house, full of Claire's belongings.

They were together in the kitchen, after dinner, and it
was past time to tell the bad news.

"I lost my job," he told her. There it was. He'd been
trying to get the words out since the previous morning,
when it had happened, and had failed every time.

Claire set the last of the dishes in the sink and turned
to look at him. "Why?" she asked.

"I was late again. It was the time too many. Leo gave
me two weeks' pay and a little extra."

She came over and sat down across the table from him.
"I'm sorry," she said.

He started to say something by way of accepting her
condolences, but she held up her hand and he stopped
himself.

"Steven," she said, "it isn't working for us, we both
know that. This is just one more thing. I am sorry you
lost your job, if you care at all, but . . . well, maybe it'll
turn out to be the best thing that's happened to you
lately." She paused. "I suppose that sounds trite, doesn't
it?"

"I don't know," he said. "In what context?"

"I've watched what you're doing to yourself and . . . I
don't think I can watch it anymore. There's something
broken inside of you, and when it broke, it took away
whatever made you who you were before."

"Yeah, I guess. You might not have liked who I was."

"That doesn't matter. Steven, you're an intelligent man

who takes the crummiest jobs and can't even hold *them*. You won't do a single thing to improve your life. As God is my witness, I care for you, and I believe that you are a better man than you let yourself be, but I just don't love you enough to be able to make it happen for you. And I can't hold on for the time it's going to take for you to do it. I don't have that kind of strength."

There was a long moment of silence when it seemed the inevitable might not happen, then the spell was broken. The alternative possibilities melted away under the blue fluorescent kitchen lights. Somewhere outside a dog barked savagely, and their lives started lining up the way they were actually going to be played out.

The rest seemed to Kirk as if it were taking place underwater. They embraced; they kissed one another with genuine warmth; they decided who would do what and when.

It was all very civilized. Kirk felt briefly that there should have been more in the way of screaming and throwing of pots and pans, as Susanna would undoubtedly have done in similar circumstances.

But it was wrong to compare the two women, and he knew it. It was especially unfair to Claire. Susanna had been his only wife; Claire had been a misguided attempt at replacement, though she had proven to have far more heart than he'd ever bargained for. Claire he would miss, yet the feeling would pale next to the pain from the loss of his wife and child, an agony that hadn't perceptibly diminished since the day they were killed.

An image leaped abruptly into his head, a treasured image: Susanna sitting in the backyard, the late afternoon sun turning her bare skin to gold, tiny Scottie nursing greedily at her breast. He remembered the peace he had felt watching his son fill himself with his mother's life.

He pushed the image away as Claire said, "I'm going to go visit my sister for a couple of days. Are you . . . okay?"

Kirk nodded and Claire walked out of the kitchen. In truth, he felt awful. He was alone and homeless, with no job and no prospect of one. All the various aches had coalesced inside him, forming a large ball that floated at the center of his consciousness. Around the ball there was a vast, empty space, devoid of even the possibility of feeling.

He sat down again at the kitchen table and tried to think his way through to whatever came next. He could hear Claire in the bedroom, packing that ratty plaid cloth bag of hers. He stared down at the scratched and yellowed Formica, picking at it with his fingernail, and thought of his father. It was inevitable, he supposed. He was adrift once again. Those were the times when he tended to think of the old man and the only place in the world that was any sort of home to him.

Charles Worthington Kirk, the elder statesman. Adviser to presidents of the United States.

Whereas his son lived a few short blocks from derelicts and grade-school addicts. In a cement house with cracked stucco exterior, in a city that should have been a desert.

Claire came back into the room with her sad little bag. "Well," she said, clutching the bag with both hands, "good-bye."

She said it the way she might have when going away for the weekend, but Kirk knew that she meant it to be forever.

He got up. "Good-bye," he said.

He kissed her lightly on the lips, and then she was gone. Her scent, the sense of her presence, lingered for a moment, but soon they too were gone.

He was alone.

He didn't have much to pack. His few personal items would fill a small corner of the Chevy's trunk. But there was no place to take them, and he wasn't about to go apartment-hunting before morning. What, then?

Two hours later, the effects of the drugs had slackened enough that he was able to answer the question. He wanted to be mindlessly entertained, and he didn't want to have to put forth much effort to make that happen. All he had to do was navigate the Caprice a half mile down the road. Okie Bob's place would just be cranking up for the night.

Okie Bob's was about as mindless as they got. It featured a shitkicker band—whether of quality or not—every night of the week. It attracted displaced Texans and Oklahomans from all over the low-rent district in which Kirk lived. Mostly men. Mostly men who didn't exactly listen to the music, but were uncomfortable if it wasn't playing in the background of their lives.

The parking lot was filling up when Kirk arrived.

He liked shitkicker music, though he hadn't been to Bob's that often. One reason was that Claire didn't like the place; few women would. Another was that Kirk rarely drank much anymore. Alcohol mixed dangerously with the drugs he took, but that in itself probably wouldn't have stopped him. It was the dehydration. That made the headaches worse in the morning, and the pain was already bad enough. So when he did drink, he generally nursed a couple of beers through the evening.

Sometimes, though, he would lose track.

There was space at the bar when he first got there, but soon there were bodies wedged between the stools. A dozen dust-cracked voices vied for the bartender's attention. Every table was littered with mugs and pitchers and overflowing ashtrays. The collective smell was getting raunchy: sweat and tobacco smoke, unwashed Levi's, and tasteless American lager beer.

The band wasn't bad. They played the usual stuff— "Whiskey River," "I've Always Been Crazy," "Good-Hearted Woman." The few hard-looking women in the place were up and dancing with their equally hard-looking men. Or else the men were trying to entice the women away from their friends. There was one fight.

By the middle of the band's second set, Kirk had had six beers. He hadn't been drinking purposefully, but he also hadn't been counting. The alcohol, combined with the drugs, had created a seamlessness to reality in which there was little distinction between what was outside his head and what was inside. He gave no thought to what the morning might be like because for now there was an absence of pain.

The band played on, behind a protective net of chicken wire. Okie Bob had put it up one night and never taken it down. A lot of flying bottles had crashed against that wire over the years, and a lot of emergency trips to the hospital had been avoided.

As they kicked into "A Country Boy Will Survive," a Hank Williams, Jr., standard, Kirk drummed his fingers on the bar, more or less in time to the music. He loved those guys up there, picking and strumming and singing their hearts out for the people. He loved the people too.

"Play it, you Okie bastards!" he shouted.

The two men jimmied into the tiny space between Kirk and the next barstool looked much alike—lean and sinewy, with sun-browned hatchet faces—and were apparently friends. One of them shoved his nose close to Kirk's and shouted, "What did you say?"

Kirk repeated himself, adding an "Eee-hah" for good measure.

"You got something against Okies?" the man said.

"Hell, no," Kirk said. "They may be dumb, but the motherfuckers can play!"

"That so? What if I was an Okie?"

"Better than a Texan," Kirk said with a grin. In truth, there was no longer a functional connection between his brain and his mouth. "Dip their wick in any rattlesnake hole." He laughed.

The hatchet-faced man jerked his thumb at his friend. "My buddy's from Texas," he said.

Kirk realized he'd said something wrong, but couldn't figure out what it was. He just sat there, grinning like a fool.

"You laughing at me?" the man said.

Kirk didn't reply. It seemed like a rhetorical question. Yet it obviously wasn't, because in the next instant he was flying off his barstool. He hit the wooden floor hard, but didn't feel a thing.

The two men jumped him, but before they could land a punch, a pair of very large bouncers arrived. They both had mustaches and were wearing identical "Okie Bob's" T-shirts that threatened to split across their chests and biceps.

The larger bouncer picked up the Okie and the Texan, and stuffed one under either arm. His partner lifted Kirk from the floor with one hand. The crowd rippled apart as the three combatants were hustled from the club.

Outside, the first bouncer rapped the Okie's and Texan's heads together and dropped the dazed men on their butts. The second threw Kirk belly-down onto the sidewalk.

"See you don't come back," the first bouncer said to all three, and then he and his partner went back inside.

Kirk got to his feet, still a little unsure of what had happened, and headed for his car. He almost made it.

The two hatchet-faced men were hearing bells inside

their skulls. Someone was going to pay for that, and it wasn't going to be the very large bouncers. They got to Kirk in the parking lot.

Down he went again, this time from a vicious cross-body block thrown by the Texan, who for a moment thought he was back playing free safety for Wichita Falls again. Then the two men began to stomp him. Kirk didn't know what was going on, and he was hardly feeling the blows, but his instincts weren't totally short-circuited. He managed to get himself into the tuck position. Then he lay there on the gravel as the angry men aimed kicks at him.

A few people passed by on their way to the club, but no one intervened. Okie Bob's didn't attract the sort of person who involved himself in someone else's fight. Nor was it likely that anyone would call the cops.

In their rage, the two men might well have killed him. Except that there was a slight, inoffensive crunching of gravel and then a man stood near them. They hadn't noticed him arrive, but they heard him speak.

"That's enough," he said.

The Okie looked over at the stranger. He saw a man of medium size with slightly thinning brown hair and high school plastic glasses. Although it was still quite warm, the man was wearing a topcoat.

"The fuck are you?" the Okie said.

"It's not important," the man said. "Stop what you're doing and leave now."

It didn't appear possible that the man could successfully fight a child, much less a couple of hardened oil-field roughnecks. Yet there was something in his face. . . .

The Okie hesitated for a moment, but then said, "Beat it."

The stranger nodded as if he'd been through this all before. He unbuttoned his topcoat and reached up under his arm. When his hand emerged, it held a 9-mm Walther semiautomatic pistol. He cocked the hammer and aimed the gun at the Okie. His calm manner suggested that he both knew how to use it and was prepared to do so.

"Uh, wait a minute," the Okie said. Both he and his Texas buddy had reflexively raised their hands. They stopped kicking Kirk.

"Now," the stranger said, and he motioned with the gun toward the entrance to the parking lot.

The Texan pointed in the other direction. "Our car is—"

"Now!"

The two roughnecks skittered away from Kirk and the man with the gun. When they felt they could turn around, they dropped their hands and began to run. They didn't look over their shoulders. In a moment they were around the corner and gone.

The man in the topcoat replaced the Walther in its underarm holster and knelt beside Kirk. Kirk was a little bloodied, but he was breathing easily. His eyes were closed.

"Steven," the man said.

Kirk knew that voice. From where? He wasn't sure he wanted to know. If he ignored it, it would probably go away, and he could sleep.

But then he heard his name called again. There was a hand on his shoulder, shaking it. Reluctantly he opened his eyes. And wished he hadn't.

Even with the drugs and the alcohol and the beating he'd just taken, he wished he hadn't opened his eyes.

"Ah shit, Smith," he said wearily. "What are you doing here?"

8

Smith clucked his tongue.

"Steven," he said. "A couple of punks like that? Time was, you would have handled them without breaking a sweat."

"Yeah," Kirk said. "Well, times change."

He propped his back against the rear tire of an old white Cadillac. All things considered, he didn't feel that bad. His body would be funny colors in the morning, but he couldn't feel any broken bones and he hadn't taken any serious shots to the head.

He looked up at Smith. The bland, expressionless face was just as Kirk remembered it; Smith could have been a world-class poker player if he'd wanted a respectable profession. Kirk forced himself to admit that his old adversary had just saved him from being beaten to death, and he tried to find some trace of gratitude in himself. He searched, but there was none there. Smith was still the last person on earth Kirk wanted to see.

"You're a long way from the home office," Kirk said.

"Come on, Steven," Smith said. He hooked his hand under Kirk's arm and helped him to his feet, seemingly without effort. Smith was a lot stronger than he looked, Kirk reminded himself.

He staggered a bit at first, but soon found his legs. He tested himself by walking across to the next row of cars. Fine. He leaned against a battered Ford pickup and faced Smith.

"I don't have anything to say to you," he said.

"Five minutes," Smith said. "You owe me that for keeping you out of the emergency room."

"I'm not going back with you. You know that."

"We need to go somewhere and talk," Smith said. "Please?"

Kirk thought about it. How much was the debt? What was his life really worth?

"All right," he said finally. "We can go ho— We can go to my house."

"Good," Smith said. "I'll meet you." He turned and crunched off across the gravel. He didn't appear to be walking fast, but in a few moments he had vanished into the night.

Didn't even ask directions, Kirk thought. They knew where he lived. Of course. It made him angry, but he realized he was too tired and sore to lead Smith on a chase around the city, so he drove straight back to the bungalow.

Smith was waiting for him when he got there, and the two men settled themselves in the small living room. Smith unbuttoned but didn't remove his topcoat.

"We need you," he said.

"Sure," Kirk said. "Like the last time and the time before that. Forget it."

"Will you at least hear me out?"

"Look, I don't like you and I don't like your organization and I don't like anything about my former existence. I wouldn't work for you again if it meant my life. Now, you saved my butt tonight. Okay, thanks. Beyond that, I don't owe you a damn thing."

"You walked out on me, Steven."

Inside, Kirk smiled at the memory. Sure, he'd walked out. One night in a little town on the Chesapeake he had, for once, gotten the better of Smith. He had left the agency man to sort out an arms smuggler, a crooked sheriff, several members of a Colombian drug gang, and a corpse or two. It must have taken some judicious sorting, even for someone like Smith.

"I guess that makes my word about as good as yours," Kirk said. "You still carrying the grudge?"

Smith dismissed the thought with a wave of his hand. "Forget it," he said. "Like I said, I took a little flak. But some good came of the affair. We got a man in place in the drug trade, which we were able to turn to our advantage in C.A. Perhaps you heard."

Kirk shook his head. "My stock of product is kind of low. And I don't give a shit about Central America any more."

"A pity. With your background, the Spanish, and the family history, we could use— Ah well, that's not worth the thinking, is it?" When Kirk didn't respond, he continued, "And beside the point, too. I'm not here about C.A. I'm here about the U.S.A."

Kirk chuckled. "Oh, really? You boys aren't going domestic, are you?"

"Special directive," Smith said. Clandestine domestic operations were nothing new, of course, but that was something he would never admit in open conversation.

"I'll bet."

"We have reason to believe that the United States is under attack by international terrorists. Is that special enough for you?"

"I don't really care, Smitty," Kirk said. Smith hated nicknames.

"It's your country, too," Smith said.

"I've given service."

Smith drummed his fingers on the arms of his chair, a

gesture calculated to annoy the listener as well as give the false impression that he was thinking something over.

"Steven, this is SCI," Smith said as though he'd come to a decision. He used the agency acronym for sensitive compartmented information. "Most highly restricted access. I shouldn't be saying a thing about this to someone with zero clearance."

Kirk sighed. "But you're going to anyway," he said. "Right?"

In a matter-of-fact voice Smith gave Kirk a capsule history of the missing Stingers. Kirk was unsurprised. He knew that the missiles had been widely available in the international black market for years, a fact denied by the government and underreported by the media because no one wanted the American people to know how scary the situation really was.

When Smith had finished, Kirk shrugged. "I warned you about this way back when Reagan started handing the things out like he was trading nylons to the natives for sex. It was stupid then and it's stupid now. A Stinger isn't a glorified hand grenade. It's only been blind luck that they haven't come home to roost before now."

"If it does you good to feel superior, go ahead," Smith said. "But Reagan has nothing to do with what's happening now."

"Oh yeah?" Kirk smiled. "Looks about the same to me. You got someone in the Big House nearly as old and just as incapable. What's changed?"

"Steven, look, this is all beside the point. The thing that matters is that three hundred and two Americans were shot out of the sky. Doesn't that do anything to you?"

It had when he'd read about the crash, yet Kirk found himself saying, "Frankly, my dear, I don't give a damn. It's on the President's head, and the Director's, and yours. Besides, what do you want me to do about it? Get 'em back for you?"

"Yes," Smith said, "that's exactly what we want."

"Ah, for Christ's sake."

Kirk got up and walked to the kitchen, where he poured himself some iced tea. The fog induced by the alcohol and the beating he'd taken was rapidly dissipating. After filling his glass, he lingered for a moment, thinking over what he'd just been told. On the surface it was a simple matter. But Smith was not a simple man. His real objective always lay several levels below the surface, well out of sight.

Kirk stopped himself. It was useless trying to outguess Smith.

When he went back into the living room, Smith was sitting calmly, his hands folded over his stomach, looking as though he was prepared to wait as long as it took.

"I don't know, Smitty," Kirk said condescendingly. "You must be slipping. You didn't seriously expect that I'd agree, did you?"

"I don't have expectations anymore," Smith said. "With you, well, you obviously don't care much about your life, but I had hoped that you still cared enough about your country that you'd help her out when she needed you."

"Don't make me puke. You're not here because of your concern for the country. You're here because of your concern for your own precious ass, period. You screwed up and you need the best man for the job to bail you out. No thanks."

"Uh-huh. And why exactly did you start using your own name again?"

The question took Kirk aback. He didn't really know why he'd started doing it, except that he was tired of pretending to be someone else. "What's that supposed to mean?" he said.

"Oh, I don't know," Smith said. "Some people might think it was like advertising for employment."

Kirk chuckled. "You guys don't miss a trick, do you?" he said. "That's a good one. It really is. The psyche of Steven Kirk revealed. Well, let me make it very simple for you, Smith. Read my lips: I-am-not-going-to-work-for-you."

"I see. Are you quite sure?"

"What are you getting at?" Kirk said.

"Susanna and Scottie," Smith said.

Kirk's hands made reflexive fists and his jaws tightened. There were no dreamlike images of mother and child this time, only the remembrance of what the innocent pair had become, two human husks burned beyond recognition and zipped into plastic body bags.

"What about them?" Kirk said through his clenched teeth.

"We have reason to think that the same people who hijacked the Stingers—"

Kirk sprang from his chair and threw himself at Smith so quickly that he couldn't possibly have reacted even if he'd wanted to. The two men sprawled backward over the chair, with Kirk on top. He pushed himself up slightly with one hand; with the other, he slapped Smith viciously across the face. The man's glasses went flying and blood welled from his split lip.

He didn't resist. Kirk grabbed a handful of his shirt-front and raised his hand again. There were several killing points within easy reach, as Smith well knew. Still, he didn't resist.

"God damn you," Kirk said in a strangled voice. "I should kill you. What do you know about them?"

Smith's calm hadn't been dented. "If you'll let me up," he said, "I'll tell you."

Damn him, Kirk thought. Damn him and the whole miserable organization he worked for. But he let Smith go. The two men disentangled themselves, got up, set the furniture aright. Then Smith retrieved his glasses and they sat down facing each other. Smith took out a handkerchief and blotted his split lip until it stopped bleeding.

"Talk," Kirk said.

"I was trying to," Smith said. "What I wanted to tell you is that the same people who hijacked the missiles may have been involved in the . . . deaths of your wife and child."

Kirk stared coldly at the other man, waiting.

"I'm sorry," Smith went on. "I know how you must feel."

"No, you don't," Kirk said.

"All right, I don't know exactly how you feel. But I do know you, and I know that they were important to you, and I know how much you must want to find out what happened to them."

"So you saw your chance for a deal. I help you with your problem, you give me information. You sonofabitch."

"Steven, it's not like that. I would have contacted you as soon as we had anything solid about your family. The hijacking had nothing to do with that."

"Sure. And the surveillance was just routine; you weren't hanging on to me in order to buy me when the need arose."

"I'm not that callous," Smith said, a little defensively.

"I can't imagine why I don't believe you."

There was a long pause. Kirk was seething inside, but he knew that he had to maintain control. Smith had sucked him in, and now he needed patience.

"Steven," Smith said finally, "I know you don't trust me. But whether or not you believe me about the surveillance we had on you, the fact is I may be able to help you find the people you'd . . . like to get your hands on. Will you listen?"

Kirk sighed, he hoped not too theatrically. "Yes," he said. "I'll listen."

"Thank you," Smith said. "Right now the most likely candidates for the hijack are an ultra-left faction within the Nicaraguan government. We doubt that the Sandies themselves would take the risk. Too much chance of retaliation, which would be disastrous for them.

"Unfortunately, we don't know what they intend to do with the Stingers. They may have some kind of blackmail scheme in mind." Smith paused. "Or worse, they could just be planning on randomly blowing up planes.

"Whatever happens, the Sandies are going to take the heat. There'll be the usual fools who start screaming for an invasion. The agency doesn't want that, no matter what you might think. We believe a land war in Central America would be a disaster. But those people's voices are going to be loud. And persistent. There's no telling whose advice the President will follow.

"We've got to get those missiles back, Steven, before this thing gets out of hand."

Kirk had listened, trying his best to read between the lines. "You think some splinter group would provoke an invasion of their own country?" he asked.

"No," Smith said. "But they might well want to embarrass the more moderate Sandies. Either cut themselves a bigger piece of the pie or push the Sandies further to the left. Or, they might simply hate us so much that they're just striking out without worrying about the consequences."

"How'd you target the group?"

"We've got a good network inside the country. There are plenty of insurgent sympathizers. We didn't have this specific faction penetrated, but we know a lot about them. They're ideologues and violence-prone. They've put consistent pressure on the Sandies to become less defensive-minded."

Kirk felt himself beginning to tense up once again. "And what's the connection to . . . my family?" he said.

"We have a B-6 report that this group may have been involved."

Smith was using standard agency code for data classification. The letter designation graded the reliability of the informant; the number estimated likelihood of truth based on other factors. B meant that the informant was usually reliable, while the 6 meant that accuracy could not be cross-confirmed.

"I've assumed all along that the car bomb was meant for me," Kirk said.

"That would be our assumption too," Smith said. "Although with these people, we can't discount a more insidious form of revenge."

"All right. But either way, the ultimate target was me. Why?"

Smith paused, then said, "Because of Grenada."

"*Grenada?*" Kirk stared at the other man in disbelief. "I don't understand."

And he didn't. The Grenada operation had been his last for the agency. During it he'd been an unwitting pawn in the Reagan Administration's larger game plan, which had resulted in the counterrevolution of the Coard/Austin faction, the assassination of Prime Minister Bishop and his top aides, and the subsequent American invasion. The lives of a lot of people had been sacrificed. Decent, pro-American people, many of them. Kirk's friends and fellow operatives.

After the betrayal Kirk had walked away from the agency for good.

Some lost years had followed, as he tried to erase his past. He'd changed his name and wandered from one dead-end job to the next, until at last he found himself in a small Virginia fishing village, pursuing the illusion of an untroubled waterman's life.

It was there on the shores of the Chesapeake that he'd

met Susanna, the woman who had become his wife, so young, yet with the wisdom to finally show him that there were things worth living for. It was there, too, that he'd last crossed swords with Smith and, with Susanna's help, turned the tables on his former boss for the first and only time.

So long ago, it seemed now, though the details were there in his memory, vivid as ever, any time he wanted to recall them:

The apoplectic look on Smith's face when he realized Kirk was going to leave him to clean up the mess with the arms smugglers by himself, and his own parting words. "Come on, Smitty, think how much fun you're gonna have trying to find me again."

The escape down the bay to Norfolk aboard Susanna's uncle's fishing boat, *Murphy's Law*.

The long, languid trip west, during which they'd transcended infatuation and really fallen in love.

Setting up house as Mr. and Mrs. Carson. Living anonymous and happy, with no reference to Kirk's former existence.

And the nervous moment of greatest joy, when he'd taken the six-and-a-half pound newborn boy in his arms and tried so hard not to drop him that Susanna had had to gently say, "Steven, please. You don't have to crush the life out of him."

Then, six months later, the explosion. The body bags.

"They blame you," Smith said.

"Who blames me?"

"The people in the group, we call them Grendies. Some of them are former Sandinistas who had particularly strong ties to Grenada. They've been joined by some Grenadians who fled to Nicaragua after the counterrevolution."

"That's insane. I tried to *help* Bishop."

"Come on, Steven. They don't see it that way. They think you set him up by giving him a tie to Washington. So Coard and Austin could then come in and knock him down. They're actually convinced the counterrevolutionary faction was on our payroll."

"I don't believe that," Kirk said.

"Think about it."

There was a pause as Kirk appeared to do just that.

But what he was really turning over in his mind were the implications of what Smith had revealed. Susanna and Scottie had died because of what had happened long ago, in Grenada, in what now seemed to Kirk another lifetime. Assuming that Smith's information was accurate. And was it? Well, the "Grendies" had persisted for many, many years in tracking him down. Yet if he'd been fingered as the saboteur of their revolution, their memories might be long indeed.

But the truly chilling thing was this: the blame would have to be shared. Because if it all went back to Grenada, the man responsible for what had happened there (if you didn't count Reagan) was Smith.

Smith had killed his wife and child.

Indirectly, yes. But he was ultimately as guilty as if he'd wired the C-4 plastic explosive himself.

It took only a few moments for Kirk to commit himself. He would have his revenge, and it would be complete. First, find the actual assassins and deal with them. Then he could turn his attention to Mr. Smith.

"All right," he said evenly. "Let's say the 'Grendies' are the people I want. You sure they're also involved in the hijacking?"

"There's no hard evidence yet," Smith admitted. "But consider this. If the Grendies and the hijackers *are* two different groups, they're both probably operating out of Nicaragua. In which case, they know each other. So when we catch the hijackers, either you've got your killers or you've got people who can put you onto them. Wouldn't that be better than nothing?"

"What's the deal, Smith? I help you recover the missiles. We nail the hijackers. Okay, what do you do for me?"

Smith looked Kirk right in the eye and said, "You have as much time alone with them as you need."

There it was. It might all be bullshit, of course. But it was an offer that made sense in context. Smith needed the Stingers back. No one would bitch if Kirk was traded a few terrorists in return.

Even if Smith was double-dealing, he was still putting Kirk into the field. He wouldn't be able to exert much

control over what Kirk did if and when he found someone he was interested in.

"Pretty sure of yourself, aren't you?" Kirk said.

"Not entirely," Smith said. "But I look at you and this
is what I see. You start using your own name again, you
let your personal life go to hell, you can't hold a job. It's
like you're trying to tell the world that you can't pull
yourself together until you come to terms with what
happened to your family. I'm offering you that chance.

"And I want you, Steven. I need you. You won't be
the only man out there, obviously, but you're far and
away the best man for the job. That's why I came in
person."

"You came in person because you knew damn well no
one else would've gotten in the door."

"That, too."

Another pause was called for, and Kirk let it happen.
Above all, he must not appear eager.

After a decent interval he sighed and said, "All right,
Smitty. I want to know what happened to Susanna and
Scottie. Is there a plan?"

Smith never missed a beat. His face betrayed no sense
of triumph, or anything else. He continued as if their
conversation had been one of unbroken accord. "Lacking
any communication from the hijackers," he said, "we're
going to have to try to anticipate them under worst-case
scenario, which is random, unannounced attacks until the
Stingers are gone. They'll have two months' time before
the self-destruct mechanism kicks in, and that mechanism
can't be disconnected without destroying the guidance
system. They probably know that.

"We also have to assume that they're targeting the big
cities. They've hit Boston. That doesn't mean they won't
hit it again, but it's likely they'll go elsewhere, too.
Therefore, the agency is putting officers into the field in
every major metropolitan area.

"I want to assign you to Washington. It's got to be on
the hit list and you're the best person I can think of to be
on-site. I'll provide a safe house, open account, anything
you need in the way of hard- and software, and whatever
else you ask for. Your methodology is up to you. You
keep something like Boston from happening in D.C., and
no one's going to care how you did it."

"Okay," Kirk said, "we can work out the details as we go along. When do we leave?"

"Tonight. The late flight to Washington," Smith said. He glanced at his watch. "We'll make it."

"And I suppose you went ahead and bought two tickets?"

Smith nodded.

Kirk just shook his head. "Christ Jesus," he said. "All right, let's go."

9

March 16

As soon as the 747 had taxied out to its place in the queue, Smith had gone to sleep, and he slept for nearly the entire flight.

Kirk, however, remained wide awake. For one thing, his body hurt in too many places for him to sleep comfortably in an airliner seat. But more important, there were so many conflicting scenarios bouncing around inside his head that even the lingering effects of the alcohol couldn't fog his mind. He was wired.

Smith, he knew, would be thinking days or weeks or even years into the future. If he wanted to deal with the man on anything like equal terms, he had to build himself a similar frame of reference.

He sorted through what he knew, and what he'd been told, and formed some preliminary conclusions. The first one would have to be that there actually were two dozen Stingers missing and that he was really being hired to find them.

True, the entirety of Smith's story might have been a lie, a ruse to get Steven back to Washington, but it didn't play as well that way. There was no reason for Smith to have waited this long if, as seemed certain, he'd always known where Kirk was. Much more likely was that Smith had been keeping tabs on Kirk in order to recruit him for just such a genuine emergency as this one. Besides, if everything Smith had said was phony, then he was a dead man, and he was probably aware of that.

Then there was what had happened in Boston. All Kirk had known was what he'd seen on TV. There had been a big plane crash. Hundreds of people killed. But no public mention yet that the aircraft had been shot down. Was it true? Kirk decided that he'd know soon enough. No one could keep a story like that from the media for long.

That left Smith's tale of the exiled Grenadians in Managua. Smith, Kirk knew, rarely told a story without having something solid to back it up if need be. But did this one make sense? Kirk ransacked his memory, going over everything he could remember from his last months of work as Smith's field man, searching for any kind of clue.

He'd been assigned to Grenada for the avowed purpose of secretly trying to normalize relations with the revolutionary government headed by Maurice Bishop. Then he'd been betrayed by Smith and other members of the Grenada Task Force. They'd leaked information about what he was doing to Bishop's rivals, the hard-liners headed by Bernard Coard, an action which led directly to Coard's counter-revolution, Bishop's assassination, and the U.S. invasion that had been the administration's goal all along.

A tear coursed down Kirk's face as he recalled his narrow escape from the island by boat, and the dark smiling face of Quartermain, a Grenadian agent and friend who'd saved his life, pulling him out before the Revolutionary Military Council could punch his ticket. Loyal Quartermain, who'd bled to death in Kirk's arms as the two awaited chopper evacuation on a tiny hunk of rock off Grenada's south coast.

For a few moments, the anger burned inside him. Anger at Smith and Bill Casey and Ollie North and all the other thugs who'd been in on the deal. Anger at himself for failing to see what they were up to. Anger at the Grenadian counter-revolutionaries who'd slaughtered their own people and who, just maybe, had stretched their spidery arms over the long intervening years and snuffed out the lives of his wife and child.

The anger burned itself to cold ash. It was the one emotion which must be absolutely controlled.

Kirk had looked hard, and had found no clues. There were now no further choices to be made. He could only commence doing what had been asked of him. Until then he would learn nothing more about his family.

And what Smith really wanted him for would remain an open question.

There was a car waiting for them at National Airport, a black car with tinted windows and, Kirk suspected, armor plating and bullet-resistant glass. He had brought only a carry-on bagful of clothes with him, and Smith traveled with nothing but a briefcase, so neither man had to wait for luggage. Within a few minutes they were being driven into the city.

It had been a long time since Kirk had been to Washington. As they rode along the parkway, he looked across the Potomac at the white marble buildings and monuments. His connection to the city stretched back a long way, as far as the days of his childhood. He remembered how proud he'd once been of his father, who'd moved through the halls of those stately buildings as though they'd been erected just for him.

Charles Worthington Kirk. Steven had first idolized him, then tolerated him, then hated him, and finally, ignored and avoided him.

However, he'd made a decision on the plane. If he was going to succeed at what Smith wanted of him—and everything else depended on that—he'd need command of as many resources as possible. And few people could open as many doors as the elder Kirk.

There was something else, too, and Kirk had struggled with it during the entire cross-country flight. There was no one in Washington he trusted. Certainly not Smith, his nominal control. No one who might still be working at the agency. None of his other government contacts or the friends of his youth.

He was alone. That was fine in terms of going into the field, doing the job, but an operative had to have *some* other person. Someone to call when the tunnel got so narrow he needed a hand from the other side to pull him through.

He'd turned the problem over and over in his mind, and the only person he could come up with was his single blood relative, Charles Worthington Kirk. Father and son might be antagonists of long standing, but at least, Kirk felt, if it came to a crunch, his father's first impulse wouldn't be to betray him.

Smith had been quiet for hours, but now he said, "You'll be wanting to contact your father, I expect," as though he'd been sharing Kirk's mind all that time.

"Maybe," Kirk said.

"I think it's a good idea. He's still as C.A.-knowledgeable as they come. The PFIAB makes a lot of Latin American recommendations based on his judgment. Plus he knows the Latin groups in D.C. and where to find them."

Kirk nodded. His father had advised a long string of Presidents on Central America. An independently wealthy career diplomat, Charles ostensibly had worked for the Department of State. But his ties to the agency had been many and deep.

After he'd "retired," he'd been appointed to serve on the President's Foreign Intelligence Advisory Board. This was an informal, nonpartisan group of fourteen senior Americans with extensive foreign policy experience. Its clout varied greatly from administration to administration, but the current occupant of the White House called regularly on its collective expertise.

"Whatever's required," Kirk said.

"Of course," Smith said.

The black car turned into a narrow, block-long street called Duddington Place, S.E. It was on the south flank of Capitol Hill, a five minute walk from the houses of Congress. Unpretentious two-story row houses lined both sides of the street. There were a couple of trees. Kirk's impression was that middle-level bureaucrats and upwardly mobile young government careerists would live on a street like this. For the former it would represent a realized goal, for the latter a stepping-stone on the way to the real power enclaves of Georgetown.

They stopped in front of one of the row houses. Its white-brick exterior was in need of sandblasting and the enamel on the wrought-iron railings was peeling. A trough had been worn into the marble steps leading to the first floor.

"Completely sterile," Smith said.

Kirk looked at Smith as if to say that there hadn't been any other possibility, and Smith nodded that he understood what the look meant: from here on, the relationship must be professional to the highest degree.

They got out and went into the house. Like its neighbors, it was small and narrow. There were two bedrooms upstairs, a living room, dining room, and kitchen on the first floor. The basement was half below street level and half above; it consisted of two large rooms with nothing much in them.

The furnishings looked as though someone had gone to Hecht's and bought everything at once, which was in fact what had happened. Things matched. They were neither expensive nor shabby, and gave the place the ambience of a Holiday Inn.

A safe house might be expected to feature the latest in space-age security gadgets. In fact, though the first-floor windows were barred, the house presented few challenges to a competent B&E man. Its locks were simple drop bolts, backed up by only a rudimentary alarm system. "Safe" merely meant that it was a closely guarded secret that the house was agency property. The transients using it were expected to have the capability of fending for themselves. If a fortress were required the agency would provide it, but somewhere more isolated than Duddington Place.

One thing the agency did provide was communications capability and serious protection against outside surveillance. The hardware was on a small desk in the corner of the living room, and Smith showed it to Kirk.

"Your terminal," he said, indicating an IBM PC. "And modem. There are instructions in the desk on how to send me electronic mail. Burn after memorizing, of course."

Kirk nodded.

"Then the Tektronix spectrum analyzer," Smith said. "Still the best." He looked at Kirk and raised an eyebrow.

Kirk nodded again. He knew how to use the unit. It was top-of-the-line in the countermeasure department and would detect virtually any transmitting device.

"We've been sweeping the house once a week," Smith said. "Never found anything, but I wouldn't get complacent. From now on, you're responsible for your own security. No one will come here after today."

"My sentiments exactly," Kirk said.

"Now, the phone," Smith said, indicating the unit on the desk, "is as secure as we can make it. But we see no point in taking any chances, so . . ."

He showed that the phone wire wasn't plugged into the wall jack. Instead it ran to a hole drilled in the back of the desk. A second wire emerged from the hole, and that one went into the jack. He opened one of the desk's side drawers. Inside was a small white box, into which the input and output wires had been plugged.

"TSU-3000," Smith said. "Between the phone and the line. You used one?"

Kirk shook his head. "After my time," he said.

"It's good. Nothing revolutionary, it just combines all the best features in one unit.

"You've got three basic components. First off, this control here lets you listen downline. That'll defeat infinity-transmitters and the like.

"Then you've got an adjustable voltage-spreader. We've got it keyed to the line now, so you shouldn't have to fool with it. It'll keep most remote-start recorders from switching on.

"And last, you've got this." He indicated an LED bar graph. "It's a variable noise-flooding generator. Sends out random static in the speech-frequency range while you're talking. Set it on 8 and nobody can get anything from a recording, but it's a little tough for *you* to hear. At 5 they get a word or two here and there. You decide."

"Nice," Kirk said. "You're getting better equipment these days."

"They're producing better equipment these days. I'd recommend jamming every call you make or get, to some degree. Anyway, the defensive items are all we have in the house. I assume you'll be wanting more. You still have a full kit?"

"No," Kirk lied. In fact, he did have access to some of the tools of his former trade, but he preferred that Smith think he was starting from scratch.

"What do you need?"

"Hmmm. It's a little early to say. Suppose I think about it and make up a list. I should be able to get it to you tonight or tomorrow morning."

"Fine. All right, how about strategy? You want to talk about that?"

Strategy for *what*? Kirk thought to himself.

But he said, "I was thinking on the plane. There's not a lot I can do until we know for sure who we're dealing with. If the hijackers never step forward, it's almost certainly going to be just blind chance for discovery. Some guy in a mobile unit who catches them firing one of the missiles. Then we take it from there.

"But assuming the Sandinistas are involved, it won't hurt to start penetration of whatever infrastructure they have right away. I've got a couple of ideas for that. And I'll see what kind of contacts my father has in the city. What about you, you got anything to give me?"

"We're working on it," Smith said. "So far we've been able to backtrack a couple of steps in the channel we set up for the missiles. Whoever lifted them is efficient. We're pretty sure he's killed everyone who might have been able to identify him up to that point. The Hondurans in Roatan, the shrimpers who carried the merchandise, and the delivery people he met in Corpus Christi.

"But he couldn't have taken out the *entire* network. Right now we're looking for a man named Ruben Tellez. He was our private sector cutout between the military and the domestic shipper."

"You bury the Stingers in a sale of Pentagon surplus?"

"Something like that. Tellez is a refugee Nica businessman. He's as anti-Sandie as they come. We had him classified as Category A reliable. He agreed to shuffle the papers and take the fall if the shipment was discovered."

"Where is he?" Kirk asked.

"We don't know. He's disappeared. He was operating out of the exile community here in town. No one's seen him since the hijacking. But we have no reason yet to believe that he's dead."

"You think he might have been turned?"

"Possible. Or he may have been doubling all along. But my guess would be that he knows who's behind this and that the opposition has him on its hit list. Under those circumstances he'd be well advised to lie low for a while."

"Any leads?"

"Yes, we feel that we may be getting close to him," Smith said carefully.

"Give him to me first if you find him," Kirk said.

"Of course. As long as you remember that he *is* an ally until proven otherwise."

"Let's both try to keep our priorities straight."

Kirk held Smith's gaze just long enough to make his point.

"Let's remember that they do converge," Smith said. He paused, checking his watch, then added, "I've got to get over to Pennsylvania Avenue. I'm . . . glad you're working on this, Steven."

"Skip it," Kirk said. "Just keep your end of the bargain."

Smith nodded and left. Kirk watched him out of the front window: the shambling figure in the nondescript topcoat, walking as if he barely had purpose, seemingly oblivious to his surroundings. But Kirk knew that not a single detail of life on Duddington Place at that moment was escaping Smith's eye.

10

The small plane banked and leveled off, and Javier Vega had a brief but unobstructed view. The island was a glorified sandbar, really, four miles long and a mile wide. There was a slight rise at the west end, where the compound was located, its whitewashed buildings starkly defined by the harsh glare of the subtropical sun.

If most things appeared puny when viewed from the air, this sand spit seemed particularly so, an insignificant splotch of white and brown and green resting on a sea that shaded off from the turquoise of the reefs to the indigo of deep water. Give me a truckload of C-4 plastique, Vega thought, and I could sink the whole business.

The flight from Georgia in the Aero-Commander 720 had been an uneventful one. The plane was a gem, top of the line for a light twin. Air-conditioned, fully pressurized, plush-carpeted, with roomy swivel seats, a well-stocked bar, and a beautiful brown-skinned woman to wait on its single passenger.

Vega had taken the long, slim, innocuous-looking box—his only luggage—into the cabin with him. He wasn't about to let it out of his sight.

He'd had some mild apprehension about the short hop out to the tiny island off Great Abaco in the Bahamas. What he had in the box, and on the videotape in his briefcase, would be more than enough to earn him a death sentence if he were caught with them.

They weren't likely to be out here looking specifically for him, but the U.S. military presence in the area was substantial, as a result of the government's so-called war on drugs. It was not unheard-of for a private aircraft to be forced down and searched. It would be ironic if Javier Vega, who hated drugs, were to have all his hopes dashed because he was mistaken for a smuggler.

The flight was a calculated risk, then, but one that Vega had decided was minimal. The aircraft was Bahamian, a clear flight plan had been filed, and the pilot had scrupulously stuck to it. The Americans were rarely interested in a plane going from the mainland to the Bahamas. It was the return flights that tended to draw their attention.

And when Vega returned, they could search whatever they wanted. He'd be clean.

The plane descended, flying into the prevailing winds, and touched down smoothly onto the runway.

There was no passenger terminal at this airport, just a single low, corrugated-roofed maintenance building. Parked in front of it was the only other aircraft in sight, a camouflage-painted helicopter. A Huey. Vietnam surplus, Vega surmised.

A Jeep was waiting to carry him and his box over the bumpy mile of dirt road to the compound. He sat in the back and didn't speak with the driver. It was necessary to mentally prepare himself for what was going to happen next.

Going in, Vega felt confident. The missiles were the bargaining chip and he had them. He could act as tough as he wanted to. And, fortunately, he thought, you don't have to be brilliant when dealing with Americans. All you have to do is think two steps ahead, which is one more than they're capable of.

God, he hated having to work with these people. They

were so arrogant, so childish, so in love with their war toys. He suspected that they had to keep creating wars, if for no other reason than a desire to field-test the fruits of their genius for inventing lethal gadgets.

They'd tried out their latest on his homeland many times over the years. They'd invaded and occupied, politically controlled and economically strangled, and they'd spilled much blood. Few countries had they treated so much like a colony as Nicaragua. He loathed them for that.

On the other hand, the Americans were easy to manipulate. All you had to do was tell them what they wanted to hear and they would throw their money at you. You had only to *seem* to be exactly what they were looking for.

It was especially true with all the amateurs in the field. "Private sector," they were called in the terminology of the trade, and there were a lot of them. Rich men and women with nothing better to do with their money than cause trouble in other countries. People willing to detour around the official branches of the U.S. government. Left wing, right wing, name your cause. There was American support for it somewhere out there in the private sector. There was money, there were armaments, there were mercenaries for hire. You could always finds someone to foot the bill.

Someone like the owner of the island. "Sherman," as he had code-named himself. And Vega was "Mosby." Cute. Playing dumb, Vega had allowed Sherman to patiently explain to him the derivation of their names. As if Vega had been able to take his degree while sidestepping "American" history.

And as if Vega somehow lacked the intelligence or resources to discover the man's real identity. What foolishness. Within twenty-four hours he had had a complete dossier on Sherman, a.k.a. Henrik Bruderdam, an extraordinarily wealthy expatriate American who ran a worldwide beer and soft drink empire from his Bahamian headquarters, and who had strong historical ties to Nicaragua.

Now Bruderdam was having an attack of . . . of what? Was it liberal guilt? Or, more likely, was he just a pragmatic businessman? Or might he be playing his own double game, using the hijacked missiles as leverage with the Americans?

It didn't matter. Vega smiled to himself as the Jeep came to a stop on a circle of crushed coral—the terminus of the long driveway through the compound. In the circle's grassy center was a *lignum vitae*, the heavy, resinous Bahamian national tree.

The structure that fronted on the circle was an imposing two-level house with broad Carrara marble steps giving outside access to the second story. Gleaming white stucco exterior, the windows framed in teak and fitted with hurricane shutters. Red tile roof.

To the left of the main house was a long, low residence building that housed the owner's staff. To the right were the generator building and the desalination plant. On the way in, Vega had passed a number of other, smaller structures that were obviously used for storage of one kind or another. Defensive weapons, long-term emergency food caches, spare parts, housekeeping items, he guessed.

There was a shed for vehicle and equipment maintenance, with one visible gasoline pump. Underground would be an enormous fuel tank—or, more likely, several large independent ones—and a sizable cistern to supply potable water should the desalinator become disabled.

The whole had been carefully planned with an eye toward independence. In normal times the island's stock levels were maintained by regular air and sea deliveries. But should a real crisis develop, the compound was prepared to be entirely self-sufficient for an extended period of time.

Vega got out of the Jeep, taking his package with him. He was met by a man in an off-white linen suit. The man led him up the polished marble steps and into the house.

The second-floor living area was light, cool, and airy, oriented to take full advantage of the prevailing breezes. Louvered bifold doors stood open all along the western wall. Above them was a series of stained glass fanlight windows.

Vega followed his escort to the north wing of the house, which on this floor was one huge room, forty feet by thirty. Command central for the Gustavia Brewing Company, Regal Soft Drinks, and other branches of the owner's farflung empire. Temperature and humidity were controlled by finely calibrated automatic monitoring devices. An oak door with a steel plate at its core was the only visible way in or out. The walls were foot-thick reinforced concrete. Windows were a plastic/polycarbonate laminate, framed with steel. They would stop almost anything short of heavy artillery.

Nevertheless, the room had a spectacular view. Vega glanced out over the rear of the property, across the glinting swimming pool to the carefully tended lawns that ended at the island's final low bluff. Beyond that were the protected waters and uninhabited islets of Abaco Sound.

Vega strolled to the far end of the room—past laser printers, FAX machines, telexes, magnetic-tape disc backups, UPS units, and old-fashioned heavy steel filing cabinets—and stood before a large teak executive's desk that sat on a slightly raised platform and suggested the throne of the Emperor of all the Indies. The desktop was uncluttered, its principal features being three personal computer monitors and keyboards, and a twenty-line PBX phone system.

The man behind the teak desk was smiling as he got up and came around to greet Vega.

"Mosby," he said, gesturing at the long, skinny box, "this is it?"

"This is it," Vega said. "Sherman."

What an idiot, Vega thought. And immediately cursed himself. The man might be overly fond of code names and all the other little trappings of secrecy, but it was no idiot who had raised himself to a position of such power.

"Ah, excellent," Bruderdam said. He dismissed the man in the linen suit without a word and when he and Vega were alone, began to open the box.

Not going to win any beauty contest, is he? Vega thought.

He was looking at a short, squat man in his late fifties. The man's head was bald on top, with a light brown fringe of hair grown long and hanging down the sides, like some aging ex-hippie. He had bright blue eyes, which appeared perpetually amused at something, set deep in a square, fleshy face.

The overall image was one of a jovial, friendly brother-in-law who liked backyard chicken barbecues and would work thirty years at the same job because he didn't like challenges. That impression was further enhanced by the man's plaid Bermuda shorts, a clashing flowered print shirt and cheap zoris.

The way he dressed made no attempt to conceal the aftermath of the eczema that had turned his skin scaly and driven him to seek the arid Bahamian climate in the first place. Vega thought of an iguana resting on a sun-baked rock.

Bruderdam took from the box the Stinger components—grip stock, headphones, and missile-containing launch tube—fondling each piece of hardware with reverence before setting it on his desk.

"And you took down a 747 with this," he said to Vega.

"Yes," Vega said.

Bruderdam shook his head slowly. "I don't know," he said. "It looks so . . . puny."

"It isn't. It probably determined the outcome in Afghanistan."

"Ah yes, our beleaguered Russian brethren."

Vega didn't say anything. He opened his briefcase, took out the videotape, and handed it over.

Bruderdam received it with a smile that might have meant anything. He set the missile launcher down and carried the tape over to a nearby cabinet containing a VCR, audio tape deck, amplifier, and hi-fi control unit. A Sony video projection system and screen descended from the ceiling.

The VCR whirred to life and the tape ran. It wasn't a long one, but what with the giant screen and surround-sound, it was almost like being there again.

The cameraman had done an admirable job, considering the light level and the rolling boat. He had filmed the entire sequence without a cut. First an establishing shot: the airport, the distinctive structures of Logan, what could be seen of the city. Then a pan to a close-up of the launcher, balanced on the shoulder of an unidentifiable individual. The launch itself: a quick zoom to the 747, far away but readily recognizable. The moment of impact and the exploding engine. The trail of smoke and flame as the crippled jet fell from the sky.

There could be no question but that it was a faithful recording of what had happened in Boston.

"Excellent, Mosby," Bruderdam said.

Vega shrugged. "When we succeed," he said.

"Oh, we will, we will. The President isn't going to have any choice on this one. If he doesn't buy them back, he'll have riots in the streets."

There was a pause while Bruderdam ran the tape again. He liked it just as much the second time. Then he said, "And where are the rest of the missiles now?"

Vega had prepared himself for this moment, but still felt a slight quickening of his pulse. He willed himself to betray not the least sign of nervousness. "They're safe," he said.

Bruderdam was still watching the TV screen as the tape rewound. "Of course," he said distractedly, "but where are they?"

Vega didn't say anything. The tape clicked to a stop. Bruderdam looked up, and when he saw the set of Vega's face he said, "What's going on, Mosby?"

"I have them in a safe place," Vega said.

"I'm to know where they are. That's the plan."

"The plan has changed."

There was a pause. The two men watched each other's expressions carefully, but neither gave a thing away.

"I see," Bruderdam said. "And whose decision was this?"

"Mine," Vega said. "I'm taking the risks, so I'm underwriting the insurance policy."

"Do I need to remind you that you need my . . . facilities?"

"No more than I need to remind you that you need me in the field, Mr.—ah, Sherman. Don't worry. As soon as we have control of the money and the rest of the response is in motion, I'll tell you where they are. I won't have any use for them at that point."

Bruderdam studied the other man for a long moment. Then, abruptly, a broad smile appeared on his face. He got up and clapped Vega on the shoulder. "You're a careful man," he said. "I like that. I knew you'd be right for this job."

Go ahead and patronize, Vega thought to himself. We've only just begun.

"What now?" Bruderdam asked. "You want to stick around for the show?"

"I don't think so," Vega said. "I need to scout out the next location. Can your man fly me back this afternoon?"

"Sure, sure, no problem. Why not relax a little bit beforehand, eh? Have a drink, take a swim. And I've got some girls in from . . . Panama, I think it is this week."

"No, thank you," Vega said tersely. He knew from his Bruderdam dossier that the wealthy American liked to import poor Third World girls to be his sexual slaves for short periods of time. He hated the smug bastard for that.

"Suit yourself," Bruderdam said. "You will tune in tonight, though?"

"I'll rent a room."

"Good. You'll enjoy sharing the moment, I'm sure. It's *your* artistry, after all."

Vega nodded.

"And one other thing," Bruderdam said with the friendly smile still firmly in place. "Don't cross me, Mosby. If you're doubling for the other side you'll wind up with a mouthful of your own balls. Eh, *amigo*?" He raised a single eyebrow.

Tough guy, Vega thought, who doesn't begin to know tough. "My sentiments exactly," he said.

Bruderdam laughed. "A marriage made in heaven," he said.

As if by chance, the man in the linen suit returned. Bruderdam directed him to see that the visitor was taken back to the plane right away.

When he was alone, the first thing Bruderdam did was place the missile and launcher on a table he'd had brought in for that purpose, since he wanted to be able to look over at them whenever he cared to. Besides which, outside of the basement this was the most secure room in the entire compound.

Mosby was such a fool, he thought to himself. He had had plenty of experience dealing with the type, and they were so predictable: Third World macho men figuring *cojones* was all it took to play with the big boys. Simply stroke their egos and show them the kind of cash they'd only dreamed about before, and they would end up licking your hand whenever you held it out.

Except this one had nipped at that hand instead. Just for a moment, the rage boiled up inside Bruderdam and he knew that, had the Stingers not been so important, he would have ripped out Vega's throat with his bare hands for the affront. How nice it would feel to do some dirty work personally for a change.

But then he shook his head and walked over to his desk, his cheap rubber zoris slapping the tile floor. No, it was a minor annoyance, nothing more.

He sat down before one of his Sun 386i micro-computers. Like the other two, it had eighty megabytes of hard disc storage and *Tempest* shielding, which would defeat the sophisticated remote eavesdropping devices that "listened" to a computer's signature radiation. The micros were connected to a VAX mini-computer that was located in the basement, two stories below.

Bruderdam composed a quick message on the small terminal and routed it. What happened next was a sort of miracle.

The message was first routed to the VAX, where it was encoded in a datastream that would be unintelligible to anyone with fewer facilities than the National Security Agency. The datastream was transmitted via a four-thousand-watt transmitter and Bruderdam's satellite uplink, a five-meter dish located in the compound's west grounds. The indispensable centerpiece of his business (and other) operations, that dish was testimony to the American axiom that enough money will buy anything you want. It had been constructed to its owner's specifications, using proprietary technology not legally available outside the military. Duplication of its capabilities using normal civilian-sector hardware would have required a highly obtrusive rig at least twice as large. As it was, Bruderdam's dish was so small that few observers would see it as anything other than an average home's TV-receiving unit. And with its sand-colored camouflage, it was virtually invisible from the air.

From the up-link, the encoded message was beamed to a Westar satellite, which relayed it down to a receiver at the New York corporate headquarters of the Gustavia Brewing Co. The Westar channel involved was one which had been rented by the brewery solely for its use.

One of the beauties of the system was that any phone calls made, or electronic messages sent, from the compound were untraceable. The Westar would, of course, record that it was being used, but it would be unable to pinpoint the source of the transmission any more closely than within a circle of five hundred miles' diameter. And once calls and messages reached the mainland, regular phone lines could be employed, so that the point of origin would always appear to be New York.

If further deception was required, the original datastream could be encoded to trigger a predetermined response in one of the mainframe corporate computers, causing spurious information to be added to the "D" control channel before the message entered the national phone system. Anyone running a trace would blank out at a dummy source in the Nevada desert or wherever else desired.

Bruderdam had as secure a communications system as it was possible to build. In this instance, he had invoked the highest level of security: top-grade encryption with dead-drop sourcing. He wanted no known link, either personal or corporate, between himself and the message's recipient.

The message read:

Mr. Grant—Order received here, but balance warehoused by seller. No problems expected in completing deal at later date. Sherman.

11

"All right," the President said, addressing his hurriedly created task force, "we're running short on time. Let me just make one other thing perfectly clear. You all know how much I support the cause of democracy in Nicaragua. It's imperative that we back our allies there. But that support does not extend to breaking the laws of *this* country on their behalf. No matter how worthy the goal, I will not tolerate the sort of thing that went on during Boland. Is that understood?"

No one said that it wasn't.

"Good," the President said as he got up. "I want to know how these missiles got loose, but more important I want them back. Pool your resources, do what you have to, and get the job done. Keep me informed through Miss McBain."

The President walked quickly out of the Cabinet Room. The others gathered up their notes and papers and, in no organized fashion, followed him.

Diane McBain took Chief of Staff Tom Read aside.

"Tom," she said, "I think we should talk."

A few minutes later they were seated in his office. McBain came right to the point.

"He's getting worse," she said.

"Oh? How so?"

"Come on, Tom. Being kin doesn't make you blind, does it?"

"What's that supposed to mean?"

"You know what it means."

"Look, Diane, I'm only the President's brother-in-law, not his frigging doctor. If you want a medical opinion, why don't you go to the proper source."

McBain waved a manila folder at him.

"Cut the crap, Tom!" she said. "Will you? You were there today." She ticked her points off on her fingers. "He never made the connection on his own between the missing Stingers and the shoot-down. He doesn't know the difference between the PLO and the Army of God. And at the end he didn't have a clue as to what we were discussing. Don't talk doctors to me!"

"I spend a lot of time with the President," Read said. "He's fine."

"Look," she began, then stopped. She massaged her temples for a moment. Finally she sighed heavily.

"I don't know," she said. "Tom, I don't want to see this administration go down the tubes. And especially not because we failed to act decisively when we should have."

"Well," Read said, "that's up to you and me, isn't it?"

"You and me." Pause. "And maybe the Vice President."

"Ah, come on, Diane. Walter Brust doesn't know his ass from a nectarine. If you can't fuck it or knock it into a hole, he's got no use for it. Dan Quayle knew more than Walter, for Christ's sake."

"Yes, but we've got a major crisis and the Vice President is going to have to be with us every step of the way. Just . . . in case."

Read gave the National Security Adviser a long look, then said, "Of course we should keep him fully informed. Was there anything else you wanted to talk about?"

McBain got up.

"No," she said, and she walked down to her own West Wing office, where Seamus Croaghan was waiting for her.

"How'd it go?" Croaghan asked.

McBain settled herself wearily behind her desk. "About as expected," she said. "This is the buck-passing stage. The Director swears the agency's clean. Defense swears they are, too. But I don't think anyone's underestimating the magnitude of this thing."

There was a pause, then she added, "I just hope the President can hold it together," and filled Croaghan in on her meeting with the chief of staff.

"Shit," Croaghan said. "It *is* getting worse. Read has to see that, doesn't he?"

"Sure," McBain said, "he sees it, but he's not going to advertise it. What would be in it for him? The way things are, he gets all the benefits of the top spot without having to take the heat. And, as we all know, *Mister* Read wants that next seat on the Supreme Court. He certainly won't get it by telling the world that his boss is exhibiting symptoms of Alzheimer's."

"Pompous old bastards," Croaghan muttered. "Maybe one of them will do us a favor and die."

"Seamus!"

"Well, why not? Then Tom could move onto the Court and you could have his job. You'd be a damn sight better at running the country than he is."

"You mean, you could inherit my job," McBain said angrily.

"God damn it, Diane! My brother was on that plane!"

There was a tense silence, then McBain's expression softened.

"I know," she said. "I'm sorry, Seamus. Don't worry, we'll get them. We may just have to take the initiative, that's all."

* * *

Smith's apartment at the Watergate, overlooking the Potomac, was starkly furnished. A table here, a chair there, a small desk. A hi-fi system, personal computer, and a bed. No attempt at aesthetics. But then, Smith hadn't acquired the place in order to impress. He never entertained and did little more than sleep there himself.

No, he was in the Watergate for the convenience and for the pleasant view. He liked the irony, too, of living in the place where the careers of so many of his former colleagues had begun to destruct. He often gave them an invisible toast when he entered his apartment. They were gone, but he'd survived the various purges. More than just survived, prospered.

The Watergate wasn't where he kept things of importance, of course, like the computer setup that housed his data bank. That was at the farm out in the Virginia countryside. No one, as far as he could tell, knew about the farm. He'd completely obscured his ownership. When he went there, normally only on weekends, he took elaborate precautions to ensure that he wasn't followed. His security personnel were there when he wasn't and absent when he was; they never saw him and were paid in cash.

It'd probably be awhile before he saw the farm again, he thought as he hung up his jacket and crossed the short hall into the living room. It would be critical to stay as close to the action as possible until the Stinger thing played itself out.

The phone rang as soon as he sat at his desk. It was Kirk.

In one of the apartment's few concessions to the need for security, Smith's phone, like Kirk's, was fitted with a TSU-3000. The result was that their conversation began in complete static, as the machines competed to see which could more effectively defeat a tap. The two had to fiddle dials for a few moments to adjust their units' noise-generation levels so that they could hear each other.

Kirk presented Smith with the list of things he wanted. It was a compact list, but complete. Weapons, surveillance devices, a few electronic gadgets, and some special articles of clothing. Smith was impressed; Kirk had not forgotten the tricks of the trade.

And one other thing, Kirk added. He needed a car. Inconspicuous, of course.

Smith promised that everything would be delivered the following morning, and as soon as Kirk hung up, he made the proper arrangements. It took awhile, but Smith was used to the drill. He bypassed official sources for most of the kit. When he'd finished, he was assured that Kirk would get his goods and, more important, that the supply line could never be traced back to him.

Then he got out his alto sax.

It was still too cool to play outside, but he did the next best thing. He pulled a chair over by the sliding glass doors that let onto his private balcony. From there he could look out on the lights of the Parkway and the dark mass of the Potomac beyond.

He was working on "Le Souk," the haunting melodic inventions of Paul Desmond, *the* giant of the alto. The way Desmond had intuitively grasped the staccato rhythm of Near Eastern music and blown it straight into his solos. The precision, the disciplined genius of the man. It might be heresy to say it, Smith had long maintained, but screw the Bird. There wasn't one of Parker's erratic flights of fancy that could stand up to something like "Le Souk."

Smith put on his scratchy copy of *Jazz Goes to College* and listened to the entire cut a couple of times to refresh his memory. Then he blanked his mind and tried to blow.

He played Desmond's opening solo right through to the end. The notes seemed to bounce and skitter off the walls like a roomful of random ping-pong balls. When he'd finished, he licked his lips. Not bad, he thought. Des needn't feel threatened, but considering it was a very tough piece, not bad at all.

If he closed his eyes, he could almost see the snake rising up out of the basket.

Phil Edwards was looking forward to a slow night.

Actually, most nights were slow nights. Although his job as broadcast technician in the main Home Box Office facility was an important one, he was there primarily for the times when something went wrong. And something rarely did. The HBO operation was computer-driven and as bug-free as it could possibly be.

There had been a major equipment malfunction only once in the two years Phil had had his job, a problem with the up-converter that he had corrected in a matter of minutes. Corporate headquarters had been pleased with his reaction time.

This would be a particularly nice night for nothing to go wrong. The company, after months of tough negotiating, had finally acquired the rights of first telecast to *Heaven's Child*, as well as the right to future videocassette distribution. The film, a gentle fable about an extraterrestrial who assumes an earth child's form in order to lead mankind away from the path of self-destruction, had struck a major responsive chord among the public. In its theatrical release it had been one of the biggest smash hits of all time, grossing over two hundred million worldwide. Now it was making its TV premiere. HBO confidently expected that the broadcast would attract a host of new customers.

Though he was acutely aware of the importance of the evening's going smoothly, Phil personally didn't care for *Heaven's Child*. It was too corny for his taste. He was unable to believe in stories where the good guys triumphed by being more peaceful than the bad guys.

He preferred something where the people who kicked ass the hardest were the ones who came out on top. And he'd choose sophisticated weaponry over the voice of reason anytime. So he was a great fan of *Armed*, the most popular techno-thriller comic of the day, which chronicled the adventures of a superhero who had lost his right arm to some terrorists and now sported in its place a device that was a combination automatic rifle, long-range surveillance system, communications center, and missile launcher.

He was a third of the way through the latest issue of *Armed*. He had one eye on the comic and the other on the monitor, where the extraterrestrial-in-child's-clothing was getting an early introduction to the peculiarities of earth ways from its "mother." *Mary*, for God's sake, he thought. How cornpone could you get?

Suddenly the screen went black.

Oh Jesus, he thought. Not now. He dropped his comic book.

But before he could do a thing, some words in red appeared against the black background:

PLEASE STAY TUNED FOR AN IMPORTANT MESSAGE

He stopped cold. This was obviously not some kind of glitch in the equipment. The signal was clear and steady. Had the company decided to insert something smack into *Heaven's Child*? It was unthinkable. But it was the first thing to check.

He picked up the phone and dialed the corporate offices of the giant communications conglomerate that owned HBO. There was someone there around the clock.

What was going on? he asked the woman in charge of the night shift.

She didn't know, any more than he did. This was *not* a company message.

Phil thought immediately of the famous Captain Midnight, who'd jammed an HBO broadcast years earlier, in protest against their scrambling their signal. It wasn't that hard to do if you had the requisite hardware. All satellite users lived in fear of their signals being overridden, but the Captain Midnight incident had proven to be an isolated one. Nothing similar had happened since.

What should he do? Phil asked.

Boost the power, he was told. It was standard operating procedure when there were routine problems with the signal.

Carefully, the woman added.

Phil kept the phone to his ear and began to turn up the gain. Normally, the broadcaster used one hundred twenty-five watts of power, which was more than sufficient. Phil doubled this, then doubled it again.

Heaven's Child didn't return. Instead the message in red was replaced by some film footage. Water, an airport, a city skyline. Phil wasn't sure what city it was.

What level are you at? the woman wanted to know.

Five-hundred, Phil told her.

She thought for a moment. A plane could be seen on the monitor, preparing for takeoff.

All right, she said. Run it to two thousand.

His hands trembling, he doubled and redoubled the power again. This was a very hairy situation. If the signal was too strong, damage could be done to the satellite. And that could be a ten-million-dollar mistake. He didn't like that kind of sword hanging over him, and he was sure the woman at the other end of the phone didn't, either.

But even at two thousand, Heaven's Child failed to show his angelic face. He asked for further instructions.

The plane had taken off. There was some footage of a man with a long tube balanced on his shoulder. Then something shot out of the tube faster than the eye could follow, leaving a smoke trail behind.

Abandon ship, the woman ordered. Return power to one twenty-five and wait it out.

Phil was relieved. He sure didn't want to be the guy who discovered how much power it would take to wreck a satellite. He rolled the gain back down.

As he stared slack-jawed at the monitor, the plane exploded and fell to the earth. Then the screen went black and the red-lettered message reappeared.

My God, Phil thought. Was that real? Did I just see a 747 shot out of the sky?

And then the film ran again, this time with a narrator. The man's voice—if in fact it was a man's—had obviously been electronically distorted.

The voice said:

"People of the United States. We are the Committee for the Furtherance of Peace in Central America. What you are seeing is a faithful taped record of the events that took place at Logan Airport yesterday morning. We regret that innocent parties had to die in this manner, but we did not hesitate to do this and are prepared to do it again, if necessary. It is the only way in which to call attention to the untimely deaths so many innocent persons in our own country are suffering every day because of the misguided policies of your government. There is no need for further killing. We ask only for an end to the illegal and immoral war being waged against us. After this broadcast, we are contacting your president to inform him of the specific steps that must be taken immediately if there is to be no repetition of the Boston incident. On behalf of us all, let there be peace."

Phil was stunned. Lord God, it was real. HBO had been temporarily taken over by terrorists.

The plane crashed as it had before. The screen went black. This time the red letters spelled out a different message:

PEACE IN CENTRAL AMERICA

The message held for about fifteen seconds. Then it vanished, and in its place appeared the otherworldy face of Heaven's Child. It was looking up at Mary, its earth mother, and saying, "But Mother, I don't understand. Why do humans do such things?"

12

Kirk had recited nearly his whole list to Smith when he realized that he didn't have the Caprice any longer. He had no way to get around. He quickly added a car to the list and reminded himself that he was going to have to start thinking more clearly. He was working again, and not in a spare parts warehouse.

Things would improve a lot once his system got straight. He'd begun the physical training, a personally developed holistic regimen of aerobics, isometrics, stretching exercises, and martial arts routines. Ridding his body of the drugs would also help, he thought. And that shouldn't take long. Though he still ached from the beating he'd taken in the parking lot, his head hadn't bothered him all day. He hadn't felt the slightest urge to visit the downer bottle, which was good, because he'd left his stash behind when he'd gone with Smith.

Looking back, there was no way to tell which had come first, the headaches or the need to dull his senses. But the two had quickly become intertwined, one reinforcing the other and the drugs dealing effectively with both.

He had been an addict, whether physical or psychological didn't matter. Now he wasn't. Early in the evening, he'd taken a walk around Capitol Hill and was amazed at the sudden clarity with which he was seeing things. And that, of course, was a recognition of how fuzzy his perceptions had become.

All in the mind, he thought.

Smith had promised to fill his order by morning. In the meantime he had things to do, and Washington finally had a decent subway system. He walked the three blocks from his safe house to the Capitol South Metro stop. The station was clean and well lighted, as they all were, and he had to wait only a few minutes for a train.

He got on and then, at the last minute, hopped off. It was the quickest way to check for a tail. There was no reason anyone should be tailing him, but still . . . Good habits were good habits. No one mimicked his little maneuver.

When the next train arrived, he took the Blue Line to Metro Center, changed to the Red Line, and rode out to Friendship Heights. From there, it was easy walking distance.

Kirk took it slowly. He wanted to be absolutely sure he wasn't being followed. Besides, he was in no hurry to get where he was going and, as always, he marveled at the enormous changes the area had undergone in twenty-five years.

What had happened was a result of the building code inside the District of Columbia, which prohibited structures any taller than the Capitol. Because of this, office and living space in the city proper were inadequate to cope with its explosive growth in the post-World War II era. Stymied developers decided to start putting up dense clusters of high-rises in Maryland and Virginia. For reasons of convenience, they decided to spot these as close to the D.C. line as possible.

The Rosslyn area, on the Virginia shore of the Potomac, was first. Friendship Heights in Maryland was soon to follow.

As late as 1968, Friendship Heights was a modest residential area of steep, twisting roads and spacious, pre-war frame houses with wide verandas. That was the way Kirk remembered it from his teenage years, when his father had shuttled back and forth between Washington and overseas assignments. Now it was a blue-chip hunk of real estate. It had a Metro stop and several square blocks packed tight with apartments, condos, and commercial mini-skyscrapers, not to mention a cluster of upscale stores with names like Saks, Gucci, and Brooks Brothers.

Kirk walked two miles west from the Heights, crossed Little Falls Parkway, and passed between a pair of hickories that flanked the entrance to Kenwood, one of the capital's most exclusive suburban enclaves and home of the finest collection of ornamental cherry trees outside of the Tidal Basin. By then he knew there was no tail.

Kenwood was within a stone's throw of the city, and no one would ever know it. Its thickly tree-lined streets were quiet and strictly traffic-controlled. A glorified drainage ditch ran through its center, and was called a brook. The homes all had lawns and gardens tended by professional groundskeepers. The dark Mercedes and Jaguars and Caddies were spit-shined. Often they were parked next to Ford Escorts that were used for expeditions into the less savory parts of town.

Kirk hated everything about Kenwood except the cherry blossoms, which were still buds awaiting that warm afternoon a week or two in the future.

He felt very conspicuous as he walked the last few blocks. As a pedestrian he was instantly under suspicion, of course. Then there was his longish hair and the blue jeans and UCLA sweatshirt.

Fortunately, he had on a well-worn pair of Reeboks. So, when the inevitable police cruiser came alongside him, he merely flicked the boys a quick wave and began to jog as if he were into some walk/run conditioning program. That satisfied the cops and they left him behind. Kirk shook his head as he slowed again. The jogging craze, he was willing to bet, had saved more than one burglar's ass.

Though his pace had been leisurely, Kirk's pulse was still racing when he reached the house. It had been a long time, and he had no idea how he was going to react when the old man finally appeared in front of him.

His father's home was perched on a slight knoll at the end of a short, looping driveway. It was a massive, solid presence, constructed entirely of fieldstone, with a few heavy exterior timbers, a weathered slate roof, and a huge Chicago bay window. It occupied its rise in the land like a feudal warlord, daring one to challenge its authority.

A foolish notion, Kirk thought. And yet . . . He shook

off the uncertainties the place aroused in him, walked briskly up the drive, and rang the bell.

Esperanza answered the door. Of course. What had he expected, Charles himself?

Kirk looked down at the diminutive Salvadoran and felt . . . what? It wasn't hatred. No one disliked Esperanza. She was a kind, gentle woman who'd made the best of a life that had offered very little in the way of hope. But Kirk could never warm to her, either. It was hardly her fault, but it had been she, and not his mother, who had come out of San Salvador with Charles after the debacle there. It was she, and not his mother, who had shared Charles's home—as housekeeper and, he was certain, mistress—for more than two decades.

He remembered the day as if it had been only a week ago. The searing heat, the flies. Mr. Agnew, the lifeless math teacher at the American school, droning on and on about nothing. Cindy St. James, the girl across the aisle who continually flirted with him. The roof of the building next door, with its chipped and cracked red tiles.

The teenager of that day had grown into a man whose bitterness the intervening years had barely eased. Though he'd been in class when it had happened, in his mind the sequence of events had the clarity of an eyewitness account:

His mother and father getting into the limo at the embassy, for the ride down to the Plaza de los Diplomaticos. His mother pleading that they not go because of the death threat. His father insisting that in his profession he couldn't live his life behind glass, and that if his wife wished to share that life she must also share its risks. End of discussion.

Then the Plaza, and the horror scene itself, each detail as vivid as arterial blood. Father standing there, waiting his turn to speak. And mother . . . Mother stepping forward unexpectedly to retrieve the hat that had blown from her head. Taking in the heart the first bullet, meant for her husband. Mother falling, the life already gone out of her. Father turning, being hit in the shoulder by the second bullet and knocked flat on his back.

After that, the soldiers' response as they loosed their automatic weapons. The screams. The panic of the crowd. Four people trampled to death in the Plaza, another killed by errant Army gunfire. The bullet-shredded body of the assassin put on display as a warning to his comrades.

And so Charles Worthington Kirk returned to the States with Esperanza, who was unquestionably a fine person, but not Steven's mother.

Esperanza looked up at him uncomprehendingly for a moment, and then recognition came into her face, a face that seemed to have aged only a few months since he had last seen her.

"Steven?" she said, very tentatively reaching out and embracing him.

He gave her a perfunctory squeeze in return, then held her at arm's length. "Hello, Esperanza," he said.

"You are . . . looking well," she said. "It is good to see you again."

"Thank you. Is Charles here?"

"Yes. Of course. He doesn't . . . go out much these days." She gripped her hands in front of her. "Please. Come in."

They stepped into the parquet-floored foyer. The hanging lamp overhead was an antique Tiffany, but it contained a modern halogen bulb that simulated sunlight.

"Steven," Esperanza said, "this is such a surprise. Your father will be thrilled."

Sure, Steven thought.

"Can I get you something?" she continued. "Coffee? Or a drink? We don't keep any of those Rolling Rocks around anymore, but there's probably some kind of beer."

"Nothing, thank you," he said. "He's in his study?"

She nodded and let him go. He walked through the living room, with its loud, monotonously ticking grandfather clock, and across the short hall. The door to his father's study was ajar, and he went in without knocking.

The elder Kirk was seated behind his mahogany desk, entering something on his computer terminal. He looked up when his son entered the room, and stared.

Steven was surprised at how he felt. He found himself wanting to say *Hello, Father*. They were words he hadn't used in twenty years.

"Hello, Charles," he said.

The man behind the desk was a slight, almost frail seventy-five-year-old with a small head, angular features and sunken blue eyes. His hair was close-cropped and the silver color his son could undoubtedly expect later in life. There was a cane close by his swivel chair.

"Well," he said, "an unlikely visitor indeed." He leaned back and had a long look at his son, then added, "Whatever you've been doing doesn't suit you much."

"Yeah," Steven said. "Well, there hasn't seemed to be much point, not since . . . you know."

"Yes, I do know. And I'm sorry, more than you probably think. But I would have thought you'd be a little better prepared. Life does go on, Steven. Mine did."

"I don't need the lecture. You make your choices, I make mine."

"Very well. What do you need?"

"I need your help, Charles."

The elder Kirk just stared for a moment, then he began to chuckle. "How very odd," he said. "Well, it must be something truly extraordinary."

"Fortunately," Steven said, "it's not for me, or I wouldn't have asked you."

"Really? And who is the lucky person?"

"It's not a person. It's the country. I assume you still believe in her."

Charles paused, then said, "Steven, what are you up to?"

"I'm not up to anything. I'm working again."

"I don't believe it."

"I hardly believe it myself, Charles. But it's true. You can check with your agency contacts if you don't trust me. There is a certain Mr. Smith whom I think you know."

Charles smiled and nodded, and indicated that his son sit down, which Steven did. There was a brief silence as Charles signed off whatever job he'd been doing and powered down his computer. Then he gave his complete attention to his visitor.

"Now, what's wrong with the country that you can fix?" he asked.

Steven gave his father a condensed version of the tale that Smith had told him the previous evening, and related what he and the agency man had done since then. Charles listened attentively, breaking in only to clarify a couple of technical questions. Steven felt that, for the most part, the old man was remarkably conversant with the ins and outs of modern weaponry. And of course he was permanently wired into Central America. It had been his life.

"Damn Reagan," he muttered when Steven had finished.

"Reagan?"

"Sure. If he'd gone in in force in '81, we'd have a friendly government there now and things like this wouldn't be happening."

"Maybe, maybe not. We still can't be sure that it's the Nicaraguans who have the missiles."

"I'd say it was pretty damned certain after that TV show."

"What TV show?"

"You didn't hear? The people with the missiles took over HBO and played a tape of the airliner being shot down."

"What?"

Charles told him about the satellite jam that had been engineered earlier in the evening. "I didn't see the original myself," he said, "but HBO taped the override and made it available to the networks. It's about the only thing on right now. You want to see?"

"Of course," Steven said.

Charles picked up a remote control unit and turned on a TV in the corner of the room. He only had to flick through a couple of channels before he encountered yet another replay of the tape. Steven watched, fascinated. When the tape had run and the commentator returned for some speculative "analysis," Charles turned the TV off.

"The Committee for the Furtherance of Peace in Central America," Steven said. "I've never heard of them."

"They probably didn't exist last month," his father said, shrugging. "It's pretty sure to be just a Sandinista front."

"I don't know, maybe."

"Well, whatever it is, it would appear to have us in its power. Which brings me to my next question: what exactly is it that you want me to do for you?"

Steven had to think about it for a moment, then he said, "I guess I need a contact. Smith's my case officer. Or at least he recruited me and he thinks he is. But . . . well, I don't trust the sonofabitch. You know damn well what he did to me in Grenada."

Charles chuckled again. "And you trust me?"

Steven grinned sheepishly. "More than Smith, I guess," he said. "Look, I've been completely out of this shit for years and now suddenly I'm somehow valuable to them again. I don't like the smell of it."

"Why not? You speak Spanish, you were raised in C.A., and you're top-notch in your field. You're a logical choice."

"Yeah, but I think I know Smith a little better than you do. He never does something just because it's logical. He does it because he expects to get something out of it."

Charles shrugged. "He expects to recover the missiles," he said.

"I hope that's the extent of it," Steven said. "But I doubt it. If he's got something else planned for me, I don't want to be caught without any insurance."

"And I'm your policy. That's pretty amusing, Steven."

"There's no one left in the agency I trust."

"I'm retired, son."

"Oh come on, Charles. You sit on the PFIAB. You've still got your contacts. And you're my . . . father."

"Well, well. You can say the word without choking on it."

"Please," Steven said. "Give me a break. This isn't easy for me, you know."

"Swallowing one's pride seldom is. Actually I'm flattered, though I'm not sure I have the clout you think I do. But all right, I'll help you if I can, Steven. So again, what exactly do you want me to *do*?"

Steven relaxed, just a little. "First of all," he said, "if Smith is running some kind of multiple con on me, I want to know about it. Whatever you can find out, though I realize that part isn't going to come easy." Charles nodded.

"Second, there's your Central American expertise. I haven't figured out yet the best way to proceed, but at some point I may need to tap into that." Charles nodded again.

"And third, I want you to be my ghost control. I'm going to have to depend on Smith to direct me in the field. Fine, I can deal with that. But suppose I come up with something he doesn't want to hear? I can't afford to trust him to pass it along. Hell, the *country* can't afford it. I need to know that you'll be there to act as a conduit to the President if necessary."

Charles nodded a third time. "Those seem like reasonable enough requests," he said. "I suppose you'd also like me to keep you alive, if that becomes a question."

Steven smiled. "Yeah," he said. "That too."

Charles got up, leaned on his cane, and hobbled around to where his son was sitting. "Thing is," he said, "I don't work with any man who won't shake my hand."

Charles held out his right hand and Steven, after a moment's hesitation, took it.

"Welcome home," Charles said.

13

If the Oval Office is the heart of the official White House, then its brain is the Situation Room, with the adjoining offices the central nervous system. The Situation Room itself is rather small, and it's the only room in the White House with entirely contemporary furnishings. Which is fitting, since it's there that the most important strategic real-world decisions are made.

The Situation Room sits at the end of a string of offices that contain elements of the most sophisticated communications network in the world: computers, TVs, telexes, printers, phones. The noise and activity levels are high, and there is a perpetual air of confusion. The disorder is more apparent than real, though, because it is the function of this peripheral equipment to supply the data upon which intelligent action can be taken.

As Donald Walker strode purposefully toward the Situation Room, people got out of his way. Not only was he the Attorney General, he was also an imposing, broad-shouldered black man. The youngest member of the Cabinet at forty-six, he'd been in the Justice Department since graduating from Harvard Law, following a tour of combat duty late in the Vietnam War. The drug trade had been his particular obsession, and he'd stepped into the national limelight when he'd broken up a huge Colombian-Italian cocaine cartel.

As a direct result of his investigation, persons unknown had lobbed a hand grenade through Walker's living room window one night. He'd lost an eye and the left side of his face had been badly scarred. He now proudly wore an eye patch and a neatly trimmed beard.

Walker found the man he was looking for, the evening's duty officer, just outside the Situation Room. This man, along with his other-shift counterparts, had one of the most sensitive jobs in government. If unexpected emergency news came in, he'd be the one to inform the President.

"Nothing yet?" Walker asked the duty officer.

"No, sir," the Navy captain said.

Walker nodded his large head. "Good," he said. "You're set to plug directly into the Cabinet Room if anything does come in?"

"Yes, sir. And if it comes by phone, we'll start the trace immediately. With the priority we're using, we should be able to pin it down within a minute."

"Very well. Thank you, Captain."

The duty officer moved away and Walker stepped over to the Situation Room door. There was a sign over it which could be illuminated to read: MEETING IN PROGRESS. The sign was dark. Walker punched a number into the keypad next to the door and opened it. He glanced inside.

One long table, swivel chairs, recessed lighting. But no people. Walker nodded his head as if he'd confirmed something, then made his way to the Cabinet Room.

The Cabinet Room is a long chamber with draped French doors that look out over the Rose Garden. It contains a working fireplace with mantel, ornate chandeliers, a collection of flags, and some fake torches in sconces along the walls. Navy stewards in blue blazers adorned with the Presidential seal move quietly about, topping off cups of Jamaican coffee.

Whereas the adjacent Oval Office tends to be used for ceremonial gatherings, the Cabinet Room more often hosts meetings of substance.

A large, oval mahogany table runs the length of the room, with brown leather chairs grouped around it. Each chair has a nameplate on its back, inscribed with the name of the appropriate Cabinet member. The President's chair, slightly taller than the rest, stands at the end of the table.

Filling that chair was a large bear of a man, still a reasonable facsimile of the heavyweight wrestler he'd been in college. His head was bald on top, with a fuzzy white fringe around the sides, and his face was weathered and kindly.

Fifteen years earlier, he'd been one of the country's top executives. Almost singlehandedly he'd transformed the American steel industry, bringing it back from the second-rate status to which it had fallen, and making the domestic product once again competitive in world markets. He'd gone on to write a best-selling book recounting his experiences in business, and extolling the virtues of hard work, self-sacrifice, and fiscal conservatism.

His high visibility and huge national popularity had not, of course, gone unnoticed by his political party, and when it came time to award the most recent nomination, he received it despite scattered misgivings about his age. The election was a laugher. As had been the case with Reagan and others, Americans were in the mood for a grandfather figure.

The President turned seventy-one the day after he was sworn in.

As with Reagan, it mattered. His subordinates ran their departments any way they wanted.

When Walker arrived, five men and a woman, the highest-ranking officials in the Administration, were seated around the oval table. Glancing at the empty chair to the President's right, Walker said, "Sit Room's set. Where's Walter?"

Chief-of-Staff Read shrugged. "I told him if he wasn't here on time he'd be shitting golf balls instead of hitting them." Read was a stern-faced·man in his late fifties, with thinning gray hair and slate-gray eyes. He spoke slowly, in a voice made gravelly by close to four decades of a two-pack-a-day cigarette habit.

Just then the Vice-President entered, stumbling slightly as he tried to straighten his tie. "Sorry, guys," he mumbled as he stuffed himself into his chair.

Walter Brust was an affable fifty-year-old who stood six feet eight inches tall and had once been the finest white power forward in the NBA. Though a fair amount of his basketball muscle had gone to flab, he hadn't really ballooned out like so many of them did. He had the bleached hair and ruddy skin of the committed year-round golfer. In fact, with his freckles and youthful face, he looked a great deal like a slightly magnified Jack Nicklaus.

Talk around the table was desultory, concerned with *what if* this and that, or with whatever small progress was being made concerning *the* problem. Everyone knew that little of substance could be done until the hijackers revealed themselves, and more than one member of the task force thought there must be better uses to which present time could be put.

But the President wanted them all there. He was certain that some word was going to come down soon. He had a feeling.

And the President was right.

The message came by telephone, on a line whose number was known to only a highly select few. Which now included terrorists.

By the time the call had been shunted to the Cabinet Room, the trace was well under way.

The caller must have known that, but he didn't seem concerned by it. A calm voice said, "Good evening, Mr. President" through the speakerphone that allowed everyone in the room to hear.

The voice was clear. State-of-the-art digital reprocessing, National Security Adviser Diane McBain thought. The guy would never risk sending his real voice down a telephone line. If it even was a guy. For the new machines, obscuring gender was just one of the possibilities.

Damn, she thought. If he had that kind of equipment, the trace wasn't going anywhere either.

"To whom am I speaking?" the President asked.

"I represent the Committee for the Furtherance of Peace in Central America," the man said.

"How do we know that?"

"Does every crank have this number?"

The President glanced at McBain, who mouthed the word "More," and then at his DCI, who nodded agreement.

"I don't think that that is sufficient identification," the President said.

"All right. You have seen the videotape, I trust. So you will have noticed that the incident was caused by a Stinger missile."

"Probably. But anyone could guess that."

"Not anyone would know where the missile came from, Mr. President. It was part of a shipment of twenty-four that was hijacked in Roatan. Does that satisfy you?"

The President checked with the same two members of his staff, and both nodded. "I believe that it does," he said.

"The only other thing I could do," the voice said, "is to tell you when and where we intend to use the next missile. And, frankly, we'd like to avoid that if possible."

"So would we. But you must know that it is our policy not to negotiate with terrorists."

The caller chuckled. "Excuse me," he said. "I think that you will be forced to reconsider your policy. Otherwise the friendly skies are no longer going to be safe for American travelers. Wouldn't it be better if we could come to an agreement in private?"

"God damn it! What do you *want*?" the President said.

"That's simple. We want peace in Central America, beginning with Nicaragua."

"And you think you'll get it by killing innocent people?"

"Whether anyone in your country can be considered truly innocent is an interesting point of debate, but moot. What we *are* doing is negotiating from a position of strength, as some of your predecessors liked to put it."

The President looked around the room for some word of advice, but nobody had one. "All right," he said wearily. "I assume there are some terms coming."

"I'm glad you see things our way," the voice said. "Our list of requirements is very short, actually.

"First, there will be an immediate cessation to all operations, covert and overt, directed against the government of Nicaragua. The forces that you are supporting will henceforth receive no supplies of any kind from the United States.

"Second, you will assist in the mandatory repatriation of all Nicaraguan nationals currently fighting against their country."

"I have no control over the Contras!" the President snapped.

"You must exert some nevertheless. They will be humanely treated, but they have to understand that they are being *permanently* disbanded this time. Their mercenary friends will be permitted to return to the U.S., of course.

"Third, you will within thirty days sign a treaty guaranteeing in perpetuity the sovereignty of all Central American nations and denying military use of the region to any outside country.

"And fourth, you will pay in reparations to Nicaragua the sum of one billion U.S. dollars, details of the transaction also to be worked out within the next thirty days."

There were low murmurs around the table. Even in a time of trillion-dollar budgets, a billion was a sizable amount.

"And in return?" the President said.

"You will get the Stingers back, and the far more important gift of peace in Central America."

"If we refuse?"

"You must show good faith by doing something of substance during the next two days. Otherwise, there will be a second incident. After that, if there is still no progress, the frequency of incidents will escalate. As I'm sure you know, the missiles have a life expectancy of only sixty days. We will use them all before they self-destruct, if we have to."

"How do I contact you?"

The man chuckled again. "Don't be foolish, Mr. President," he said. "I contact you. I will do so again in forty-eight hours. I hope some progress will have been made by then."

The line went dead. There was immediate cacophony until the door opened and the duty officer from the Situation Room was shown in. Then there was a sudden and complete silence.

"Yes, Captain," the President said. "What have you got?"

The officer merely stood by the door, his hands clasped in front of him. "I'm sorry, Mr. President," he said. "I'm afraid the trace was . . . inconclusive."

"What do you mean?" the President said angrily. "We didn't have the bastard on the line long enough?"

"I'm sure," McBain said, "that what the captain means is that the call is untraceable. I suspected that it would be."

"Yes, ma'am," the duty officer said. "We dead-ended at a filling station pay phone in the Nevada desert. It wasn't being used at the time. We rang it."

"How in hell can a call be untraceable?" the President demanded.

"With the proper equipment and the necessary expertise," McBain said, "a call's point of origination can be made to appear as other than what it actually was. The Nevada desert or wherever."

"Yes, ma'am," the duty officer said.

"Jesus Christ," the President said. "That's all we can do?"

"I'm afraid so, Mr. President," the duty officer said.

"This is a very sophisticated operation," McBain said. "Tell me, Captain, could we make a satellite intercept?"

"It's technically possible, ma'am, but that's assuming the caller is using a satellite channel at all. He might not be. He could be sending a false code right down the line from the other side of Pennsylvania Avenue. At the very least, we'd have to have a pretty good idea of when the next call was coming. And then we'd have to be damn lucky."

"All right, Captain," the President said. He waved his hand and the officer left the room.

When the door had closed, there was pandemonium again. The President finally had to slam the palm of his hand repeatedly against the tabletop.

"God damn it, shut up!" he shouted.

A semblance of order slowly returned to the Cabinet Room.

When he could be heard without raising his voice, the President looked directly at his DCI and asked for a rough assessment of the situation.

"Well," the Director said, "I'd have to check with the Latin Am section, but I've never heard of this Committee. I doubt that they exist except to do what they're doing. The question is who they're working for. I'll put my best people on it right away."

"Oh, come on!" Enzo Carini said. The dapper Secretary of State was a short, trim man in his late forties, with black hair that was still naturally so, hazel eyes and a boyish face. His pale gray Armani suit served to set off nicely his tanning-parlor skin, which at the moment was more red than bronze. "They're fronting for the Sandinistas. They've got to be."

"We don't know that," the Director said.

"They want a billion dollars for Nicaragua!" Carini said. "What more do you want?"

"I want to know where the money's actually going," the Director replied.

"I think Enzo's right," Monty Banks said.

Army General Montgomery Banks, the Chairman of the Joint Chiefs, was a short, wiry man in his late fifties. His crisp uniform had rows of decorations, and his wintry blue eyes were set deep in a leathery, stoic face that gave away nothing for free.

"The Sandie Intelligence Directorate's fingerprints are all over this," he said. "We should have cleaned those bastards out years ago, before they *had* a military. Now we've got Communist dictators on the run everywhere in the world but our own backyard, where we tolerate *two* of them."

"Diane?" the President asked his National Security Adviser.

"Well," McBain said carefully, "it certainly looks like a Communist operation. And the terms primarily benefit Nicaragua. Though the Salvadoran left would be pleased with them, too."

Chief of Staff Read said, "I don't know what kinda dick-wads we got here, but I'm inclined to agree with the Director. Only thing that matters in this world is where the money goes."

"Assuming it does go to Nicaragua," McBain said, "the Sandinistas still might not be behind this. It could be one of their . . . allies."

There was a pause. No one wanted to voice what everyone was thinking. The thaw in relations with the Soviet Union had become an accepted geopolitical reality, and the prospect of a fresh confrontation with the Russians was a particularly ugly one.

General Banks broke the silence. "Well, I don't believe it," he said. "The missiles were on their way to the Contras. The hijack took place in Honduras. That's Nicaraguan agents at work, not the KGB."

"Or Cubans," Carini added. "Same damn thing."

"Shit," the President said. "I can't cave in to a bunch of terrorists. It'll be Iran all over again."

"If I might," Gunther Schule said.

The Secretary of Defense was a slightly rotund man in his early fifties, with dark hair that was gray at the temples. He wore a Brooks Brothers suit, including a vest with a gold watch chain, and smoked his cigarettes through a tortoiseshell holder. He was a soft-spoken man, but he was ceded the floor as soon as he interjected himself into the discussion.

"I think, Mr. President," he said, "that we need to remember that this group still has twenty-three Stingers left. They have the potential to kill thousands of innocent people. The ramifications of that have to be weighed against the negatives of cutting a deal.

"Fortunately, it seems to me that they're taking the political problem into account. By not publicly revealing the terms of negotiation, they're giving you the option of resolving the situation in secret. That just might keep the fallout to a minimum and it's worth consideration, in my opinion."

"Oh, for Christ's sake, Gunther," Carini said. "How in the hell do we keep something this big from leaking?"

"We keep it strictly within the room," Schule said.

The members of the group looked uneasily at one another.

"We're being asked to move a *billion* dollars," McBain said.

The Director puffed on his pipe, nodded, and said, very matter-of-factly, "We could deal with that."

"The rest of the terms could probably be handled on a business-as-usual basis," Tom Read said. "The President's ongoing efforts to bring real peace and security to the region, etcetera. The public only knows about the one missile. If we can stonewall the full hijacking, we just might keep the cutworms from the cabbage."

Vice President Brust finally spoke. "Righto," he said. "The sooner these people get what they want, the sooner we can get the country back to normal again." He looked at the President, seeking approval, and was ignored.

"Nuts!" General Banks said. "You deal with a black-mailer today, and tomorrow he's right back on your doorstep with his hand out."

"Hear, hear," Enzo Carini said.

"Just what are you gentlemen suggesting?" McBain asked.

There was a pregnant silence. No one wanted to be the first to say the words *military action.*

"All right, look," Tom Read said. "Let's admit that it's a little early to be rattling the fucking sabers, okay? Why don't we open a confidential channel to the Sandinistas, try to persuade them that it's in their best interest to hold the Committee back for a while. Promise them we won't take any action against them so long as there are no more incidents. You *imply* you're ready to use force, it usually works better. We can also tell them any kind of lies about what we'll do after the crisis is over. Maybe we can buy enough time that the agency or the bureau'll recover the Stingers."

The DCI and Attorney General both nodded. "The Director and I are coordinating," Donald Walker said. "Wherever the rest of the missiles are, we'll find them. Soon."

The tone of his voice suggested that God help anyone who was found along with them. "But we need a little breathing room," he added.

"I agree with Tom," McBain said. "We should try to buy some time. When the guy gets in touch again, I think you should do your best to stall him, Mr. President. A few days may be enough. And I'll talk to some technical people, see if there isn't some way to put a more efficient trace on."

Gunther Schule cleared his throat and once again everyone looked his way. "Speaking of phones," he said, "there's one other thing we haven't talked about. Our caller, as he so kindly pointed out, reached you on a secure line, Mr. President."

The President looked at his Secretary of Defense blankly.

"Well," Schule said, "how did he get the number?"

"A lot of people know the number," the President said.

"A lot of people within our government. It's well protected against unauthorized users, isn't it?" Schule asked the Chief of Staff.

"Of course," Read answered. "The lock on the distribution list is tight, as far as I know."

"What in hell are you saying, Schule?" Carini asked. "That these bastards have inside help?"

"The possibility exists, Enzo. It'd be foolish to deny it."

"Gunther's right, Mr. President," McBain said.

"Who's on the damn list, anyway?" the President said.

"I'll go over it with you," McBain said quickly. "In the meantime, I think we should launch an immediate investigation. If someone on our side did leak the number, he or she might lead us right to the terrorists."

"All right, do it," the President ordered. "And if there's treason involved," he said to his Attorney General, "throw the goddamn book at them." Walker nodded.

"Now, anything else?" the President asked.

"Well," Read said. "You're going to have to make a public statement, sir. I'd suggest some vague booshwah about terrorism and an offer of federal assistance to the families of the victims. And I wouldn't take any questions from the media."

"All right, write it out," the President said. "I'll speak from the Oval Office in the morning. No press access except for the camera crew. Screen them good, Tom."

"Yes, sir," Read said. The President waited, but no one raised any further points.

"I want everyone back here tomorrow evening," the President said. "And try to bring some good news with you."

14

"Steven. This is Frank and that's Bud," Smith said. "From IAD."

Kirk nodded toward the van's cab, a perfunctory acknowledgment to the two men whose real names he had just not been given. He'd never had much use for the foot soldiers of the Operations Directorate's International Activities Division. They were support staff that worked outside of the bureaucracy and were called in when some kind of specialized knowledge was required. The request could come from anywhere in the world, it didn't matter. The IAD man who was dispatched would be an expert in demolition or psywar or marine ops; he wouldn't know (or necessarily care) jackshit about Lebanon or Honduras or the Philippines.

IAD people—as close to a true mercenary force as the United States officially maintained—were dangerous, because whoever controlled them had a strong and highly functional power base under his command. For years that person had been Smith.

Kirk had received Smith's message just before midnight. It had been brief and to the point. The satellite sweep had activated a signal from the missing Stingers. They were in Washington, somewhere within a circle of five miles' diameter centered over the northeast section of the city. That was as close as the satellite could pinpoint them, and it was close enough; from there, a mobile ground unit could easily home right in on them.

There was now going to be an attempt to retrieve the missiles, and Smith wanted Kirk to be part of the recovery team.

That was it. There had been no mention of the fact that IAD personnel would be tagging along. Not that there should have been; Smith was merely exercising need-to-know precautions that were entirely proper.

And not that it was any great surprise. Smith wasn't going to chance an encounter with international terrorists with only Kirk at his side. So he would have turned to the IAD, the most logical source of readily available help. That meant using agency resources right there in the nation's capital—a clear violation of the law—but so what? Niceties of distinction such as *domestic* and *foreign* were for more theoretical moments.

Since his requested weapons hadn't yet been delivered to Duddington Place, Kirk felt relieved when Smith handed him two items, a 9-mm Walther semiautomatic pistol and a suppressor.

"Full clip," Smith said. "It's not the one you ordered, but we were on short notice tonight."

Kirk held the gun in his hand for a moment to get the feel of it. Then he screwed the silencer into its nose. It was a smooth, tight fit. He checked that the safety was on and slipped the pistol behind his belt.

The van was a bland-looking black Chevy, with no windows in its sides and opaque curtains over the rear ones. There was a large whiplash antenna that suggested nothing more sinister than a CB.

Inside, a bench ran along one wall and shelving along the other. The shelves contained an array of surveillance and other electronic equipment. There was a monitor connected to a hidden motor-driven, high-definition periscope that tilted and swiveled so as to afford nearly complete visual coverage of the surrounding area. There were video and audio recorders. There was a small refrigerator, a color TV, and a chemical toilet.

Most important to the van's present task was a microwave transmitter and receiving unit with extremely sensitive tuning capabilities. This sent out the signal that activated the transponder in the Stinger pod and received the answering signal. The small dish that made it all possible was mounted directly behind the grille in the van's highly customized engine compartment.

The receiver's homing device was a VDT that displayed a series of concentric circles with a cross at its center. The point of origin of the transponder's signal was represented by a large, glowing dot. When the dot lay directly over the cross, the van was headed in precisely the right direction. In addition, a digital readout at the bottom of the screen gave the range and compass bearing of the target. It automatically updated every four seconds.

The van went out North Capitol Street, then turned east on New York Avenue. This was a part of Washington that tourists avoided: crumbling brick row houses with bartizan turrets; store- and housefronts sealed up with plywood or cinder blocks, many of them vacant since the 1968 riots; overflowing trash cans at the curbs of streets strewn with smashed bottles; liquor stores and dingy carry-outs on every corner; here and there, the 'dozers of urban renewal moving in.

Smith tuned in the receiver. The dot appeared, pulsing in the upper-left-hand quadrant of the screen. In the soft green glow from the VDT, Kirk saw one of Smith's infrequent smiles cross his face. It passed as quickly as one of the street lamps along the road.

Smith directed Frank, who was doing the driving. As they proceeded west, the dot migrated slowly toward the center of the screen. The bearing was more or less correct. Target range: eighteen hundred meters.

Kirk blanked his mind of expectation and merged with the moment, relaxed but ready to react on an instant's notice.

They passed a jarringly modernistic McDonald's and turned north as the dot dropped below the screen's midline. They were soon in an area of dilapidated warehouses just beyond the freight yards. There was no other traffic on these back streets at this hour, just the van and behind it a dark Ford that was obviously also a part of the operation. Glass crunched beneath their tires.

The glowing dot slid along the screen's center line and then, as the van made one last turn, positioned itself directly over the heart of the cross. The road they were on was aimed directly at the target. Range: two hundred meters.

The van passed between a tire recapping business and an open yard filled with rusting auto parts. There was a sign on the yard's chain-link fence that read ATTACK DOG—TRAINED TO KILL. The recapper leaked the odor of burned rubber into the air.

Range: seventy-five meters. The van pulled over to the curb, crushing an empty can of Jolt. The Ford followed suit, and both vehicles turned off their engines. Neither had been running with lights for some time.

A few moments later, a man got out of the Ford. He looked around nervously, but saw nothing except some scraps of paper being blown down the street by the slight breeze. There was some vicious barking from the direction of the junkyard and the screech of a cat in distress.

The man hurried over to the van, opened its rear door, and got in.

Kirk found himself looking at a man who had red hair and an ugly, acne-scarred face and was wearing a plaid topcoat. Though built like a grizzly, he was obviously an amateur and skittish as hell.

"What is this man doing here?" Kirk asked Smith.

Unsurprisingly, he got no response. Smith merely said to the stranger, "Sit down," and Seamus Croaghan did, on the bench next to Kirk. Kirk eyed him coolly and Croaghan looked down at his feet.

Smith was busy with the radio, letting someone know exactly where he was and which building was suspected of hiding the missiles.

When he'd finished he said to Croaghan, "The channel's going to stay open. If there's any trouble, just give them a Mayday and they'll send in the Marines."

"Shit, Smith," Croaghan said, "you really think the Stingers are in there? Look at the place. Damn thing's ready to fall down if you blow too hard on it."

"Sometimes the least secure place is the least suspicious," Kirk said. "But I agree. This doesn't seem like a very likely hiding place."

"We know they're in there," Smith said. "Or at least the transponders are. If we don't recover the missiles, whoever owns the building may be a lead."

"All right," Kirk said. "Let's go."

Smith took a rifle with a Starlite scope from under the bench. "Frank," he said, "you come in from the back. Bud, see if there's a loading dock or something on the far side and go in there. Steven, you take the front. I'll cover you from here. And you," he said to Croaghan, "see that your men are ready to move."

Bud and Frank checked their silenced Uzis and slid back the bolts, jacking live rounds into the firing chambers. Croaghan called the Ford with details of the plan.

"Now, stay by the radio," Smith said to Croaghan. Then to the other three he said, "Don't take any chances. If they've got a good defense, retreat and we'll call for reinforcements. Take someone alive if you possibly can. Keep in touch with each other. And for God's sake, if the place is empty, be careful of booby traps."

He then handed out two additional items. First, belt-clipped twenty-thousand candlepower Streamlight flashlights. Kirk held his by its knurled, sure-grip handle. A nice piece of equipment, he thought. The Streamlight had a sealed beam quartz halogen bulb that would provide plenty of illumination, not to mention a blinding surprise for anyone waiting in the dark. It had a lenscap with an adjustable black diaphragm that could be stopped down to a pinhole. And it was tough enough to use as a club, if necessary.

The second item was an Ear Mic, the modern successor to the walkie-talkie. A sub-miniature transmitter/ receiver, the Ear Mic looks like a hearing aid and is worn in the same fashion. It allows hands-free communication between people tuned to the same frequency by translating the vibration of the ear bones into a usable signal and sending that signal to any other Ear Mics within range.

Each man, including Smith and Croaghan, fitted himself with one of the devices. When they'd finished, Smith said, "Let's do it."

He looked at the other four in turn and they all nodded, acknowledging that they had heard him both normally and through the Ear Mic. Then each spoke for a moment in a low voice to make sure his own unit was transmitting as well as receiving.

After a final few words of encouragement from Smith, Bud and Frank slipped quietly out of the van and disappeared, their dark clothing immediately blending with the shadows. Kirk and Smith went out the sliding side door. Smith knelt down next to the right-hand wheel well. From there, he was catty-corner to the warehouse and had a clear field of fire to its front.

The street was poorly lighted, but details of the building could still be made out. Made of corrugated steel, it had a couple of large windows at the right front and three steps up to a landing and small door on the left. Two posts were all that remained of the railing along the steps. Above the door, B&B DISTRIBUTORS was lettered in faded white paint. There was no indication as to what they had distributed.

Smith scanned the building through the Starlite scope. "The door's padlocked," he said to Kirk. "But the hinge looks useless."

He leaned his rifle against the van and went back inside. In a few seconds he emerged with a large screwdriver, which he handed to Kirk.

"That ought to pop her," he said. He retrieved his rifle and took up position behind the fender again.

Kirk bent over and sprinted down the sidewalk. The stripped shell of a Pontiac sat directly opposite the warehouse and he stopped and crouched behind it, peering through the holes where its windows had once been.

There was nothing to see. A distant, muffled sound of metal on metal came from the far side of the building.

134 • *Doug Hornig*

Bud or Frank making his entry, Kirk thought. It was time for him to give support.

He moved quickly across the street and up the wooden front steps. The top step cracked as it gave under his weight, but his momentum carried him onto the landing. In one fluid motion he slid the screwdriver under the hinge and wrenched it from its screws, muffling the sound with his sleeve. The unlatched door creaked open of its own weight and he slipped inside. He immediately squatted down, leaning his back against the front wall.

The air was musty, tinged with the faint odor of something rotting. Kirk steadied his breathing as his eyes adjusted to the lower light level. He listened carefully, but no sound came from within.

He had entered what had once been a small office. All that was left was an overturned metal desk, a pile of heavy glass that was probably the remains of a water bottle, and a file cabinet, lying on its side with its twisted drawers protruding. There was the ghostly shape of a wall calendar, but Kirk couldn't make out the year. A large hole in the rear wall had likely contained a glass partition at one time.

Adjacent to the former partition was a door into the warehouse proper. It was open.

Kirk didn't particularly want to show any light, but he had no choice. If there were any tripwires in the building, this was one place he'd be apt to find them. He unclipped the flashlight from his belt and twisted the lenscap counterclockwise as far as it would go. When he turned it on, the flashlight produced a beam no wider than a pencil point.

Even this he hid with his hand until he'd gotten down on all fours. Then he uncovered the light and quickly scanned the area between himself and the inner door, looking especially for something that would strike him between the ankle and the knee.

No tripwires. And no sense of presence, either. No feeling that anyone had been in here in a very long time.

Cautiously he crossed the office and looked through the open door into a vast black space beyond. The light coming through the front windows revealed that the interior was probably one huge room, though Kirk couldn't be sure since he couldn't see too deeply into it. It appeared to be open from floor to roof, and there was a second story that ended about fifteen feet short of the front wall.

Across the way a crack of light was showing in the wall. That would be where Bud had come in. There was no indication that Frank had made his entry at the rear.

But then Kirk's Ear Mic came to life.

"Frank," Bud said, "where you at?"

"Back of the building," Frank whispered. "I can see all the way to the front and this place is about empty. There's a few big drums of something and some stairs along the near wall here. I'll check out the second floor if they're clean."

Kirk saw the narrow beam of light as Frank searched the stairs for a tripwire.

"I'm going up," Frank said.

"You're covered from the side," Bud said. "Where you at, Steve?"

"Front," Kirk said. "I've got it covered. There's an empty office and that's all. I don't think there's anyone else here."

"Agreed," Bud said. "You take it careful, Frank."

Frank went from the ground floor to the second without a sound. A moment later a tiny point of light appeared up there.

"Hay bales," Frank said. "This place is full of hay bales. I'm going to full light. There ain't nobody up here."

"Frank, you watch out," Bud said.

"Nothing," Frank said. They could hear him now, walking above them. "No, wait a minute. I'm over in the back corner. There's a pile of long, skinny crates. Throwed every whichaway. It looks like they pulled the missile pods out of them already, but I'm gonna have a closer look."

"Wait a minute, Frank," Kirk said. "We better get someone in here to—"

But Frank's next step landed him squarely over a pressure detonator.

The blast blinded Kirk as it lifted him from his feet and slammed him down onto the building's cement floor. His head bounced once and he lost consciousness.

Above him the hay bales were a sheet of flame. A

billowing cloud of dense white smoke quickly filled the entire warehouse. The beams supporting the second floor, buckled by the explosion, began to give way. The roof timbers started catching fire, as did the plywood nailed to them. In a matter of moments the second floor was an inferno.

Kirk came to with a violent cough. There were bits of burning debris all around him. He managed to turn himself over, pressed his nose to the concrete and took a breath. Acrid smoke laden with some chemical filled his lungs and he gasped. That only caused another coughing spasm.

His eyes were streaming tears and his right shoulder ached. Inch by agonizing inch, he pulled himself across the floor to where he thought the door to the office should be. He hit a solid wall. The door was there somewhere, but where? If he went right, some autonomic part of his brain told him, he'd find either the door or the end of the office wall. He went right.

He groped along. The wall was getting hot, hotter . . . and then it ended. The door was back the way he'd come. He turned, tried to push himself to his feet, but fell. His conscious mind was shutting down from the oxygen starvation. Desperately he lunged forward. Once, then again.

"Steven, where are you?" came the voice in his Ear Mic. He tried to respond, but managed only a slight croak.

"Bud?"

No response. The voice didn't ask for Frank.

The entire second floor collapsed with a tremendous crash, and the fire seemed to double in intensity. Kirk threw himself forward one final time. His fingers wrapped around the door jamb. He gripped it, unable to move any farther.

He began to curl up and go to sleep. . . .

Then a brilliant flashlight beam sliced through the smoke. Powerful hands grabbed his forearms and he was being dragged out through the office, out into the cool, crisp night air. Air he could breathe.

Kirk was laid gently on his back. Through his blurred eyes he could see the ugly stranger in the plaid coat standing over him. The man who'd saved his life. He was fighting to catch his own breath. Kirk tried to say something, but found that he couldn't.

He vaguely heard the sound of running footsteps and then Smith was standing above him as well.

"Get him *out* of here!" Smith commanded. "Then pull your men back! We don't know what in *hell* is in those drums Frank saw!"

"We couldn't find—"

"Everything fell on top of him! Come on, *move,* for Christ's sake!"

The burly redhead picked up Kirk as if he were a child, ran with him to the van, and threw him in the back. Then he raced to the far side of the building, returning a few seconds later with three men strung out behind him.

Smith started the van, wheeled it in a squealing U-turn, and accelerated down the street without a backward glance. Behind him, the dark Ford did the same thing.

The two vehicles were well under way when the warehouse blew. Its four walls smacked flat against the earth, and its galvanized steel roof popped like a champagne cork, spun through the air and crashed to the ground, smothering the stripped Pontiac across the street. A column of smoke and flame rose up two hundred feet, as if the site had just been nuked. Chunks of concrete and metal rained down on the neighborhood.

Smith clung to the steering wheel as the van was buffeted by the concussion from the blast. For a long moment he felt like he was driving through a hurricane. Then the turbulence passed.

He checked the rearview mirror. The Ford had escaped as well. He aimed the van toward the heart of the city.

15

Carla Stokes could barely contain her excitement. She'd
sat by the phone in her apartment for hours, not daring
to go to bed, knowing that she had to be getting a call
from Smoking Gun. A man she'd never met. Just a raspy
phone voice, but her personal pipeline into the White
House.

Why he'd chosen her over all the other high-powered
Post newspeople she'd probably never know, and she
didn't really care. All that mattered was that he had
come to her, six months earlier, with the first leaked
story and that, on average, he'd fed her another about
once a month.

They hadn't been major stories, true, but they'd con-
sistently outflanked her competitors and they'd been one
hundred percent accurate. Her source had legitimate access to the President.

Everyone had seen the videotape of the Aer Lingus jet
being shot down. The networks had played it over and
over. But beyond that, the public and the media were
still in the dark. What was this Committee for the Furtherance of Peace in Central America, and what did it
want? Had it, as promised, contacted the President? If
so, what sort of conversation had they had?

As an investigative reporter, Stokes believed that
these were questions that the people deserved answers
to.

But beyond that, there was the magnitude of the story.
This was going to be a monster, the sort of story upon
which a resourceful person could build a career.

Though only thirty years old, and fortunate to be on
the staff of the *Post* at all, she was chafing to break out of
the pack. She looked above her and saw people who

didn't have half her natural ability. And what was more, they were nearly all white. That situation she fully intended to change.

Which was why she was willing to sit on her butt for hours waiting for a raspy voice on the phone that called itself Smoking Gun, for God's sake.

When the call finally came after midnight, she knew that the wait had been worth it.

It was an easy story to do. She didn't bother to recapitulate the details of the HBO override, nor did she engage in any analysis. Let the editorial page writers have their field day with that tomorrow.

She kept it brief: "Sources close to the President" have revealed a blackmail plot involving Stinger missiles obtained in some illegal manner. The blackmailers threaten to shoot down additional aircraft unless the President takes the following action.

Stokes iterated the Committee's four demands. Then she restated the President's position of non-negotiation with terrorists and closed with a notation that there were differences of opinion among the President's advisers and that an appropriate response to the blackmailers was still in the process of being worked out. The American people should rest assured, the "source" had said, that an accommodation would be reached without further loss of life.

That was enough, Stokes knew. First of all, it would scoop the hell out of the competition. And second, it would establish her as boss lady for the duration of the crisis. Her byline would ride Page One above the fold. She would be in demand for the Sunday talk shows. By the time the story played out, she'd be a risen star.

When she'd finished sending in her copy, she leaned back in her chair and stretched, lacing her fingers behind her head.

She'd pondered the question of Smoking Gun's identity before, of course. He—assuming it *was* a he and not a vocally talented female—had to be fairly close to the President. That meant Cabinet-level or a member of the immediate White House staff.

For a while she'd been convinced it was Seamus

Croaghan, the NSC staffer, but she'd gotten to know him a little, through incidental contacts, and he had such a sense of integrity that she couldn't believe he was a snitch.

Then she thought it might be Diane McBain herself. But that was unlikely. Diane McBain was an ambitious, wily lady who wouldn't want to risk the consequences exposure as a leak would bring.

Currently, she was flipping a coin between Attorney General Walker and Secretary of State Carini. Walker had the gruff, don't-give-a-damn personality for it, and the President highly valued his ability to get things done. Don Walker was a real possibility.

Enzo Carini might be an even better one. The Secretary was a radical ideologue who was known to be frequently at odds with his more moderate colleagues. It'd be natural for someone like that to try to use the press to further his own interests.

The informant's identity was an interesting question, but more interesting still was that the President of the United States was being blackmailed. That was a delicate matter, one which had necessitated a conference call with the *Post*'s top brass before she had begun to write her story. The balance between legitimate national security concerns and the public's right to know had had to be carefully weighed. The decision to go ahead and publish had won out but, she believed, it had probably been a close call.

So what was Smoking Gun doing leaking a story as sensitive as this?

He'd told her, off the record, that despite the blackmailers' list of conditions he believed it was not the Sandinistas who were behind the plot. However, he was personally interested in seeing the Sandinistas come to the bargaining table with more good faith than they'd shown for the Arias Accords and subsequent attempts to end the strife in their country. If the details of the demands were made public, he felt the Nicaraguan government would be unable to resist the pressure from both the United States and the court of world opinion to act in a conciliatory manner.

It made sense, but the problem was, the truth could

just as easily be the opposite. Smoking Gun could be hoping for a public clamor that led to direct American intervention in the Nicaraguan civil war.

To hell with speculation, Carla thought as she headed for bed. She wanted to be at least somewhat fresh for the fantastic reception she was going to get at the office in the morning.

PART III

CROAGHAN

And the light of a candle shall shine no more at all in thee; and the voice of the bridegroom and of the bride shall be heard no more at all in thee: for thy merchants were the great men of the earth; for by thy sorceries were all nations deceived.

—Revelation 18:23

16

The fourteen-year-old boy sat cross-legged, glaring at the mat. Sweat ran freely down his body beneath the stained white *gi*.

"What is it, Steven?" the old man asked him. "What is causing you to lose your focus?"

"I hate this, *sensei*," the boy said. "I don't want to do this anymore."

"Your father wishes that you continue," the old man said.

The boy looked up at his teacher, his face a wooden mask hiding childish fury. "And why must I do as my father wishes?" he asked.

There was a pause, during which the master waited for his pupil's anger to wane. It did not. "You are young," the old man said finally. "You cannot yet recognize your father's wisdom. What you are learning will serve you well in life. The skills are only a means to an end. Someday, yes, you may have to call on them in battle, but the highest achievement will be never to have to use them."

The boy stared straight into his *sensei*'s eyes. "I *will* use them," he said coldly. "I will use them to kill my father. He murdered my mother and I will kill him."

The old man recoiled from the boy, the horror clearly visible in his eyes. . . .

Kirk came awake with a jolt. He was sweating and gasping for breath. The dream had closely followed real-life events, although he had never spoken his wish to kill his father out loud.

He looked around. A strange bed, some sort of machine next to it. There was a tube hissing oxygen into his nose. He was in the hospital.

Then he remembered what had happened. The explosion, the smoke, passing out on the concrete floor. But it was over now. His breath came a little raw, his head was stuffy, and he had a dull ache in his right shoulder, but he was okay. There was no reason for him to be in a hospital.

He was alone in the room. Good. He removed the oxygen tube and tested out his breathing. He could still taste the acrid, chemical flavor of the smoke. It had been a vicious trap, with more in those bales than just hay. His lungs were working abnormally hard, but they were functioning. He could survive without the oxygen supplement.

Next he carefully detached the IV needle from his arm and turned off the drip. If he needed a shot of glucose, he could eat an ice cream cone.

He sat straight up, slipped from under the sheet, and slung his legs over the side of the bed. Nothing happened. He didn't get dizzy, didn't begin to retch. So he dropped to the floor.

It was a little odd to be on his feet. And the floor felt a bit strange, like a more uneven surface than it really was. Which meant his sense of equilibrium was slightly screwed up. No problem; he could adjust for that.

He slipped into his shoes and tottered over to the closet, where someone had been kind enough to hang his clothes. They stank of smoke, which made him momentarily nauseated, but he put them on anyway.

Then he walked out of the room and out of the hospital, just like that. He had an instinct for getting out of strange places without attracting attention, and he used it. Smith could settle his account later. That's what a control was for.

When he hit the street, Kirk discovered that he was on Pennsylvania Avenue. He'd been taken to Columbia Hospital.

He dug into his pocket and smiled. Smith had left a handful of bills in there, anticipating that his field man might have a need for some ready cash when he woke up. Whatever else he might be, Smith was a professional. After a moment's thought, Kirk walked down to the Foggy Bottom Metro stop, took the yellow line three stops east, and changed to the red.

An hour after leaving Columbia Hospital, he was in his father's study, having showered and put on some clean clothes he'd once considered fashionable. They still fit him passably. He'd related to his father the events that led up to his hospitalization, beginning with the late-night phone call from Smith. He left out nothing that he could remember.

In return, Charles filled him in on all that had happened while he'd been asleep.

First, the morning *Post* had broken the story of the blackmail plot. The public now knew that the terrorists had the means to make further attacks upon civilian aircraft. And they knew what price was being asked to prevent that.

Then the President had delivered a hastily prepared speech over the national networks. He was obviously stunned by the *Post* story and railed against the treacherous unknown person who had leaked it, as well as the newspaper for having thoughtlessly published it. He strongly suggested that if more innocent people were to die, the *Post* was looking at a major lawsuit and the leak artist was facing a long jail sentence.

He went on to say that a number of options were being considered to deal with the terrorist threat. In the meantime, increased security had been ordered around all major airports, and the FBI had launched a massive effort to locate the perpetrators. The country wasn't going to be big enough to hide in.

Furthermore, negotiations were under way with the government of Nicaragua, with the hope that there would be early successes on the diplomatic front.

Beyond that, he asked the American people for their patience. He knew that they wouldn't want him to publicly tip his hand as to the full extent of what he was doing. Let them rest assured that every effort was being made to resolve this crisis immediately.

After the speech, Charles had gone to the Hay-Adams house for an emergency meeting of the Foreign Intelligence Advisory Board, and the President had dispatched National Security Adviser McBain herself to brief the PFIAB.

McBain, Charles said, had reported that the governments of Nicaragua, Cuba, and the Soviet Union had all contacted the President in the wake of the previous evening's broadcast and the *Post* story. All three had vehemently denied any complicity in the blackmail plot. And the Cubans and Soviets had warned they'd take a dim view of any U.S. military moves against the Sandinistas.

The President, as he'd truthfully said on television, was considering his options. Members of Congress were making noises appropriate to their particular political philosophies.

By early afternoon, CBS had conducted a quickie poll of a small, "representative" cross-section of the voting populace. It reported that a plurality, nearly half of those questioned, favored retaliatory military action in Nicaragua.

That was where matters stood at the moment. There were two things, Charles believed, that were still not public knowledge. One was the original source of the Stinger missiles. The other was Steven's mission of the previous night. The explosion in the warehouse in northeast D.C. had made the morning news, but no cause had been assigned to it and there was no indication it had been involved in any way with an effort to recover the missiles.

"Good," Steven said. "That'd be all we need, for the people to find out that someone lured us to the booby-trapped missile crates and killed a couple of agency men."

"It might tend to inflame the public," Charles said.

"What does the PFIAB think?"

"We're sleeping on it. We'll meet again tomorrow morning to work up our recommendations for the President. One of the things that didn't make the paper was that the blackmailer intends to call back in forty-eight hours and expects some progress to have been made. So we want to have our two cents in by then."

"And what do *you* think?"

Charles leaned back in his chair. "It's a tough call," he said. "You know I favored toppling the Sandinistas years ago. If we have to go in now, the price will be terrible, but the President has to be prepared for the possibility. At the least, we need to make a *show* of force down there. We can't sit back and let a backwater like Nicaragua undercut us like this."

"You're convinced it's the Sandinistas?" Steven asked.

"Yes. Or some other, more radical faction, it doesn't matter. They may be preserving their deniability, but they know about it. It's imperative that we recover the rest of those missiles, and soon."

"Otherwise . . ."

Charles shrugged. "Otherwise," he said, "we could be looking at a very ugly land war in Central America. The Cubans will almost certainly aid the only allies they have left. And if the Russians decide to come in, then it could escalate faster than anyone could control. Even if they don't intervene directly they could punch our buttons elsewhere, and the confrontation could spread to every hot spot in the world in no time. One hates to use the domino analogy, but . . ."

"Spare me," Steven said. "All right, I'm a believer. Let's talk about getting the Stingers back. Can you still tap into WALNUT?" WALNUT was the agency's complex data-retrieval system.

Charles nodded.

"I want your access codes."

The younger Kirk watched his father carefully. This was a delicate moment. Charles was bound by law and loyalty not to release his access codes to anyone. Nevertheless, Steven wanted them badly. He could have asked Smith to assign him some personal codes of his own, of course, but he would not have known what he was getting. Smith could give him something that provided only limited access, or that contained encoded diversions away from sensitive compartmented information, or that activated any one of a number of gimmicks detrimental to his purpose.

What Steven needed was the kind of blanket access his father had. He had to be able to get a reliable answer to any question he asked. And he wanted to test how far his father was willing to go to cooperate with him.

"They could hang me for that," Charles said coldly.

"It's an extraordinary situation," Steven said. "Besides, you know I'll protect them. Afterward you can deactivate and lock me out forever. It's pretty low-risk."

There was a long pause. The old, old feeling came over Steven, that the decision here, as always, depended solely on its positive or negative relation to some ever-distant goal, not on the accident of paternity.

"All right," Charles said finally.

And that was that.

Steven pulled his chair around behind the desk and sat down at the terminal. With Charles's help he carefully threaded his way into WALNUT.

Primarily he wanted to see how the codes worked. But once into the database, there was no reason not to put it to immediate use. He called for a list of Sandinista operatives known to work out of Washington. Their locations, descriptions, habits, weaknesses, etc. That was as good a place to start as any.

The list was fairly short. Steven made a hard copy that he'd commit to memory, then destroy.

He needed nothing else from WALNUT—at least nothing that he was willing to have his father looking over his shoulder for—so he exited the system. He was about to leave the house when he thought of something else.

"Oh yeah," he said to Charles, "one other thing. That ugly redhead who showed up at the op last night. Do you know who he is?"

"Sounds like it could only be Seamus Croaghan," Charles said. "He's on the National Security Council. A top assistant to Diane McBain."

"She's the National Security Adviser?"

"Right, the dragon lady. Protector of the President's lair, you know. Plus I think she wants to move up in the Administration, and I doubt that she cares how she does it."

"What about this Croaghan? What was he doing out there last night?"

"Well," Charles said, "he's the NSC's Central America expert. That might be the link. But I wouldn't be surprised if there was a personal favor involved somewhere. His brother was on that Aer Lingus jet."

"Hmmmm . . . What's your take on him otherwise?"

"I don't know. Ugly as he is, he had to have been tough to get where he's gotten. Supposed to have a brain too, I've been told. Why the interest?"

Steven shrugged. "Good to know who else is in the field," he said. "Besides, he carried me away from that warehouse. I might want to thank him for that someday." He got up. "I'll be in touch."

Kirk left and took the Metro back to the house on Duddington Place. When he got there, he found the items that he'd requested waiting in his living room. There was also a set of keys to a three-year-old beige Eagle that was parked out on the street. A good choice, he thought. Unobtrusive, but a fair amount of power and, especially, that four-wheel-drive if he needed it.

Next he called a special number and left a prearranged coded message. Half an hour later Smith got back to him.

"Secure line?" Kirk asked.

"Yes," Smith said. "How are you doing?"

"A few aftereffects, but nothing serious. I left without paying my bill."

"That's fine. It'll be taken care of."

"Do we know what happened?"

"The enemy obviously knew we'd come looking for the transponders. Just a little reminder of how serious he's playing the game. What else is there to know?"

"Who owned the warehouse?"

Smith named one of the country's largest corporations. "They bought it five years ago," he continued, "and hadn't gotten around to renovating it yet. I don't think they're the people we're after."

"What about B&B Distributors?" Kirk asked.

"We're checking, but I doubt it's going to lead anywhere. I believe the hijackers knew the warehouse was abandoned and they just used it, don't you?"

"Yeah, probably. But let me know what you find out anyway. Are Frank and Bud . . . ?"

"They're in the rubble someplace. The fire spread a bit after the explosion. An hour ago it was just coming under control. Did you hear about the blackmailers' terms?"

"Uh-huh. I bet the President's pissed."

"Yes, there would appear to be a rather substantial leak, no pun intended."

Smith just made a joke, Kirk thought. Sonofabitch.

"You want to tell me what the redhead was doing there?" Kirk tried, hoping to catch Smith before the good humor faded.

"No."

Kirk sighed. The man protected need-to-know better than God.

"All right," Kirk said. "Any speculation on who the leak is?"

"Steven, look," Smith said, "the internal problems of the Administration are not relevant to—"

"The hell they aren't! It's my ass out here, Smith. If there's a chance somebody is going to try to sabotage my efforts, I'd like to have an idea which direction to watch."

"I'm sure the President is trying to plug the leak," Smith said coolly. "If there's any personal threat to you, I will take care of it or let you know about it. You may trust that."

Sure, Kirk thought. "How about Tellez? Have you located him?"

"Not yet. But we're reasonably certain he's in the city. It shouldn't be long."

"Okay, I need one other thing. The Central American solidarity groups, here and in the suburbs. When they meet, who the upcoming speakers are, whether they're Communist megaphones, all that kind of stuff. Have someone dig it out and get it to me ASAP. I'll stay close until I hear."

"No problem. Anything else?"

"Don't worry," Kirk said. "I'll call you."

An hour later Smith's men delivered the information.

Kirk was in luck. There was a Nicaraguan solidarity rally scheduled for eight that night at a church on 16th Street. There would be Sandinista representatives present and, though none of the names matched his list, it could be an excellent point of infiltration.

He lay down, to give his battered body some rest while he devised a plan of attack.

17

Seamus Croaghan sat behind the desk in his small West
Wing office, trying to decide what to do next.

He'd attended a meeting of the abbreviated version of
the Central American Interagency Task Force. Just himself, Smith, Derek Trane, the man from State, and Colonel Webber of Army Intelligence. They'd agreed on basic
strategy for stonewalling the source of the Stingers and
other elements of damage control. When Croaghan had
tried out the notion that there might be a foreign agent
highly placed within the Administration, he'd gotten the
same response he had from his boss: a respectful hearing
for his idea, but that had been it. His suggestion that the
CAT initiate a top-secret probe, aimed at rooting out the
traitor, had been unanimously voted down.

Now, sitting in front of his computer terminal, he was
troubled. He'd had reservations when he'd first been
drawn into the CAT, but basically had believed in the
necessity of maintaining a covert presence in Central
America.

With regard specifically to Nicaragua, he believed it
was in the best interest of the U.S., as well as that
country's neighbors, to keep the pressure on, until the
Sandinistas became persuaded that democratization was
the way to go.

Over the time he'd been working with the CAT, though,
he'd learned an important truth: there was a certain
protection to be had in accountability. The more covert
the operation, the more likely that those involved in it
would act out of their own self-interest.

Smith, for example. Croaghan was convinced that he
never did *anything* for other than personal reasons. And
Trane. His involvement with the CAT had undoubtedly
been to help him get closer to Diane McBain, with whom

he wanted both a sexual and political alliance. And Webber was a very ambitious military man, with those silver stars in his eyes.

He suddenly thought of his brother, and realized that he wasn't much different from his fellow CAT members. The thing was not just political for him either, it was very personal.

He stared at the blank face of the CRT.

Ah, what the hell, he thought. He didn't need Diane McBain's permission to investigate a serious potential breach of national security. Nor did he need her cooperation. He could go it alone. All he required was his desktop PC.

When it came to computers, hardly any of his coworkers understood what he could actually do.

They would have been surprised, for example, to find out that in the late seventies and early eighties he had belonged to the elite "Inner Circle," a loose confederation of the most daring and ingenious computer hackers in the country. These youths—ranging in age from mid-twenties down to early teens—grew up at the dawn of the new age of personal computing. They were irresistibly drawn to the field, as the finest minds of prior generations had been mesmerized by the intricacies of atomic physics or the challenge of manned space flight.

Compared to that of an astronaut or particle physicist, however, a hacker's path to understanding was shorter and a whole lot cheaper. Hackers could and did master their subject in the privacy of their own bedrooms. The only physical requirements were a terminal and a modem. After that, you were on your own. An entire world of electronic intelligence was open to you if you had the brains, the inclination, and the persistence to figure out how to get at it.

Seamus Croaghan had blazed a lot of trails in those early hacker days, but had decided after college that there were more interesting things to do with his life. So he'd taken his language fluency, his background in politics and history, and his fascination with gadgets, and he'd entered what used to be called public service before it was so routinely used for private gain. Over the years he'd also kept in casual touch with his childhood friend

Diane McBain. When her star had unexpectedly begun to ascend, he'd hitched a ride.

It was odd how things worked out. Here he was, sitting in an office in the West Wing of the White House, a respected Presidential adviser, and he felt like he was twenty years old again. What he was about to do was cash in what he'd learned during his "Inner Circle" days.

There were so many questions. About the hijacking itself, the blackmail scheme, the deadly leak within the Administration. And somewhere, within the vast, linked, information retrieval systems of the U.S. intelligence network, were answers.

True, they might not be precise ones. But lacking that, there would be footprints pointing in the proper direction. No one in the electronic age could possibly cover his tracks completely. The very complexity of the system worked against it; there were too many nooks and crannies where the odd bit of incriminating information could get stuck.

A seasoned tracker, with enough time and energy, could follow the trail back to its source.

He logged on to his personal computer and set to work. The first step would be a comprehensive review of his own files, memos, PROF notes, etc. There might well be something in there that had escaped notice initially, but would now jump out at him. If not, then he could think about exploring the larger databases and, finally, surreptitiously penetrating other people's files.

He activated a program that would search for occurrences of a key word.

Then he punched in the word: Sunflower.

The search began.

18

Kirk's internal alarm went off at six o'clock, and he woke from his nap feeling a good deal better. He walked to a small restaurant two blocks from the safe house, fought his way through the happy hour crowd, and picked up a couple of sandwiches to go.

He carried his dinner to the beige Eagle Smith had left for him. Before going anywhere he searched the car thoroughly, inside and out, looking for a directional transmitter. He didn't find one. So he started the Eagle up and, while he munched on the sandwiches, checked out his new wheels. Around the side streets, down Pennsylvania Avenue, then back along the Southeast Expressway to see how the car handled at speed. It was adequate.

He left the Expressway at Twelfth Street and drove back into the heart of the city, parking illegally in front of the Farmers and Merchants Bank on Fourteenth. He'd requested that Smith set him up at a bank that had late hours of operation and Smith had obliged. Farmers and Merchants was open until eight every night of the week except Sunday.

Kirk went inside and asked to see the status of his account. When the figures came up on the teller's CRT, he was pleased. The agency wasn't skimping. Just to make sure it was real money, he tried to close the account. No problem. It was real.

He took the entire amount away with him in the form of a cashier's check. He walked around the corner to the offices of Capitol City Trust, which was also open late. There he converted most of the money into short-term CD's, which he stored in a safe-deposit box that he rented. He kept a little cash and put the balance into an account with a different identification number.

After completing these transactions, he went back out

to the Eagle. No ticket. He drove west two blocks, then went straight north on stately, tree-lined 16th Street, and arrived at his destination with twenty minutes to spare.

The Good Fellowship Unitarian Church—on a street overloaded with imposing religious structures—didn't look like a church. It was a stately old white-frame building set back from the road, with extensive flower gardens at the front. There were no stained glass windows, not even a cross nailed to the roof. But there was a large, illuminated glass case near the sidewalk, with its inside done up to resemble an open book, presumably the Bible. The book's white pages had lines into which black plastic letters could be slotted, to spell out the subject of Sunday's sermon or, in this case, a particular special event.

TONIGHT, the book announced to passersby, AT 8 P.M. AMERICANS IN SOLIDARITY WITH THE PEOPLE OF NICARAGUA. GUEST SPEAKERS. SLIDES. REFRESHMENTS. THE PUBLIC IS INVITED. COME AND BEAR WITNESS!

Kirk shook his head sadly. They were undoubtedly decent, concerned people. But they were dabbling in matters of which they had so little understanding. Witness? How could you bear witness to something you hadn't been within a thousand miles of? How could a bunch of outsiders, no matter their good intentions, ever hope to understand the centuries-long oppression that drove the people of Central America to do what they did?

Hell, he thought, the maintenance costs alone on that building could feed a dozen *campesino* families. Was anyone going to bear witness to that?

He walked the block immediately surrounding the church to familiarize himself with the neighborhood. It was an instinctive precaution. He found himself in a quiet, upper-middle-class section of the city. The homes were large but not ostentatious, their modest grounds well tended, with expensive cars parked in their driveways. A few people were parking on the street and heading back toward the church, but otherwise no pedestrians. The particulate-ridden air was cool and damp, and the sidewalks had a slick, grayish patina to them that held the impression of each passing foot for a moment.

Kirk made his circuit and returned to a point directly behind the church and a block over. Here an alley ran between two brick houses and terminated in a small graveled parking area at the rear of the church. He walked down the alley. There were no streetlights; the only illumination came from a naked bulb over the church door.

From the parking area he walked around the side of the church, across a yard dominated by a pair of venerable oaks, down a curving garden path layered with bark mulch, and back through the arriving crowd to Sixteenth Street.

Satisfied, he retrieved the Eagle, drove it to the mouth of the alley, and parked there. Then he returned to the church via the main sidewalks. He took his time without being obtrusive about it, and by the time he'd reached the entrance he'd seen enough to disturb him.

The crowd attending, and presumably sympathetic to, the rally was a mixed bag. A good number were graying middle-aged folk, veterans of protest, many of them sporting peace buttons that they'd probably had since the Sixties. And there was a fair number of the younger set—the ones who'd actually have to fight the war in Central America if there was one—in their raggedy blue jeans and Vietnam-era Army jackets with their fathers' names stenciled over the pockets in fading black ink.

He had expected as much. What bothered him was another distinct group of people. They were exclusively male, wore dark, anonymous clothing, and were scattered here and there on the side streets, slouched down in their cars for the time being.

One logical explanation was that the slouchers were there to disrupt the rally. Given the inflammatory nature of the day's news stories, this was no great surprise. In fact, if the solidarity people had been on the ball, they would have anticipated a disturbance and postponed the gathering until tempers had cooled. But they hadn't.

That left Kirk with a dilemma. His original plan had been to maintain as low a profile as possible. He intended to try to identify someone who seemed like a strong potential point of entry into the local Nicaraguan community. Then, after the evening's activities, he could tail the chosen person and, if necessary, use his powers of persuasion on him or her.

Though the plan might appear to be nothing more than

a shot in the dark, it was the sort of thing that, with a little luck, could quickly yield some highly useful information. There was always somebody at these rallies who knew something, somebody who was monitoring them for the other side, somebody with Sandinista or Cuban or even Soviet contacts. Kirk was confident that he still had the know-how to single out that person.

Now, however, he had to consider the consequences of a disruption and answer one simple question: should he warn the event's organizers that there was trouble on the way?

It was a tough nut. All of his training urged him to hang on to that low profile at any cost. He had a goal that took precedence over considerations of the moment. But he was not the man that he had once been.

He decided, as he walked up the church steps, to alter his plan.

Just inside the door were a couple of people handing out leaflets. Kirk approached one of them, a plump young woman with a face like Sally Field and a permanent toothy smile. She handed Kirk several sheets of paper. He folded and slid them into his back pocket without looking at them.

"Excuse me ma'am," he said. "Who's in charge of organizing this?"

"Oh, we don't have that kind of structure," she said. "We all work together here." She nodded, her smile still glued in place.

"Okay. Who will be introducing the speakers, then?"

"That would be Mr. Elkins. This is his church. I mean, it's really the people's church, but he—"

"And where would I find him?" Kirk cut in.

The young woman pointed through the inner door. "He's the tall man in the gray turtleneck," she said. "Do enjoy the program, and thank you for your support."

Kirk went through the inner door and down the long aisle to the front of the church, where the man in the turtleneck was talking to a middle-aged couple. Elkins was a tall and lanky man with gray hair curling over the top of his collar and steel-rimmed bifocals perched on his nose. He was holding forth on the counterproductive trade consequences of the U.S.'s misguided Central American policy.

When there was a break in the conversation, Kirk said, "Reverend Elkins?"

The man turned to him and said, "Oh, just Mr. Elkins, please." As he shook Kirk's hand, his smile was as broad and continuous as that of the Sally Field look-alike at the door. "Or just Bob would be even better. We're all equals here."

"Scott Craik," Kirk said. His use of his former alias was unplanned, but the name came out easily. "I think it's great what you're doing here tonight. Very positive. I'd like to help if I can."

"Pleased to meet you, Scott," Elkins said smoothly. "Yes, we're doing the best that we can to counter the negativity of our elected misrepresentatives. How would you like to help?"

"I've just returned from Nicaragua," Kirk said.

"Oh, how wonderful. Where were you?"

"Esteli," Kirk tried, crossing his fingers.

"Marvelous. For how long?"

"Nine months."

"Doing what?"

"The scientific and technical exchange program. I was helping them build a new road. I'm a civil engineer. And you're right, it *was* marvelous. Esteli has such a proud revolutionary tradition, and the people's hearts are as wide as the mountains."

Elkins was beaming. "Wonderful, wonderful."

"Anyway," Kirk said, "I'd be happy to share some of my experiences with the people here tonight. It's just one person's story, but I think it might help."

"Why, certainly. We'd be honored to have you. You must have some very informative things to say if you were down there that long. Let's see, how about if we put you second? Our featured speaker is a marvelous young Nicaraguan unionist. We want her to go last, but you could talk just before."

"That'd be fine." Kirk paused. "The only other thing is, uh Bob, you don't expect there's going to be any trouble, do you?"

Elkins laughed. "Trouble?" he said. "We're here to try to prevent trouble, not cause it. We may be informal, but this is still the house of God, Scott."

"What I was thinking was, what with all this terrible

stuff in the news, I'm sure there are people out there who don't feel especially well disposed toward Nicaragua right now. Don't you think it might be a good idea to have someone keep an eye out for troublemakers? Maybe have them near a phone, just in case."

Elkins looked out over the crowd. "No, I don't see any troublemakers here," he said. He put his hand on Kirk's shoulder. "Don't let paranoia take you over, my friend," he continued paternally. "It's merely another false path, due entirely to the troubled times in which we find ourselves. And don't worry, if any bad apples do show up, why, we'll just win them over." He winked, then looked at his watch. "It's about time to get this show on the road. Come on, I'll introduce you to our other speakers."

Kirk followed the clergyman to the dais. Things hadn't gone quite as well as he'd hoped, but he was satisfied. He'd gotten himself into a position where he'd have an unobstructed view not only of the audience, but of whoever entered the hall. Under the circumstances—considering that his pitch had been completely improv—it was about the best he could have done.

Now he just had to be careful to stick to his hastily conceived cover story. He had enough background knowledge of Esteli to be able to fake that unless someone quizzed him closely on current conditions there, and even then he could probably generalize enough to get away with it. He shouldn't trip himself up on his name; he'd used it for years. And he could still call up his civil engineering training if anybody wanted to know how you built a road.

His fellow speakers were already seated in their folding metal chairs on the dais. Elkins introduced the pair who were due to go first, a young married couple who had been to Nicaragua for two weeks as part of the Witness for Peace program. The couple seemed to be afflicted with the same smile disease as the two organizers Kirk had met. They wore tiny gold crosses in their lapels and buttons for LORD JESUS and JUSTICE IN CENTRAL AMERICA on their matching polyester sport shirts. They oohed and aahed politely when told of the extent of Kirk's Nicaraguan experience.

Kirk dismissed them as inconsequential to the task at hand and forgot their names immediately. The evening's final guest, however, was another matter entirely. She was introduced as Piedad Andino, a native Nicaraguan.

Kirk found himself looking down at a woman in her early thirties, dressed in khaki shirt and trousers, with heavy boots. She was short, but had broad shoulders and an athletic build, with small breasts and powerful-looking legs. She had brown eyes and thick black hair cut short around a dark, flat-nosed, predominantly Indian face that would hold a kind of timeless beauty for those who liked the type.

Something about the woman—a vaguely similar body type, something in the eyes—reminded Kirk for a fleeting instant of his late wife, Susanna. Then the feeling was gone.

"We are most honored to have Ms. Andino with us tonight," Elkins was saying. "She is truly an extraordinary person."

Andino showed neither pride nor embarrassment at Elkins's description of her. She continued to look at Kirk, coolly but intently, as if she were trying to read his mind and expected to find something of interest there.

"This courageous woman was a hero of the struggle against Somoza," Elkins went on. "She fought in the front lines. After the people's triumph, she helped found ANDEN—that's the Nicarguan Teachers Union—and was one of the guiding forces behind AMNLAE. That's—"

"The National Women's Organization," Kirk said. "I know. I had the pleasure of meeting some of its members."

"Of course. Excuse me, Scott. Our Mr. Craik was in Esteli under a technical exchange program," Elkins said to Andino.

"It's nice to meet you," she said. She had a deep, husky voice that seemed to rise up from the vicinity of her belly. "Did you know Ivonne Lacayo or Reyna Mayra Laguna?"

Kirk shook his head. Always better to deny than to risk admitting acquaintance with someone who didn't exist. "No," he said. "Who are they?"

"Members of AMNLAE," she said. "In Esteli."

"I'm sorry, no. But I didn't get to meet everyone. I was in the field most of the time."

She nodded, but kept her gaze on him, her expression

neutral, and he was by no means certain that he'd passed the test. He decided that if no better prospect showed up, this was the person to follow after the meeting.

"Well, I'm sure you two can catch up on mutual friends later," Elkins said. "I think it's high time we got this thing in gear. I'll just say a few words, and then turn it over to all of you."

Kirk took an empty seat that put the young Jesus couple between him and Piedad Andino. It might have been Elkins's chair, but Kirk didn't care. He knew that if he sat next to the Nicaraguan woman he'd be overly conscious of her presence, and that would interfere with his surveillance of the hall.

Elkins stuck to his promise and kept the opening remarks brief. Then he introduced Mr. and Mrs. Fiedler, the Witness for Peace people, to the general audience. The young witnesses were obviously flattered at the applause they received.

They were also obviously unaccustomed to public speaking. But they gave it a game try. They hemmed and hawed their way through a twenty-minute description of how they had become involved in the program, the places they had visited and the political lessons they had learned.

Then they set up a screen at the back of the dais and a projector at its front, and launched into their slide show. As photographers they weren't much better than they were as speakers, but the audience was with them. There were boos when a slide showed the aftermath of a Contra mortar attack on a small village. There were cheers for a picture of a member of the local militia, a boy about sixteen years old, proudly holding a bolt-action rifle that was nearly five times his age.

There was a hush as a picture came up of a small child, his leg wrapped with a bloody bandage. In the child's face you could see his determination not to show his pain.

The intruders slipped into the hall when it had been semi-darkened for the slide show. There were nine or ten of them. They seemed to have entered unnoticed, since everyone's attention was directed forward at the screen.

Or nearly everyone's.

Kirk had been certain they were coming and never

turned his back on the front doors. He glanced over at Piedad Andino. She hadn't either.

One of the women who had been handing out pamphlets tried to show the newcomers to some empty seats, but she was pushed roughly to the floor. Before most people were aware of what was happening, three members of the group marched down the center aisle between the row of seats. The others were split between the left and right aisles.

The woman who had been shoved got up and ran after them, shouting, "Hey, you can't just barge in here like this!" She grabbed the shirt back of one of the men, and he turned and cuffed her on the side of the head. She dropped like she'd hit a wall.

The men reached the area between the audience and the dais. They fanned out so that a couple had their eye on the speakers, the rest on the crowd. In the dim light Kirk could make out short clubs in some of their hands. They all wore leather gloves. Assume that the gloves are weighted, he thought. They were amateurs, low-end hired muscle. But they might not be entirely untalented. He relaxed and took some deep breaths. In a few moments he had emptied his mind of all extraneous considerations.

Elkins jumped down and confronted the center group and its apparent leader, a short, blocky man. The minister waved his arms as if giving a particularly fiery sermon.

"What do you think you're doing?" he shouted. "This is a church!"

"Show's over, pops," the blocky man said.

"All you Commie lovers go home!" one of his friends shouted.

"Will you gentlemen please remember where you are?" Elkins said. "This is a peaceful gathering."

The blocky man snickered. "You want peace," he said. "Then you got to talk to the bastards in the only language they understand. Like this."

He launched a quick punch to Elkins's mid-section, doubling him over, and followed with a short uppercut. The reverend stumbled backward and fell, ending up half on and half over the carpeted edge of the dais. He lay like that for a moment, then dropped to his hands and knees, and wobbled groggily around like a dog who'd just lost the scent.

Pandemonium erupted in the hall. Some people screamed and tried to claw their way to the door. Others just screamed. Still others waded into the fray. Fists and clubs began to fly.

One of the intruders vaulted up onto the stage, yelling, "You like those murdering bastards so much, why don't you go live with them?"

He grabbed the Witness for Peace couple and was about to slam their heads together when Kirk came at him from the side, delivering a perfectly placed kick to his outer left thigh, six inches above the knee.

The blow was an effective but not permanently disabling one. It traumatized the nerve clusters in the area, tore the lateral vastus muscle, and dislocated the man's hip joint. The man fell to the dais, howling with pain and clutching his useless leg.

His cries were lost in the general din, but one of his companions saw what had happened and began to cautiously work his way to Kirk's rear. No one had yet thought to turn on the lights and for a fleeting moment the photograph of the boy with the bloody leg bandage was starkly displayed on the man's chest. Then he slid back into the gloom, holding a nightstick loosely in his right hand, close to his body.

A blond teenage girl in blue jeans and a paisley shirt that had been torn down the front staggered toward the dais with a stunned expression on her face. Blood streamed from an open scalp wound and dripped onto her bare chest. She turned one way, then another, her hands held out in front of her.

Kirk had his arms around the shoulders of the witness couple and was herding them to the side when the man with the nightstick charged him from behind. He could read what was happening in the sudden horror of the young woman's face. It was as good as having eyes in the back of his head.

He released the couple and turned on the ball of his foot just as the man swung the club at his head. Kirk stepped into the path of attack, catching the crook of the man's elbow on his right forearm, and turned again. The blow meant for Kirk's head ended harmlessly in midair, and the man crashed to a halt against Kirk's back. Kirk immediately grabbed the club with his left hand and with his right elbow delivered a quick, hard backward strike to the man's sternum.

It was his best available maneuver at that moment, but it was a tricky blow to control. If too much force were used, the sternum could shatter, driving bone fragments into the chest cavity and causing internal bleeding and death. Just because this man was a thug wasn't sufficient reason to kill him. So Kirk drew the punch a little.

The man teetered for a moment as shock messages from his heart, lungs, and pulmonary artery made their way to his brain. Then he collapsed.

On the other side of the stage, two men were circling Piedad Andino, steadily closing on her. With her obviously Central American features, she was a particular target, and the men were smiling as they moved in. One of them had a club. The other had a long, skinny knife held at waist level, palm up.

When the two got within striking radius, she seized the offensive. She whirled completely around, drawing her right leg in, then lashed out with the sole of her foot, the full power of her thigh muscles behind the blow. She caught the one with the club just below the knee.

The man's left tibia snapped like a brittle stick. His mouth formed a small, surprised O before he stumbled and began to moan.

She had immediately shifted her attention away from him and returned to a balanced fighting stance. She faced the man with the knife. He hesitated, eyeing her warily, but kept edging toward her. From time to time he flicked the knife in a sudden, sweeping motion. Each time she would pull back just enough that he'd miss her by an inch or two.

"Murderer!" he said. "Bitch! Come on!"

Frustrated, he beckoned with his knife hand. That was a mistake. The gesture froze his hand in place for a moment and that was all Andino needed.

She scissor-kicked, getting excellent elevation and driving her toe into the man's wrist. The kick didn't do any great physical damage, but the knife went flying into the air and turned end over end in a great, lazy arc before falling back to the floor.

The man turned this way and that like a catcher looking for a foul pop fly, but in the semi-dark there was no

clue as to where the knife had gone. Not that it would
have done him any good in any case. Andino was far
quicker than he was.

She stepped forward, inside his reach, and hammered
him with a sword hand strike to the side of his neck. Like
Kirk, she knew the potential of the punch and delivered
it with less than maximum force. Even so, the trauma to
the carotid artery knocked the man unconscious at her
feet.

In the meantime Kirk had taken out the short, blocky
man who seemed to be the leader of the group. Kirk had
simply jumped down, sledgehammering the man with the
bottom of his fist. He aimed the punch at the fontanel
area of the top of the man's head and hit reasonably
close to it. The blocky man sat down hard, then toppled
over onto his side and lay still.

Half of the intruders were now out of commission, and
the rest of them were starting to realize that something
was going terribly wrong. They began to try to push their
way to the exits. But now the crowd was after *their*
blood, and it had become increasingly bold with the
improvement of the odds. A full-scale brawl was under
way.

In his peripheral vision Kirk had seen what Andino
had done to the men who tried to take her. So, after
disposing of the blocky man, he caught her eye and
motioned with his hand toward the rear of the church,
where a door stood open. She hesitated for a moment,
looked at the confusion all around her, then nodded.

He pushed himself back up onto the stage and had
taken a couple of steps before a gunshot rang out. Everybody froze.

Kirk glanced to his left. Elkins was standing at the far
end of the dais, looking shaky but steadying himself with
one hand on the raised platform. In his other hand was a
pistol that he'd dug up from God knew where. He was
waving the gun, though keeping it pointed in the general
direction of the ceiling.

"Stop it!" the lanky minister shouted. Slowly he lowered the gun to about waist level.

Both Kirk and Andino were out of his direct line of
sight, so they began to move as unobtrusively as possible
toward the open door at the far end of the hall. In a few

moments they had slipped out unnoticed. They crossed a small, dusty storage room, went through another door, and found themselves outside in the parking area at the rear of the church.

"I've got a car," Kirk said, and he led her down the alley to where he'd parked the Eagle.

19

As Kirk pulled away from the curb, the first police sirens could be heard in the distance.

"I assumed that you didn't want to talk to the cops," Kirk said to his passenger.

"And I would assume that you don't either," Andino said.

He grinned. "You speak English very well," he said. "Where did you learn?"

"In Managua. Do you think we don't have competent teachers there?"

"On the contrary," he said, switching to Spanish. "If you are any example, I'd say you were very competent. What is it that you teach, tae kwan do?"

It was her turn to smile. "You were peeking," she said, sticking to English.

"Couldn't help it," he said, returning to his native tongue. "You sort of stood out in the crowd. Those two thugs couldn't have been handled any better."

"The ability to fight is an important survival skill. Everyone in the people's militia must practice it, for the good of oneself and the country." She paused, then said, "And where did you learn your Spanish, Mr. . . . Craik? The accent is not Nicaraguan. And it certainly isn't Mexican. El Salvador, perhaps?"

"Or somewhere," he said. "So . . . what do we do now?"

"I was watching you as well. I think we talk."

"Fine. Let's see . . ."

He had been aiming the Eagle downtown, so he kept heading in that direction. In a few minutes he had parked, and the two of them settled themselves on a bench in Lafayette Square, directly opposite the White House. The square was about as safe a place as one could be after dark in the city. Because of its proximity to the White House, one group or another was always demonstrating, camping out, holding a candlelight vigil or whatever. And because of the square's high media visibility those groups were tolerated, an official nod to the principles of freedom of speech and assembly.

But that didn't mean they weren't being watched; the President's mansion was, after all, right across the street. At any given moment, the area could be under the eye of the D.C. police, the FBI, the Secret Service, or any combination of the three. Not to mention the odd intelligence outfit that might have an interest in what was going on there.

Kirk chose a spot in the northwest quadrant, near the Von Steuben statue, away from the busier Pennsylvania Avenue side where tonight some noisy shows of anti-Nicaraguan sentiment were underway. This also put them outside the zone most likely to be covered by any surreptitious audio surveillance.

When they were seated, Andino said, "One thing. I believe it would not be wise to engage in the use of force, yes?"

"Yeah, you've got a point there," Kirk said. "Bound to be unhealthy for one of us."

There was a pause while the two of them studied each other. She would be a tough nut to crack, he thought, if it ever did come to that.

"Good," she said finally. "Now, I do not think you have recently been in Esteli, Mr. Craik."

"Well, begging your pardon, I don't think you're really a schoolteacher, ma'am."

"In my country, it is necessary to wear many hats, as you say. Preserving the integrity of the Revolution demands it. I am not your enemy. *We* are not."

"If you say so. Then which hat are you wearing today?"

"Why don't we just be frank with each other, Mr. Craik? Wouldn't that be easier?"

"Sure. You go first," he said with a smile.

"Will you then be honest with me?"

"If you are."

"Don't patronize me, please. You are a professional and so am I. We both recognize this. And I believe that in this instance we are both working toward the same end."

"Which is what?"

"The recovery of the missiles, of course."

That took him by surprise. He wasn't sure what he'd been expecting, but it wouldn't have been a forthright discussion of the missing Stingers. He paused.

In the distance, a swelling chant could be heard. *"Block-ade! Blockade!"* the crowd was shouting.

He decided to be cautious. "I don't understand," he said.

"I asked you not to insult me," she said impatiently. "You are a professional and you show up at a Nicaraguan solidarity meeting with some ridiculous cover story about building roads in Esteli. You can only be trying to track down the missiles. Who are you with, the FBI or the CIA?"

"I work for myself."

Andino sighed. "All right, you are a highly trained, concerned private citizen. Fine. Let's assume you have 'accidentally' made some contacts in the trade. How's that?"

He shrugged. "What if I have?"

"Then perhaps we can cooperate. Unofficially, of course, due to the hostility that exists between our governments. But with the understanding that we would eventually link up with official channels."

"I don't know," he said. "This is very strange. You seem to be so sure of why I was at that meeting tonight. Why were you there?"

"I am a spokesperson for the Revolution, here to help correct the mistaken impressions your people have about what's happening in Nicaragua. My appearance at the church was planned a month ago, as a part of my current tour. Believe me, I hardly expected to become involved in anything like the current . . . situation. In fact, I almost decided to cancel out tonight, but then I had the same idea that you apparently did. There was always the chance that someone from the *other* side might show up. That is what you were thinking, isn't it?"

"Maybe."

"And what did you plan to do then, kidnap me, torture me? Well, you don't have to. Here I am."

He looked into her defiant black eyes. "This is pretty confusing," he said.

"Why?"

"You hijack our missiles, blackmail the President, and now you're telling me that you'll work with me to get them back. It doesn't make any sense."

"Oh for God's sake, Craik, you don't seriously believe that *we* have your missiles, do you?"

"What am I supposed to believe? The money is to be paid to your government. The other conditions are exactly what I would expect from you."

"Look," she said intensely, "we don't kill innocent people. We're a civilized government, not a gang of terrorists. And even if you don't trust that, you should realize that we're not *insane*. We might be able to give you a pretty good fight for a while, but in the end we're no match for you. How can you possibly think that we'd risk your taking military action against us?"

"It depends. You might if you'd prearranged with your . . . allies to back you."

"Don't be ridiculous. You of all people should know the folly of trying to fight a war on the other side of the world."

"You have allies closer to home."

"Sure. The Cubans are just waiting to hand you an excuse to take them on as well." She shook her head sadly. "You really don't give us much credit, do you?"

"All right," he said, "let's pretend for the sake of argument that you don't have the missiles. Then who does?"

"I don't know who does. If I did, we wouldn't be having this conversation. I would have gone and gotten them and given them back to you."

"And to continue our hypothetical argument, why is all this happening?"

"That's a good question. I think there are two possibilities. One, somebody's just after the money, and they tricked out the rest of it to shift the blame. Or two, someone's deliberately trying to provoke the United States into invading my country."

"Or both?"

"Or both."

"Could be," he said. "But isn't there a third possibility too? How about some splinter group, either within your government or on the fringes of it? They might think they could actually pull it off."

Andino spat out her reply. "If there is such a group, they are traitors."

The chant drifting over from the other side of Lafayette Square was now: *"Bomb them! Bomb them!"*

Kirk didn't know what to make of the woman's story. He didn't dare accept what she was saying at face value, yet he had to admit the logic of it. He tried to figure what her motivation would be if she were lying. Nothing came to him. Unless . . . Unless she wasn't a Sandinista at all.

Fortunately, he ought to be able to verify her credentials.

"What are you proposing?" he asked.

"That we work together," she said. "We are both already in the field, though you may not choose to admit it. Okay, I have certain resources; you have the support of your people, I assume. All we need now is to recognize our common interest. Which is to get you back your missiles, yes, but most important to prevent any foolish military action from taking place."

He thought about it. It would be a mutually mistrustful alliance at best, if "alliance" was even the proper word at all. "Do you have a plan?"

"We are investigating at home and in Honduras," she said. "In the hope that we may turn something up at that end. And I'm using my local resources to look at this end."

"What resources?"

"No insults, Craik. Remember?"

"It's not an insult. I can't cooperate with anyone who's actively engaged in domestic spying. You know that."

She paused, then said, "The best I can offer you is that none of our efforts are directed against American citizens. Is that good enough?"

"You think it's an exile group?" he said.

"Let us say the thought has occurred."

The thought had occurred to him, too, but the more he'd considered it, the less he'd liked it. Sure, the Contras would be motivated to try to provoke the U.S. into invading Nicaragua. Plenty motivated. And no question that they'd be ruthless enough to go about it in this way. What they lacked was the means. This had been a smooth and sophisticated operation, well planned and well executed. The level of expertise—and U.S. government penetration—involved made him doubt they could have pulled it off. Unless they . . . had help.

"If any Americans are involved," he said, "then it's my problem. Immediately."

"Of course."

"And just answer me one other question. You must realize that I could have you deported for what you've said. Why are you taking a chance on me like this?"

She shrugged. "I saw how you defended the people in the church," she said. "You acted without hesitation. It was a very professional response, but it was also instinctively directed against terrorism. It means that whatever our political differences, we are on the same side."

She gave him a searching look that made him uncomfortable.

"All right," he said after a pause. "I guess I could use all the help I can get. How do you want to work it?"

"It's too volatile a situation for dead drops," she said. "We need to be able to get in touch faster than that. And maybe more frequently as well."

After a consideration of pros and cons, they agreed to exchange phone numbers. They assured each other that their respective phones were secure.

She got up. "You aren't going to insult me by trying to follow me, are you, Craik?"

Kirk shook his head and, without another word, she headed north, toward H Street.

He didn't try to follow her; at this point there was no reason to. He waited for a few minutes, then retrieved his car and drove back to the safe house on Duddington Place. He wasn't so trusting that he didn't check to see that *he* wasn't being followed. But there was no tail.

Once in the house, he immediately made two calls.

The first was to Smith. Kirk requested that any calls made to the phone in the safe house be routed through a dead link, so that any attempt made to correlate phone number with address would fail.

Smith told him not to worry, that that had already been done, as a basic precaution. The number of record was part of a switchboard at one of the agency's dummy corporations, and the forwarding itself was controlled by agency computers. Kirk's phone was as secure as it could be made.

"Why the concern?" Smith said.

"I'm beginning to move," Kirk said. "And I wanted to be certain."

"Anything to report?"

"I was at a church on Sixteenth Street tonight, where they were having a pro-Nicaragua rally. I thought I might be able to infiltrate, but some antis showed up and there was a riot. Did you hear about it yet?"

"No."

"You will. Some people are going to need hospitalization. And I didn't want to have to deal with the cops. I was using the name Craik to work my way in with the sponsors. You might want to get in touch with the cops on the quiet and let them know not to look too hard for Craik."

"Jesus, Steven. This is your idea of a low profile?"

"I couldn't help it, Smitty. And I didn't hurt anyone except in self-defense."

Smith sighed. "All right," he said, "I'll take care of it. Did you at least get something useful?"

"I don't know," Kirk said. "I want to look into this group a little more closely. I'll let you know."

Kirk's second call was to his father. He gave Charles the phone number Andino had offered him and said that he wanted an address to go with it ASAP. He told his father that absolutely no one else had a need-to-know on his request. Charles promised to try to have an answer by the following afternoon.

Then Kirk sat down at his computer terminal, engaged the modem, and did a remote dial-up.

It had been a long time since he'd been on his own inside WALNUT, but he found that the accessing procedures came back to him rather quickly. His father's account number and password, as he'd expected, carried a high level of clearance. There were restrictions: he wouldn't be permitted to manipulate files, alter data, or compile programs. As far as simple retrieval went, though, he doubted that anything he really wanted would be denied him.

Slowly, methodically, he made his way through the system.

He wasn't that familiar with the Central American section—Charles had wanted above all for his son to carry on in C.A., and so of course a much younger Steven had taken a job in Africa—but the different regional files were set up in basically the same manner. And they could be searched using a flag word or combination of words, or any number of more complicated methods.

After some trial and error, he was able to key his request specifically to *Nicaragua*, subset *government field officers*, subset *active in the United States*. Then he entered *Piedad Andino* as the flag words and asked for *all occurrences of*. The system would automatically check the name both as a primary and an alias. He pressed *Return* and waited.

It took about ten seconds. The agency's software was among the most sophisticated in the world and its mainframe computer was among the most powerful.

The lines scrolled down on the screen:

Andino, Piedad
Age: 32
Height: 5-1 Weight: 110
Hair: Black Eyes: Black
Background: Active in the military effort against Somoza regime, beginning as a teenager. Numerous commendations for bravery. Post-revolution in-country training as teacher—history and politics. Fluent in English. One of founders of ANDEN teachers' union and AMNLAE women's organization. Formal military training, including small arms, communications, and unarmed combat. Strong opponent of elected UNO government and active in HS replacement by FSLN.
Current position: Believed to be highly placed Sandinista official. Member of Security and Defense Council. Frequent visitor to U.S. because of language proficiency. Lectures to "solidarity" organizations as a "teacher." This is perceived as possible cover for clandestine activities, though none have yet been clearly identified.

Weaknesses: Potentially susceptible to offerings of
    money.
Risk category: A
Prospect for recruitment: Unknown
Recommended course of action: Though subject is
    classified in Risk Category A, it is not recom-
    mended that she be excluded from U.S. except
    in wartime. Should be considered as having
    positive potential for interrogation prior to ex-
    pulsion, should such become prudent.

Kirk read the Andino dossier and then reread it. Now
he didn't know what to believe. She appeared to be
exactly what she said she was.

20

March 18

At two in the morning, Seamus Croaghan was still sitting
in front of his computer terminal.

Over the course of the evening, he'd been sifting through
data on Sunflower, both the legit and black sides of the
operation. He'd collated and cross-indexed the data, arranged it chronologically, and stored it on his hard disk
in a file that was password-protected. Having become
paranoid about what he was doing, he'd even taken his
security precautions one step further. He'd written in a
logic bomb, a tricky piece of programming that would
automatically destroy the file if someone gained access to
it without following a complex procedure that he kept
only in his head.

Some of what he'd learned was intriguing, but the
frustrating thing was, there was nothing that truly surprised him. And it had to be somewhere, he knew it did.
There was something very, very wrong within Sunflower.

An operation didn't go as haywire as that one had without leaving some indication of what had happened.

Where were the tracks?

In the back of his mind he had been pondering that question all night long. He'd thought about the CAT, and about each of its members, the person's political leaning, affiliations within the Administration, possible private motivations.

The answer might lie with any one of them. Nevertheless, when crunch time came, the place to look for the author of a snafu was invariably the agency.

That meant Smith.

It'd be just like the man from Operations, Croaghan thought, to get something screwed up worse than the Democratic Party, and then come on helpful as you please while he was busily passing the buck behind everyone's back.

There were two basic questions to settle. What, if anything, did Smith know about Sunflower that Croaghan, and possibly other CAT members, didn't know? And, did the secret knowledge interface with the hijacking and/or blackmail plot?

The answers might be found buried in WALNUT somewhere, but Croaghan doubted it. Smith, he reasoned, was a careful man and could be expected to give his operations maximum protection. He would use WALNUT only up to a point.

Still, he would not be able to accurately monitor *any* operation without some kind of record-keeping. And so the first procedural question was: where would he maintain his most secret files?

Well, Croaghan figured, there would be a lot of intrinsic security problems with on-site agency storage. So assume that he maintained the files at some remote location, perhaps an apartment to which only he had the key. That would make more sense than Smith's Watergate residence, which was public knowledge and legendarily spartan.

How to discover that remote location, that was the problem.

Croaghan tried to approach it like the whiz-kid hacker he'd once been. Since Smith would need to be able to

178 • Doug Hornig

access his private system from the Watergate or from his agency offices, it would have dial-up capability and therefore it was vulnerable. But its number would be heavily guarded, known only to—

Of course. Smith would know his own number. That was it, the way in.

Croaghan could call Smith's Watergate computer, just as Smith could call the one in Croaghan's office. They needed to be able to send each other electronic mail, and other little goodies.

He looked at his watch. Two-thirty in the morning.

The risk was that dialing Smith's Watergate computer would alert him that it was being accessed *if* Smith happened to be watching or using it at that time.

Croaghan decided that it was a chance worth taking. For one thing, the man had to sleep sometime. For another, even if Smith realized the computer had come on, he'd have no reason to suspect it wasn't for some legitimate purpose. After all, a serious crisis was playing itself out, and electronic mail might come anytime.

Croaghan dialed in.

After a half ring, Smith's modem connected him. Now came the hard part. Persons accessing Smith's computer were naturally authorized only to do simple things, like leave messages. They couldn't fool around with his personal files, couldn't even see what those files were called.

Unless they knew the password.

Guessing someone's password was the first and foremost hacker challenge.

The computer prompted Croaghan. *Function?* it asked. At this point it couldn't differentiate between a random user and Smith himself.

Instead of the more usual *Mail*, Croaghan typed *Logon*.

Username? came up next. *Smith*, Croaghan replied.

The computer accepted it. So far, so good. Smith, like most computer users, employed his own name as one possible point of entry.

Then came the prompt for *Password*.

This was where Croaghan had to summon all his hacking expertise. Standard passwords were between one and eight characters long. They could contain numbers, letters and symbols in any order desired. If you wanted your password to be *mftbslk3*, that was fine with the computer, and anyone trying to crack it would get old and gray in the process, even with a random-string generator to help.

Such a meaningless collection of characters was, however, awfully difficult to remember. It would probably have to be written down somewhere, which entailed the risk of its being lost (meaning Smith lost access to his files forever if he couldn't recall it) or being seen and stolen by someone else who wanted it.

So most people devised passwords they could easily recall. The laziest used a single letter. Those a little more security-minded used their name, or their birth date, or their dog's name, or such impersonal staples as *love*, *sex*, *money* and, yes, *password*. A hacker would try all of these and any others that could be arrived at by the process of deduction. Often enough the hacker eventually succeeded, or there never would have been such a thing as hacking.

Croaghan was one word away from entering Smith's system. Now he had to figure out what that word was.

He typed the letter *a*. Smith's computer responded: *Access denied. Password?*

In this way, Croaghan quickly went through the alphabet and the numbers zero through nine. No luck. He hadn't really expected Smith to make it so easy, but it was worth a shot.

He graduated to words and tried all the commonly used ones. He thought *power* might be a particularly good guess. But in each case he still came up empty.

Stymied, he used the glowing screen as a point of focus and attempted to drop into a relaxed state where the obvious word would suddenly suggest itself. Nothing came.

Then he tried every agency buzzword he could think of. No go.

What next? He thought about Smith, tried to remember everything he knew about the man, and realized that he knew damn little.

Smith played the saxophone, so Croaghan tried *sax*.
Access denied.

What kind of music did Smith play? *Jazz.* That wasn't
the word, though. So how about a jazz musician, a sax
player? Croaghan made a list of every sax virtuoso he
could think of whose name was eight letters or less, or
who had a well-known nickname like *Bird*. One after
another he tried them.

And he hit it.

When he typed *Desmond*, the system logged him on.
He felt the old hacker's rush that always came when he
outsmarted the guy at the other end. He'd done it. The
hardest part, hopefully, was over.

After a couple of prompts he was looking at a listing of
the files stored on the Watergate computer. Now, if his
assumptions were correct, the key to further explorations
was here somewhere.

What he had reasoned was that Smith, being an efficient sort, would have some form of easy access to his
primary database, wherever it might be located.

This was a common need among people who worked at
home and made frequent dial-up use of a remote unit.
And several software companies had stepped forward to
meet that need. A number of time-saving programs had
been written that would automatically activate the modem, do your dial-up, and perform logon procedures for
you. All you had to do was customize them to your
particular systems. After that you merely commanded
your home computer to *run* such-and-such, and you were
quickly connected to the remote system.

Croaghan was betting that he'd find such a program
filed away here, one that would allow Smith to talk to his
private computer with minimum hassles.

The file in which the program was stored could, of
course, be called anything. Croaghan studied the list.
A number of files, things like *Calendar*, could be
quickly eliminated. Others were more enigmatic, especially three at the end of the list named simply *x-1*,
x-2, and *x-3*.

He decided to look at *x-1* first and asked the machine
to display the file for him. Sure enough, it was a BASIC
program. He went through it, becoming more excited as

he did so. There was the modem activator, a phone number, logon instructions. It was just the sort of routine he was looking for.

He directed Smith's computer to run *x-1*.

A few moments later he was inside WALNUT. This wasn't it. He immediately logged off the agency super-computer.

Next he took a look at *x-2*. It turned out to be another automatic dial-up program. So he ran it.

He waited, and then he was looking at a screen that displayed only two things, the word SMITH and a request for the password. This was it, Croaghan was sure of it. Once again he tried the word *Desmond*.

And was admitted to the system.

Now all that remained was to verify that this was indeed the system he was looking for.

First there was a menu, asking him what he wanted to do. He requested a file listing. There was another menu, giving him some more specific choices. He asked to see the names of files created during the previous month. When the list scrolled down, he knew he was in the right place.

It was time to get out. He logged off of SMITH, which returned control to the Watergate apartment. Then he had that computer send him a copy of *x-2*. Finally he broke the modem connection. Now the Watergate unit would shut down and he no longer risked being accidentally discovered using it.

And he had a personal copy of the software that would allow him into SMITH whenever he wanted, without having to go through Watergate first.

There was only one other consideration. Did SMITH only allow one user on at a time? Croaghan had no way of knowing, but he suspected that it did. Smith would likely have set it up that way, in the belief that only he would ever have access to it.

That being the case, Croaghan had to be very careful. If Smith dialed up his system and found that it was in use, then he'd know that his security had been breached. He'd immediately change the password and perhaps take even more drastic steps to ensure that the unauthorized user would be denied future entry.

Croaghan knew that he had to make his raids on SMITH when it was least likely that the system's owner would also be trying to use it. He looked at his watch again.

Quarter to four.

He had no idea what time Smith went to bed and got up, though he suspected that the agency man slept little. Still, this hour of the morning ought to be among the safest of times. He was dog-tired himself, the words on the screen were beginning to blur a little, but . . .

Croaghan sighed. He got up, did stretching exercises for a few minutes, and made himself a strong cup of coffee.

Then he sat back down at the terminal and ran *x-2*.

He began to pick his way through SMITH.

21

When Diane McBain entered Croaghan's office at nine-thirty, she found her top deputy slumped over his desk, his head resting on his forearm. For one horror-stricken moment she thought that he might have shot himself. The atmosphere in the White House was that tense. But there was no blood, no gun, and she then saw the steady rise and fall of the man's massive shoulders.

He was asleep, rumpled brown corduroy suit and all.

She went over and gently shook him. Croaghan came awake with a start, spinning in his swivel chair, his meaty hand clamping down on her wrist. He yanked on her arm, pulling her toward him, and was raising his other hand when she shouted at him.

"Seamus!"

The sound froze him. He blinked, stared at her uncomprehendingly for a moment, and then recognition finally came into his face.

"Seamus!" McBain repeated. "You're hurting me."

He let go of her wrist at once. She stood above him, rubbing it.

"What were you, dreaming or something?" she said.

He continued to blink the sleep out of his eyes. He massaged his cheeks, pulled on his lower lip, stared blankly into the middle distance. His mind was turned inward, chasing some thought that had been at the edge of consciousness when he'd awakened but was now retreating so fast he couldn't gain ground on it.

Finally he said, "Yeah, I guess so." He smiled. "I have these dreams where I'm the last honest person left in the government. I always wake up as the bad guys are closing in on me."

"What are you doing here, anyway?" she asked. "Didn't you go home last night?"

"I guess I didn't. I was going through all the old Sunflower records to see if there was some clue to what happened to the Stingers. Didn't find much." He looked over at the featureless computer screen. "At some point I must have taken a break from the terminal and laid my head down and . . ." He shrugged. "What time is it?"

"Twenty-five to ten. We just had a strategy breakfast in the Cabinet Room."

"Any new developments?"

"Yes."

Hearing the concern in her voice, he looked up and saw it in her face as well. He motioned her over to the small conference table he maintained in his office and started the coffee maker.

"Coffee in a minute," he said, folding his hands on the tabletop. "What's up?"

"The President talked to the General Secretary on the MosCom first thing this morning," she said. "The Russians are denouncing the whole thing as part of a regressive American plot to invade Nicaragua."

His face turned a brighter-than-normal shade of red. "By killing our own *people*?" he said. "That's *insane!*"

"Of course it is. But if they can conceive of doing it themselves, they're not going to put it past us." She took a deep breath. "They're saying that their so-called ally has been framed by the present Administration's expansionist foreign policy, and that they're going to back the Sandinistas to the max."

"Holy shit."

"We don't know *what* they mean, but some ships *are*

headed east from Cam Ranh Bay and there's movement in their sub fleet. We're tracking the whole thing as best we can."

He abruptly shoved his chair backward, got up, and walked over to the coffeemaker. He returned with two cups of coffee, unsweetened for himself, one sugar for her.

"It's not the naval presence that worries us, of course," she continued. "The Soviets don't have the firepower to confront us that way, and they know it. But if they get the Cubans to transfer over a wing of fighter/bombers, then we're in real trouble."

"What about the agreement?" Croaghan asked.

The agreement he was referring to was an unwritten one that reached all the way back to the Reagan Administration. The U.S. was allowed to meddle in Nicaragua as long as the American military didn't become directly involved. In return, the Russians promised not to supply any MiG fighters, no matter how much the Sandinistas pleaded for them.

The agreement might, however, have been rendered obsolete by the hectic rush of world events, especially the new Soviet/Nicaraguan treaty. After the army-backed ouster of the elected UNO government, the FSLN had sought to buttress its shaky power base by concluding a formal pact with the Soviet Union, committing its ally to the defense of the Revolution if it was threatened by outside powers. The new General Secretary had gone along in what was widely viewed as a desperate attempt to hang on to some shred of international prestige after the hammering the Soviets had taken on the home front. How far Moscow was prepared to go to back the accord, no one knew.

"Well, we hope we still have one," she said. "But the General Secretary said they'd take whatever steps were necessary to honor their obligations, and he stressed that they hadn't ruled out *any* options. If they feel that Nicaragua needs a real invasion defense, *and* they're determined to provide it, then the only way to go is land-based planes."

"I can bet what Monty Banks wants to do," Croaghan said.

She nodded. "He says the Joint Chiefs are in agreement," she said. "They believe the Soviets are running a bluff, but the arms buildup in Nicaragua is real. They want to invade before the country is turned into a fortress and the casualty risk becomes too high. At the least, the military wants to make some preemptive strikes on the Nica airfields to make sure the MiGs couldn't be landed. The possibility of American pilots facing Cubans or Russians in the air has everybody freaked."

"The Soviets are shipping in more ground weapons, too?"

"We assume so."

He scratched the back of his head. "Jesus, where does Defense stand on this?"

"Schule believes we can negotiate our way out of the mess. But I think he's afraid, Seamus. I've never seen him like this. I think he's convinced that once we start shooting it's going to escalate faster than we can control, and we're going to end up in the middle of a very real war."

"Nuclear?"

McBain nodded slowly. "Yes," she said. "We like to believe that those days are behind us, but the possibility's still there."

"And Mr. Carini is siding with the Chairman?" he said.

She nodded again. "Odd, isn't it? We have a Secretary of State who wants to fight and a Secretary of Defense who wants to negotiate."

"Sounds like the battle lines are drawn," he said wearily. "Well, my opinion is that we better start moving some bodies into position. Whatever else happens, we can't let the Russians back us down just because they growl a little."

"I agree. And so does the President. He ordered five thousand troops into Honduras this morning, and put them on full alert. The Hondurans are being very cooperative. Basically, they're scared shitless.

"He also ordered a carrier task force from the Seventh Fleet, the *Independence*'s, to stand off the Nicaraguan Pacific coast. That'll give us a very heavy presence in the area."

"With that much juice, we could blockade them if we absolutely had to. How did the President and the General Secretary leave things?"

"I'd say our relations are in danger of going back into the freezer," she said with regret. "But the President didn't really have any choice. We've got to be firm in our own backyard."

"Yeah." He thought for a moment. "You considering any economic moves?" he asked.

"The President ordered Carini to sound out our allies on a complete embargo. That'll give Enzo something real to do and, hopefully, it'll help him keep himself under control. Anyone who loses it at this point is going to be a real danger.

"Domestically, it's the crapper. People are canceling their airline reservations all over the place. Everyone's afraid to fly. The carriers are in a panic. If business stays off this badly for long, a lot of them could go under."

"Jesus, the President's really screwed there. He can do a lot of things, but he can't force people to travel."

"Right. And then there's the damn leak. If we don't find out who it is pretty soon, I'm afraid the paranoia's going to start eating us up."

Croaghan felt overwhelmed. During every Adminstration in the past twenty years, a crisis that had started out small kept growing, until it threatened to become the one event by which the entire term of office wound up being judged: Nixon and Watergate; Carter and the hostages, Reagan and Iran/Contra. Only this time the President was headed for a direct military confrontation with the Soviet Union.

"We've got to find the missiles, Seamus," McBain said.

22

It was a moment that Kirk was continually forced to relive:

"There's no need for you to identify the . . . bodies," the homicide detective had said. "You . . . wouldn't be able to, anyway."

Still, Kirk demanded that the man take him down to the refrigeration room, where the corpses, name tags tied to their big toes, were filed away in heavy steel drawers. Except that these, of course, were different. The attendant pulled out the drawers and there were no big toes. Just a couple of pathetic-looking plastic bags.

"Open them," Kirk told the attendant.

The man looked to the detective for guidance.

"Mr. Kirk," the detective said, "you don't—"

And Kirk said again, "Open them."

The policeman shrugged and walked back out into the corridor. He'd been a detective for ten years, and he knew that it was going to take at least three cigarettes to numb his sense of smell as much as he wanted. There was no need to torture his eyes, too.

Inside the refrigerator room, Kirk discovered what remained of human bodies after an explosion of C-4 plastique, followed by a gasoline fire. The detective had been right. No visual identification would have been possible. His wife could be identified from her teeth. His son . . . His son didn't even *have* teeth yet.

At the time he had been unable to forge the emotional link that connected those charred remains with the living, laughing creatures they had once been. What was in the plastic bags was one thing. The fact that Susanna and Scottie were gone forever was another.

Between the two there was only a dark hole into which Kirk had willingly fallen, and at the bottom of which he had stayed until the night Smith walked back into his life.

Now, the scene in the refrigeration room stood once again still and clear in his memory, and he felt what he might have felt then had he been able to.

It was rage. Not the hot-blooded rage of present anger, but the cold, controlled rage that grows from a savage wound that has never healed. A rage that would be pitiless when its moment came.

He walked to the window, parted the curtain slightly, and looked out on Duddington Place. The street was empty between the rows of parked cars. There was only a single pedestrian, a white-haired woman walking a poky white-haired dog. As he watched the old woman, he slowly cleared his mind's eye of the vision of those once-human husks.

He had called Smith in order to get a brief update on the situation. Smith also told him that he wouldn't have to worry about the D.C. police looking for him, but that he should be very careful about staying out of further trouble. The agency had only so much influence.

He had also tried the number Piedad Andino had given him. All he had gotten was a recording that read the number back to him and instructed him to leave a message after the beep if he wanted to. He didn't.

Charles had checked in, too. He had an address to go with the phone number Kirk had given him. Kirk thanked his father and asked if he might be able to dig up the owner of record for that address. Charles said that he'd try.

Then Kirk had called a cab and had it drive him by the place. He didn't want to risk either himself or the Eagle being seen, but wanted to know where he might possibly locate the woman if he needed her.

The building was a narrow, empty storefront in the Hispanic section off Columbia Road, with two floors of apartments stacked above it. It told him nothing except that she might well be using a forwarding machine herself. Still, he had familiarized himself with the neighborhood, just in case.

Now he let the curtain fall back across the window. He returned to his desk. He'd been hoping to hear from Andino, since she was still the best lead he had, but there'd been nothing.

He was mentally reviewing the Sandinista operatives' dossiers he'd memorized when his train of thought was interrupted by a knock on the door.

There shouldn't be unexpected knocks at the door.

He slipped a pistol out of the desk drawer and moved quickly to the side of the window. The visitor could be a lure to get him to put his head in the middle of someone's crosshairs. Without moving the curtain, he peered down through the space between it and the window.

The angle just allowed him to make out the profile of a burly man in a rumpled corduroy suit. The man knocked again, then looked nervously left and right. When he did so, Kirk saw who he was: the ugly redhead from the raid on the warehouse. What had Charles said his name was? Croaghan. From the National Security Council.

"Jesus Christ," he murmured.

He put the gun away, hurried downstairs to the door and let the man in.

"What in the *hell* are you doing here?" he said.

Even inside, Croaghan looked reflexively over his shoulder. "I-I'm not sure," he said, shrugging. "I needed someone to talk to."

"And you happened to pick *me*?"

Croaghan looked him in the eye. "No, I didn't *happen* to pick you. I did it intentionally. Can we talk?"

Kirk shook his head. "Jesus," he muttered again under his breath. "Yeah, I suppose so."

He turned and led the way into the living room, where Croaghan sat stiffly on the couch. Kirk took a chair across from him.

"Ah, take off your coat," he said. He couldn't sustain his anger. This man had saved his life, at some risk to his own.

As Croaghan removed his jacket, Kirk said, "You mind telling me how you knew where I was?"

"It's a long story," Croaghan said. "And I'd like to start at the beginning."

Kirk studied his visitor. Croaghan's nervousness had been replaced by the self-confident air of a man who wanted to get down to serious business. If one overlooked his amateurishness, Kirk thought, Croaghan possessed a quiet solidity that was rather appealing. And an intelligence behind the eyes that couldn't be concealed.

Then there was his face. Ugly, florid, with an expression that suggested perpetual irritation. That would put a lot of people off. It would also be a tool that a clever man could put to good use, the functional equivalent of Smith's deadpan.

The first thing Croaghan said was, "I know about Grenada."

Kirk just stared at him. "What?" was all he could think of to say.

"I know what happened in Grenada," Croaghan repeated. "I know what happened down on the Chesapeake and . . . since then. I know what you're doing now. And obviously I knew where to find you now. It's all in your dossier."

Kirk shook his head. "WALNUT?" he asked.

"No. Your WALNUT file is nowhere near so complete. I've been into Smith's private database."

Again Kirk could only stare. He'd assumed that Smith had secret files stashed away somewhere, but . . .

"I won't bore you with the details," Croaghan said. "Suffice it to say that I know a lot about computers. Their security systems aren't nearly as secure as people would like to believe. And that includes Smith's.

"Anyway, the point is this. Smith has quite a little dossier on you, among others. Among a *lot* of others. You're an interesting man, Kirk. Considering your past relationship with your control officer, I'm pretty surprised to find you here."

During the time Croaghan had been speaking, Kirk had shifted gears. He'd been taken by surprise, which was unprofessional but understandable in this instance. When you were taken by surprise, though, the one thing to do was recover quickly.

"I love my country," Kirk said.

Croaghan chuckled. "Fine," he said. "Your motivations are your own business. Of course. But I presume that you really are trying to get the Stingers back."

"Yes, I am. Look, Croaghan—"

"Ah. I have seen your dossiers and you, apparently, have seen mine."

Kirk thought about it, then decided he had nothing to gain from playing dumb about Charles. Smith's files would certainly contain family data. "My father knows everyone in Washington," Kirk said. "Including you."

Croaghan nodded. "Fair enough," he said.

"What I was about to say was that you know what I'm doing here. Care to return the favor?"

"To make a long story short?"

"If you want to."

"I'm here," Croaghan said, "because I no longer know whom I can trust."

"Meaning that you trust *me*?"

Croaghan paused for a long moment, then said, "Yes."

"How in God's name . . ."

"Oh, it's pretty simple, actually. I read your dossier, remember. Anyone who's as deep on Smith's shit list as you are *has* to be one of the good guys." He grinned and added, "Besides, I saved your life, you sonofabitch. You owe me."

Kirk laughed. Whatever game the NSC man was playing, he had his cover story down cold.

"I surrender," he said. "What do you want, Croaghan?"

The Irishman's demeanor became instantly serious. "How much do you know about the circumstances of the hijack?"

"Just what Smith deemed I needed to know."

"Which probably means damn little. Okay, here's a bit of background for you."

Kirk listened intently while Croaghan told him about the CAT, its makeup and its missions, and about the specific operation known as Sunflower. It was a Contra supply op, he said, with the legitimate nonlethal aid program masking the black aspect, the delivery of arms. Croaghan denied, however, any knowledge that Stingers were involved and swore that he would never have gone along with a plan to supply them.

"Then who?" Kirk asked.

"That's the disturbing part," Croaghan said. "Smith's files seem to indicate a network of people, powerful people, who run operations like this on their own. I don't know who they are, because he's got code names for all of them, and I don't know how far their reach is, because I didn't have time to fully track it. But at a guess, I'd say there are a couple of agency people—including Smith, of course—some military, and some private-sector, probably formerly of the Pentagon. And possibly someone on the White House staff, as well. A goddamned shadow government."

Kirk merely nodded.

"What's that supposed to mean?" Croaghan said.

"Of course there's a shadow government," Kirk said. "As you call it. I'm pretty surprised if you didn't know."

Croaghan looked defensive. After a pause, he said, "Okay, I've heard the rumors. But frankly, I always put them down to liberal paranoia. What do you know, Kirk? Tell me."

"It's not a very well-kept secret," Kirk said. "There's a loose coalition of agency people, current and former military brass, mercenaries, international money men, exile Cubans, and a few other splinter groups. All anti-Communists. They've been around since the early sixties. They make their money from drugs and illegal arms sales, and they use the profits to tinker with the affairs of other countries. They aid the opposition in places like Nicaragua and train the police in places like Chile." He shrugged. "They unquestionably have the ability to set up operations like the Stinger shipment."

"That pisses me off. The CAT has been their pipeline right into the White House. Which means that I've been their tool."

"Sure. It's useful for them to have people inside the Administration who can truthfully deny any knowledge of things like the cocaine-for-arms deals that kept the Contras alive in the early eighties, as Ollie North did so convincingly in his day. And just like Ollie had to play the scapegoat, you may have to, too."

"Shit." Croaghan paused, his angry expression growing even angrier, then said, "You know, Kirk, my brother was on that 747 in Boston."

"I'm sorry," Kirk said.

"And what really gets me is that this shadow government is ultimately responsible for those missiles falling into the wrong hands in the first place." He looked Kirk squarely in the eye. "That makes me partly responsible, too. I want to get the sonsofbitches who fired that Stinger, but I want to nail the other bastards just as much. I don't know, maybe more. They're Americans, for Christ's sake."

"That's a tall order," Kirk said. "These people are tough and they're smart, they sell each other out, and they won't hesitate to kill you if you become a nuisance."

"I don't care," Croaghan said defiantly.

"Uh-huh. But you need help. And that's why you're here."

"You're good. I can tell that from your files."

"Look. My job is to recover the Stingers, Croaghan. Maybe knowing where they came from will help us, maybe not. The important question is, who has them now?"

"I realize that. But we're going to be uncovering this shadow government's operations. It's inevitable. After we do get the missiles, I'm not asking you to hold my hand. You know Smith. Just show me how to put a noose around his neck, too."

"What does your boss think about what you're doing?"

"Diane? I haven't told her. I . . . I've known Diane

since I was a kid, but I couldn't swear to you that she wasn't a part of this thing. She's ambitious and . . . maybe ruthless, too. I just don't know."

Kirk closed his eyes for a moment and massaged his temples while he thought things over. On the one hand, the fewer people he was involved with, the better. On the other hand, the operation became more complex with every step he took. First Andino, now Croaghan. Neither of them could be trusted because both had some personal ax to grind, yet either could prove to be highly useful.

A further consideration was that the fox was already in the henhouse. Since the NSC man had access to Smith's files, anything Kirk told Smith was eventually going to find its way to Croaghan. Or so Kirk would have to assume. Thus it would be impossible to turn Croaghan away entirely.

"I can't be a part of your personal vendetta," Kirk said. "Like I said, my job is to find the missiles, period. If we can cooperate on that, fine, but once we locate them, I'm gone." He paused, then added, "However, I'll go this far. If I do turn up anything you can use to get what you want, I'll give it to you."

Croaghan let out a breath he hadn't realized he'd been holding. "Thanks," he said.

"One other thing. You'd better understand that if you take these people on, you're going to need some pretty powerful people on your side. Or a few mercenaries of your own."

Croaghan nodded. "Where do we begin?" he said.

"We begin by understanding something," Kirk said. "I'm out in the field, which means that I'm likely to get my ass shot at any day. Which means I don't let people know what I'm doing. Which means I don't tell you.

"On the other hand, you have to help me all you can. Anything you find out, anything you hear at the White House, anything odd that turns up in a computer file, the smallest scrap of information that seems relevant, you pass it on to me right away. I'm sorry if that sounds like a one-way street, but it's how we'll get the job done. I'll do what I can to see you're not completely in the dark.

"Now, I assume you know how to get in touch with me."

"No," Croaghan said. "The phone number wasn't in the file. That's why I came here."

"Well, don't come here again, *ever*, unless I ask you to." He gave Croaghan the phone number. "Consider all the phone lines in the White House to be unsecured. You need to call me, use a pay phone in some out-of-the-way place. I guess it goes without saying that if you choose to trust me, you can't trust anyone else."

"I understand that."

"And I'd recommend that you get a gun if you don't already have one."

Croaghan nodded.

"Okay," Kirk said. "Now, I want you to tell me everything you found out in your computer searches. Everything. Names and dates and places. Whatever you can't remember, send me by electronic mail later. I'll open a file for you called 'Red.' "

For the next hour he listened as Croaghan spilled out everything he could recollect. Kirk interrupted as little as possible and paid as much attention to the way in which the story was presented as to its content.

When Croaghan had finished, Kirk said, "I want to see Smith's files myself."

"How computer-literate are you?" Croaghan asked.

"I can use WALNUT."

"Not good enough. WALNUT's full of user aids. Smith's database doesn't have any. You have to be pretty good to get around in it."

"Can you teach me?"

"Yes, but not in five minutes."

"I've got as long as it takes."

Croaghan shook his head. "Not now," he said. "It's too risky. If Smith catches us on the system, he can rig it so I can never get in again. The safest time is when you expect him to be in bed, or if you know he isn't going to be near a modem."

"All right," Kirk said. "As soon as we can, though."

Croaghan got up. "Okay. I've got to go now."

The two men shook hands warily, and Croaghan left.

When he'd gone, Kirk tried to sort things out in his mind. The only things that had been suspicious were one, Croaghan's reluctance to let him into Smith's files, and two, the man's professed ignorance about the shadow government. But his explanation for the former had been plausible. And as for the latter, well, Croaghan wouldn't be the first person Kirk had met who simply didn't *want* to believe.

Unfortunately, the man could be entirely on the level and still be dangerous.

Kirk sighed to himself. It was a familiar situation: all parties working at cross-purposes and no one's goals completely clear. Maybe it was just Washington.

The truth, the half-truth, and nowhere near the truth.

Welcome back, Kotter. Welcome back.

PART IV

ANDINO

We have seen the best of our time: mach-
inations, hollowness, treachery and all
ruinous disorders follow us disquietly to
our graves.

—*King Lear,* I-ii

...Worst of all, they were bent on eradicating all the
...of the Revolution was simply couldn't permit that the

23

The two Guatemalan girls were eighteen and seventeen, respectively. The older was a little taller, though neither was much over five feet. Both had glossy black hair and dark mestizo faces on which was written the conflict between the heritage of Maya and the corruption of Europe.

They were identically dressed, in distressed American blue jeans, T-shirts, and thong sandals. One's T-shirt belatedly promoted BRUCE SPRINGSTEEN, THE TUNNEL OF LOVE TOUR, 1988, while on the other's were the five interlocking rings that formed an equally dated advertisement for the Winter Olympics in Calgary.

Henrik Bruderdam watched them from his bed as they stood shyly in front of him, shifting their weight from one foot to the other, trying to keep friendly smiles on their faces, obviously hoping that they weren't about to screw up in some major way. He scratched idly at his eczema-scarred arm.

The girls had never seen anything quite like this short, squat, scaly-skinned man with the sparse fringe of hair hanging down the sides of his head. They had only arrived the night before, after their first plane ride ever—in fact, their first trip away from their home village—and weren't at all sure what was supposed to happen next. But the man looked pleasant enough, and they were going to earn more money than they could have dreamed of at home. Perhaps, if they were very good girls, they wouldn't have to go back. Maybe they could stay in this wonderful place, where no guns were being fired, no soldiers were tramping past in the night.

Through the windows they could see the sun setting over Abaco Sound and a scattering of clouds along the horizon. A bold red light like blood had filled the room for a few minutes before fading to a more sedate rose that lingered on, giving their skin a pronounced coppery hue.

"You," the man said, pointing to the shorter girl, "undress your friend."

He pantomimed what he wanted done. The girls were always supposed to speak enough English for the basics, but he could never be positive of what he was getting.

The smile on the girl's face began to fade. Uncertainly she looked first at Bruderdam, then at her companion. The former made an impatient motion with his hand for her to proceed. Her friend just nodded slightly.

The younger girl grappled with the other's T-shirt, trying to pull it out of her waistband, but lost her grip. She licked her lips, then set about the job again, concentrating this time. The T-shirt slid up over the torso of the taller girl, who raised her arms obligingly so that her friend could peel it off.

Bruderdam looked on impassively.

The older girl was wearing a thin nylon bra that wasn't terribly necessary, and her friend nervously fumbled with this next. Finally the bra fell to the floor, revealing small, pear-shaped breasts with dark areolae the size of fifty-cent pieces and protuberant nipples.

Bruderdam nodded.

Her friend's belt was another tough go for the shorter girl, but eventually she got it unfastened, the underlying button unbuttoned, and the jeans unzipped. The older girl helped by nudging off her sandals and raising each foot in turn so that the jeans could be tugged from her legs.

She now wore only a pair of white cotton panties. Hesitating, the younger girl looked nervously at Bruderdam.

"Come on," he snapped. "Get on with it."

The taller girl shrugged and tried to take off her own panties, but she was stopped by a harsh word from Bruderdam, who gestured that no, her friend was to do it.

Which, reluctantly, she did. Now her friend was naked, standing in a pose that reflected uncertainty, pride, and innocent flirtation in equal measure.

Bruderdam motioned that he wanted her to turn around,

slowly. She did, her awkwardness conflicting with her desire to please.

Her body was still slender, though she was much longer through the trunk than below the waist, and there was just the suggestion of the stockiness that would come with age. Her hips had not yet fully spread and her rear end was still firm and globular, like a ripening apricot. Her legs were muscular and ended in small, delicate ankles and feet.

Bruderdam shifted his attention to the other girl. "Run your hands over her body," he said, again pantomiming the action he wanted.

The younger girl backed away from him, shaking her head.

"Miserable little witch!" he shouted. "What the bloody hell do you think you're here for?"

He jumped out of bed, dragged her over to her friend and shoved the two of them together.

"Do it!" he said.

Slowly, indecisively, the younger girl caressed her friend's body. Bruderdam stood over them, pointing out what he wanted her to do, where he wanted her to linger. The older girl stood stiffly, but her nipples hardened even more and a sheen of sweat appeared on her breasts and belly. Goose bumps formed along her arms.

When the younger girl came to her friend's pelvis, she turned instinctively away, but Bruderdam forced the older girl's legs apart and pushed the other's hand up between them, indicating how he wanted the girl rubbed, slowly, back and forth with the index finger, until the area became wet and musky and the finger slid without friction. The younger girl whimpered, but did what she'd been instructed to do.

Bruderdam reached inside his robe and took hold of himself. He was pleased to find that he was satisfyingly hard.

Next he had the two girls shuffle over to the bed and indicated that the older one was to lie on her back, her legs spread slightly apart. The girl complied. She had a minimum of pubic hair, not enough to even slightly conceal the slick cleft that had begun to part as a result of her friend's rhythmic finger music.

Bruderdam never touched the naked girl. The younger

one was now staring at him in horror, with no comprehension of what she was supposed to do. Bruderdam
dragged her roughly by the hair and pushed her down on
the bed, forcing her face between her friend's legs. The
girl squirmed and whimpered, trying to pull away, but
Bruderdam held her there.

"Kiss her," he commanded, his face close to hers. And
he demonstrated what he wanted her to do with her
tongue.

She shook her head. No. This wasn't—

He forced her in more closely until her cheeks were
pinned between the other girl's thighs. Her friend's rich
odor filled her nostrils and the tip of her nose was wet.

"Kiss her," Bruderdam repeated. He pulled back the
girl's hair and pushed her head forward so that her lips
were crushed against her friend's labia. The moment the
taste came into her mouth, she gagged.

Bruderdam pulled harder, until the girl felt that her
neck would snap. She closed her eyes and let the tip of
her tongue poke out of her mouth, just a little. She
moved it around, fighting hard against the gorge rising in
her stomach.

The man let go of her hair and stood up. She lay there,
watching him out of the corner of her eye, her slightly
extended tongue still describing its tiny circles. The man
dropped his robe. Underneath, he was hairy and naked.
He had a long penis that stuck straight out.

The girl gasped when she saw it and immediately shifted
her gaze, which left her looking right at her friend. She
tried closing her eyes, but found that she couldn't keep
them shut. The man grabbed her hair again and shoved
her forward, burying her face in her friend. It was a
suffocating, dark, wet prison.

She twisted her head and saw the man standing there,
pulling on himself until he leaned forward and erupted
over her friend's face.

The older girl reached up and tried to wipe the semen
away, but Bruderdam slapped her hand and she lay still.
Then he touched her for the first time. He brushed the
sticky fluid until it pooled over her lips. He pulled her
mouth open so that it dripped down her throat. The girl
swallowed dutifully.

Bruderdam smiled. He smeared what was left of the

semen over the girl's face, then put his robe back on and walked over to the table that stood next to his bed. He pressed a button on its underside.

In a few moments a man in a linen suit came through the bedroom door.

"Get them out of here, Thomkins," Bruderdam said. "And no food tonight. They need to learn how to be a little more . . . cooperative."

When the man and the two Guatemalan girls had gone, Bruderdam went into the oversize bath that adjoined his bedroom and took a long, cool shower. Then he shaved and powdered his body. He dressed in a floral print shirt and khaki shorts and rubber zoris. He didn't wear underwear, believing that it lessened a man's virility.

He took his time with this, and lingered over dinner as well. There was no hurry. The President could wait while Bruderdam enjoyed some of the small pleasures of his life. The invigorating afterglow of sexual release, the feeling of cool needles of water against his skin, the taste of fresh lobster tails dipped in garlic butter.

After dinner, Bruderdam carried his snifter of cognac with him to the second-floor office in the north wing of his house. The door to the office was locked, as it always was when he wasn't inside. There was a keypad to the right of it, on which Bruderdam entered a four-digit number. Changed every morning, the number was known to himself alone. Should business for some reason take him off-island, he could disconnect the mechanism entirely and an explosive charge would be needed to enter the room.

A buzzer sounded and the door opened. Bruderdam locked it behind him, as he always did when he was going to deal with particularly sensitive matters.

It took him a few minutes to engage the appropriate software, set up the voice modulator, and gather his thoughts. He'd made a few notes and these he set in front of him on his desk. He looked at his watch. Nine-thirty, Eastern Standard Time. The President should be in a sufficient stew by now.

What a ridiculous old man, Bruderdam thought, and he saw a brief fantasy image of the President stripped naked, electrodes wired to his shriveled nuts. He chuckled to himself.

Then he punched in the White House number he'd used before. The signal was relayed to Washington over local phone lines after being encoded with false point-of-origin information, so that the call would appear to have been made from a shopping mall pay phone in Scottsdale, Arizona.

As a result, a very surprised Scottsdale housewife—like the Nevada gas station operator two days earlier—was going to have a long and meaningless encounter with her local FBI agents.

The President, meanwhile, was pissed. He was accustomed to having his every wish attended to instantly. So, though his advisers were assembled once again in the Cabinet Room, the President himself chose to remain in the Residence with the First Lady. When the call came, the caller would just have to wait while the President made his way downstairs.

The duty officer summoned him just after nine-thirty.

When the President arrived in the Cabinet Room, there were respectful nods all around, but an undercurrent of discontent was running very near the surface. Looking at his colleagues' faces, the President thought that everyone probably had his or her own idea about the way things should be going. But fortunately, his was the only one that counted.

"This is the President," he said into the speakerphone.

"This is the Committee for the Furtherance of Peace in Central America," said the man at the other end.

Though the timbre of the voice was different than it had been the first time, the cadence was familiar.

Still the President said, "Identify yourself."

"Roatan," the voice said. That information had not yet been made public.

"All right," the President said.

"There appears to be a leak at your end," the voice said. "We're not happy about that. We had hoped that the negotiations could be carried out privately."

"I'm sorry." The President's jaw visibly clenched. "I've tightened security and I trust that it won't happen again."

"Good. But that would appear to be the lesser of our worries. I don't find that any progress has been made with regard to our requirements in the past forty-eight hours."

"These things take time."

"Not for the President of the United States."

"I have negotiators who are prepared to meet with you at a time and place of your choosing."

"Your negotiations are with the Nicaraguan government," the voice said. "Not me."

"We have been in serious discussion with them," the President said.

"That is not the information I have received. I would say that you are dragging your feet, Mr. President. Perhaps you do not believe that we are serious. Or perhaps you think that you can prevent any further use of the Stinger missiles. In either case, you are being very foolish, I assure you."

"We are negotiating in good faith."

"That remains to be seen. When next we talk, I'm sure it will be more clear."

"When is that?"

"I don't know. You will hear from me after you begin to transfer the money. The money will be paid to the Provident National Bank on Grand Bahama. A special account has been set up in the name of the Committee. The bank will then supervise its disbursement to the intended recipient.

"Naturally, the missiles will not be returned until well after this transaction takes place, so I would strongly advise you not to attempt to interfere with the bank's activities. Likewise, any intervention by the Bahamian government will be considered to be at your instigation and will be dealt with accordingly. Do I make myself clear?"

"Quite," the President said.

"Good. I think we understand one another pretty well, Mr. President. But I also think that you need to be reminded of the gravity of your situation. Therefore, I'm afraid that we are going to have to act again. I do hope that this is the last time that it will be necessary. Good night, Mr. President."

"Wait—"

But the connection was broken.

Bruderdam took a sip of cognac. He smiled to himself. Okay, Mosby, he thought, let's see how true your aim is this time. Then he called Thomkins and asked that the Grenadian girl be brought to his bedroom.

Silence reigned in the Cabinet Room. The President looked from face to face, but nearly all eyes were cast down at note pads or across to the draperied windows.

"What's your assessment?" he asked the DCI.

"I'm sorry, sir," the Director said. "But none of my people has been able to get anything solid. The Sandinistas said they didn't do it and then sealed up Managua tighter than a drum. All indications are that their militias are being mobilized as if an invasion were imminent."

"Give me your best guess, then," the President said.

The Director puffed on his pipe a few times while he gave it some thought, then said, "My best guess is that the Sandies aren't doing it directly, but they're manipulating the people who are. That way they can plausibly deny responsibility and still reap the benefits."

"Which are?"

The Director ticked them off on his fingers. "Money. Ridding themselves of the Contras. Raising their status in the Third World. Perhaps most important, testing our will in the region."

"Don't they believe we'll act?"

"No, I don't think they do. Our intelligence on their state of mind is pretty good, in my opinion. My analysts suggest that they study American opinion polls pretty carefully, and that they've concluded that public sentiment is so overwhelmingly opposed to a land war in Central America that you wouldn't dare risk it."

"And what do you think our course of action should be?"

"Well," the Director said, "they have to be careful. Shooting down civilian aircraft is bad for their image in most places. I don't believe they'll do it again—despite what the Committee person said—unless they're convinced that we're not legitimately negotiating."

"When did he say he was going to do it again?"

"It was more an implication," Diane McBain said quickly. "He said *act* again, which may or may not mean another missile attack."

"Come on, Diane," Secretary of State Carini said. "Of course he means another attack." He looked around. "Does anyone here really believe there isn't going to be one?"

"I didn't say there would never be another," the DCI said. "Merely that the man's current threat is probably a bluff."

The President turned his attention to the Chairman of the Joint Chiefs.

"What's our state of military preparedness?" he asked.

"Depends on what you want to do," General Banks said. He shifted his wiry frame around in his chair. "The *Independence* won't be in place for another forty-eight hours or so, but if you wanted to make a preemptive strike, we could do it using land-based aircraft. We're nowhere near being able to go in with troops, though. We need more and they would have to be better positioned.

"Still . . . if we don't let the enemy get too fortified, an occupation is feasible. We would have to air-drop into Managua in strength, take the city, and hold it. Concurrently, we'd have to open a secure supply line from the sea and probably another from Costa Rica. Once all that was in place, it shouldn't be too difficult to pacify the countryside. We anticipate massive defections to our side."

"General," Gunther Schule said quietly, "if you don't mind my saying so, that's the biggest crock of shit I ever heard."

Banks glared at the Secretary of Defense. "Yeah, I do mind," he said.

"Mr. President," Schule said, "that is a very faulty analysis of the situation. My staff people have assured me that the vast majority of the people of Nicaragua, whether or not they like what the Sandinistas are doing, would fight to the death to keep a foreign invader out. Any attempt to take Managua would mean we'd have to go in in strength, which would be a very bloody proposition by the overland routes and might well be beyond the capabilities of an air drop.

"And that doesn't even take into consideration what the Russians might do. They're quite capable of committing their fighters, just like they're threatening. Do we want to go to war with the Soviet Union?"

The rotund, nattily dressed Secretary paused, but nobody wanted to speculate about World War III. "Besides," he added, "I don't think we should even remotely consider military action before we're absolutely sure who's behind this."

"Jesus, Gunther," Enzo Carini said, grateful for the change of subject. "You heard the Director. If the Sandies aren't in the field themselves, it's their stooges."

"I'm not convinced of that just yet," Schule said.

"Then what *should* we do?" the President asked the group.

Attorney General Walker spoke. "How about warning them, sir? Saying that we'll hit any further arms shipments that come in, but that we'll hold off if they put a freeze on."

"Never work," Carini said. "They'd just say they were medical supplies and they'd keep 'em coming."

"And there's no way to trace those damn phone calls?" the President said.

Chief of Staff Read shook his head ruefully. "I had our best man brief me," he said. "It may sound ass-backward, but in the end our technology betrays us. The harder it gets to tamper with the phone system, the better you can screw things up if you know how to do it. Our caller has some highly advanced equipment. If he's using one of the communications satellites, we *might* be able to pinpoint his general area, say within two hundred miles, but that's about it."

"That's ridiculous," the President said.

Read shrugged. "Maybe so," he said, "but the phone companies have billions invested in the present system. They're about as likely to change their ways as a couple of pit bulls in a dirt circle."

"If I may," Diane McBain said, "the real ticking clock here is the Stingers. We locate them and we defuse the whole situation. We don't and pretty soon the entire country's going to be clamoring for blood."

The President grunted. "Uh-huh," he said. "Any progress?"

"I think there has been," McBain said. "We've identified the last person in the chain that led to the hijack who isn't known to be dead. It's just a matter of time before we find him. Indications are he may be hiding, in which case he probably knows something of importance. Hopefully, we'll soon know what he knows.

"In addition, although our attempt to recover the pods failed because they were booby-trapped, we're very quietly having a crack evidence team from the D.C. police go through the remains of that warehouse. There's a good chance they'll come up with something.

"And we've also set up excellent surveillance of the international departure points. If anyone with a remotely terrorist profile tries to leave the country, we're going to pull him in."

"General Banks," the President said, "how long do you think we can afford to wait?"

"I'd call a strike as soon as possible, sir," Banks said.

"You think with the firepower we're sending we could have an effective blockade?"

"Yes, sir," the general said. "A naval blockade. But we'd still have to decide what to do about the airlift."

"I realize that," the President said. He paused, then continued. "All right, I don't want *any* military action taken without my specific approval, is that clear?" Banks nodded. "And no covert actions either." The Director nodded. "It is one of the primary goals of this Administration to avoid being drawn into a war in Central America and I intend to stick by that goal.

"But it is also important to maintain our posture of non-negotiation with terrorists. I'm not going to lie to the American people the way Reagan did. We don't pay any money and we don't sign anything. Bottom line. However, it's possible we can buy some time by *appearing* to talk treaty with the Sandinistas. Enzo, I want you to get with their ambassador and make it look like we're willing."

Carini nodded, though obviously he was not pleased.

"Otherwise," the President said, "I want those damned missiles back, Miss McBain."

"Yes, sir," she said.

24

March 19

The phone awakened Kirk just after midnight.

"Andino," the voice said. "I need to talk to you."

It had taken a moment, but Kirk was now fully functioning. The urgency in the woman's voice sounded real.

"Where?" he said.

"You tell me."

Kirk thought about it. It could be a trap, but she was leaving the details of the meet up to him, which put certain limitations on what she could set up ahead of time. She knew enough to know that that was the only way he'd trust her even a little. Very professional. He named the first place he thought of.

"The west end of the pond near the Vietnam Memorial," he said. "Just off Constitution Avenue at Twentieth Street. You know the city well enough?"

"I'll find it."

"There are some benches there. Forty-five minutes?"

"Right."

Kirk dressed quickly, in basic navy blue, with a windbreaker over his heavy wool sweater. There were still three days before the first day of spring, and the weather had turned chilly.

He spent a few moments thinking about what to take from the kit Smith had provided him with, and decided that the less he took, the better. He settled on the two pieces of equipment most likely to do him good.

The flashlight was a twenty-thousand-candlepower Streamlight, identical to the one he'd carried into the booby-trapped warehouse. If necessary, it would temporarily disable a Starlite scope.

His gun was a silenced Model 459 Smith & Wesson 9-mm semiautomatic pistol, with a fourteen-round magazine and the customization package favored by Kirk—and by so many others that the weapon had become more or less the professional's standard choice.

Lighter and smaller than the over-the-counter version, it had an easier, smoother trigger pull and relocation of its center of gravity closer to the palm. There was Teflon coating throughout, making it virtually jam-free. A knurled forefinger trigger guard and magazine pinkie extension allowed for a more steady aim. The hammer spur and safety had been removed. Both the grip and the magazines were transparent plastic, for instant verification of cartridges remaining. And a special gutter sight encouraged aiming with both eyes open.

The pistol felt like a true extension of a person's hand,

and it fired like one. Kirk hefted it for a moment before slipping it into a shoulder holster under his windbreaker. He always took care when he handled it, acting as if there were a chambered round even when there wasn't; when there was one, the gun would most likely go off if he dropped it. The silencer went into his jacket pocket along with a couple of spare clips.

Then he drove to the Mall.

He arrived twenty minutes after he'd hung up the phone. He parked on Constitution Avenue and walked in, circling the Vietnam Memorial and coming at the pond from the west, the most protected approach. He stayed behind the trees along the asphalt footpath and kept a close lookout. As far as he could see, he was alone.

Fifty yards from the pond loomed a large wooden rest-room building. Kirk checked it out, found it locked all around, then huddled down next to it and surveyed the scene in front of him.

Nothing moved but a pair of ducks bobbing on the surface of the water. Kirk studied the area's prominent features: the pond, with a concrete apron and wooden benches ringing it; a few circular plastic tables with holes for umbrella poles in their centers; some slat-sided cylindrical trash receptacles; and a shuttered kiosk. Old-fashioned lamp posts lined the paths, but the overall light level was low.

His position was a good one. He held one of two points of high ground, the other being a knoll directly across from him to the north. The rest rooms protected his back, and he was in deep shadow.

Satisfied, Kirk settled in to wait. He slowed his breathing and let his mind fall into a state of no-thought, or maximum alertness. In this state he created a zone of awareness around himself. At any motion or sound within the zone, he would react instantaneously.

Piedad Andino, when she came, approached from the east. She moved quickly, but with an irregular step and a constant shifting of her attention.

Kirk wondered if she had as little idea of what to expect as he did. He slipped the pistol out of its holster and quietly screwed the silencer to the barrel. Then he tucked it behind his waistband. It was a dangerous place for a gun with no safety, but risk and accessibility were trade-offs.

Andino approached the kiosk warily, stepped into its shadow and disappeared from Kirk's sight. Five seconds later she emerged around its back side, stepping cautiously. If she was carrying a gun, it wasn't evident.

When she'd completed her circuit of the kiosk, she looked around—impatiently or nervously, Kirk couldn't tell. For a moment her eyes rested on his—though she couldn't see him—and in that moment there was something in the shape of her, the way that she stood, and the image of Susanna once again flashed to the front of Kirk's consciousness. He pushed the image away.

The woman was apparently alone, and Kirk didn't want to leave her standing there for too long. He stepped from the rest rooms into a thin grove of oaks that stood between him and the kiosk.

As he did, a slight breeze sprang up, ruffling the surface of the pond and bringing with it the smell of . . . what? The tang of oil? It was barely detectable even to someone whose senses were as acute as Kirk's, but he knew for certain that it didn't belong. He stopped.

At that moment a tiny red dot appeared on Andino's jacket, at belly level. It traveled quickly upward and stopped just over her left breast.

"Look out!" Kirk yelled.

Andino reacted instantly, throwing herself to the side, rolling off her shoulder and scrambling for the protection of the kiosk. Behind her, there was no audible gunshot, just the sound of a bench splintering as the bullet struck it. A second bullet tore a hole in one of the plastic tables and a third thudded into the kiosk three feet from where she'd plastered herself against it.

Kirk had moved quickly to his left and dropped behind the largest of the oaks in the vicinity. As he did so, he yanked the Streamlight from his belt with one hand and pulled his pistol with the other.

Personally, Kirk had never had much use for laser spots. They were useful primarily against amateurs, where the fear factor was important. Against a professional such an aiming aid would most likely only give away his adversary's position. And if he was carrying decent countermeasures, that would be disastrous.

As Kirk was securing cover for himself, he was simultaneously noting the source of the laser spot: the knoll to his north. By the second shot he had the gunman's position pinpointed. And by the time of the third he was ready to go on the offensive.

His left hand was gripping the Streamlight, thumb facing him, the hand jammed hard against his right wrist. His right arm was fully extended. It was a very stable shooting posture.

He flicked on the Streamlight. The spot on the knoll was illuminated in a blinding glare, revealing the crouching gunman. The man had just turned his attention away from Andino and was searching with his Starlite scope for whoever had shouted the warning.

When the light hit the man, he rolled backward in a hurry. Kirk squeezed off three quick shots. There was a groan from behind the knoll and then scrambling sounds heading west.

Kirk switched off the light. The man would probably be at least partially blinded for several minutes, and his scope would have fogged out, rendering the rifle essentially worthless.

Andino, seeing what had happened, reacted instantly. She raced down to the edge of the pond and hurried north, putting herself between the gunman and Constitution Avenue, cutting off escape in that direction. Good instincts, Kirk thought to himself. Then he slipped cautiously out of cover, across the asphalt and partway up the knoll, moving parallel to the gunman's direction toward the Vietnam Memorial. He and Andino had the man pinched between them, with Kirk steadily cutting down the angle.

Kirk blocked out the traffic noise from the avenue, and listened intently for the telltale sounds of the retreating man. He analyzed what he was hearing. The man was doing his best not to give himself away, but was failing. If he was reasonably competent that meant he was hurt, perhaps badly, and was trying to find himself some workable defensive position.

His quest was hopeless. The area on the other side of the knoll was an open grassy field. Still, Kirk had no way of knowing what the man had to defend himself with.

Kirk decided to get in front of the man and wait for him. He headed south through a thicket of oak and sycamore to the asphalt footpath, where he could move silently.

And almost ran head-on into a jogger.

Kirk's initial instinct was to shoot first and ask questions later. No one should have been out jogging at this hour. But in the split second during which he made up his mind, he decided that the guy was for real.

The jogger was middle-aged, with sparse curly hair and a neatly trimmed beard. He was wearing a designer sweatsuit with reflective stripes on the sleeves and pantlegs. A terry cloth sweatband was wrapped around his forehead. There was a tiny flashlight attached to a Velcro wristband.

He screamed once when the gun-wielding stranger materialized in front of him, then took off in the opposite direction as fast as he could run.

Kirk swore to himself. The guy was sure to report an attempted mugging. But how quickly? He might wait until he was safely home, or he might make a beeline for the nearest phone or flag down the first passing police car. Assume the worst. Assume that time was rapidly running out.

Kirk moved quickly down the path and into the shadow cast by the statue of the three American foot soldiers. He looked down at the Vietnam Memorial itself.

The Memorial is a long, chevron-shaped wall, fashioned from one hundred and forty slabs of polished black granite. At the chevron's vertex the wall is ten feet in height, and it tapers outward from there until it is no more than a few inches high. The names of all fifty-eight thousand American dead from the Vietnam War are cut into the wall.

A cobbled path along the wall slopes downward into the vertex, and then upward along its other edge. Tiny lights set in granite blocks provide illumination. The whole way, there are flowers and mementoes in front of or leaning against the Memorial, left there by family and friends of the deceased, or those who simply choose not to forget.

The gunman was crawling toward the monument's low

point. Perhaps he thought that with the wall at his back, he'd be as protected as he could be. He was moving slowly and with obvious effort.

Kirk flanked him by climbing to the top of the wall. He crouched and ran along the open grass until he estimated himself to be just above his target. Then he got down on his belly and slithered to the edge.

The gunman was below him and slightly to the right. About a five-foot drop.

Kirk pushed himself up and sprang over the edge. He hit the gunman hard, first with his feet to the lower back, then with knees to the ribs. Something cracked. The pistol the man had been holding skittered away over the stones. His rifle had apparently been abandoned.

The man twisted violently under Kirk's weight, but there was no real strength in him and Kirk held him pinned facedown until he quieted. Andino arrived at the east end of the Memorial and hurried down toward the two struggling men.

"We've got to get him out of here," Kirk said. "Someone saw me."

He tried to turn the man over. As he did, the man pulled a belt knife and lunged at Andino. The knife sliced through the fabric of her pants and bit into her leg as she jerked backward, and the man fell on his face. She jumped into the air and came down hard, driving the heel of her foot into the man's hand. He gave a little yelp as the medial nerves were traumatized and bones shattered.

The knife lay useless beneath his palm.

"Come on," Kirk said urgently.

He got a hand under one of the man's arms and Andino did the same with the other. Together they lifted him to his knees. And then they saw how badly he was wounded.

The front of his clothes were soaked with blood and there was a widening pool of it where he'd been lying. His head lolled forward, his chin resting on his bloody chest.

"Pigs," he muttered in Spanish.

He began to cough. Hard, wet coughs. At first the blood sprayed from his mouth, then it flowed. His body jerked convulsively a couple of times and was still. He hung from his captor's grip as though crucified.

Andino grabbed the dead man's hair and pulled his head back. She stared at him, her expression grim but unsurprised. Then she spat into the lifeless face.

"Murdering bastard," she said in Spanish.

Kirk felt that he was truly on the outside, looking in. But he, too, had recognized the dead man.

25

After a hurried consultation they dragged the body into the trees and abandoned it. Kirk asked Andino how badly she was wounded, and she told him she was fine.

Then they made their way back to Kirk's parked Eagle. They pulled out into traffic and were a couple of hundred yards down Constitution Avenue when the D.C. police car arrived to begin looking for the mugger.

Kirk—without any kind of plan except to get away and somehow gather his thoughts—drove east, straight toward the Capitol. He didn't speed.

Somehow he hadn't been shocked when he saw whom he had killed.

The man's name was Tomas Herrera. He was an anti-Communist Nicaraguan, a former high-ranking member of Somoza's *guardia*. He'd fled the 1979 revolution and surfaced in South Florida, where he hung out with other exiled Somozaists, as well as with an activist group of Cubans who schemed to take their country back from Castro.

Herrera had been for hire for particular kinds of enterprises. The book on him was that he was a can-do person, tough, ruthless, fervent in his beliefs and prepared to die for them. He'd been on the agency payroll during the Contras' first organizational days in the early eighties, and was rumored to have handled some of the risky business of the cocaine-for-arms swaps. However, with the passage of time, Herrera had moved into more legitimate fund-raising activities and had acquired some of the aura of respectability that adhered to the Contras' elder statesmen.

He'd gone back to Managua after the 1990 election and been imprisoned when the FSLN retook the government. Later released, he'd returned to the U.S. and resumed his anti-Sandinista activities.

Kirk didn't know anything else about Tomas Herrera, except that now the man was dead.

And the important question was: what was he doing on the Mall in the middle of the night, shooting at Piedad Andino? Kirk didn't believe in coincidence in such matters. The attempted murder had to have something to do with the present crisis.

The easy explanation was that Andino was a target because she was suspected of involvement in the hijacking and subsequent blackmail attempt. The exiles were pissed off and wanted to make an example of her.

Another possibility was that she was part of the plot and had been ordered killed by her own people, with Herrera the poetically just assassin.

She might have been telling Kirk the truth, though. Perhaps she genuinely wanted to help him find the missiles, and the Nicaraguan government was innocent of involvement in the plot.

"Where are we going?" she asked him.

"I don't know," he said. "We need to talk."

"That was the second attempt today," she said in a professional, matter-of-fact tone. "Can you take me someplace safe? I will trust you."

The yellow light blinked steadily in Kirk's head: caution, caution.

"The embassy?" he suggested.

"No," she said, "not tonight. The risk is too high. I can contact them in the morning."

"Motel?"

"If you say so."

He nodded and put the Eagle through some basic maneuvers to determine that they weren't being overtly followed. Then he stopped on a deserted side street. Very carefully he inspected every area of the car where a transmitter might have been placed. She doublechecked him.

Finally satisfied that they weren't the object of a remote tail, he drove out New York Avenue, passing near the remains of the booby-trapped warehouse. Several motels were located out there, situated to attract tourists who couldn't afford downtown Washington prices. At this time of year, before the cherry trees had blossomed, rooms would be available.

They selected one and Kirk went inside alone. There was no reason to risk a motel employee seeing Andino with her bloody pant leg.

He registered them as man and wife and took the room for two days, paying in advance in cash. The desk clerk did the paperwork quickly. The new guests had interrupted his viewing of an R-rated teen sex pic on the Movie Channel—Kirk could see the bouncing young breasts through the door to the inner office—and he was anxious to get back to it. He failed to notice that Kirk got into a car other than the one he'd specified on the registration card, and that the license plate numbers didn't match.

Kirk fetched a couple of cold sodas from the drink machine and they went up to the room.

It was done in standard American motel decor: floral spreads on the two double beds, a cheap color TV, fake wood dresser, shrink-wrapped plastic glasses on a tray next to an ice bucket. Above the beds hung a framed print of the Tidal Basin awash in cherry blossoms.

Kirk went over to the air conditioner, set it to FAN ONLY, and turned it on. Then he switched on the TV. He found a station where there was only static and turned the volume up until the room was filled with white noise.

Andino watched him, shaking her head slowly, then joined him next to the TV.

"I thought this place was random," she said.

"Force of habit," he said.

There was little chance that anyone was intentionally listening. But this was still Washington. There was always that one-in-a-million shot that they had inadvertently stumbled into the wrong place at the wrong time and might be accidentally overheard.

"How about the leg?" he said.

She nodded and they went into the bathroom. She took off her boots and pants—with the ease of someone who was used to living in close quarters with men—and sat down on the edge of the bathtub. For a moment he was irresistibly aware of her as a woman. The seductively unself-conscious way she undressed, her smooth, muscular thighs so reminiscent of Susanna's, her dark pubic triangle showing through the thin fabric of her white cotton underpants. And as their eyes met briefly, he felt that she was reading his mind.

Dangerous, intrusive thoughts. He buried them as he turned away from her and got a washcloth down from the wire rack on the wall.

With soap and water he cleaned her wound. It was, as she had indicated, not a deep one, but it must have hurt when he soaped it. She didn't wince.

When he'd finished, he tore one of the hand towels into strips and fashioned a bandage that he tied around her leg. She nodded her appreciation as she pulled her trousers back on. When the two of them had returned to the front room, Kirk pulled the room's two chairs close to the TV set. Sitting there was essentially as good as sweeping the room for bugs.

"Okay," he said. "Let's talk."

"Okay," she said. "First of all, thanks."

"For what?"

"Warning me."

He dismissed it with a wave of his hand. "You said it was the second attempt," he said.

She nodded. "That's why I called you, because of the first one. There was a car sitting across New Hampshire Avenue as I was coming out of the embassy this evening. Someone inside it had an automatic pistol."

"Which obviously missed. You think—"

"Missed *me*," Andino cut in. There was a sudden anger behind her dark eyes. "The woman standing in front of me was not so fortunate."

Her words took a moment to sink in, then Kirk said, "I'm sorry. That was insensitive of me."

"In any case it is done," Andino said grimly. "She will live. What we must make sure of is that it not happen again."

In the pause that followed, some of the tension between them drained away.

"I was wondering if you were sure it was the same guy," Kirk said. "There's a lot of anti-Nicaraguan sentiment out there."

"I don't know. I thought about that. But after what happened in the park I'd have to assume, if not the same person, the same people."

"How'd they know about the park?"

"I thought about killing you."

It was an unexpected response, but an effective one. She was letting him know that she felt she'd had a legitimate reason to mistrust him and that she hadn't acted on it. He found that he instinctively moved a couple of steps toward her corner.

"Thanks for not," he said, tacitly acknowledging that she was probably good enough to have done it. "How close did I come?"

She smiled for the first time and held her thumb and forefinger about two inches apart. Then she was serious again.

"I didn't think they could have followed me," she said. "Which meant that I had walked into your trap. You recognized the man in the park, didn't you?"

He nodded. "Tomas Herrera. I've seen his picture on the evening news, like everyone else. I've never met him, though, and I certainly didn't set you up."

She looked at him searchingly before saying, "That's what I decided."

"That I wasn't going to shoot my . . . ally?"

"Not really. I thought about the way you took him out. You reacted on pure instinct. If you'd known he was going to be there, you'd have betrayed that, one way or another."

"Which leaves us with the question of how they knew."

"Somebody's phone isn't secure," she said. "In the current circumstances it's probably mine. I won't use it again. But here's the point, Craik. However Herrera came to be there, the important fact is that it was him. Now do you believe what I've been telling you?"

Kirk found that he wanted to. It was the simplest explanation of all. But it was also the ugliest. America's friends trying to goad her by secretly killing Americans. Who would want to believe that?

"Because he was a Contra?" he said.

"Yes," she said. "I'm getting close to finding out what happened, I can feel it. I think that's why they decided to eliminate me."

"Maybe."

"Craik," she said, exasperated, "what is it going to take?"

"I don't know. Can you tell me how you're trying to track the missiles down?"

"We've infiltrated the exile community. Naturally, our sources are very nervous right now; it's not a time to appear unusually inquisitive. But we've been able to establish for sure that the perpetrators are in the Contra structure somewhere. It shouldn't be long before we get some names."

"Which you'll share with us."

"Of course. You think we're so crazy that we'd try a retrieval mission here in the States by ourselves?"

"No, I guess not," he said. "How close are you?"

"We're next to people who knew about the operation but weren't involved in it, and we think they may know who was. It's not the sort of thing you can come right out and ask for. We may end up having to compromise the potential informant."

Kirk didn't need to know Sandinista methodology for compromising an informant. He had a question he desperately wanted to ask, and it might best be dropped out of the blue.

"I heard there are some exiled Grenadians living in Managua," he said.

She stared at him, taken aback. Besides the puzzlement in her expression, though, he saw something else, too. Something a lot more powerful. Try as he might, he couldn't quite read it.

"Yes, there are," she said carefully. "A few."

"I also heard they might have allied themselves with some of the more radical Nicaraguan elements."

"They can associate with whomever they want. Your country seems unwilling to recognize that our goal is a free and open society."

"It is kind of hard to tell."

"Listen, Craik, I'm sure you don't approve of what we had to do, but I'm equally sure you don't understand why we did it. The FSLN is still by far the biggest party in my country. The United Nicaraguan Opposition was a ridiculous coalition of political groups from one end of the spectrum to the other. They weren't competent to *gov-*

ern. Worst of all, they were bent on eradicating all the gains of the Revolution. We simply couldn't permit that. Believe me, the majority of our people supported their ouster."

"Well, we won't know that until the next election, will we? When's that going to be?"

"Look, let's not talk about this, okay? It has nothing to do with why we're here." She'd become animated when defending the FSLN's actions, but the earlier, wary expression returned as she asked, "Why did you mention the Grenadians?"

"Is there any possibility they could be involved in the hijack? Behind your back, I mean."

Now her face clearly reflected what was going on inside her: dawning recognition. "Who are you?" she said coldly.

"I told you," Kirk said. "I'm working—"

"No. *Who* are you? What is your name?"

Kirk stared at her.

"My God," she said. "I know who you are." Unconsciously she started to cross herself. Nicaraguans come in all political colors, he thought, but underneath they were Catholic to the core. She stopped when she realized what she was doing. "You're Steven Kirk."

Her whole posture had shifted. She was ready to fight if need be.

"Wait a minute," he said, holding up his hands. The hair on his arms had stiffened. "Wait a minute. What's going on here?"

"You know what they call you in my country?" she said in an angry, rasping half whisper. "The Butcher of Grenada." Her fingers had involuntarily crimped themselves into claws.

Images from his past flashed in his mind. The ill-fated Grenada mission. His betrayal by Smith and the entire foreign policy apparatus. His personal failures. The innocent people who had died there—his friends.

Of course they would know about him in Managua. They wouldn't know that he had walked away from it all. And somehow found Susanna . . . Or would they?

"Keep calm, Piedad," he said as gently as he could. "I'm going to sit on my hands now."

Very carefully he raised himself up, slipped his hands

well under his butt, and sat back down. The gesture was clearly submissive, taking away his ability to strike the first blow, giving her just enough of an edge to put her firmly in control.

Anger still showed in her face, but it was now mixed with confusion. Oddly enough, he found himself responding to her sudden hostility with the feeling that here was yet another indication that she was telling the truth. And he felt a sudden, very unwelcome flush of sexual attraction.

"What you've heard isn't true," he said. "I was set up. What happened in Grenada was exactly what I was trying to prevent."

She looked at him suspiciously, but he had the distinct impression that she wanted to believe him.

"The agency doublecrossed me," he went on. "They told me I was going in to work covertly for improved relations with Grenada. Instead they used me to ruin Bishop's credibility with the radicals, and the rest just followed. I regret what happened more than anything I've done in my life. But by the time I realized what was going on, it was too late. All I could do was quit."

"And now you're working for them again."

He paused and they looked at each other in silence. It was a critical moment, he realized. There was a choice he was probably going to have to make eventually, and he was being compelled to make it now.

"I'm not working for the agency," he said. "I'm working for myself."

"You're not after the missiles?" she said, obviously perplexed.

"Yes, I'm trying to recover the missiles. But not for the agency, for me. I lost my wife and child six months ago, to a car bomb. I've been led to believe that the Grenadians living in Nicaragua may have been responsible for that, as well as for the hijack. That's why I asked you about them. Do you think it's possible?"

She just stared at him, her mouth slightly open.

"I want the people who killed my family," he said. He would have forced some fury into his voice if he'd had to, but he didn't. It was there.

She swallowed hard. "I don't know who killed your family," she said. "It could have been them. They hate you. But they didn't take the Stingers. The Contras did."

For an instant the image in Kirk's mind linking the Grenadians and the car bomb was replaced by one featuring the Contras. He quickly dismissed the notion. They might have hijacked the missiles, but why in the world would they have murdered his wife and child?

"May I get off my hands now?" he asked.

She nodded and he withdrew his hands from beneath him. He shook them a little to get the circulation going.

"I've told you the truth," he said.

"And I've told you the truth," she replied.

The white noise from the TV set still filled the room, but the static level between the two of them had dropped markedly, and they both knew it.

"It's late," he said.

"Herrera was well known," she said. "Will the agency be able to control this?"

"I don't tell the agency anything they don't need to know. The jogger won't be able to describe me; he was too busy looking at the gun. And the cops know the Contras. When they find the rifle with Herrera's prints all over it, they'll figure some kind of drug deal was going down. The case'll end up at the back of somebody's file somewhere."

"Are we still working together?" he asked.

"We're still working together."

"Good. The deal is this: we help each other find out who's holding the missiles and where they are. But if I come across the people who planted that car bomb, I don't care what their political leanings are, I don't owe you anything. I do what I think is appropriate. Okay?"

"Except for one thing," she said firmly. "I can't let you harm a Sandinista in my presence."

He thought for a second, then decided he had nothing to lose. "Excepting that," he said. "Anyone else, I want to go in with you when you locate them."

"All right, then."

"How do I contact you?"

"Same number. I won't go near the phone myself, so just leave the word 'sting' for a callback. But I'll probably be in touch with you first."

Getting up, he nodded once in her direction, then left the motel room.

On the drive back to the safe house, he thought about what had happened. The shootout on the Mall had to be connected to the Stinger crisis, one way or other. Andino either had some answers, or was close to them.

And if she was close, so was he.

26

The President was furious. He waved a copy of the front section of the morning *Post* in his Chief of Staff's face, almost as if he were going to slap him with it.

Smoking Gun had struck again. The headline read:

TERRORISTS THREATEN FURTHER ATTACKS

And the subsequent story contained all the details of the previous night's communication from the Committee for the Furtherance of Peace in Central America.

"God damn it, Tom!" he said. "I thought I made it clear I didn't want any repetition of this shit!"

They were in the Presidential study, just across the hall from the Oval Office. It was an intimate, book-lined room, the only place in the West Wing the Chief Executive could go for privacy. No one—no matter how important his business or how intimate he was with the President—ever entered the study without knocking first.

"I'm sorry, sir," Tom Read mumbled. "But security is about as tight as we can draw it. We're pulling only the most trustworthy people for duty in the Situation Room. My guess is that there's an Albanian in the woodpile."

"One of the people who was in the room when the call came in?" the President said.

"Or their most senior aide. It wasn't supposed to go any further than that."

"Who?"

"I don't know, Mr. President."

"I know you don't know, Tom. You want to hazard a guess?"

"Hell, it could be anybody."

"All right," the President said with exasperation, "let me take a guess. Seems to me they'd want to have a motive. Which could be to stir up the public. Which suggests Enzo or Monty Banks."

"Mr. President, you can't go jumping to conclusions. Somebody could've told somebody who wasn't supposed to know. Or it could've come out of the agency. I'll be sucked dry if they don't always seem to know exactly what's going on. And there's lots of Casey's people still in there who think Reagan should have pressed the invasion button back in eighty-one."

"You know what I really don't like about this, Tom? If there's somebody working against us, there's the possibility he's working for the other side."

Read thought that over, then said, "If he is, then our tit's in the wringer either way. We don't catch him and he continues to make fools of us. We do and you're gonna have a scandal that'll make Watergate look like the two-bit burglary it was."

"I can't have a traitor in my Administration!" the President said.

"Well, I wish I could advise you, sir, but chances are the leak is a patriot and thinks he's doing what's best for the country."

The President got up and walked over to the small fireplace, where he stirred a heap of glowing coals with a poker. He turned back to Read.

"Well, what do you think we should do?" he said.

He suddenly realized he was shaking the poker at his Chief of Staff and replaced it self-consciously in its stand.

"I think you ought to have Don Walker stand up at the next meeting and read the riot act. Make it clear that if there's another leak during this business, and if we find out who it is, we're going to prosecute them. For gross violations of national security." He paused, then added, "Or treason, if you want to go that far. And that whoever's office it came out of is going to be held responsible, too."

The President thought about it. "That's good," he said. "The sight of Don on the warpath ought to put the fear of God in them. Unless he's the one, of course."

Read shook his head. "I doubt it," he said. "Our sieve is a stone snitch, when you come right down to it. And whatever else that one-eyed bastard is, he ain't that."

"Okay, let's do it, damn it. Will you take care of the details?"

Read nodded.

The President gave his Chief of Staff a long, searching look, then said, "I'm trusting you, Tom. You're my little sister's husband and you're my friend, and I'd be shocked to my boots if you were the one. But I swear before God, if you are, I'll fry your ass as crisp as I would anyone else's. No offense."

"No offense taken," Read said. "It isn't me."

"Good. Anything else?" the President asked.

"Ah, maybe . . . This is kind of a delicate subject sir, but, well, I can think of something we could have the Attorney General try."

"Come on, Tom. You think you're going to shock me?"

Read cleared his throat. "No," he said. "It's not illegal or anything. It's just, well, I don't want you to think I'm a racist, Mr. President, but the lady reporter who's been writing up all the leaks, she's black."

The President looked blankly at his Chief of Staff.

"Well," Read continued, "she's our best lead on the leak, so *some*body ought to take a meeting with her. Maybe try to lean on her a little. Let her know how much damage she's doing, if nothing else. And if pressure don't work . . ."

"If pressure doesn't work, what?" There was still no sign of comprehension on the President's face.

"Walker's a very impressive black man," Read said. "You have to admit. And from what I hear, the Stokes woman is a looker. They're both single." He shrugged. "You never know."

"Oh, I see," the President said. "If they were to . . . hit it off, we might get some control over her."

"That's the general idea, sir. If we can't block the stories, at least we could be a little better prepared for what's coming."

The President chuckled. "You're not only a racist," he said. "You're a sexist. It's a good thing Diane's not here."

"I believe it's a practical move, Mr. President. Like I said, somebody from our side is going to have to visit her anyway."

"You're right, of course. So it might as well be Don. Everything else aside, he's the logical choice. Tell him I want him to go see her ASAP, will you?"

"Yes, sir."

"Now—"

The President was interrupted by a knock at the door. "Who is it?" he called.

A voice from outside said, "Captain Troy, Mr. President."

The President looked at his Chief of Staff and Read said, "Duty officer."

"Jesus, what now?" the President muttered, then called, "All right, come in."

The door opened and a young man in starched whites entered the study.

"Excuse me, Mr. President," the man said.

"What is it, Captain?"

The officer handed over a single sheet of paper that the President quickly read. When he'd finished he looked angrily at Tom Read. "Convene the group," he said tersely. "Immediately. The bastards have hit another plane."

By the time the President's advisers could be gathered in the Cabinet Room three hours later, Diane McBain was able to provide a thorough account of what had taken place that morning.

An American Airlines 737 had taken off from the Atlanta airport just after eight o'clock in the morning. As in Boston, the Stinger had been fired during the plane's initial climb to altitude. This time, however, the pilot had been more fortunate. The missile had either impacted the exterior of the engine housing or had exploded prematurely for some other reason.

As a result, there had been only minor damage to the target engine. The pilot had been able to shut down the affected fuel line before there were any secondary explosions and had maintained control of his hydraulics. He'd brought the plane safely back to ground. The passengers had ended up with just a very bad scare.

Everyone in the Cabinet Room spontaneously cheered when McBain finished detailing the failure of the missile attack.

"Gentlemen, please?" she said. "We're all grateful that no one was hurt. But I'm afraid I'm not through yet.

"Unfortunately, there was no mystery this time as to what had happened. Atlanta officials tried to keep a lid on it, but the story was all over the airport in a few minutes and the media had it within an hour. And this is the result." She took a deep breath and let it out. "Over half the passengers on that 737 turned in their tickets. That was just the beginning. As the story hit the national news, the airlines' phones jammed up. Not just in Atlanta, either. The cancellations are flooding in all over the country." She paused, then added, "People are becoming flat-out afraid to fly."

"My gosh," Vice President Brust said. "Isn't that something?"

"Except for the airline executives," Read chipped in. "A delegation of them was put together in a hurry and it's on its way here now. All the biggest companies. They want a meeting with the President, which they probably deserve."

"And there's no word out of the pilots yet. But if *they* start getting the willies . . ."

"Damn it, we've got to get those Hawks back!" the President said.

After a moment of uneasy silence, McBain said quietly, "Yes, we have to recover the Stingers, Mr. President."

The President nodded vigorously.

"If civil aviation in this country freezes up," Tom Read said, "there won't be a sector of the economy that's untouched."

"At least the sonsabitches'll self-destruct in sixty days," General Banks said.

"Yeah, but let's remember that in sixty days we could have twenty-two more planes shot down," Read said to the diminutive JCS Chairman. "We will have had a panic on Wall Street and I don't know what all else. This ain't something that's happening on the other side of the world. It's a war on our own soil. I don't think the American people are prepared to accept that."

There were concurring murmurs around the table.

Then McBain said, "There's also the Soviets to contend with. As most of you already know, the President received a communication from the General Secretary this morning. The Soviets are blaming us for the missile attack once again. They're citing their treaty with the Sandinistas and promising that they're ready to transfer the MiGs from Cuba if we show any further sign of aggression towards Nicaragua."

"They wouldn't dare," Banks said. "It's a bluff."

"The General Secretary was emphatic," McBain said.

"And if they do?" the President said.

McBain deferred to the DCI, who puffed once on his pipe and said, "Nicaraguan pilots have been trained on the MiGs, but they don't have much practical experience. We'd take some losses, but we could wipe them out in short order. But if Russians or Cubans were flying the planes, we'd have a real fight on our hands. Not to mention what the political ramifications would be."

"What if they used their own pilots rather than Nicaraguans?" the President asked.

The Director responded without in any way indicating that he'd already answered the question. "Our intelligence estimate is that that is extremely unlikely," he said. "However, even if they do use indigenous pilots, there is the possibility that the Soviets would consider the loss of their aircraft to be the same as a direct attack on them."

"Nuts!" General Banks said. "They can't maintain a six-thousand-mile supply line, and they know it."

"Monty's right," Carini said, plucking an imaginary piece of lint from his Armani suit. "But all we really need to do is destroy the Nicaraguan airfields. We do that first and the question is moot. They'll never try to attack our fleet from Cuba. We'd engage them every mile of the way, and we'd win."

Secretary of Defense Schule tapped his tortoiseshell cigarette holder against the edge of a cut-glass ashtray. "A preemptive strike gains us nothing," he said. "We look bad in the eyes of the world and we ensure that there will be a dangerous confrontation. I suggest we negotiate in good faith and see what happens."

"We have anything from Managua?" the President asked the DCI.

"Just that the Sandies are gearing up for an invasion," the Director said. "They expect one. But nothing on who's behind the blackmail plot. Whoever's running the operation is doing a damn good job of keeping the hood over it."

"I just want to say that I'm against negotiating with terrorists," Attorney General Walker put in. "I believe we can lay our hands on those missiles soon. Then the rest is history."

"Look," General Banks said, "sooner or later, we're gonna have to clean that country out and it might as well be sooner. With the Contras' help, there's no reason it can't be done quickly and efficiently. Once we get some occupying forces in there, then the terrorists here will have no reason to carry on with this thing."

The President held up his hands. "All right," he said. "Thank you. I appreciate your candor. Let me think about it. And let me say that I am sure of one thing. I am *not* sending American boys to die in Nicaragua."

He looked directly at Banks as he said it and the general stared back stiffly.

"However," he said to the group at large, "it would seem prudent at this time to give the Contras a fuller measure of support. So this morning I met with joint Congressional leadership to request forty million in emergency military aid for the resistance, to be airlifted down there immediately. I was assured by members of both parties that approval on the Hill would be forthcoming without delay. Any opposition?"

There was none.

"Excellent," the President said. "Now, there's one other thing. Don?"

Walker got to his feet and leaned forward, resting his palms on the table before he began to speak. He towered over the others.

In an impassioned but controlled voice, he expressed the President's deep concern about the leak and made it clear what was going to happen to the offender when he was caught. Not *if*, he emphasized, *when*. He used the word "treason." People began glancing surreptitiously, and nervously, at their neighbors.

Almost as an afterthought, he added that he intended to plug the leak at Carla Stokes's end, if he could. By the time Walker finished his speech, it almost seemed as if the leak were the real problem, and the Stinger-armed terrorists of secondary importance.

"Thank you, Mr. Attorney General," the President said. "I take it everyone's clear that he has my complete backing in this matter." There were no sounds of dissent. "Good. Now, for the time being, we wait. Tom, you let me know when the airline people get here. I want you to be with me when I meet them."

"Yes, sir," Read said.

"And I'd appreciate it if somebody came up with a fresh idea on this thing."

Late that afternoon, the President and his Chief of Staff were back in his private study, alone. They'd had a one-hour meeting with the hastily assembled delegation of airline executives.

"What'd you think?" the President asked.

"They're obviously scared piss-dry," Tom Read said. "Which I'd say they have every right to be."

"You think they're that close to the edge that a temporary drop-off in business would push them over?"

"A lot of them, yes, especially if the drop-off's steep. The big jets, it's very damned expensive not to run them. Once the companies start folding, we could have some real vultures picking at the remains. We could wind up with two or three airlines left, and maybe no one with Christ's first idea of how to run them.

"I agree about the pilots and flight attendants, too. If they start refusing to go up, then you got chaos; we'd have to help out with the military, which we really don't want."

The President rubbed the top of his bald head, massaged his temples. He sighed.

"I'm tired, Tom," he said. "Christ, I'm tired. And I forget things. You know that I know that, don't you?" Read nodded. "I just want it to be over."

The President gazed with unfocused eyes at the fireplace, now filled only with cold ashes.

"Reagan's critics were right," he said. "I never thought I'd say that, but they were. This is no job for a seventy-year-old man."

Read stared down at his feet.

After a pause the President said, "Promise me one thing, will you, Tom?"

"Of course," Read said. "What?"

"Don't let me look like a fool."

27

Henrik Bruderdam's phone system was just as efficient at protecting incoming calls as outgoing ones. Those employing the special number—which was changed as often as necessary—were routed to the computer at corporate headquarters, where they were prompted for the proper access code. If it was forthcoming, the computer would link them via the secure satellite channel with the facility on the island.

Javier Vega had been briefed on the procedure, and in the early evening after the Atlanta miss he put his call through.

"Mosby," Bruderdam said, "what happened?"

"There is a certain amount of luck involved," Vega said. "We had it the first time and not this. But the desired effect is achieved whether the plane comes down or not. Each time there is greater public concern and more pressure on the President to act."

"Nevertheless, I want another success before I talk to him again. How soon can you get set up?"

"The third site isn't far. I can move into position there tonight. We can be ready by tomorrow morning."

"Good. Do it. Pick a nice, fat one and let's hope luck is back on our side."

"All right," Vega said. "But I want to see some evidence that you are keeping your bargain as well."

"The U.S. government is hard to move, Mosby," Bruderdam said. "There is a lot of inertia. But we will move it, you have my word. My people are busy."

"All right, you'll have your plane tomorrow. But each of these is becoming riskier. Everyone in the country is watching for us, and I don't dare do anything but stay close to ground between strikes. The sooner we get some results, the better."

For a long time after Vega had hung up, he pondered how things were going. Not having access to the White House, he couldn't know for sure. The President must be squirming like an eel by now, and yet he showed no signs of acting. Well, after another plane was taken down, he'd have no choice.

Then there was Bruderdam. The man was a real pain in the ass. A patronizing pain in the ass, at that. He was also expendable, once the operation had achieved its goals.

The more immediate problem was the woman. She was too close to being able to identify him, and Herrera had failed to get her. That was astonishing. Either she was very, very good or she'd had some highly competent help. It was bad both ways. It might be something else he would have to personally attend to.

Scowling, Vega started preparing for the trip to Washington.

What a fool, Bruderdam thought after his conversation with Mosby. As if the Nicaraguan were in a position to be making threats. All the same, he was a potentially dangerous fool.

Bruderdam sat down at his computer. Before entering anything, he pondered matters of strategy and tactics, taking his time, considering every detail he could think of.

Then he composed three messages. They were encoded and transmitted as electronic mail, using the same route as his phone calls. Each of the recipients' decoders would automatically destroy the message once it was read.

The first message was:

Stonewall—Mosby showing signs of intransigence. We should make every effort to negate his advantage by locating merchandise and relieving him of control. Suggest you may wish to give your people more assistance in finding him. Sherman.

The second was:

Mr. Grant—Best for all if we could move more quickly in this matter. CEO is dragging his feet. Suggest you use your influence with him to speed things up. Also have suggested to Stonewall that

*those pursuing Mosby be given a boost, with an eye
toward regaining control of inventory. Your choice
to assist. Sherman.*

And the third was:

*Burnside—Things moving too slowly. Suggest you
pick up pace of planted news stories. Disinformation
may be way to go. Sherman.*

All things considered, Bruderdam thought after he'd
sent his messages, it was going well. But he had to exert
maximum effort to maintain a sure-handed grip on things.

28

"You need to act faster than this," Kirk said.

Seamus Croaghan had just responded to Kirk's midday
message to call the "warehouse."

"I had to go to Boston," Croaghan said. "There was a
memorial service for my brother, before they return his
remains to Ireland. I just got back."

There was a pause, then Kirk sighed and said, "Ah,
I'm sorry, Seamus. That was very insensitive of me."

"Don't worry about it. You didn't know."

Croaghan's initial anger at Kirk had quickly dissipated.
The man couldn't be expected to keep track of what was
happening in Croaghan's life. Besides, he had initially
contacted Kirk, not the other way around; it was up to
him to hold up his end.

"I know what I've gotten myself into," Croaghan continued. "And I'm in it to the end now. Going to the
funeral only strengthened that. From here on out, I get a
call from you and I'll get to a safe phone as soon after I
receive the message as possible. Okay?"

Kirk was still subdued. "Yeah, sure," he said.

"Come on, Kirk. Let's get to work. What do you need?"

"I want to know everything there is on Tomas Herrera," Kirk said.

"Herrera? The guy whose body they—? Were you—?"

The Nicaraguan exile's violent end had played second fiddle to the Atlanta missile attack, but it was right there on the front page. Croaghan had read about it on the plane ride back from Boston. The police as yet were admitting to no leads, but speculation centered on a Contra/cocaine connection. To Croaghan, it was one suggestive event in a long chain of them.

"No, I wasn't," Kirk said smoothly. "But it's a damned strange coincidence that he turns up shot to death at this particular moment."

"I thought so, too," Croaghan said.

"I tried a WALNUT search on him, but didn't turn up much. You know the system better than I do; maybe you can find something. You might also try Smith's files. He's on his way over here, so access should be safe for a while.

"What I'm particularly interested in is when Herrera last worked for the agency. WALNUT says '86, which I don't believe. See if you can find any connection between him and Sunflower. Also, I want to know what other special assignments he seems to have carried out. And look for any indication he may have been doubling."

"All right, I'll see what I can get you. . . . Kirk, I've been doing a lot of thinking, and there's something else I've got to say. I feel like I'm under a lot of pressure here."

"You want to tell somebody," Kirk said.

"Well, what if what I've found out *is* relevant? If I sit on it, that makes me almost an accessory. I couldn't live with that."

"It could turn out badly either way, Seamus. Who would you tell?"

"The President, if I could. But I can't." Croaghan took a deep breath. "Kirk, sooner or later I'm going to have to decide if I trust Diane."

"And right now you think you do?"

"Yeah, maybe," Croaghan said.

"Tell her what you've discovered if you think you should," Kirk said. "Just don't tell her that you're working with me. Or even that you're aware of my existence."

He paused. "Plus if she thinks she's the only one you've told, you might find out very fast if she's trustworthy."

"You're probably right. . . . Damn, I don't know if I want to know!"

"You do. I'll talk to you later."

Kirk meditated for the next fifteen minutes, and by the time Smith arrived he felt clear, ready to deal with his "control." Kirk hadn't seen him since the warehouse explosion two and a half days earlier.

At least he knocked, Kirk thought as he let Smith in. The way the man moved, you expected him to keep an appointment with you by suddenly materializing at your side.

Kirk led Smith into the living room and the two of them sat down. The moon-faced agency man didn't take off his topcoat. He could sit in the room for hours, Kirk knew, and not break a sweat. Because Smith had come in out of the damp, cool night, though, he was obliged to polish his glasses.

"You're looking better than last time," he said.

"Yeah, I feel better," Kirk said. "It wasn't until this morning that I finally got my wind back. Sometimes I can still taste the smoke when I breathe."

Smith nodded in such a way as to suggest that Kirk's welfare was important to him. "Things are tightening up," he said. "I don't want you out there at less than full strength."

"Tightening how?" Kirk asked.

"A lot of bad feeling is coming out. Last night we lost one of our good friends. Murdered down by the Vietnam Memorial, of all places."

"I know," Kirk said, choosing his words carefully. "I saw the afternoon paper. Who's out killing Contras, do you think?"

Smith shrugged. "The police are writing it off against drugs," he said, "which it's best we let them believe. But I think it has to do with the Stingers. Herrera used to work for us, and he was a bit of a cowboy. I'd bet he decided to try to find the missiles himself. He probably got close enough to set up a trap for the terrorists down on the Mall, but they outsmarted him and blew him away."

Kirk listened attentively, aware that his reaction was being judged. When Smith had finished, he nodded. "Makes sense," he said, then added suspiciously, "You had no idea he was in the field?"

"If I had, you'd have been the first to know about it, Steven. I don't jeopardize my officers. You get every-thing you need to know. I resent your suggestion."

"Consider it withdrawn. If the terrorists killed Her-rera, we have to assume they're in Washington, then."

"Or at least some of them are."

"You expecting them to hit Dulles or National?"

"I certainly hope not, but the Director and I agree that those are possibilities, along with BWI. The Director has advised the President, and it's up to him to decide on countermeasures." Smith paused, then said, "How about you? Are you making any progress?"

"Some," Kirk said. "Charles and I have identified the Sandinista operatives working in the city and I've been tracking their movements. If I can penetrate the net-work, I will. Otherwise, we think the best move is to cut the weakest one out of the pack."

"How close are you?"

"I don't know. A couple of days, maybe."

"Do you want me to have interrogation facilities ready?"

"Just on a standby basis. Don't worry, Smitty, if I need to snatch somebody, I'll ring for help. If there's anybody left to snatch. It's a little counterproductive for people to be taking pot shots at the Embassy." That story, too, had made the front page, but below the fold. "Wouldn't know anything about that, would you?"

"Steven," Smith said, "look. I am not the enemy here, despite what you may think of me. I'm not going to get in your way. But you have to realize how much anger is building up out there." He gestured vaguely at the rest of the world. "It seems likely that the attack on the Nicaraguan Embassy was the work of a right-wing extremist group. We certainly didn't have anything to do with it."

"Well, if it was an extremist group, you ought to be able to nail them, which I'd appreciate. They're just going to make the ones we want that much harder to find."

"I understand the problem. We'll do what we can, but we're not really in control. There are a lot of hate groups for whom this is the perfect excuse to get out the guns."

Kirk nodded. "Okay," he said. "What about Tellez? You turn him up?"

"Not quite," Smith said. "But we're sure he's in town. And the way he's gone to ground, he must know something."

"I have to say, I haven't stumbled across his name yet."

"That's not surprising. He helped move the missiles along, but he's not a Sandie unless he's doubling. There's a good chance he wasn't involved in the hijack at all. So he may only have seen something that makes him a liability."

"You still think the Sandinistas are responsible?"

"Do you have reason to believe otherwise?"

"No. But I think there's room for doubt."

"I'd be wary of getting too far afield, Steven. Keep the goal clear in your mind."

Kirk understood the warning. His goal was information about his family. Getting it meant attaining Smith's goal first. That was going to be the sequence of events and he'd better not screw around with it.

Smith had been observing him carefully. "Yes?" he said.

"Yes," Kirk said.

"Good. What was Seamus Croaghan doing here?"

"God damn it, Smith! You're watching a *safe* house?"

But Smith was unperturbed. "Of course not," he said. "I would never risk drawing attention to this place by putting it under surveillance. I do not unnecessarily jeopardize my field men, as you ought to know by now. Croaghan, however, is not one of my field men."

He raised an eyebrow at Kirk, but Kirk didn't say anything.

"I'm your control officer and I want to know what you're doing diddling around with the National Security Council," Smith said.

"What are *you*?"

The question rankled Smith, though only as careful an observer as Kirk would have picked it up.

"Are you familiar with the CAT?" Smith said.

"No," Kirk said.

"Central American Interagency Task Force. CAT, for short. Representatives from the agency, State, Defense, and the NSC. It handles detail work."

"I can imagine."

"Croaghan's a member of the CAT, and so am I."

Damn him, Kirk thought. What he'd done, of course, was to plant a seed of suspicion about Croaghan in Kirk's head. And even though Kirk knew that that was what he was doing—as well as knowing that it was being done in order for Smith to retain control of the situation—the seed was nevertheless planted.

"What's that supposed to mean?" Kirk asked.

"It means that he and I work together," Smith said innocently. "That's all."

"And you want to check on what the other guy is doing."

"Of course. You're my field man, not the NSC's. I have a need-to-know about this."

"And I have a need to know what the CAT's involvement in all this is. That damned missile shipment was illegal."

"We were engaged in providing humanitarian assistance to the Contras. Which as you know was perfectly legitimate. The Stingers were being supplied by someone outside that framework. Not the agency."

"But . . . ?"

Smith shrugged. He wasn't about to say that some other member of the CAT might have been involved in illegal arms shipments, though he was quite willing to let the inference be drawn if Kirk desired to do so.

Another seed. Through sheer willpower Kirk maintained his composure. "Glad to see there's such a level of trust in your group," he said acidly. "The fact is, I invited Croaghan here. I wanted to thank him for saving my life."

"Oh please, Steven," Smith said.

"No, you wouldn't understand something like that, would you?"

Smith sighed. "How'd you find out who he was?"

"I described him to Charles. It's not easy to make a mistake with Croaghan."

"So you thanked him and then what?"

"Just what you'd think. He knows I'm working on getting the Stingers back. He's inside the White House. I thought it'd be useful to have a contact there." Kirk paused, wondering whether he ought to twist the knife a little, then went ahead and did it. "If I'd known about the CAT, I would have consulted you, of course, but I didn't."

It felt good.

Smith nodded, unperturbed. "I see," he said. "Well, I wouldn't discourage you from establishing whatever contacts you think you need. But now that you understand the . . . situation, you will know enough to tread a little lightly?"

"I get the point," Kirk said.

"Good." Smith was on his feet before Kirk quite realized that he'd gotten up. "Keep me informed, Steven," he added and then he was gone.

29

Carla Stokes's apartment was the top floor of a townhouse just west of Dupont Circle. It was a quiet area of older residential buildings, art galleries, embassies, and traditionally elegant hotels. It was also close to a Metro stop and a fairly safe ten blocks from the offices of the Washington *Post* so that, if she had to, she could even walk to work.

She had chosen this particular apartment primarily because of the living area: by day a bright, airy space under the old-fashioned skylight, yet intimate at night when the working marble fireplace became its centerpiece. The natural-finish contemporary maple furniture was set off nicely by the scattered pieces of Dogon art she'd managed to acquire since moving up to the *Post*.

She had never been formally introduced to the Attorney General of the United States, but she'd seen him around, had heard him speak, and was fairly impressed with him. He was a black man who'd risen to a very high government position without, apparently, kissing anyone's ass. That was remarkable. He was also intelligent, and a handsome, imposing figure who effortlessly dominated a room full of people. And he was single.

So when Don Walker had called her, Stokes had canceled her evening's plans without a second thought and invited him to her apartment.

He was coming on business, of course. He hadn't specified what, but it would be the business of her stories about the missile crisis. Which was interesting, because he himself was one of her leading candidates for the role of Smoking Gun.

But business or not, one had to make the most of one's opportunities. She lit a fire in the hearth and dressed herself in a flowing, gold-embroidered white silk caftan that alternately revealed and concealed her body as she moved. For jewelry she chose some simple gold hoop earrings and a brown seed necklace a friend had brought back from Jamaica. She looked great, and she knew it.

They talked next to the crackling fire, over a bottle of Chardonnay, recounting the stories of their lives. Her childhood had been spent in a poor section of northeast Washington, his in an equally slummy area a few miles away, along the Anacostia River. Both had struggled for the college education no one in either's family had ever had. Though both were ambitious, they shared a genuine commitment to ideals. She believed in the crucial role of the press in a free society, he in the ability of the American system of justice to effect change.

They could have passed a very pleasant social evening, but eventually Walker got down to the nut.

"The President wanted me to talk to you," he said.

"The terrorist story." Stokes shrugged. "Well, you know how I feel. The people have a right to know what's going on."

"Carla, look. The President is in an awfully tough spot here. There are some very delicate negotiations going on. On the one hand, he's responsible for the safety of air travelers. On the other, he's trying to prevent a land war in Central America, which he knows the people don't really want no matter how much they might start screaming for it. We feel that running these stories is highly counterproductive."

"Then why is there a leak? It's got to be coming from close to the top."

"I don't know why there's a leak, damn it! If I did, I'd be getting ready to prosecute."

"Oh?"

"Yes, we're invoking national security. We take it that seriously."

"Are you threatening me?"

There was a pause, then Walker said, "No, I'm not threatening you, Carla. The violation of law is usually to be found in the leak, not the reporting."

Now that was ambiguous, wasn't it? she thought, her professional ire rising. She didn't care at all for the word "usually." At the same time, though, she unconsciously drew herself a bit closer to the fire. She'd never before confronted the possibility of prosecution for something she'd written. She had no idea if she'd stand by her principles when it came to the crunch, but jail terrified her. That she did know.

She took a healthy swallow of the musky white wine. "You want me to stop writing about this thing?" she asked.

"No," Walker said, "but the President would appreciate it if you would stop publishing confidential information."

"If you want us to stop printing it, I'd suggest you stop leaking it."

She raised her glass to him and smiled to make sure he understood that it was neither an insult nor an ultimatum, merely a good-natured challenge from one person who was good at her job to another who was just as good at his.

Walker stared at her for a moment, then he chuckled. "You know a good plumber?" he said. "No pun intended."

They both laughed at that, and the tension that had come between them began to abate. Walker loosened his necktie.

"Take it off if you like," Stokes said, her dark eyes gleaming over the top of her wine glass.

Walker shed both his necktie and suitcoat, and rolled up his sleeves. "All right," he said, "let's talk serious. Just you and me without the white folks around."

Stokes shook her head in mock wonder. There was a big smile on her face.

"What it is," Walker said, "is that we both have things we want, and nobody knows better than us the kind of trouble we're gonna have getting them." He raised an eyebrow and she nodded her assent. "Okay," he continued, "you got your principles and I got mine, etcetera etcetera. It'd be nice if you'd stop writing up the President's private meetings, but I know you won't if you keep on getting the minutes. I'm not even sure but what you've got the right to do it, and I probably wouldn't stop you if I could."

"I'm touched," she said sarcastically.

"Come on, give me a break. I'm trying to tell you that while I don't like what you're doing, and would prefer that you didn't, I don't entirely disapprove of the fact that you're doing it. Whereas with the leak—"

"Which isn't you?"

He looked at her with astonishment. It was too abrupt, she thought, too genuine to have been faked. She decided on the spot that the Attorney General was an unlikely Smoking Gun.

"Me?" he said.

"No," she said, "I guess not. Just a thought. So what you want me to do is betray my source. You know I can't do that."

"Your source is a traitor," he said, visibly angry. "I think what *you're* doing is hurting the country, but it's your right. There's no excuse for what *he's* doing. That's the difference. You see what I mean?"

"Sure I see what you mean. But I've gotten a lot of good stuff from this guy. I wouldn't want to betray him even if I knew who he was. Which I don't."

He had no answer for that. She studied his rugged face, trying to deduce what it was he was really after, and realized with a start that that was probably exactly what he was thinking about her. She also felt a growing awareness that the attraction he exerted on her might be reciprocated.

Her brain flashed some warning signals about mixing business with the personal life, but she decided to ignore them. This was Washington, where the two were so intertwined as to be, for all practical purposes, one.

"Carla, let me put it this way," he said. "Like I said before, without the white folks around. We got a woman here who wants to be, what? Editor of the *Post*? Or maybe something even better than that?"

She smiled.

"And we got us a man," he went on, "who wants to

be, oh, something or other, let's say the President, for the sake of argument."

She chuckled. "Okay," she said. "Mr. President."

"Now, neither one of these people is likely to make it without a little help from their friends. And who are their friends? Let's take the lady. Is it," he asked, pausing a moment for dramatic effect, "some white dude voice at the other end of a telephone line?"

Stokes laughed out loud at that.

"You get the picture," he said. "Carla, I want that sonofabitch. You I can live with; him I can't. And you don't believe for a minute that he's got a dime's worth of loyalty to you, do you?"

"No." As she shook her head, the golden hoops tugged at her earlobes. "Of course not."

"Then help me nail him. He doesn't deserve anything more than he'd give you, I'm sure you'd agree. And you'd be doing me a very big favor."

She considered his argument. She'd been asked to betray sources before, by cops and politicians and other reporters. And she'd never done it; it was considered journalistic suicide. On the other hand, she'd never been propositioned in quite this way before. Walker was good, damn good, but what was the bottom line?

"Interesting," she said. "The Attorney General asking me to give him a career boost."

"Ouch," he said. "Okay, maybe I deserved that. But don't get me wrong, I really do want the guy."

"I'll accept that," she said. "Which leaves us with the question of the moment. What, as they say, is in it for me?"

"Fair enough. It just so happens that the Justice Department media rep is leaving in July. I'm going to need to replace him, and I don't have anyone in mind right now. Beyond that, who knows? No promises. But if the President is reelected, I understand his press secretary has been saying privately that four years will have been enough. I . . . always like to see my people move up."

There was a long pause. Both of them drank some wine and stared at the fire. The dangled prize was a big one.

"I really don't know who he is, Don," she said finally.

"I believe you," he said, "but you're the only one who

talks to him as the leak. What we'd want you to do is try to entice him out into the open, where we can see his face."

"Well, all I can say is that I'll think about it."

"Fine. Just don't take too long. Deal?"

"Deal," she said firmly. "Now, can we change the subject?"

He grinned. "Sure," he said. "What did you want to talk about?"

"What time do you have to be home?" she said.

30

Kirk was awake this time when Andino called. The conversation with Smith had left a sour taste in his mouth and he'd been thinking ever since, trying to assemble the puzzle so that it made some kind of sense.

Smith and Croaghan and Andino. Ruben Tellez and Tomas Herrera. Contras and Sandinistas and Grenadians. The hijacked missiles, the blackmail plot. The shadow government. Susanna and Scottie.

He concluded that although the pieces fit together in a number of ways, that number was steadily diminishing. Someone was bound to be telling the truth; others were not. It could only be a matter of time before he was able to separate the two.

"It's me," Andino said over the phone. "We should talk." He noted that she no longer felt comfortable identifying herself by name.

"Where?" he said.

"Same place. Take care. Please."

She was telling him to make certain he wasn't followed, and he respected her request. Though he was reasonably sure that no transmitter had been planted in the Eagle, he didn't take it. Instead he walked out to

Pennsylvania Avenue, where he went into one of the Capitol Hill watering holes and called a cab.

His driver was an Afghani with a single gold front tooth. Mahmoud didn't speak all that much English, but he understood the fifty-dollar bill Kirk handed him and the instruction to lose any tail. In Washington, he probably heard that twice a day.

Kirk settled back and buckled his seat belt. Of all the nationalities represented in D.C.'s multi-ethnic cabbie corps, an Afghani was absolutely the best one could do in a random draw. It might seem pathetic that the best horsemen in the world were jockeying cars through the city's streets, but the Soviets had left many of them with no alternative and they had transferred their skills smoothly from animal to machine.

Mahmoud was no disappointment. He raced the cab down the back streets, across the grain of traffic into sudden turns, through shortcuts and alleyways that Kirk would never have known were there. All the while he spoke calmly in his halting English of how he was trying to get a stake together now that the hated Russians were gone. He wanted to have enough so that when he returned to his country he could help to rebuild his village, which had been ravaged by foreign bombs. Kirk promised him another fifty when they got where they were going.

Within five minutes Kirk knew that anyone trying to tail the cab had been left muttering obscenities to himself, so he directed Mahmoud out New York Avenue, Northeast.

As a final precaution Kirk had Mahmoud drop him off at one of the other motels along the strip. He gave the cabbie the second bill and wished him good luck in the long trek home. After Mahmoud drove off, Kirk went into the motel lobby and bought a newspaper from the vending machine. He loitered until he felt the desk clerk was about to ask him what he was doing there, then walked purposefully out into the night.

A few minutes later, Andino let him into her room. He caught himself feeling happy to see the dark, half-Indian woman, and quickly quashed the feeling.

"I've found out some things," she told him. "Somehow they got a line bug on the phone I was using before. That's how they knew where we were going to be."

He nodded. "Who did?"

"The Contras, of course," she said testily.

"No, I mean specifically. Do you know that yet?"

"We have a pretty good idea. It's an activist exile group that works closely with the anti-Castro Cubans and the Contras, both here and in Central America. They raise money and arrange weapons shipments, but don't often go into the field themselves. A lot of them are officers from Somoza's *guardia*."

"I can imagine how you feel about *them*."

"Yes," she said bitterly, "I did not agree with the Directorate's decision to abolish capital punishment."

"Most Americans never even knew about that," he said.

"Most Americans know *nothing* about my country."

"It's not just you. It's the whole world. Our perceptions tend to be defined by what fits comfortably into a thirty-second spot on the six o'clock news."

Among other things, Kirk thought. He was intimately acquainted with the relationship between public ignorance and governmental disinformation. He was a veteran of Grenada.

"How's the leg?" he asked.

"Better," she said. "I got some antibiotic ointment and proper bandages. I don't even notice it."

She went over to a small knapsack that was lying on the dresser top, and took out a sheet of paper that she handed to Kirk. It was a list of names printed in ink.

"I was thinking," she said. "You know, the Contras have never received Stinger missiles. Not during the eighties, and not now."

He nodded. "They've always been under sanction."

"In that case I thought it was unlikely that there would have been very many people trained in their use."

Of course, he thought. A simple idea, but brilliant. If she were telling the truth, and the Contras had in fact hijacked their own missiles, then pinpointing exactly who had the skill to take down planes should be relatively easy.

He realized that the idea would have occurred to him, too, if he hadn't been so swayed by the logic of the Smith scenario.

"So I had our people find out who was known to have received advanced weapons training," she went on. "When we separated out all those still in Nicaragua or Honduras, we were left with a pretty short list." She gestured at the paper Kirk held in his hand.

Kirk looked at the names: Ernesto Rivera, Victor Hugo Tijerino, Javier Vega, and Eden Cabrera Cruz. All graduates of Fort Bragg.

None of the names meant anything to him.

"We're checking them out," she said. "If you have access to CIA files, you might want to do the same."

"I'll see what I can do," he said. "Thanks."

"And look, Kirk, if you need some help, you know, with your Spanish . . . I mean, it's very good but . . . it's Salvadoran. There are some differences."

She was also offering to help with an interrogation, and he knew it. There'd be some things she'd be willing to do that he wouldn't.

"Yeah, I may need you," he said.

"I was thinking about something else, too," she said after a pause. "What you said to me about . . . your family. I'm sorry for you, Kirk. No matter what happened in Grenada, they did not deserve to die like that."

"Please," he said. "Don't—"

She shook her head. "No, listen to me. I know about losing family, all right? What I am saying to you is this: there are those in your country who wish to overthrow our Revolution by force and you, in your way, are working to prevent that, which is done by recovering the missiles. I am doing the same and we will be successful, I believe. Afterward, then, I will do what I can to help you find out what happened to your wife and son. If any Nicaraguans were involved, they will be punished, I promise you."

"If not?"

"If not, I will help you do . . . what you need to do."

They were looking into each other's eyes. He felt that once again they had crossed some invisible line.

"Thank you," he said. "I appreciate the offer. ı don't really know what I'd do if I got my hands on them. But I think I'd probably want to be alone."

"I can understand that."

The moment was threatening to become a little too intimate, he knew, yet he was wavering. It had been a long time since he'd been with anyone he thought might have a genuine empathy for what he'd been through.

I know about losing family, all right?

"I have to go," he said.

"I'll phone you if we are able to narrow the list," she said.

"Good. Thanks again."

He was careful to use a pay phone in the motel lobby to call for a cab.

31

March 20

Seldom had an official visitor to the White House been searched as thoroughly as was the Nicaraguan ambassador, but she remained unruffled throughout. It was nine in the morning when she was finally shown into one of the President's private offices in the basement of the West Wing.

The ambassador wasted no time in coming to the point.

"The government of Nicaragua condemns this latest attack on a civilian aircraft in the strongest possible terms," she said to the President. "In no way is my government involved. It is contrary to our policy to condone terrorism by anyone, and I am prepared to extend to you our full cooperation in finding those responsible."

The President was still numb from the morning news, and it took a few moments for the ambassador's words to register.

Just after dawn, a DC-10 had taken off from Dulles, the international airport west of Washington in the Virginia countryside. Security had been increased in the area, but the airport was surrounded by woods and farmland. There were a lot of places to hide.

The DC-10 had been hit by a missile just after clearing the tree line. The tail engine had exploded, shearing off the entire tail assembly and rendering the plane unflyable. The pilot had done exceptionally well to crash it in a freshly plowed cornfield, away from human habitation.

In part because of the public's crisis of confidence, only eighty-nine people were aboard. All were killed. The perpetrators of the crime left no trace.

"I'm sorry, Madame Ambassador," the President said. "What did you say?"

"I said that we are prepared to help, however we can, to find those responsible and bring them to justice," she said.

"I see. Then tell us who the Committee for the Furtherance of Peace in Central America is."

"We don't know, Mr. President. If we did, we would tell you instantly, but this group is as much a mystery to us as to you. In no way does it have our cooperation or support."

"They are nevertheless acting on your behalf."

"No," the ambassador said angrily, "they are not! What they are doing can be of no benefit to our country. If you think otherwise, you are very mistaken."

"Then . . ." The President spread his arms helplessly. "Why?"

"There can be only one reason. It is the work of our enemies, who seek to coerce you into taking military action against us, such as your naval presence and the troop buildup in Honduras."

"You understand that I've had no choice in what I've done."

"Yes, I understand that. But it must go no further, Mr. President. Any military involvement between our countries is the last thing on earth we would want."

"I . . . just don't know what to believe anymore."

His face was drawn, for he hadn't been able to sleep well since the Boston tragedy, and God knew when he would get some rest again. Every last one of his many years pressed down on him.

The ambassador spoke gently, saying "Mr. President, I know how you are feeling. You would like some sign that we are not involved. Let me try to give it to you.

"I won't say that we don't seek many of the same accommodations as are contained in the terrorists' agenda. We do. But we don't want your money. Tell this 'committee' that you refuse to pay. Tell them in our name that you refuse. Then if they continue to insist on these 'reparations,' you will know for sure that it is not us. You will know them for the criminal blackmailers they are."

"But if I continue to resist their demands," the President said, "how many more people will die? Can you tell me that?"

"No," the ambassador said. "I'm sorry, Mr. President. I cannot."

"How'd it go?" Croaghan asked.

Diane McBain slumped in her chair and kneaded the back of her neck, tucking away a few stay blond hairs. She'd just returned to her office from another emergency meeting of the President and his advisers. "I don't know," she said. "Not good, I think. I've never seen the President looking so shaky. Or so . . ."

"Old?"

"Yeah, I guess old. He's in a no-win situation, Seamus, and I don't know how much longer he can stand the strain. I'm worried." She paused. "And how about you? How are you holding up?' "

Croaghan looked at her questioningly.

"I haven't seen you since the memorial service," she said. "Are you okay?"

That brought it all back. The pain as he absorbed the finality of his loss. The casket that couldn't be open because of how little was in there. The stupid platitudes mouthed by the mourners. The loneliness of the flight back and the long night by himself in his apartment. He hadn't talked to anyone about it except for the few impersonal words he'd exchanged with Steven Kirk.

"He was always there for me, Diane," he found himself saying. "When I was a kid. Before he decided to go back to Ireland." He gestured at his scarred face. "It was hard, growing up like this. But it would have been a lot harder if he hadn't always been there, standing up for me. I'm not sure I would have survived. You know how it was. You remember, don't you?"

She swallowed the lump in her throat. "Yes," she said. "I remember."

He chuckled as he wiped away a tear. "It's funny," he said. "Dermot Croaghan, the toughest kid on the block. Like he was destined for a cop from the Year One. And he turns around and becomes a priest on some rock pile in the middle of nowhere." He shook his head. "Only the Irish, right?"

She nodded, unable to speak. There was a pause. Finally he clapped his knees and said, "Well, it's over. And the best thing we can do for my brother, God rest him, is find the sonsofbitches who killed him. What happened at the meeting?"

"Well," she said, "we talked about the airline situation, of course. After the DC-10 went down, *everybody* canceled their reservations. Planes are sitting on the ground all over the place, so even those people who absolutely have to fly are having major problems. The companies can't afford to subsidize flights for a dozen passengers." She smiled ironically. "On the other hand, Amtrak and Greyhound can't begin to meet the demand. I think we're going to have shootings over a seat on the Metroliner."

"And there's nothing we can do about it."

"Not a lot," the National Security Adviser said. "Except to try to restore the public's faith in air travel. And I don't know how the President plans to do that. Everyone has at least a little fear of flying. Something like this just brings it right to the surface. Anyway, then there was the story. You hear about that?"

"Oh, no. Which story?"

"Tom Read had a copy of the midday edition of the *Post*," she said. "It had all the gory details on the shootdown at Dulles, which was bad enough. But it also had another story, by that Stokes woman, quoting her usual 'reliable White House source.' She wrote that the terrorists had contacted the President today and threatened a stepped-up series of missile attacks if he doesn't meet their demands. The damn story was a complete fabrication. Our leak is now spreading lies, Seamus."

"Jesus," he said.

"Yeah, the President's ripped. Not to mention Don Walker. But in any case, there was no counterbalance; the edition went to press too early to have reported the Nicaraguan ambassador's visit and the networks quoted Stokes's account verbatim. So the story's having a predictable effect. The crowd in Lafayette Park is growing. The calls and telegrams are starting to pour in; they're running fifteen to one for bombing the Sandinistas back to the Stone Age. Even our bleeding-heart *Post* is editorializing that it may be time for the President to take a harder line."

She shook her head sadly. "You know," she said, "I love this country, Seamus. God damn me if I don't. But once the American people get loaded for bear, Christ but it's hard to get them to put the guns away . . . ." She gazed at the far wall.

He waited a tactful moment, then said, "What did you decide? Anything?"

"I don't know," she said. "The can-do boys are pushing hard for some sort of military statement, of course. The rest are waffling around, waiting to see which way the wind's going to blow before they jump.

"The President is sticking to his guns. No further military moves. And he instructed Carini to work with the Nicaraguan ambassador to set up a timetable for negotiations. His point is that we're negotiating with the Nicaraguan government, not terrorists, since we don't really know who the terrorists are yet.

"And the President's also decided to follow the ambassador's recommendation about the money. The next time the blackmailer calls, we're going to let him know that the peace negotiations are in process but that we refuse to pay the billion."

"That's an awful risk to take," he said.

"Tell me about it. Anyway, he's at a meeting of the PFIAB right now, to see if they've got anything constructive to offer. And he's going down to the Hill this evening to address a joint session on the crisis. National TV. The only problem is, I don't think he knows what to say."

"You going to help him with the speech?"

She nodded. "Tom and I."

She gave him a look that meant it was time for her to get to work on it, that she wanted to be alone.

He cleared his throat and said, "Diane, I know this is a real bad time, but I've got to talk with you."

She looked him in the eye, then sighed and said, "More bad news? Come on, Seamus, give me a break."

"I don't know how bad it is, relatively. But it bears directly on the crisis and you ought to know about it. And I think, so should the President. If I keep it to myself any longer I . . . I'm going to feel liable."

She sighed again. "All right, what is it?"

He took a deep breath and told her everything he'd learned about the operations of the "shadow government."

When he'd finished, she looked at him strangely. "What's your source on all this?"

"You know me," he said. "I've got a way with computers. I looked at a lot of old agency files and stuff. In some cases, I put two and two together."

"Uh-huh. Well, I've got to tell you something, Seamus. This is not news."

"I don't understand."

"Oh, for God's sake. You knew perfectly well there was a black side to Sunflower. You helped *run* it. Why on earth do you think I put you in the CAT in the first place? So that the White House would have an eye on what was going on."

"Sure, but . . . Diane, making certain the Contras have enough bullets to stay in the field is one thing. The President wants that. But dealing them advanced weapons systems that there are supposed to be very tight controls on is something else entirely, isn't it?

"What's worse is that there's a pattern here, stretching back at least twenty-five years. These people have been making their own policy all that time. They do what they want to do, no matter who's in the White House or what restrictions the Congress lays on. You think the President would have given his 'tacit approval' if he'd found out they were shipping Stingers?"

"He wouldn't have been able to, no."

"Dammit, that's not the point! It wouldn't have crossed his mind. Not something that . . . illegal. Immoral. I don't know, something. He's not that kind of man."

"Look, this is the modern world. Sometimes things have to be done that don't look great in the short run so that—"

"Diane, two American airliners have been shot down," he said through gritted teeth.

"That's not our fault."

"Oh, yeah? And whose is it?"

There was a pause, then she said, "I don't know what you want me to do, Seamus."

"I think you should tell the President," he said.

"Tell him what, exactly?"

"I don't know. That there are a bunch of former agency people and ex-generals and international money men out there running their own foreign policy, I guess. And that they're doing it with the cooperation of their counterparts inside the government. I don't think he knows that."

"You don't."

"No, I don't. And I think he'd be damned upset to find out, but I think he'd want to know."

"I see," she said coolly. "All right, thank you, Seamus. I'll take it under advisement. Now, if you don't mind, I need to get to work on the President's speech."

Croaghan just looked at his old friend. No, he thought. She's not a part of it. She can't be.

Carla Stokes was clicking keys at the computer terminal in her cubicle at the *Post* when the phone rang.

"Stokes," she said.

"Carla, it's Don Walker."

"Well, hello, Mr. Attorney General," she said warmly. But he was all business.

"Have you thought over what we talked about last night?" he asked.

"Yes. Haven't made my mind up, though."

"Try this on, then. That story you wrote this morning, it's a goddamned lie. From start to finish. Your Smoking Gun is beginning to make them up."

"I don't understand. He's always—"

"Yeah, well, he isn't this time. Don't ask me why. What he's telling you to print is causing a lot of pain in the White House and unnecessary anxiety out in the country. Not to mention that the bastard is obviously setting you up to play the fool. Come on, help me, Carla."

There was a very long pause, then Stokes said, "All right, we can at least talk about it."

32

Kirk drove to Kenwood this time. He gave the Eagle a quick once-over out on Duddington Place and made a couple of routine tail-shaking maneuvers along the way, but he didn't feel the need for a high degree of caution. No one was gaining anything by tracking him to his father's house.

He'd arrived a half hour later than their agreed time, but when Esperanza let him in, Charles wasn't there. The meeting of the President's Foreign Intelligence Advisory Board had run a little over, she explained. And then they'd hastily scheduled a consultation with the President himself, which necessarily had to be brief. Charles was expected back shortly.

Would he care to wait?

Yes, he would, Kirk said.

Esperanza made him a cup of coffee and the two of them sat down in the living room.

For a few moments the only sound was the measured ticking of the grandfather clock in the far corner. The room was full of ghosts for Kirk. The most prominent being his mother's, of course. Her photograph, framed in gold, still rested on the mantel above the veined marble fireplace. She hadn't aged a day since that morning in the Plaza de los Diplomaticos.

Next to her was another ghost: himself as a senior in college, smiling wryly as if he understood what the world was about. Just before he'd dropped out of his father's life entirely.

There was no picture of Esperanza, though. Charles had never remarried, and the fiction that Esperanza was simply the housekeeper had been meticulously maintained. That one thing, Kirk thought, probably summed up his father better than any other.

He looked around some more. The furnishings too had an almost spectral appearance. They hadn't changed much in the nearly twenty years since he'd gone off to school. After El Salvador Charles's diplomatic wanderings had begun to wind down and his possessions had begun to acquire permanence.

Having taken in the room, his gaze rested on Esperanza. The petite Salvadoran was smaller than Piedad Andino, though built along the same lines. She also showed more Spanish blood and less Indian. She was not unattractive, and a good twenty years younger than his father.

"You still do not like me very much, do you, Steven?" she said.

He didn't really know what he felt.

"Nor your father," she continued.

Her tone was gentle. Some long standing hostility might have been lurking behind her dark eyes, but what she was saying lacked the force of accusation. When he still didn't reply, she added, "Your mother was a wonderful person, Steven, and what happened to her was a terrible thing. But it wasn't my fault, or yours. And it certainly wasn't your father's."

"I don't dislike you," he said neutrally. "Or Charles."

"You shouldn't," she said. "He is a decent man. If it were not for him, I would most certainly be dead. The leftists killed my father, you know. A teacher. Not even a political man. Just because he didn't oppose the government."

"Yes, I knew that. I'm sorry."

She smiled grimly. "And my brother joined the guerillas. Did you know that?"

He shook his head.

"The death squads got him." She shrugged. "Murderers on both sides. So what chance would there have been for me?"

"I don't know," he said. Who *could* know? he thought.

On the wall opposite him was a map of Mexico and the tiny republics of Central America, looking for all the world like a funnel with a long, snaky hose attached. And blood running through it, blood without end—he could almost see it. Suddenly he felt that he'd made a terrible mistake coming east with Smith. His own personal life had been so twisted up with the history of that tortured region, and it wasn't going to yield up its secrets without exacting its toll. He'd been a fool to think otherwise.

"Charles Kirk gave me a home when I had none," Esperanza said. "More than that, he gave my life some peace. You can never know how much that means."

Kirk didn't say anything. But what he thought was, you couldn't be more wrong, Esperanza. He may have given you peace, but he took mine away, and it was returned to me only years later. First by Susanna, then even more so by my son. I do know how much that means, because I would trade the rest of my life to have it back for a couple of days.

They looked at one another across a few feet of suburban Washington living room, and a chasm of centuries empty of understanding.

"My country, too," Esperanza said. "Your father has worked so hard to bring peace to my country."

God, Kirk thought, how could she so sincerely believe so monstrous a lie? The man must share nothing with her. Nothing but his tainted money and perhaps, occasionally, his sexless bed.

He stopped himself. He was blaming this woman for what she did not know, and that was wrong.

Esperanza studied him for a long moment, then said, "I can see that you believe you understand things about which you know nothing. In Salvador, such a belief would soon bring your death. I hope that it is not also true here."

He gestured at their surroundings and said, "You lost your family, Esperanza and you've found another. I've lost mine and have nothing."

"I know that, Steven. You may not believe it, but I have wept for your loss as if it were my own. We are much alike, you and I, though there is one thing you have not yet seen: it is rarely wise to unbury the dead."

Kirk stared at her. "What are you trying to say, Esperanza?" he asked.

But the moment was gone. Her expression changed to that of a pleasant, easygoing service person.

"Some more coffee?" she said.

By the time Esperanza had rustled up the second cup, Charles Worthington Kirk had hobbled through his front door, leaning heavily on his cane.

Kirk looked at his father, the bent back, small head, angular features, close-cropped silver hair. Like a frail, wizened bird, just barely able to scratch up meal from the dirt.

But the image faded quickly once Charles's gaze fell on his son. Charles's deep-set, deep blue eyes still burned with the fire of a much younger man.

"Hello, Steven," Charles said.

"Charles."

Esperanza helped the master of the house out of his tweed overcoat. Beneath it, Charles was dressed in the "diplomat's uniform," as Steven had come to think of it over the years: dark grey, chalk-striped worsted suit; pale blue broadcloth shirt; silk Rep tie in red/silver on navy; mirror polished black wing-tip shoes.

"Business?" Charles said to his son and Steven nodded.

The older man led the way to his office, slowly and with obvious difficulty. Only when he'd settled himself into the dark leather chair behind the mahogany desk did it seem that he might be relatively free of pain.

"Are you all right?" Steven asked.

"Of course," Charles said. "I tend to think of arthritis as God's way of reminding us that our minds so often outlive our bodies' usefulness. What can I do for you?"

"Esperanza said you were at a PFIAB meeting."

"True enough. There's very little that will drag me out of this house these days. But for the President . . ."

"The Council of Elders deliberates. And what conclusions does it draw?"

There was just the slightest hesitation before Charles said, "We feel that some kind of military intervention is inevitable. Don't you?"

"I would hope not," Steven said.

"Unfortunately, hope is in very short supply in the world. Other things work a great deal better."

"You're assuming the Sandinistas are behind the hijack," Steven said. "What if it's somebody else?"

Charles raised his eyebrows like they were the golden arches. "Is that what you believe?"

Steven paused. "I don't know."

"Well, do you have a theory?" Charles asked.

"I have a lot of them, but one rather obvious one is—"

"The Contras."

"Uh-huh. And the anti-Communist Cubans, or some combination thereof. The Contras know they've got a tough fight before they're restored to power, if they are. So why not prod the Americans to invade and then waltz in behind them?"

"Yes," Charles said, "it's possible. Except for one thing. I have very good connections in the exile community. I think if an operation of this magnitude had been planned, I would have heard about it."

"Even if it was completely compartmented?"

"I think so. We're talking about some pretty tight circles here."

"Still, I can't write the Contras off. They were the ones

the missiles were going to, so they were in the best position of anyone to hijack them." As Charles nodded uncertainly, his son hurried ahead, "You see, that's the problem I have with this one. Access. How would somebody on the outside find out about an operation as clandestine as the Stinger shipments?"

There was a pause as Steven allowed his words to sink in. Then Charles said. "You're not thinking . . ."

"I have to. Whoever it was could have had an accomplice within the Contra network, of course. Or . . . or it could have been an American, Charles."

"I don't buy that."

"I'm not trying to sell it. But at least consider it. Don't we have enough crazies right here at home? And wouldn't a lot of them like to see the Sandies fall? And don't a lot of them have sufficient resources?"

"It's still hard to swallow."

"Murder and treason are. On the other hand, a billion bucks can buy a lot of time to forget what you've done."

Charles picked up a pen and started doodling on the pad next to his telephone. He drew a circle, then a line through its center and another line at right angles to that one. Then he bisected those angles, and the ones that resulted.

Steven took from his shirt pocket a piece of paper with the names Piedad Andino had given him on it. He handed it to his father. "You know these men?" he said.

"Sure," Charles said, "they're all members of the resistance. What about it?"

"They're all highly trained military people. I want to know which of them is capable of mounting an operation like this one."

Charles looked his son in the eye. "Where did you get this?" he asked.

Steven didn't say anything.

"I thought we were working together," Charles said.

"We are. I'm asking you for something that might help me out in the field. If we were doing this by dead drop, our whole conversation today would have consisted of one question."

"I see," Charles said, though he obviously didn't like what he saw. "Any of them is probably competent enough. What else do you need?"

"Dossiers on all of them. Whatever you have in

your private files that's not in WALNUT. And their whereabouts."

"Steven, I don't keep track of—"

"A few minutes ago you were telling me how tight your connections in the exile community were."

Charles's jaw muscles tightened. "Don't try to badger me, son."

"I'm not," Steven said. "I would think this is a pretty simple request. Either you have the information or you don't."

"I can only try."

"Fine. Now?" Steven gestured at the desktop computer.

Charles scowled at him, but he booted up the computer and began clacking keys.

Fifteen minutes later Charles's dot-matrix printer made some buzzing noises for a while and then a seven-page, single-spaced document was in Steven's hand.

Steven scanned it, nodded and said, "Thanks, Charles."

"Oh, any time," his father said.

33

Only three of them took the call in the Cabinet Room: the President, his Chief of Staff, and his National Security Adviser. The call had been unanticipated, and there hadn't been time to assemble the crisis task force.

The voice had been altered once again, but they could not mistake the cadence of the spokesperson for the Committee for the Furtherance of Peace in Central America. It had been permanently etched in all their minds.

"Good day, Mr. President," the voice said. "I trust that you got my message."

God, the poor man looks ashen, Diane McBain thought. Though he was still a physically imposing presence, you could almost see his resources being drained out through his face.

"Is that your idea of a joke?" the President said.

"Not at all," the voice said. "We obviously didn't

communicate that well last time. I need to be certain that you take my meaning now."

"I take your meaning. You're a vicious, cold-blooded killer."

"Spare me the hypocrisy, please, and I'll spare you a reminder of the bodies of *campesino* women and children lying in ditches with American bullets in them. The point is, Mr. President, that our negotiations must begin moving forward. As long as our conditions are met, there will be no further loss of life."

"What guarantees do we have?" the President asked.

"You don't have any," the voice said. "Except that we will use all the rest of the missiles if you fail to act."

"We've halted the flow of military materiel into the area, as you requested. And we are negotiating. The Secretary of State has met with the Nicaraguan ambassador, and I met with her myself this morning. We're making progress."

"Not good enough. You say you've halted the flow of materiel, and yet your warships stand off the coast of Nicaragua and your troops are massed on her border."

"We have the right to protect our legitimate interests in the region."

"I'm afraid your actions strike us as more offensive than defensive."

"The attacks on our airliners must cease," the President said firmly. "If they do not, I will have no choice but to follow the advice of those who counsel retaliation."

"In which case the passengers on twenty-one more planes will die," the voice said. "And not all at once, I assure you, but spaced out over the life of the missiles. Your industry will remain immobilized for the next two months."

"And I can assure *you* that that will result in the destruction of the government you seek to aid. So where does that leave us?"

"With the need to resolve the situation to our mutual benefit, Mr. President. And let me just apprise you of one more fact while we're on the subject. Among the future targets is most certainly going to be Air Force One."

McBain looked quickly over at the President. The direct threat against his life was obviously not an idle one. He could of course avoid the use of Air Force One for the next sixty days. But he couldn't do the same with

Marine One—the Presidential chopper—without becoming a virtual prisoner inside his own White House.

"The risks go with the job," the President said evenly. "My life is not more highly valued than those of any of your victims."

"Admirably put," the voice said. "But you must consider whether your successor would be able to adequately fill your shoes."

There was a long pause before the President spoke again. "All right," he said, "let's stop playing *what if*. I'm prepared to meet your demands. We begin negotiating immediately. But no doublecrosses. If you don't act in good faith, there will be no alternative to a military solution."

Read was shaking his head vigorously. McBain looked at the President with surprise. He dismissed the both of them with a wave of his hand.

"Tell me what you require to be assured that we are on the right track," the President added.

"Very good, Mr. President," the voice said. "I'm pleased to find that you are a reasonable man. Now, specifically, we need the negotiation and signing of the treaty as specified, and we need to see it being done in the open, perhaps the U.N.

"Next, the demilitarization of the region must begin at once, and it must be highly visible.

"And finally, the cash must begin to flow."

"We can accede to all of these," the President said. "With the exception of the money. We're not prepared to pay ransom."

"The money is not a bargaining chip."

"There must always be points of compromise, and I believe this to be one. After relations between our countries have normalized, then we can talk about aid."

"No. We're talking about reparations, not ransoms. Money is the only thing that means anything to Americans. Paying it serves as an admission before the world of guilt for your criminal conduct in Nicaragua. This is a crucial part of the process."

"Then we have a sticking point," the President said. "Perhaps you need to discuss it with the rest of the committee."

"I don't need—" The voice paused. When it spoke

again, it was tightly controlled. "Yes," it said. "Perhaps I do. You will be hearing from me, Mr. President."

When the caller hung up, both Read and McBain tried to speak at once, with McBain momentarily deferring to the more senior official.

"I think that's a mistake, Mr. President," Read said. "Are you seriously going to try to negoitiate with those people?"

"We need to do something, Tom. There can't be any more killing."

"But there's got to be a little stall time left. It's only been four *days*!"

The President turned to McBain. "How close are we to nailing the bastards?" he asked.

"Close, I think," she said. "The Director says his people nearly have the supply route mapped out. And the bureau has its agents in place all over, just waiting for a stray word. A few of my people are in the field, too. Pretty soon somebody is going to tell somebody who tells us and we'll have them."

"Doesn't sound like we're a whole hell of a lot closer to me," the President said.

"Sir, as Tom pointed out, it's only been four days. The terrorists have probably been planning this for a year."

"I still think it's a mistake," Read said. "Now you're locked in. If you don't live up to their expectations, they're apt to cut loose a whole podful of the Stings."

"Well, it's done, Tom!" the President said. "And I expect the support of everyone." He looked at McBain as well. "Are we clear on that?"

"Yes, sir," they said in unison.

"Good. We negotiate in good faith and hope that they do the same. It is the policy of this Administration to avoid thoughtless military adventuring, whether it's in Guatemala or wherever. We should have learned a long time ago that it doesn't pay to fight other people's civil wars for them."

"I agree, Mr. President," McBain said. "It's in our best long-term interest if we can resolve this without actually going into *Nicaragua*." She put just the slightest emphasis on the word. "It's a wise decision."

"What about the money?" Read asked.

"I wanted to test him," the President said, "as the

Nicaraguan ambassador suggested. See if he was willing to compromise on that to get the other things. I guess we'll have to wait until he checks it out, which does maybe buy us some more time."

"You think he has to check it out?" McBain asked. "I wonder. The way he said, 'I don't have to,' and then cut himself off, it made me question whether this might not be a one-person committee we're dealing with."

"One or a hundred and one," Read said, "he's still shuffling to the tune the boss is playing in Managua. He isn't going near a compromise until they okay it."

The President grunted. "Probably not," he said. "In the meantime, I've got a speech to give. What am I supposed to say?"

McBain handed the President two typewritten pages that she extracted from her leather portfolio.

"The important thing," she said, "is to convey that we're doing something. The media's been portraying us as frozen in our tracks, and you need to effectively counter that."

"Right," Read said. "Stress that we moved our warships into place immediately and have a well-trained fighting force within striking distance of the border. We're talking to the Russians as well as the Sandies. Our investigative agencies are on double overtime."

"It might not hurt to make a direct appeal to the terrorists," McBain said. "As long as you can do it without appearing weak."

"Ask Congress for more emergency aid to the Contras, definitely," Read said. "There's no way they could fight you on that right now."

"And there's got to be some, I don't know, some kind of reassurance that it's okay to fly," McBain said. "I know you can't force people to, but . . . there's got to be some way to get the message across."

"How about a symbolic gesture on my part?" the President said.

McBain and Read both looked at him, first with incomprehension, then with dismay.

"You don't mean . . ." Read said.

"It wouldn't have to be Air Force One," the President said. "Maybe just to Andrews and back on Marine One. Something to show the people that their President isn't afraid to announce that he's flying somewhere and then get up there and do it."

"Mr. President, no!" McBain said.

"You mean, tell the terrorists ahead of time when and where to shoot you down?" Read said incredulously. "That's making yourself the Judas goat. It's crazy."

"But it has its appeal," the President said. "Don't you think we could protect Marine One?"

"In general, yes," McBain said. "It's got excellent evasive hardware, and we could escort it with Cobra gunships. But we're talking about your *life*. Something could always go wrong. We can't risk that."

"Well, I'm going to seriously consider it," the President said. "Every air traveler today is putting himself in danger. A real leader will assume some small part of the risk himself."

"I hope you decide against it, sir," Read said, and McBain firmly nodded her agreement.

The President got up. "All right," he said. "I want to go over these notes and think a little more about the speech. Let's meet about it again later this afternoon."

"Later, Mr. President," Read said as he headed for the door.

McBain lagged behind. "Mr. President," she said, "I wonder if I might talk to you privately just for a few minutes."

He looked at her with annoyance.

"It could be important," she added.

"Very well," he said, and he led the way to his study.

"It's about the original supply line," she said when they were alone. "For the Stingers?" The President nodded. "The agency has been telling us all along that it was a private-sector operation, privately financed by Contra supporters and run outside of official channels. But that presupposes that the missiles were bought on the black market and, well, that's beginning to seem unlikely." She went on to tell him of Croaghan's concerns about the military and its private-sector cohorts.

"And the agency might have provided covert assistance?" he asked when she'd finished.

"Yes, I'm afraid so. So we're looking at a possible crime, the illegal sale and attempted delivery of Stinger missiles. But worse than that, whoever was involved is now indirectly responsible for the deaths of all those Americans. This could be a major scandal, sir."

The President looked at his National Security Adviser coldly. "Miss McBain," he said, "the scandal is the least part of it. Innocent lives have been lost. Our civil aviation is completely disrupted. The United States is being blackmailed. If members of the military or the agency were involved then they must be held accountable."

"Yes, sir. I wasn't suggesting that we provide damage control for the Pentagon or the CIA. If they're in it, they'll pay for it." She took a deep breath and let it out. "However, all this does suggest a further possibility, too. Remote perhaps, but . . . Someone inside the Administration could be involved, too. That would be a disaster, Mr. President."

"No, God damn it! You may not under any circumstances cover this up! If any of my staff is involved, I will appoint a special prosecutor to deal with them. And I would expect the resignations to begin with yours. Is that clear enough for you?"

"Yes, sir," McBain said. "Perfectly. I'll continue with the internal investigation and I'll keep you fully apprised of its progress."

"See that you do. Now, if you don't mind . . ."

McBain nodded to him and left the study. As she walked slowly back to her West Wing office, she wondered how in hell things were ever going to work out.

34

"Congratulations, Mosby," Henrik Bruderdam said into the phone. "That was an excellent job."

Vega grunted at his end. "Save your breath," he said.

He hadn't called the pig American in order to be complimented on his marksmanship. The shoot-down at Dulles had gone well, but he'd had a brush beforehand with one of the police patrols that had almost scrubbed the whole thing. Vega was ready for some tangible results.

"Now, now," Bruderdam said, sounding like a father trying to calm an unruly child.

The young man was a surly, ignorant spic, Bruderdam thought, and he still held the location of the missiles close to his chest. It was time to force him to give up his secret. After that, he'd be more use to them dead than alive. They could set him up to take the fall as planned. What's more, Bruderdam wanted to supervise the turncoat's end personally, make it a particularly ugly one.

"Have you talked to the President?" Vega said.

"Yes, of course," Bruderdam said. "They know we're serious."

"That isn't what I want to hear."

"Mosby, who died and left you boss?"

In the silence from the other end, Bruderdam could almost make out the grinding of teeth. He sighed. "All right," he said, "what is it that you do want to hear?"

"I want to know exactly what's happening," Vega said.

"The President is moving on all our demands except the money. He's frightened and in the process of capitulating, but it's going to take a little time—"

"I haven't *got* time! Every policeman in this country is looking for me. We need some action and I thought your people were pushing for it."

"The President is an obstinate old bastard," Bruderdam said. "More so than we figured. Our people inside are pushing him and eventually he's going to come around. Trust me, Mosby."

"The hell with trust!" Vega said. "If we don't have the money or military action, one or the other, then we've got *nothing*. You know, if the President's screwing around with us, maybe we're just dealing with the wrong man."

Bruderdam paused. How had he ever let Stonewall and Grant talk him into trying to run this lunatic? he wondered. The man was a loose cannon. "Mosby," he said calmly, "we need to plan our next move very carefully. I still believe this President can be manipulated. What I want you to do is come out to the island so that we can go over everything face to face. I can have the plane in Orlando tomorrow morning."

"Fuck you," Vega said. "I don't need you."

"Look, Mosby—"

But Vega had broken the connection. Bruderdam

slammed the phone down. What did *that* mean, dealing with the wrong man? God damn the little greaser.

Bruderdam immediately set up his computer, and for the next couple of hours electronic-mail messages flashed back and forth through the Gustavia Brewing Company's satellite channel:

Stonewall—Mosby may be proceeding on his own initiative. Potential attempt to oust CEO. Suggest terminating his participation in this project ASAP. Necessary that we first take delivery of merchandise. Sherman.

Sherman—Mosby whereabouts unknown, but believe somewhere this city. Kirk active here in recovery attempt and may have skill to locate Mosby if assisted. Stonewall.

Mr. Grant—Mosby threatening project. Believe he may now be working for removal of CEO. This might not be undesirable considering caliber of deputy CEO, but further involvement of Mosby unacceptable. Stonewall trying to use Kirk to locate Mosby and recover inventory. Sherman.

Sherman and Stonewall—All assistance to Kirk to conclude Mosby participation. Merchandise must return our control, but imperative Kirk not bankrupted in process. Grant.

Burnside—Activities to date apparently unpersuasive to CEO. Advise take local supplementary action. Sherman.

Sherman—Agree on need for timely action. Local rep being retained for activity which will make CEO response unavoidable. Completion soonest. Burnside.

Security at the Capitol was as tight as it had ever been. Every outside entrance was guarded by at least two Secret Service officers. Inside, everyone had to pass through two checkpoints, each of which involved a body search and metal detector scan. Equipment and personal items were visually inspected as well as fluoroscoped. And finally, all reporters and congressional aides, even the members of Congress themselves, were required to wear special identifying credentials.

The Presidential procession to the Hill had been made down a Pennsylvania Avenue that was cleared of traffic. Police blocked the side streets and maintained a close watch on rooftops. The executive limo (itself with state-of-the-art armoring) was flanked front and back, and on both sides, by escort vehicles that had been built to withstand assault by anything short of a tank.

Before walking out into the glare of the TV lights, the President said, "I feel like a prisoner."

And Read replied, "For the time being, Mr. President, you are."

The speech itself, commentators agreed afterward, was almost entirely devoid of substance. But then, to tip one's hand in such a delicate situation would obviously run the risk of further disaster.

Toward the end, however, the President electrified the audience by proposing to demonstrate his confidence in the safety of air travel. As many people knew, he said, there was a plane flying into Andrews Air Force Base the following morning, bringing the remains of ten American servicemen that had been located by the Vietnamese government and returned home. The President announced on national TV that he would fly by helicopter to Andrews and meet that plane.

On the ride back to the White House, Read said, "I really think that was a mistake, sir."

The President shrugged. "If I don't provide leadership," he said, "who will?"

"That's not leadership. That's telling the enemy exactly when and where they can kill you."

"Come on, Tom. If they want to kill me badly enough, they'll find a way. A sniper could have done it while I was crossing the parking lot this evening. A suicide car filled with high explosives could do it in the next five minutes. The president of the United States can't become a hermit."

"This is different than the normal risks. A lot different. They've got Stingers, for Christ's sake, in case you'd forgotten."

"And Marine One's got the best electronics in creation. My mind's made up, Tom. I said I'm going to do it and I will."

"Well, I'm going to talk with Diane," Read grumbled. "And Monty. You're going to have some Cobra escort ships; you can't refuse that. But what I'd really like—and I want you to think about this—is for Marine One to take off without you actually being on board."

"Is this legal?" Carla Stokes asked.

The Attorney General of the United States had just finished hard-wiring her telephone to a Uher tape recorder in her desk drawer.

"Yes and no," Don Walker said. "It's not an illegal bug, since you've given your consent. Anyone's allowed to record their own telephone conversation. All the law says is that if you do, you have to notify anyone at the other end that you've just punched the *Record* button. I wouldn't be tempted too often if I were you."

"Basically I don't want to record anyone but Smoking Gun."

"Right. And since it'd defeat our purpose to tell him what you're doing, you're going to have to break the law."

"Well, this is a first," Stokes said. "Here's the USAG advising me on how to commit a crime."

Walker grinned. "Just one tape with his voice on it, Carla," he said. "Then we disconnect the thing. And I ain't gonna use the recording in court."

"You're going to voice-print him? By comparing the tape to what?"

"Sorry. That's beyond your need-to-know, lady."

"I'm hanging my ass out for you, Donnie boy. Never mind the cops. I'm more worried about what Smoking Gun'll do to me if I help you nail him."

Walker went over to her, put his arms around her waist, and let his hands slide downward. She had a rear end like Flo-Jo.

"Don't worry," he said. "Nobody touches that fine tight ass. I guarantee it."

She smiled at him mischievously. "Nobody?" she said.

Back in the good old days, Danilo Baez had been what Wild Bill Casey's NSC/agency cabal referred to as a UCLA, or "unilaterally controlled Latino asset." It referred to those who were completely off-line, meaning outside the normal command structure used for the direction of foreign agents. UCLAs were accountable only to the specific individuals within the greater intelligence community who had hired them.

He'd had plenty of work in those days because of his diving skills. There was the mining of the harbors, the sabotage raids. He'd done what was required of him with efficiency, and hadn't asked a lot of questions. And the men who'd used him had compensated him well.

But after Reagan left office, the demand for his services had declined drastically. Baez had had to take a job—less exciting, less well paid, though also less dangerous—guiding American scuba enthusiasts over the reefs off Roatan and the other Honduran Bay Islands.

Still, he'd kept his hand in as best he could. He had a contact in La Ceiba, forty miles away on the mainland, and he took the occasional contract that came his way when those making the decisions up in El Norte had need of his services. That was happening a little more frequently these days, with the renewal of the Nicaraguan civil war.

The La Ceiba contact called himself Joe. No surname was used. All Baez knew about Joe was that he was well connected and paid his bills promptly. Better yet, the payments were in hard American dollars.

Baez had returned from an afternoon dive excursion and was attending to routine gear maintenance when the message came through on shortwave radio.

"Your mother's sick again," the co-owner of the resort said as she handed Baez the message.

The playfulness in the way she said it suggested a lack of concern for the health of Baez's mother. It was generally believed by the resort's management that Baez's periodic trips to the mainland were other than family-related. Consensus was that a girlfriend was involved. But Baez didn't abuse his leave privileges and was otherwise an excellent divemaster, so his absences were tolerated.

The message was from his Aunt Josefina and said simply that his mother had taken a turn for the worse and he should come over as soon as possible.

Aunt Josefina was Joe. The turn for the worse meant an important job was in the offing. And as soon as possible meant exactly that.

Baez didn't bother to pack As it was, he barely made it to the airport before the Tan Sahsa DC-3 took off on the last of its daily flights to the mainland.

An hour later he was with Joe in a waterfront bar in La Ceiba, having a great deal of difficulty believing what he'd just heard. Though Joe spoke Central American Spanish very well, it was obviously not his native tongue, and Baez felt that perhaps he had misunderstood. "Could you please say again?"

Joe repeated the job offer, and it came out the same way. An American ship, a frigate escort, was currently docked at San Lorenzo—Honduras's deep-water port in the Gulf of Fonseca—while it underwent some minor repair work. Baez's assignment was to plant a magnetic mine on the ship. Since the ship was due to leave port in thirty-six hours, time was of the essence.

"I don't understand," Baez said when Joe had finished once again. "I work *for* the Americans, not against them. I thought that you did, too."

"I do," Joe said. "This assignment comes from the Americans themselves. I have checked and am convinced that it is so. All of the people involved I have worked with many times before."

"But . . . to plant a mine on one of their own ships? What good can come of this?"

Joe shrugged. "It is a small mine and not fully armed. It will not do much harm; no one will be hurt. Why they should want to do this slight damage to their ship, you can guess as well as I. They would not tell me, any more than they would tell you."

Baez looked at Joe for a long moment, then said, "They wish to place the blame on someone else, don't they?"

Joe shrugged again and didn't reply.

"I don't know," Baez said. "It does not sound right."

"The payment is fifteen thousand American dollars," Joe said. "In cash. Plus expenses, of course."

Baez's breath caught in his throat, but his face betrayed no emotion. Fifteen thousand American dollars. He quickly calculated what he could do with so much money. He could do a lot.

"Tell me some more," Baez said.

Quickly Joe outlined the plan. It was designed to be a quick-in, quick-out operation. The pay was generous, Joe explained, not because it was so terribly risky, but because it had to go off without a hitch, and on schedule. And in addition, it was a night dive without lights, a job that required a high degree of skill.

Baez thought it over.

There were obviously some complicated politics involved here. Yet in the past Joe had always been straight with him. Baez found it impossible to believe he was now being asked to work for the other guys.

And then, there was the money.

"All right," Baez said finally. "I'll do it. But it had better be as you say. No one gets hurt. We're not actually working against our friends. If you haven't told me the truth, you will regret it."

35

Kirk had left a message for Piedad Andino, but she hadn't yet gotten back to him.

He was tired of staring at words. Black words on a printed page, green words on the glowing CRT screen.

He'd spent the evening studying dossiers. First, the dossier on Tomas Herrera that Croaghan had compiled and electronic-mailed to him. And second, the files on the four names Andino had given him, the Contras who had received advanced weapons training.

Information on the latter had come first from Charles, during Kirk's last visit to Kenwood. Later, though, Kirk had run the names through WALNUT on his own. Then he'd compared the two printouts. As he might have predicted, his father's files were a little more complete.

He'd also cross-checked the info on Herrera and found that Croaghan's rap sheet was a lot more detailed than his own, especially in regard to the subject's dark side.

What Kirk had been looking for all night was some insignificant connection between Herrera, who seemed very likely to be involved in the blackmail plot, and one of the other four, who might then be presumed to be still active in it.

The problem was, there were a lot of connections.

The five men were upper-level members of the Nicaraguan exile community, which meant they belonged to a fairly exclusive club whose membership hadn't changed much since the exodus that followed the revolution in 1979: former officers of Somoza's *guardia*, businessmen, landowners, those of the pre-revolutionary elite who'd managed to escape the country with their assets reasonably intact or who'd supplemented their income with agency money. Some had tried to repatriate after the 1990 election, some hadn't. Since the FSLN had reclaimed power, they'd all been fully or primarily based in the States, and they all more or less knew each other.

Herrera had been by far the most publicly visible one of the five. He'd done a lot of out-front fund-raising over the years, to go along with his involvement in the black ops that were documented in the dossier.

There was no specific record of his role in the cocaine-for-arms swaps of the early eighties, but then there wouldn't be. Evidence of those deals had been shredded years ago, when the participants had hurried to cover their asses after the Iran/Contra scandal broke. But Kirk could read between the lines. Herrera was the type. He'd been a hired assassin, and likely a drug dealer as well.

If Herrera had suddenly started doubling for the Sandinistas, he'd fooled everybody.

Being a double agent was a delicate balancing act. You had to do enough to convince the people you were trying to con of your sincerity, but not so much as to make your real employers suspect a betrayal. Your record usually ended up looking like an exercise in caution.

That definitely did not describe Tomas Herrera. He'd committed himself to things, dangerous things at times, and he'd seen them through.

Kirk was all but forced to accept Herrera as the genuine article. Which meant what? Kirk could see only two possibilities. Either the attack on Andino had nothing to do with the hijack/blackmail plot. Or else the Contras were up to their eyeballs in it.

Then he focused his attention on the men from Andino's list.

Of the four, he'd eliminated two from current consideration. Ernesto Rivera would have been a good bet, but he was primarily a field commander and all reports placed him in the bush in Honduras at this time. And Victor Hugo Tijerino's file had been closed two days earlier. He'd been knifed to death in Miami, in a dispute police there were calling drug-related.

Naturally, Rivera could actually be in Washington, and Tijerino alive and well. But it was better to try the probables first, and question the veracity of the files later.

The remaining two names were Javier Vega and Eden Cabrera Cruz.

Cruz was a real possibility. He'd directed intelligence activities for Somoza and later worked closely with the Argentines during their initial organization and training of Contra forces. He was qualified in all manner of weaponry and was an explosives expert. He hadn't bought into the UNO's electoral victory and had remained in New York. Through all of the political changes, he had presumably continued doing what he did best.

Then there was Vega.

Kirk had been intrigued with him right away. He'd had all the requisite training (Fort Bragg, School of the Americas). His father had been a highly successful business-man and Somoza confidant; his brother had been a member of the *guardia* who was killed during the last, hopeless defense of Managua in 1979.

Vega was by far the most highly educated of the four. His father had carried out enough money to position himself in the South Florida real estate market and send his remaining son through school at the University of Miami. Javier had majored in business, and following his secret post-graduate instruction, divided his time between his father's business interests and the Contra cause.

After the election, he'd apparently seen himself as a key figure in the reconstruction of the Nicaraguan econ-omy, but the reascendancy of the FSLN had scuttled his plans. Now he appeared to be once again hard at work for the opposition.

The key word was *appeared,* because what had really caught Kirk's eye was the notation that Javier Vega was strongly suspected of being a double agent for the Sandinistas, and should be treated as such in any contacts with the agency. There was also speculation that he might be allied with a radical leftist/Grenadian exile faction in Managua that favored terrorist tactics against all foreign supporters of the Contras.

A slow chill came over Kirk when he read that, but he had to shrug it off. Personal feelings must be kept bottled up until the proper moment. That moment would come.

Looking through the file, he was struck by one other detail. The elder Vega had a prominent business partner, a man named Enrique Salazar. The latter, now near the top of the Contra chain of command, had been a colonel under Somoza. One of his brightest officers then had been the young Tomas Herrera and, subsequently, Herrera had worked closely with his old commander.

It might not be that elusive solid connection Kirk was looking for, but it was provocative.

Kirk closed his eyes and constructed mental pictures of Cruz and Vega. Not good enough. He got up and called his father.

"Charles," he said, "I want photographs of two of the men from that list. Javier Vega and Eden Cabrera Cruz."

"Still chasing shadows, Steven?" Charles said.

"I don't want anyone else to know. Especially Smith. Can you get them?"

"Mmmm, yes, I suppose so. But it might take a day or two. It'll have to be done pretty obliquely."

"Faster is better. Get them faxed to you if you have to."

Charles pause, then said, "Look, Steven, I hope you know what you're doing. You saw the President's speech tonight?"

"Uh-huh."

"He's setting himself up as a target, Steven. I don't like it. By tomorrow afternoon we could be in a much worse mess than we are now."

"I'm sorry, Charles. I can't have the missiles by morning."

"I realize that. I just hope you're on the right track, that's all. I don't want to lose the President. Or—or you."

That was about as close as his father was going to come to expressing affection. "Thanks," Steven said, "but the President is well protected and I can take care of myself. The only other thing I can say is, I believe I'm following the right trail. In any case, I need the photographs."

"I'll see what I can do," Charles said.

Less than five minutes later, the phone rang.

"Smith," the agency man said over the line. "I've got

some information for you. Ruben Tellez, the last link in the chain before the Stingers went astray? He's in Washington and he wants to come in."

"Why now?"

"He knows something. He can see these people mean business as plainly as we can, and he's got to assume they think he's already traded them for his own security. He's scared."

"Has he talked?" Kirk asked.

"Not yet. He's demanding protection first. I think he's worth it, Steven. I want you to escort him."

"All right. Where?"

"Come to my apartment at the Watergate. We can debrief him here and then arrange to have him moved to a safe house."

"Where is he?"

Smith gave Kirk an address on California Street, just off Connecticut Avenue.

"Apartment 606," Smith said.

"What's the routine?" Kirk asked.

"His code name is Winslow. You're there to take him home. That'll do." Smith paused for a beat, then continued, "The other side is looking for him too, of course. We don't know how close they are. So be careful, Steven."

"I'd planned on it. Can you take him any time tonight?"

"I'll be here," Smith said.

After Kirk hung up, he looked at his watch. Nearly ten o'clock. He decided to give Andino until midnight to check in. Then he'd go out alone.

She beat the deadline by twenty minutes, and he found that he was relieved she had.

"I've got something," he told her. "Don't want to talk about it over the phone. Can you be at the Dupont Circle Metro entrance in half an hour?"

"Sure."

"I'll pick you up there."

36

Kirk tried his best to rationalize what he was doing.

He was taking the woman along because his intuition told him it was the right thing to do. He was taking her along because her command of Nicaraguan Spanish might be useful in interrogating Tellez. He was taking her along because she was a skilled operative who could help out if something went wrong.

But it was no use.

Those things were not irrelevant, but the truth was, Andino was bait, as well. The people Kirk was after had followed her to the meeting on the Mall; they might follow her again tonight. If they did, he might be able to take one of them alive. And that might prove more valuable than bringing in Tellez.

As he wheeled the Eagle around Dupont Circle, Kirk detached himself from his personal feelings for the woman. They could only get in the way.

Andino was where she'd promised to be. She was wearing baggy fatigues and a loose denim jacket, making her body as shapeless as possible. Her dark hair was pulled back and tied behind her. There was no makeup on her face and her expression was sullen. The neighborhood was known for the diversity of its night life, but no one was going to mistake her for a pickup.

Kirk pulled to the curb and she got in. Then he drove back through a hundred-and-eighty-degree arc and headed north on the narrow strip of Connecticut Avenue that rides above the tunnel under the circle.

"I got a tip on where to find Ruben Tellez," Kirk said. "He's the last one to have seen the missiles before they were hijacked. You know him?"

"No," Andino said. "Where is he?"

"An apartment on California Street. I'm supposed to

pick him up and deliver him to our side before the other side finds him and kills him. But I thought we might have a little chat with him first."

She smiled. "That sounds like a good idea."

The commercial enterprises of lower Connecticut Avenue slid past: skinny old row buildings housing restaurants, boutiques, travel agencies. The Eagle merged with traffic coming out of the tunnel under the circle, crossed the intersection of Florida Avenue, and began up the long hill commanded by the Hilton.

Halfway to the top, Kirk turned left on California Street. He drove past the address Smith had given him, his eyes (and hers) searching methodically for anything that looked out of place, anything that in the slightest way suggested a setup.

They spotted nothing. California was a quiet residential street of small, older apartment buildings dug into the side of the hill. Few lights showed at this hour, and no pedestrians were about.

Kirk cruised some more. He turned right on Twenty-Third Street, took it to Kalorama Road, turned back onto Connecticut, and came at California from the opposite direction. Still, nothing caught his attention.

He parked the Eagle on the street and they walked back to the apartment building.

Kirk pressed the button for 606 and the speaker grille emitted a trebly "Yeah?"

"I'm here to take Winslow home," Kirk said.

There was a buzz and Kirk and Andino were granted entrance to the building lobby. Nothing remarkable about it. There were naugahyde-covered benches along the wall to either side, with potted ferns next to them. Three steps up to the elevators and hallways branching off left and right. Flanking the elevators, six-foot-high mirrors with gold flecks and a peeling gilt frame. A slight scent of sauerkraut lingered in the otherwise musty air.

Kirk watched the two of them in the mirror as they went up the stairs, the way they looked, walking together. Andino was wary, her attention flicking here and there, just as it should. Then, just for a moment their eyes met and held. And Kirk felt his stiff professional mask slide smoothly away from him, like a lost oar adrift in the fog.

She must have read his thoughts, because she gave him a little half-smile before returning to her surveillance of the hallways.

Kirk, slightly embarrassed by the wordless interchange, zeroed in on the elevator buttons and pushed the one with the black up arrow. A bell chimed softly and the right-hand doors slid open.

They rode up to the sixth floor in silence.

The door to 606 had a button in its center, with a fish-eye peephole above. Kirk pressed the button, sounding a two-note bell. Andino flattened herself against the wall, out of sight.

Kirk apparently passed visual inspection, because a few seconds later the door opened and he went inside, into a narrow entryway.

Andino was right behind him, moving fast. As the door closed and automatically latched itself, she slammed her shoulder into the small of Kirk's back. He stumbled forward into Tellez and the two men fell together in a tangled pile. When they looked up, they were staring at humanity's manufactured version of the cosmic black hole: the empty circle at the barrel end of a silenced 9-mm semiautomatic pistol.

Her face was grim. "Who else is here?" she demanded of Tellez. For emphasis she worked the slide on the pistol, chambering a round, and flicked off the safety.

Kirk stared at her in disbelief. His lips curled around the "Whh" sound, but he didn't speak the word.

Tellez was a short, pinched-faced man with heavily oiled black hair, dressed in a finely tailored flannel suit. He was also terrified. He held both hands up in front of his face.

"Nobody!" he said quickly. "I swear it. Nobody."

She paused, listening intently. "Up," she commanded. "Both of you."

The two men got to their feet, Tellez shakily, Kirk cautiously.

"Turn around," she said to Tellez. When he'd done so, she said to Kirk, "Now put your arms around his waist and lock your fingers. And *you* keep your hands in your pockets. I *will* shoot." The men did as they were told. "Now show me around," she ordered Tellez.

The men shuffled dutifully through the apartment, Andino following with her aim centered unwaveringly on

Kirk's back. Even with the silencer, the pistol was power-ful enough that a bullet would blast its way through both bodies.

It was a quick trip. There were only three rooms: living room/kitchen, bathroom, bedroom. Nowhere was there a single personal touch to indicate the place had been lived in. Andino checked carefully. Tellez had been telling the truth.

They ended up in the living room. Andino had Kirk lie prone on the gold carpet, his hands crossed underneath him, between his legs, and his head turned so he couldn't see the other two. Tellez was told to sit cross-legged. She squatted behind him and nudged the base of his skull with the pistol.

"This gun has a very loose trigger," she said to him in Spanish. "Sometimes it goes off by itself. I want you to start talking and don't stop until you've told me every-thing you know about the missiles. Now!"

In the fast-moving stream of Spanish that then poured out of Tellez, Kirk missed a word here and there, but was able to follow it.

He'd acted as a go-between, Tellez said. He'd done similar jobs many times before, with all kinds of weapons secretly bound for the war. There was no reason to suspect any complications this time.

The Stingers had been crated, marked FARM MACHINERY, and were awaiting shipment out of Norfolk when the crates were switched with the cooperation of a friendly inside the U.S. military.

"Who?" Andino interrupted.

Tellez wasn't sure, someone in the warehouse. Many people in the services cooperated with the anti-Communist effort in Nicaragua.

Andino nodded for him to continue.

It was a standard procedure, Tellez went on. A clan-destine shipment with one destination could easily be rerouted because the original intended recipient couldn't complain without revealing that they were expecting some-thing they weren't authorized for in the first place.

The diverted missiles had then been loaded into a rental truck and Tellez had driven them to Corpus Christi. There, he'd parked the truck in a designated spot and, as instructed, walked to a nearby hotel, where a room was reserved for him. The room was situated so that he could see who came to get the truck. If anything went wrong, he was to call a local phone number immediately. If everything looked right he was to return to Washington, ignorant of where the shipment went next.

The truck had been picked up within an hour, and that was when he had first begun to feel uneasy about the whole operation.

The new driver was supposed to have been a man named Vargas. But Vargas didn't show up. Another man came in his place. Tellez assumed he must have been a replacement, because he had the proper keys to drive the truck away.

"Did you recognize this man?" Andino said.

"Yes, yes," Tellez said. "So I wasn't so worried at the time. It was Francisco's boy. Javier Vega."

Kirk's sharp intake of breath was nearly audible. Andino betrayed nothing; she merely told Tellez to continue.

Still, Tellez said, it was a change in the plan, and he'd called the emergency number. There was no answer.

Now he was more concerned. He called home and passed word of what had happened into the command chain of the Nicaraguan government-in-exile. He was told that everything was okay and he could take the plane back to D.C.

Who was the superior to whom he reported? Andino asked.

He'd phoned the business office of Enrique Salazar, Tellez said. He'd talked first with an aide, but it was the colonel himself who had closed out Tellez's part in the operation.

Andino prodded her captive and he moved rapidly through the remainder of his narrative. He'd returned to Washington, still uneasy but hopeful that his concerns were unfounded. No one had contacted him about anything.

Just when his life appeared to be returning to normal, the Boston missile attack had occurred, and he knew for certain that something had gone very wrong. Fearing for his life, he went immediately to ground in this apartment, which he'd paid rent on for years without telling a soul about it.

He'd been following the story since then, waiting to see what might happen, his only sources the newspapers and TV. He hadn't dared approach anyone in the exile community, since he had no idea whom he could trust.

Finally his anxiety had become too much to bear, and he'd called Smith, his agency contact, and asked for protection.

That was it.

"That's everything?" Andino asked.

"Everything," Tellez said. "Please, let me go now."

She grunted and got to her feet. The man was a seasoned Contra go-between, but, by the level of his fear, obviously one unused to life-threatening operations. Kirk had little doubt he'd told everything he knew.

"Bend over and touch your forehead to the floor," Andino said to Tellez, and he complied.

Then she nudged Kirk with her foot. He turned his head so that he could see her. She was slipping the pistol back behind her belt and motioning him to get up. He stared at her, uncomprehending.

"Come on," she said.

Tellez started to raise himself, but she kicked him and he quickly buried his face in the carpet again. She took Kirk by the arm and led him over to one corner of the room.

"For Christ's sake, Kirk," she said in a low voice. "It was bound to work better if you believed it, too."

She grinned at him.

"Sonofabitch," he muttered to himself. "Sono*fabitch*."

"Hope I didn't hurt your pride," she said. "But seriously, what are we going to do with the bastard now?"

He shrugged. "We got what we wanted. Any reason I shouldn't go ahead and deliver him to my control?"

"You don't think he'd . . ."

"Warn Vega? Nah. Look at him. He's a lot more afraid of Vega than he is of us. He's probably worried that we're *from* Vega."

The went over and got Tellez. He was understandably hesitant about going anywhere with them, but Kirk was finally able to convince him that they were in fact headed straight for Smith.

The three of them took the elevator down to the deserted lobby, and exited the building in a strained silence.

Kirk went out first. He checked up and down the street but no one was in sight. A cold mist drifted on the light breeze that had begun blowing upriver. Here and there in the apartment buildings were solitary rectangles of yellow light, or the fuzzy glow of TV sets like phosphorescent jellyfish floating in a night sea. A lone cab crept by, as if looking for a difficult address, and disappeared in the direction of Massachusetts Avenue.

The two Nicaraguans followed Kirk a few moments later. The group slowly descended the three sets of steps to sidewalk level and turned right, heading for the parked Eagle. Kirk was nearest the street, with Tellez sandwiched between the other two. Tellez, in his haste to be somewhere else, edged slightly ahead of his companions.

Taking one last look behind her, Andino saw the man just emerging from the mist off toward Connecticut Avenue. The man was alone. He was wearing a heavy topcoat buttoned to the neck, a scarf around his throat, and a snap-brim hat, and he had only one arm. His glasses glinted briefly from reflected street light.

He had been walking steadily in their direction, but then stopped. He stared as though seeing something both expected and surprising.

There was something about the way the empty sleeve was dangling—

Andino caught his eye—

There was a fleeting instant of mutual recognition—

Then the man's missing arm was emerging from the front of his topcoat. In his hand was the familiar boxy shape of an Ingram M11 machine pistol.

Andino tried to save all of them.

She screamed once and threw herself sideways at Kirk, knocking him between a pair of parked cars. In the same motion she grabbed at Tellez's sleeve. Her fingernails clutched the fabric momentarily, then slipped off as her momentum sent her sprawling on top of Kirk.

The gutter was filthy with stagnant cold water, crankcase oil, bits of asphalt, a ruptured plastic two-liter Pepsi bottle, the shredded sports section of a three-day-old Washington *Post*.

Tellez spun around. He had time only for a quick look at his assassin and a glance at the two squirming shadows in the gutter. His last thought was that the bastards had set him up after all.

The one word, *no*, forced its way as far as his lips. It froze as the gunman squeezed the Ingram's trigger.

In less time than it would take to speak the weapon's name, the Ingram had spit ten .45-caliber rounds out through its silencer and across twenty-five yards of misty space into the target. The bullets clustered inside a circle no wider than a coffee cup.

Tellez jerked and clawed at the air as if driven by some irresistible internal disco beat. The single word that was trying to escape his throat turned into a strangled half growl. He was dead even before his backflung body hit the sidewalk.

Andino scrambled over Kirk's supine form, ramming her knee into his face in the process. Blood began to flow from his nose, but he didn't notice.

He rolled over, pulling out his own gun. Andino, hers already drawn, had positioned herself on the street side of the line of parked cars. She was carefully rising to get a fix on the man with the Ingram, every muscle tensed in expectation of another series of discreet coughs and the sudden shattering of windshield glass.

Instead they heard the sound of running feet echoing down the street.

Kirk skittered out onto the sidewalk. He could just make out the man rapidly putting distance between them as the mist swirled in behind him. The man could run, and he had a good head start.

Kirk went after him, snorting blood into his throat, slipping at first on the slick pavement, then finding his balance and hitting stride. Kirk could run too, though he didn't know if he was faster than the man he was chasing.

He wasn't.

The man veered right when he reached Connecticut Avenue, still with a good hundred-yard lead. By the time Kirk reached the busy thoroughfare, his quarry was well down the long hill that led to Dupont Circle.

Doggedly, Kirk continued to give chase. Scattered late-night pedestrians took brief note of the running men, then turned away. No need to get involved.

When a black sedan pulled to the curb near the bottom of the hill, Kirk suddenly realized what a stupid thing he was doing and pulled up. The man in the topcoat hopped into the sedan. It turned down Florida Avenue and in a moment was out of sight. It had been too far away for Kirk to make out the plate number.

He was winded, but after taking a quick swipe at the drying blood on his face, he turned and began trotting back up the hill. Andino would have seen to Tellez, of course. But even if the man was still alive, what could she have done? No one could have survived an attack like that. He cursed himself for having gotten into a foot race with someone who would obviously have had an escape plan.

He jogged down California Street, safely away from the bright lights of Connecticut. Tellez lay where he had fallen, as yet undiscovered. Kirk hunted for a pulse, though the Nicaraguan was plainly dead. And had been, Kirk judged, from the instant the fusillade ravaged his body.

Reluctantly Kirk got up and walked away. He felt the strong, instinctive human prohibition against abandoning the dead, but he had no choice. He couldn't afford to be found here. He still had too much to do, and no time to waste dealing with the slow-grinding wheels of local law enforcement. He could phone the murder in later. Anonymously.

Andino had apparently come to the same conclusion about her presence at the scene, because she wasn't waiting for him when he reached the Eagle. He didn't bother looking around for her. She was a professional and would be blocks from here by now. He got into the car and drove away.

Where would she be? he thought.

They couldn't just drift apart after what had happened. She'd realize that, too. Unless . . .

Forget it. She'd saved his life. If she'd been working with the hit man, why would she have done that? She knew enough now that he was expendable.

Where?

When in doubt, he reasoned, return to the previous rendezvous point. The Metro stop.

He drove circuitously back to Connecticut Avenue and cruised down to Dupont Circle. He went around it twice. She wasn't there. But then, she wouldn't have had time to get there unless she'd been hurrying. He doubted she would have called attention to herself like that.

He reversed direction on Connecticut, went west on R Street, then turned left on one-way Twenty-First. And found her, walking slowly but purposefully past the darkened row houses, looking only straight ahead, like a street-smart woman alone in the city at night was supposed to.

Even though she didn't so much as glance in his direction, he knew that she knew he was there. He slowed the car to her pace.

She acknowledged him with a nod. Then, after checking the street in all directions, she came around to the passenger's side and got in.

37

Kirk drove for a while without a destination, and without either Andino or himself saying anything.

It was a mutual, unspoken accord. Some time was needed. To allow the adrenaline level to drop. To deal with the deep, unavoidable, somewhat guilty sense of satisfaction that comes over the organism when it witnesses the violent death of another: *at least that was not me.* To build resistance to the overwhelming urge to reach out and enfold the nearest warm body. To confront the inevitable question: *what happens next?*

They went out Massachusetts Avenue, down to Rock Creek Parkway, then north, following the park, a long, narrow strip of woodland that snakes its way through the center of the District of Columbia.

Finally she looked over at his face and said, "I'm sorry. It isn't broken, it it?"

Without thinking, he reached up and touched the crusted blood below his nose. "It's not broken," he said. "And look, thanks for . . . knocking me over."

She took a deep breath and let it out slowly. "Did I need to?" she said.

For a moment he didn't know what she meant. Then he did. From her point of view, it was a logical and rather important question.

"You think *I* set Tellez up?" he said. "Forget it. There's nobody on our side I'd trust to be a good enough shot."

She smiled. "I don't blame you," she said. "But that doesn't mean it wasn't an agency hit."

"You're right. But I don't think so. This country is not nearly as devious as we're sometimes made out to be. Right now we're just trying to get the missiles back. It doesn't make any sense to be killing people who might lead us to them."

"I suppose not. You didn't have any advance warning?"

"Not really. My control did warn me that the hijackers might be close to finding him, but I had no way of knowing how close. If I had, I would have been trying to grab them instead of him."

"You're convinced it was Vega's people?"

"Yeah, I'm convinced."

He glanced over at her. In this combination of shadow and artificial light her features appeared far more Indian than European. They seemed set with the permanence of stone, and if there was anything in her expression to read, he couldn't discover it.

He thought about what he'd just said. Tellez hadn't lied; the man's fear had been palpable. And yet that notation in Vega's agency file had fingered him as a double for the Sandinistas. If it was an embedded lie, as it seemed to be, had it been planted in the expectation that Kirk would find it?

Deliberately he turned his attention back to Andino. "Why?" he said. "Aren't you?"

She turned so that she was facing him, leaning her back against the car door. "I know him, Kirk," she said.

She meant the assassin, of course, and Kirk found himself nodding. He was moving now in a relatively small circle. Why wouldn't she know everyone in it?

"Who is he?" Kirk asked.

"His name's Corrales," Andino said. "He was close to Herrera, and he knows Vega. He's a *Somocista*, but small-time. Another killer for hire."

"Taking orders from Colonel Salazar?"

"Maybe."

"Killing his own?"

That was the question, Kirk thought. The key.

Andino didn't speak for a long time. When Kirk looked over, he saw her apparently lost in thought, so he didn't prod her. There was a parking area to the left, with picnic tables beyond it among the trees along Rock Creek. The lot was nearly deserted.

Kirk pulled in and gave each of the other cars a quick look. There was nothing more suspicious than necking couples and teenage drinkers. He cruised to the remotest corner and turned the engine off. Then he faced his passenger and waited.

Finally she said, "They've been killing their own from the beginning. I'll bet that when you were briefed, you were told that Tellez was your government's last link to the missiles. And the reason for that was that everyone scheduled to handle them after him is either dead or missing."

He smiled at the clarity with which she saw things. "That's about right," he said.

"It's got to be a faction within the exiles," she said, nodding. "A tight little group. Salazar maybe. But definitely Vega. I didn't want to influence you when I gave you the list, but he would have been my choice. He feels like it's his birthright to be at the head of the ruling class."

"You think Vega's running the operation?"

"It makes sense. We know he grabbed the missiles personally, and then they disappeared. People immediately started turning up dead, including people on his own side. I don't know who might have been involved originally, but it looks to me like right now Vega is running out of control. Trying to use the operation for his own personal gain."

"For the money?"

"Maybe," she said. "He wouldn't turn it down. But I told you, what he really wants more than anything is power. And I believe he thinks this is the best way to get it."

"By coercing the U.S. into invading," Kirk said.

"Exactly. He probably blames the FSLN for not getting his just reward after the election and sees that the only path to the top now is to come in behind your military. Then he'd have us where he wants us. And if he *was* recognized as the person responsible for forcing us out, he'd have the rest of the opposition in his debt, as well. There'd be no one to seriously challenge him."

Kirk thought about it, slotted together every piece of information he'd unearthed since he arrived in Washington. Her theory fit the facts better than any other, but . . .

A long time passed without either of them speaking. When she broke the silence, once again she knew exactly what was on his mind. "Do we trust one another enough to go our own ways?"

"I don't know," he said.

"Well, do we trust one another enough to work together, then?"

"I guess it's one or the other, isn't it?"

"Yes, I think so. We both know what's going on now. We have the capability of helping each other a great deal or causing an equal amount of trouble."

She saved my life, he thought. And nothing she's told me yet has proven wrong. I wouldn't have gotten this far without her.

"All things considered," he said, "I guess I'd trust you if you were out of my sight. But the truth is, I'd rather have you around."

"You are a strange man, Kirk," she said. "Not at all like your American colleagues."

"It's why I got out of the trade."

She gave him an ironic smile. "It may be the end of my career when they find out I was working with the Butcher of Grenada."

"Retired butcher," he said.

"They'll never buy that."

"Then don't tell them. You were working with someone named Craik, and that's all you ever knew."

"They'll find out."

"And then what?"

"I don't know. Reeducation. Jail. I'll never be allowed the freedom I have now."

"Then come to this country."

She looked at him for a long moment, then said, "You don't understand, do you, Kirk? I believe in the Revolution. It may be far from perfect, but it is our own. I couldn't abandon it, no matter what happened. However small the part chosen for me, I'll play it."

"No," he said, "I think I do understand. I'm just not used to people who believe in anything."

"Do you not want to know what happened to your family?"

"Yes."

"Then you believe in something, too. But to answer your question: yes, I trust that we would not be working against each other. However, I also would rather be with you than not."

"All right. I have a house."

She thought that over. "How secure is it?" she asked.

"Truthfully," he said, "I don't know. You might be exposed there. But there's been no indication that my side isn't leaving me alone. And I'm sure Vega's people don't know about it."

"After tonight they'll know I'm working with a gringo. They'll eventually find out who you are, and where. They have powerful friends in Washington."

"Then we'll just have to find them first."

On the drive back to Duddington Place, they discussed Kirk's plan for locating Vega.

"You know where Salazar is?" she said.

"No, but I have a good source," he said.

"Your control?"

"No, someone else. Someone I trust more than my control."

She nodded. "Good. And how would you deal with the colonel?"

He shrugged. "What do you suggest? How tough is he?"

"He was perhaps tough once," she said. "But he is not so young anymore. And he has been a long time out of the field." She grinned. "I think he has taken to the American way of life."

"If he called, what do you think? Would Vega come to him?"

"It's worth a try. Vega may be operating on his own, but Colonel Salazar is still technically his superior. That command structure has been important to the exiles, and Vega probably respects it in spite of himself."

Kirk parked the Eagle and the two of them walked to the safe house. After showing her around, he asked that she wait in "her" room while he made some phone calls.

The first was to Smith.

"Smitty," Kirk said. "If it hasn't been found already, Tellez's body is on the sidewalk in front of the building on California Street."

There was a pause, then Smith sighed and said, "Shit. All right, it'll be taken care of. But what happened?"

"Someone hit him as I was bringing him in. I chased the guy, but he had a car waiting and he got away."

"Tellez is dead for sure?"

"Well, he took a two-second burst point-blank from an Ingram. I doubt if he even had time for a last thought."

"Did you see whoever did it?"

"Yeah, but I didn't know him. Do you?"

"What are you suggesting, Steven, that we're terminating our own informants?"

"Personally, I don't have any idea who's whacking who around here. I'm not *suggesting* anything, Smith. I'm asking you in plain English: could it have been an agency hit?"

Even over the phone, Kirk could see the wheels turning inside Smith's head. What to tell, what to conceal, how best to protect the ass of number one.

"Not to my knowledge," Smith said. "If it were, then the implication would be that someone on our side doesn't want the Stingers found."

"That's right, Sherlock."

Smith ignored him. "I find that impossible to believe," he said without irritation.

"Spare me," Kirk said, and he cited a couple of well-known instances from years past when agency officers had deliberately allowed the U.S. to be embarrassed in order to gain leverage with an unresponsive Congress.

"That was different," Smith said coolly, "and you know it. None of that involved the murder of civilians."

"Right, the bodies weren't American."

"Pretending stupidity doesn't become you, Steven. You're talking about terrorism and high-level treason here. No one has ends that would justify that kind of action."

"How about a mole?"

"The mythical Ivan?"

"Or the mythical Ernesto. Whatever nationality's the prime suspect these days."

"You're getting out of line," Smith said.

"Yeah and fuck you, too!" Kirk said. "That guy tonight tried to take us *both* out. You don't think I have a need-to-*know* about this?"

But Smith's voice was as calm as ever. "If there's a mole," he said, "we'll find him. That's our job, not yours."

"And in the meantime, it's my ass on the line. You got a major problem, Smitty, and it isn't just the missiles. If there isn't somebody actually in the agency working against you, then they're damn close. You better find them."

"That's my job, as I said."

"I warn you," Kirk added, "I don't care who it is, if I run into them again, you're gonna be cleaning up the streets after me."

"You do whatever you need to do to get your job done. That's understood."

"And you?"

"If we find anyone who's collaborating with the terrorists, we'll deal with them," Smith said, "you have my word. Now what do you intend to do next?"

"Find whoever axed Tellez, wouldn't you say? I'll need a detailed list of everyone you know who ever did business with the man. Especially people in Washington. For starters."

Smith paused, then said carefully, "I'd be careful if I were you, Steven. I wouldn't get carried too far afield with this."

"What's that supposed to mean?"

"Just that that line of inquiry is going to bring you into contact with people who won't take kindly to being suspected of involvement in a plot to blackmail the U.S. government. Somewhat, ah, dangerous people, if you follow me."

"Yeah, our *allies*," Kirk said disgustedly.

"Our friends can be a little touchy. It's wise to remember that their first allegiance is not to us, but to the liberation of their homelands. Besides . . . there is the question of what is the proper direction in which to go."

"Smith, for Christ's sake, a man was killed tonight. It stands to reason that the people who murdered him *knew* him. And if it wasn't about the missiles, I don't know what in hell it was about. How else should I go?"

"I'm not going to argue with you, Steven. It's not my

role to make tactical field decisions. I just want you to be careful and I want you to succeed."

"Thanks for the vote of confidence."

"Now," Smith said, "there is one other fairly important matter. Did Tellez tell you anything before he died?"

"Nothing of value. He was anxious to get to you, with good reason. Which is why I need some names. Tomorrow morning?"

"I'll do what I can."

After he'd hung up with Smith, Kirk immediately called his father.

"Steven," Charles said sleepily. "My God, what time is it?"

"After three," Steven said. It seemed like days earlier that he'd called Charles about the photographs.

"Can't this wait? I'm afraid I don't have your photo—"

"No, it can't. And you can forget the picture of Cruz. Vega's our man."

"You're sure?" The elderly voice was alert now. "How do you know?"

"Skip the details. I'm sure. He tried to have me killed tonight. He's the one we want. I still need a picture of him, but that's not why I'm calling. Do you know Enrique Salazar?"

"Colonel Salazar? Of course. But what's he got to do with this?"

"I have to talk to him," Steven said. "Where is he?"

Charles thought, then said, "I don't know for sure. He lives in Miami, but he has another residence here, plus his main offices. He spends a lot of time lobbying. He could be either place."

"Can you find out?"

"It would be fairly easy. Right now?"

"How about mid-morning? Without alerting anyone as to who's interested in him."

"Yes, I suppose I could do that."

"Good. And then can you get me in to see him?"

"Why?"

"We want Vega. Salazar was his commanding officer. We don't know where Vega is, but Salazar might."

"I don't know," Charles said carefully. "I'm not sure I like the way this is going. If you're wrong—"

"Then your credibility suffers," Steven said. "Big deal.

Meanwhile people are dying. How about finding him and we'll see about the details tomorrow?"

"All right. Get some sleep, Steven."

That was good advice. But there was one more call to make.

It was to Seamus Croaghan, and his assignment was a tough one. Kirk gave him four names—Herrera, Salazar, and the Vegas, Francisco and Javier—and asked for a rundown on property in the D.C. area owned by the men, or by any companies with which they might be associated.

He said that he realized the scope of the task, but that it could be vitally important. Important enough to sacrifice a little sleep? Croaghan asked. Kirk smiled to himself and said yes. Fine, Croaghan said, he'd work on it straight through.

After Kirk hung up, he went back upstairs and found Andino sitting up in bed, still awake. He trudged into her room and sprawled in a chair next to her.

"We should be able to start after Salazar tomorrow," he said.

She nodded. "Good," she said. "I think that that is the right thing to do."

They were silent then, for long enough that a certain amount of tension began to build between them.

"What are you thinking?" she asked finally.

"Nothing," Kirk said. "I was just enjoying looking at you."

"Kirk, I like you. And I think that we will work well together. But you must understand that there are times when sex is counterrevolutionary."

He burst out laughing.

"What is funny?" she asked when the laughter had subsided.

He wiped his eyes. "Now, that's one I never heard before," he said. He got up, came over, and kissed her on the cheek. "Not only that, there are times when it's downright beyond the reach of mere mortals. Good night."

And he tottered off to bed.

Corrales was nervous going into the rendezvous with Javier Vega, though he had no real reason to be. He'd proven himself to be much more of a professional than

Herrera had been. He'd taken care of Tellez cleanly and efficiently. True, he'd missed the opportunity to eliminate the Andino woman, but then he'd hardly expected her to be there. It wasn't his fault.

And he hadn't gotten the third person, whoever he was. But that might be for the best. He could easily have been someone the resistance didn't want killed. It was terribly risky to make uninformed judgments in such matters.

No, no reason to be nervous. But with Vega . . .

They met in the shifting shadows of a Japanese cherry tree on the northeast bank of the Tidal Basin. At that hour, there were no other pedestrians; the only sound was the thrum of late-night traffic on nearby Independence Avenue. The mist off the water streamed around them and headed inland. In the distance the ghostly dome of the Jefferson Memorial seemed to float unsupported in the air.

"Tellez is dead," Corrales said.

Vega nodded. "Good," he said. "There were no problems?"

Corrales thought about it briefly, then said, "No, none."

Vega fixed the assassin with his hard black eyes. "I was told that a man chased you along Connecticut Avenue," he said.

The driver had betrayed him. Corrales felt his anger rise. "There was a man with Tellez," he said. "But I did not recognize him. He must be working for the Americans, though, because Tellez was leaving the apartment building with him. The woman, Piedad Andino, was also there. I do not know why."

"She survived?"

Again Corrales hesitated for a moment. Then he said, "Yes. Both she and the man were armed. It seemed wisest to pull back."

"And you were recognized?"

"No, it was dark."

Vega swore silently to himself. The Sandinista woman had somehow gotten herself much too close to the operation. If that wasn't bad enough, they'd had two good chances to take her out of the picture. Both times they'd failed miserably.

And then, Corrales was probably lying, Vega thought.

If he had recognized Andino, the reverse was most likely also true. That now made him a risk, but one whose abilities were nevertheless of some value. Vega weighed the one against the other.

Inside his jacket pocket, his fingers closed around the device he carried there. "Describe the other man," he said.

Corrales did so, to the best of his ability.

It could be anyone, Vega thought. And he could be working for almost any of the other sides. Worst of all, he had to assume that both Andino and the man now knew everything Tellez had known. That wasn't a lot, but neither was it insignificant.

"We need the woman," Vega said. "And we need to eliminate her. After she tells us who she's working with."

Corrales nodded. She shouldn't be that hard to find.

"I will bring her to you," he said.

"She must not be allowed to cause any further trouble," Vega said.

Nor must Corrales, Vega thought. If he couldn't deliver Andino within a couple of days, his usefulness would be at an end. Vega withdrew his hand from his pocket. It was wrapped around a miniature hypodermic modeled after the infamous Saxon's Fang. He clapped Corrales on the shoulder, saying, "You are a good soldier."

The tiny hypo was a spring-loaded chemical delivery system. In this instance it contained but a single cc of DMSO, into which had been mixed one five-hundredth of a grain of ricin. The needle point barely pricked Corrales's skin. With the distraction of the slap on the shoulder, he felt nothing.

The DMSO, however, immediately went to work, carrying the ricin deep into Corrales's body. There was not even the transitory sensation of wetness.

Vega slipped the Fang smoothly back into his pocket. He would be very, very careful not to touch the needle point until the weapon had been properly cleaned, just in case any of the mixture still clung to the cold steel.

Ricin is one of the deadliest poisons known to man, and it is lethal in extraordinarily minute dosages. Best of all, from Vega's point of view, the human body reacts to ricin poisoning in a delayed manner.

Corrales now had less than three days in which to

fulfill his mission. After that, no matter whether he succeeded or not, an irreversible sequence of events would ensue.

He would become nauseous. He would experience vomiting, diarrhea, hemorrhaging, and severe pain. Then, mercifully, he would fall into a stupor.

And he would die.

PART V

THE PRESIDENT

Have him put on a garment, the robe of
life,
so that he may go back to his city,
so that he may now go the rest of the
way down his road.
Let him put on an elder's robe, and let it
always be new.

—*Gilgamesh*, XI-v

38

March 21

The night was equally as long as the day to come. During its course the leaden sky began to clear and the lingering mist to dissipate. The vernal equinox arrived with the dawn, bringing sunshine and unseasonable warmth.

At seven-thirty the President, despite contrary urgings by his closest advisers, took some morning air on the second-floor White House balcony that overlooks the South Lawn.

Marine One sat silently on its pad. The chopper had always seemed comical to the President, reminding him of an ugly, blunt-nosed man wearing a propellor beanie.

It was ironic, he thought as he looked out at the manicured grassy knoll with its beautiful fountains, tall trees, and lovingly tended gardens. Such an attractive, peaceful-looking place, yet the entire White House grounds was one vast minefield.

Most of the thousands of tourists who streamed past each day never even thought about it. They gazed at the lawn and saw a lawn, not the first line of defense for a president. They passed on by, unaware (perhaps mercifully unaware, the President thought) of the guards inside who watched *them* twenty-four hours a day, seven days a week. The guards who, at the first sign that the wrought-iron fence around the White House had been breached, would throw the switch that electrically activated the minefield. An unauthorized intruder would be blown to bits before he got within fifty yards of the presidential mansion. Any questions would be asked later.

Also invisible to the casual observer was the rest of the White House defense network. The guns and missiles (yes, Stingers) up on the roof, not only of this building but the adjacent Treasury Department and Executive Office Buildings as well.

The President sighed. These were all necessary precautions in the modern world, of course. Yet he couldn't help thinking with a kind of nostalgia of Eugene McCarthy's campaign promise that, if elected, his first official act would be to tear down the fence around the White House.

1968 had run its course in a different country, perhaps even in a different century, he thought.

And yet, had much really changed? The president in 1968 feared to make an appearance at his own party's convention. The present incumbent was advised not to show his face outside the White House.

He'd spent much of the night lying awake, wondering if he'd made the right decision in scheduling the flight of Marine One. And wondering, too, whether he should actually be on it. It would be a simple enough matter to send someone else in his place. Tom Read had even volunteered.

But the power of the presidency, after all, resided as much in the realm of the symbolic as in the more tangible world of treaties and submarines and black-tie dinners. The President himself was no less in awe of his office than the most fervently patriotic citizen out in the heartland.

Yet it was all dependent on a chief executive standing for something, he knew. And so seldom had it happened in recent years, as those elected to the office were revealed by time as having stood for nothing but their own narrow self-interest.

The President didn't know how his predecessors would have handled the Stinger crisis, but for him there was no choice. A president had to reflect the collective will of the people. If he was afraid to fly, then why should his countrymen be any different?

The President was going up in Marine One; that was certain.

He was, however, not a foolish man. So he'd accepted the proposal put forth by his Chief of Staff and the Chairman of the JCS. Arrangements had been made to have Marine One escorted by three heavily armed Cobra gunships.

Light from the first sun of spring sparkled off the tips of the wavelets out on the river.

Vega and Corrales arrived at the last minute and parked the van parallel to the Potomac in a pull-off area in Lady Bird Johnson Park. Vega had selected the spot with care. He had expected, as was the case, that there would be few other vehicles about. And the adjacent George Washington Parkway provided a convenient escape route. They would have quick access to Interstate 66 or the Beltway without having to wait for a single traffic light.

Best of all was the view. The van's sliding side door was closed now, but when it was open there would be an unobstructed line of fire to the Washington Monument, a mile away. The White House itself was out of sight, but its location was easily figured, using the Monument as a guidepost.

The attack was a terrible risk, but Vega had decided it was worth it. The President would be succeeded by Vice-President Brust, and he was a man who was much more susceptible to manipulation.

True, the police presence between the White House and Andrews would be substantial. But that was a lot of ground to cover. A properly planned strike should go off without a hitch.

Vega could feel the confidence rippling through his body. He had reached that exalted state where the operative cruises along, free of doubt, believing that he can do no wrong. It was a condition of near infallibility, bolstered by his previous successes and an absolute faith in the finely meshed functioning of his logic and his intuition. It transcended all.

There could be no failure here.

The presidential chopper was due to take off at any moment. Vega and Corrales had arrived a scant few minutes early and would wait for only a short while past the appointed time. If the chopper failed to appear, the strike would be canceled. There was too much of a chance that the van would attract attention, and to be stopped and searched would be disastrous.

The chopper's course was completely predictable. Marine One always lifted off in the same direction—south—no matter what its ultimate destination. The reason for this was simple. Directly south of the White House was the Ellipse and the Washington Monument grounds. In all other directions were public buildings. Thus, if for any reason the helicopter crashed early on, it would impact where there would likely be the fewest additional casualties.

After attaining cruising altitude, somewhere around the Monument, the chopper would then turn and take up its intended heading. In this case southeast, toward Andrews Air Force Base and the rendezvous with the jet carrying the remains of the American MIAs.

Vega waited in middle of the van, the Stinger launch tube on the floor next to him. Through a tinted bubble window in the van's sliding door he could train his binoculars on the air space around the Monument, without being seen himself. Corrales remained at the wheel, ready to kick the engine over at a moment's notice.

Five minutes passed.

"Enough," Corrales said. "Let's get out of here."

"Any cops?" Vega said.

"One just went by on the Parkway. Slowly."

"Wait."

Suddenly it rose into view from the far side of the Monument: the unmistakable shape of the Sea Stallion designated Marine One.

Vega had only seconds to act. "Clear?" he called.

"Clear," Corrales said.

Vega slid open the van door. Then he hunkered down, with one knee raised, and hefted the launch tube to his shoulder. He balanced an elbow on the upraised knee. It was as stable a firing position as he could manage.

He clapped on the headphones and peered through the optical gunsight, scanning, scanning . . .

Where was it?

There. The chopper was circling around to the west of the Monument, now heading back east—

And a man strolled past the van, heading for the riverbank. He looked up and stopped in his tracks. He was staring at the business end of a missile launcher. Though he'd never seen one before, not up close, the man knew enough to yell for help.

Vega never saw him, but Corrales didn't hesitate. He pulled a silenced pistol from under his jacket and shot the startled man three times in the chest before he could make a sound. The man's body was flung backward. It twitched once as blood welled up and began to soak its clothes.

The silenced gunshots didn't make enough noise to penetrate Vega's headphones, but it was unlikely they'd have affected his concentration in any case. He'd already activated the seeker and gotten lock-on. He held the lock for just a moment, then fired the weapon.

He had no way of observing the results of the attack. At the sound of the launch, Corrales started the engine, and he was already pulling the van out onto the Parkway as Vega dumped out the launch tube and yanked the sliding door shut.

He never saw the Cobras.

But he did see, through the van's rear windows, what was happening behind them. Several people were rushing toward the man who had been shot. Another ran instead to his car, which sported a prominent whip antenna.

Vega cursed in Spanish as he scrambled forward to the passenger's seat.

The van skittered out into traffic and sped down the Parkway, heading west. Corrales's face was a lifeless mask.

"This way!" Vega shouted, indicating that Corrales should bear right.

"Now slow down."

There was no response.

"Slow *down*!" Vega screamed.

The van slowed as the Parkway dipped downward, prior to passing under Memorial Bridge.

"More!" Vega commanded.

Corrales obeyed. The van's speed dropped to twenty-five.

"Get rid of the van!" Vega said, and he opened the door and jumped.

He hit the roadside in perfect stride, stumbled forward and tucked into a shoulder roll that eventually slammed him into the dirt. Immediately he got to his feet. He'd be bruised, but nothing was broken.

Dodging traffic, he scrambled across the Parkway and up the hill on the opposite side. Then he jogged casually across the bridge and lost himself in the crowd milling around the Lincoln Memorial.

Marine One, a CH-53 Sea Stallion, was a state-of-the-art military helicopter that had been modified for civilian use. Which meant that its passenger-carrying capacity had been reduced from thirty-eight sardined combat troops to a dozen civs traveling in plush comfort. The aircraft's avionics, however, were even more technologically advanced than in the standard military production model. That hardware's job was the protection of the President of the United States and so it was, simply, the best in the world.

The atmosphere inside the chopper had been tense but confident. Despite the high-profile nature of this particular flight, no one expected the terrorists to try anything. And even if they did, the crew consisted of the most highly skilled men the Pentagon could deliver on one day's notice.

Only two civilians were aboard: the President and his chief of staff, who had insisted on accompanying him. It had been decided that Secretary of Defense Schule, along with a representative of the Joint Chiefs, would fly in a different chopper and meet the President at Andrews. Just in case.

Lift-off had been uneventful, and Marine One rose smoothly toward its rendezvous with the Cobra gunships, high above the Washington Monument.

The radar man picked up the three Cobras, on schedule and on course. Marine One circled west and headed back to the east as the escort choppers began to move into position.

And then, far below and across the river, Javier Vega locked on and fired.

Marine One's infrared sensors detected the missile immediately. Range: two thousand meters.

If response to the attack had depended solely on human nervous systems, there would not have been enough time. But the chopper's on-board computers analyzed the threat and reacted automatically in considerably less than one second.

Several things then happened at once. Half a dozen high-intensity flares were launched to distract the Stinger's I/R seeker. A highly sophisticated ultraviolet jammer crippled its U/V homing system. And a bright red light began blinking frantically on the instrument panel of every member of the flight crew. That light meant only one thing: aircraft under missile attack. Take immediate evasive action.

The pilot did so the instant the light flashed. His long hours of training and experience kicked in and, without thinking about it, he nosed the chopper down and put it into a power dive.

The bottom dropped out of everyone's stomach. Neither the President nor the Chief of Staff had to be told what was happening. Reflexively they gripped the armrests of their seats until their knuckles turned white.

The Stinger was badly confused. The target had fragmented and its U/V signature was a hopeless muddle. Still, the missile was the best of its class. It rejected the flares. Its computer made some delicate in-flight course adjustments and it veered to the west, homing in on the helicopter once again.

Just six seconds after launch, the missile impacted its target. There was a small explosion as the payload detonated, then a much larger one as the chopper's fuel tanks blew.

The flares burned on, drifting slowly downward, like bits of fiery debris left behind by the ball of flame that now plunged to the earth.

Some of those on the Monument grounds had, out of curiosity, been watching the helicopters, and then the flares. But everyone looked to the sky at the sound of the explosion. Many stared in incomprehension. The rest screamed and began to run.

They streamed down the hill toward Constitution Avenue, dragging their children, jostling and falling and being trampled, as if fleeing a Monument that had somehow turned evil and was driving them before it.

The resultant disaster was not as bad as it might have been. The fireball spiraled down—narrowly missing the Monument and the crowd still huddled around its base, mesmerized by the falling horror—and crashed on the hillside.

Seven people died, not counting the two-man chopper's crew, both of whom had perished long before the Cobra escort ship dropped from the sky.

Aboard Marine One, the pilot's first instinct, after taking evasive action, had been to get the President away from harm. It was unlikely that the terrorists would have another missile to fire, but he could take nothing for granted. He skimmed the helicopter along at treetop level to the Potomac, not worrying where his escorts were. Then, since the attack had come from the south, he turned northwest and followed the course of the river.

Tom Read's mouth was dry, and he was still shaking a little, but he realized that the immediate danger was over. He opened his eyes and looked at the President.

The President was pale and sweat was coursing down his face. He was obviously having trouble breathing.

"Mr. President," Read said. "Mr. President!"

"Tom," the President said between breaths. "Pain in my left arm . . . I think it's serious. . . ."

Lieutenant Raffler, one of the military aides assigned to the flight, was already out of his seat. Raffler was a trained paramedic. Even as he was feeling for the President's pulse, he called for oxygen and ordered that the chopper make for Navy Med.

"It's okay, sir," Raffler said soothingly to the President. "Just relax. We'll have you on the ground in no time."

The pilot sensed intuitively what was happening. He turned Marine One more to the north and radioed the Naval Medical Center in Bethesda. The President was flying in, he said. Please have staff on full alert to deal with possible heart attack.

As soon as Vega was clear of the van, Corrales pushed the accelerator to the floor. The passenger's side door slammed shut. The van rumbled west, following the Potomac and inadvertently paralleling the course of Marine One.

Not too fast, Corrales cautioned himself. Don't attract attention.

Behind Corrales, the witness Vega had seen running to his car had called the police on the emergency CB channel, described the van, and told them in which direction it was headed.

Within moments, a diverse array of law enforcement officers was converging on the George Washington Parkway. Arlington Police, U.S. Park Police, Secret Service, and FBI, as well as others of lower profile. Every exit off the Parkway was staked out.

Corrales, though he didn't know it, was trapped. He sped past Roosevelt Island and went under Key Bridge, the high-rise glass cluster of Rosslyn up the hill to his left. He wasn't all that familiar with the area through which he was driving. He had the idea that if he could just get to the Beltway, everything would be all right.

Just past Spout Run he glanced in the rearview mirror and saw a police car holding a steady distance behind him. It could be coincidence . . . No. There are no coincidences.

He was on a limited-access highway, the worst kind of place to shake a tail. He had to get off.

Past Chain Bridge. Another official-looking car was back there now, hanging with him. His hands were clammy, but his mind was clear. Get off the Parkway, find some side streets, ditch the van, lose the pursuit.

The Georgetown Pike exit loomed ahead. Corrales wheeled the van into the cloverleaf.

And they had him. As soon as he made his move, one of the tail cars radioed ahead and two police vehicles immediately pulled across the head of the exit ramp, sealing it off. The trailing vehicles screeched into a V behind him, blocking any retreat. Men with drawn guns popped out of their cars and fixed him in their sights.

Corrales looked around him, gauging the odds. They were poor. He cursed his misfortune, but switched off the engine, placed his hands on the wheel and awaited instructions.

It took a while to sort things out. Everyone wanted to be the one to arrest the terrorist. Tempers shortened as claims of jurisdiction bumped up against one another.

Though there was no evidence that a missile had been launched from the van, there was a general presumption of guilt. Corrales became the target of a steady stream of verbal abuse as well as some physical manhandling. But through it all he merely repeated, over and over, that he was entitled to consult with a lawyer.

The question of what to do with him was resolved when a dark sedan with three men inside arrived. All were armed and were carrying high-level federal credentials which identified them as, respectively, officials of the CIA, Secret Service, and National Security Council. They declared themselves members of a joint task force that represented the President himself.

The driver of the van, they said, was part of an international conspiracy to assassinate the country's chief executive, and as such he was their property. No arguments. They were taking him into custody immediately, and anyone who tried to interfere would be considered a coconspirator and shot.

The others were stunned into silence. No one interfered as the three men herded the handcuffed Corrales into their sedan. And police cars were moved, so they could leave.

Instead of heading in the direction of the city, however, the sedan dropped back down onto the Parkway. It got off at the next exit west, which led, depending upon one's choice, to either the Bureau of Public Roads or the Central Intelligence Agency.

39

Kirk was awakened by the telephone. His head was stuffy and his mouth dry, as if he were suffering from a mild hangover. Which in a way he was, though the previous evening's intoxicant had been adrenaline rather than alcohol.

He activated the TSU-3000 and picked up the receiver. It was Smith.

"They tried to kill the President," Smith said.

"Jesus Christ," Kirk said. "When?"

"This morning. The damn fool insisted on going up in Marine One like he'd promised, and they were waiting for him."

"What happened?"

"Evasive action, which worked. The Stinger took out one of the Cobra escorts instead. It crashed near the Monument. Both of the crew were killed, and some people on the ground."

Kirk took a deep breath and let it out. "The President's okay?" he said.

"We don't know," Smith said. "He survived the missile, but it seems to have precipitated a heart attack. They rushed him to Naval Med. The doctors aren't saying anything yet."

"Jesus." He paused to let the implications of all this sink in, then said, "Does that mean that Brust . . . ?"

"The Vice-President has been notified, of course. So long as the President is . . . incapacitated, Walter's in charge. But I would guess things are still a bit confused."

"Great. That's all we need, Smitty."

"I wouldn't be so pessimistic, Steven. The system creaks a little bit, but it works."

"If Walter Brust is at the wheel, I doubt it. But where was the Stinger fired from?"

"The other side of the river. Security was tight all around the city, but we couldn't cover every potential launch site. However . . . we got one of them."

"One of the terrorists?" Kirk said. "How?"

"They fired the Stinger from a van. Two, maybe three of them. The driver killed an innocent bystander. The other one or ones jumped out somewhere, but we nailed the driver just off the George Washington Parkway."

"Where is he?"

"We have him."

"Come on, Smitty. Can you do that?"

"Of course," Smith said calmly. "This is a little too important to leave it to the local cops, don't you think? Or would you rather we read him his rights and get him a lawyer while his partner uses up the rest of the missiles?"

"I wasn't questioning your grabbing him. But half of Washington will be on your ass by tonight."

"Forget it. The press is blacked out, with authorization from the President. NSC, Defense, everyone's getting a crack at the guy. There isn't going to be any blow-back on this."

"I assume your blab specialists have had a go at him."

"He's been encouraged to talk, yes. His name is Corrales. He's done some free-lance work for the pro-democracy forces in the past, but our best sources have him turned by the Sandies about six months ago."

Here we go again, Kirk thought. How could the opposition manage to fight a war when it was so riddled with double agents?

"We believe," Smith went on, "that Corrales has lately

been working with another Sandinista double named Javier Vega. Vega's the one with the brains. We suspect that he's either behind this thing or close to it. Except that ultimately he's taking *his* orders from Managua.

"Unfortunately, Corrales is a tough nut. He hasn't told us a thing yet. We'll keep trying, but in the meantime I'd suggest you go after Vega. He's probably sitting on the missiles. If he was in that van, chances are he's still in the city somewhere. Which means they may be, too."

"All right," Kirk said. "Keep me posted, Smith. Let me know if you break him."

"Of course. And Steven, one other thing. If you locate Vega on your own, you're not to try to bring him in. And for God's sake, don't attempt to recover the Stingers yourself. Contact me immediately and I'll provide support for you. No offense, but we have to be sure he doesn't . . . slip away again. Is that clear?"

"Sure. You're the control."

"Good."

After Kirk hung up, he gave careful thought to what he'd just heard. Smith had handed him Tellez and now Vega. Maybe he was wrong about the man. Maybe Smith was calling it truthfully, the way he saw it, and someone else in the agency was screwing around with the files.

Kirk shook his head. He had too little hard data. It was like trying to learn an unfamiliar city by riding its subway system.

Piedad Andino came into the room, looking rumpled but alert. Kirk filled her in on the morning's developments, stopping short of revealing his source and other details that she had no need to know.

When he was finished, she said, "So Corrales is out of the way. Good; he's scum. Now we can get on with finding Vega and the Stingers. You have no further doubts, I trust."

"No, none."

Their conversation was interrupted by the phone. Andino by this time was used to the ground rules. She excused herself and went upstairs to have a shower.

The caller was Kirk, Sr.

He only had time for a few minutes' conversation, he said. The uncertainty surrounding the status of the President's health had produced something of a power vacuum in the halls of official Washington. Especially considering the gravity of the current crisis. Therefore, an emergency meeting of the President's Foreign Intelligence Advisory Board had been convened. The PFIAB, Charles was certain, would immediately place itself at the service of the Vice-President.

Charles was off to that meeting and whatever followed.

"The President was a damn fool," Charles said.

"Yeah," Steven said, "but there's not much point in flogging that now."

"Anyway, I've arranged for the photographs you wanted, but I don't know how long I'm going to be tied up with this, so I don't know when I can get them to you."

"Don't worry about it." It mattered a lot less now, for Andino knew what Vega looked like. "Were you briefed on what happened this morning after the Stinger attack?"

"To some extent," Charles said. "What about, specifically?"

"They got one of them. Corrales. You know him?"

"Not personally. I know who he is."

"Good. Who is he?"

There was a pause, then Charles said carefully, "He purports to be an active Contra operative, but the intelligence agencies believe that he's been doubling for the Sandinistas."

"And what do you believe?"

Another pause. "I believe that in this instance they could be mistaken."

"So now you see why I've been on that particular track."

"Yes, I understand. But you may still be wrong."

"Vega's our man, Charles."

"Perhaps. And you think Colonel Salazar can lead you to him?"

"I hope so."

"Very well," Charles said. "Salazar is in Washington right now. He does his lobbying for the Contra cause out of a downtown office on K Street." He gave Steven the address. "Americans for a Free Nicaragua, the organization's called. It's mainly Salazar doing the legwork, but he's got a network of financial backers behind him, pretty heavy hitters. Then there's his house." He gave Steven another address, this one off Broad Branch Road, North-west, near Rock Creek Park.

"Fancy digs?" Steven said.

"The colonel's adopted country has, shall we say, done well by him. As with others in a similar position, one wonders whether he would ever want to go home, even if he were successful in bringing us down again."

"Got you. What about family, he have any?"

"Yes, but they spend most of their time in Miami. They're there now."

"He's alone?"

"Except for whatever personal staff lives with him."

"Bodyguards, you mean," Steven said.

"I'm sure they have other duties, but that's essentially what we're talking about."

"How many?"

"Sorry. That's not the sort of information the colonel's loose with."

"I imagine they're well armed."

"That would be a reasonable presumption."

"Shit." Steven thought about it, then said, "What about getting in to see him? Something that wouldn't push the wrong buttons. Could you set it up?"

"That'll be trickier, and I don't have the time this morning. You could just walk into his office, of course. It's open to the public."

"Not exactly what I had in mind."

"You want an in to his house?" Charles said.

"Or a meeting on neutral ground, better yet. Or some-place advantageous to me, best of all."

"Hmmm. All right, let me think about it. I'll talk to you later, after the board adjourns."

"If not sooner. I'll plan to be here around six. Thanks, Charles." He paused, then added, "And for God's sake, please try to keep the leash on Walter Brust. He's capa-ble of doing something very stupid, and there couldn't be a worse time for it. We're getting close, I can feel it."

A few minutes later, Andino came down from her shower. Over breakfast she and Kirk swapped ideas.

In the end they decided that if Salazar was going to lead them to Vega, he was going to have to be coerced. That being the case, they would need to get him on unfamiliar turf, which meant a snatch. Charles might be

able to put them into position to do that, but even if he
could, he might not be able to act quickly enough.

Best to plan how they would do it on their own. So,
after eating, they got into the Eagle and went for a ride.

First they drove past the office of Americans for a Free
Nicaragua. It was in a six-story, steel-and-glass building
on one of the busiest stretches of K Street, near Connecticut Ave. Kirk idled the car illegally long enough for
Andino to slip in and check the building's directory. The
office they wanted was on the fifth floor.

The tacital problems involved in taking Salazar from
his office were insurmountable, as Kirk had figured. The
two of them just shook their heads, writing off the
possibility.

That left the colonel's home, which they drove to next.

It was on a quiet, upper-class, residential street, only a
stone's throw from the park. The colonel might have
posted someone at the window, twenty-four hours a day,
to monitor the traffic for suspicious-looking vehicles, but
Kirk risked a couple of circuits of the block anyway.

The house was a spacious, two-story white frame affair, sitting on about three-quarters of an acre of wooded
ground. The land sloped gently up from the road to the
house—a distance of perhaps fifty yards—and then leveled off.

A six-foot brick wall encircled the property, with two
breaks in it: one for the driveway, the other for the front
walk. Both entrances were closed by wrought-iron gates.
The driveway led directly to the four-car garage that
abutted the main house. No cars were in sight. The
ivy-covered wall appeared to be more decorative than
defensive.

The rear of the parcel reached to the next street over.
From there the back of the house could just be glimpsed
through the trees.

They saw no signs of life, inside or out.

All in all, the house looked not unlike its neighbors. It
was the sort of place that might easily be called home by
a high-level civil servant, a bank vice-president, or the
owner of a prosperous travel agency.

Kirk was sure that its innocuous exterior was mislead-
ing. There would unquestionably be systems of one kind
or another to discourage intruders. But whatever they

were, they weren't obvious. No razor wire atop the wall, no photoelectric alarms, no Dobermans on patrol.

After carefully studying the house and property, he cruised through the immediate neighborhood, surveying the lay of the land, making detailed mental notes. He didn't have to explain to his companion what to do. She knew. Later they could compare impressions and map out the best strategy.

By the time he left the area, Kirk was confident that he could find his way around in total darkness, if need be.

And he was certain that Andino could, too.

40

The lady of the moment was a young, lissome blonde, as they invariably were, though they were not always as evidently a *real* blonde as this one was. Her other physical charms included long, stunningly tapered legs, a narrow waist, and high, uptilted breasts whose firm perfection strongly implied a discreet silicone assist.

At one time the lady had been the incumbent Miss Maryland. Her talent was cabaret-style singing, and the song of her choice had been Michael Jackson's "Billie Jean." Though her voice was chronically flat and she'd completely mutilated the logic of the song, she had still managed to take the title; she'd been devastating in the Swimsuit competition. Later, in Atlantic City, she'd finished well out of the money overall—every girl at that level was a killer in the Swimsuit—but had come home with a nice consolation prize, first runner-up in the Congeniality voting.

At the moment she was naked. Her golden, tanning-salon skin stood out against the blue satin sheets like the sun in a cloudless sky. She stretched, rolled onto her side and raked her crimson fingernails gently across the long, tree-stump thigh of the naked man who was propped up next to her in bed.

Walter Brust barely noticed what the lady was doing. His gaze was fixed on the forty-inch TV screen, so large it was almost like being there.

"Look at this!" he said excitedly, and the lady dutifully turned her head in the direction of the TV, feigning interest.

He pushed one of the buttons on his complex remote control device and the action slowed down to quarter speed.

On the screen, a much younger Walter Brust muscled his way to the basket in slo-mo. He grabbed a pass and took the ball to the hoop, stuffing it through. He didn't so much beat the defender as steamroll him. It was one power forward against another, strength vs. strength, a six-foot eight-inch, two hundred thirty-pound white man in a white uniform putting his best move on an equally large black man dressed in green.

On his first dribble Walter drove his shoulder into the black man's chest, hurling the defender backward. On his third, Walter soared upward for the jam, simultaneously decking the black man with an elbow to the chin. The ball rippled through the twine and the referee blew his whistle and slashed the air with his hand: count the basket and a foul on the defense.

Walter pushed some more buttons and the tape backed up. He ran it through the same sequence one more time.

"See that?" he said to his companion. He laughed with unrestrained glee. "I almost cold-cock the poor bastard and *he* gets called for the foul!"

The lady nodded respectfully. She didn't know the first thing about basketball, but she greatly admired a white man who had enough of the right stuff to knock a huge black man on his ass.

For Walter, though, the beauty of the moment captured on that videotape was not in the legalized mayhem.

It had been the sixth game of a savage seven-game playoff series with the Celtics. And it had been Walter's night to shine. He'd scored twenty-seven points and pulled down eighteen brutally contested rebounds. The stuff shot had come after forty-seven minutes and fifty-seven seconds of play, and it had tied the score. Walter was dog tired and black-and-blue as he stepped to the charity stripe.

Foul shooting had never been his strong suit. But this time he was playing in that trancelike state athletes occasionally attain, in which they are somehow tuned to the basic rhythm of the universe and can do no wrong. Walter knew with utter certainty that he'd nail the shot, and he did.

The Celtics made one last desperate try, a thirty-foot Hail Mary heave at the buzzer, but it sailed wide. Walter was a hero. He'd delivered in the clutch.

Nothing that had come his way since could top that. Not sex with a succession of the most beautiful blondes in America. Not the wealth he'd acquired from some fortuitous natural gas investments. Not the term he'd served as governor of California. Not the surprise nomination for Vice-President, nor his subsequent election to the nation's most important duty-free office.

None of those could do what a reliving of the glory days could: make him young again.

Walter was watching The Play yet a third time, but the lady of the moment obviously had another sport on her mind. She ran her tongue lightly along his inner thigh, cupped it around the underside of his balls and wagged it rapidly like a tail.

The maneuver created a tickling sensation, but hardly an unpleasant one. Walter felt the familiar warmth spread upward from her tongue in one smooth wave, as far as the middle of his belly. He clicked off the VCR and leaned back against the headboard, closing his eyes.

The former Miss Maryland, he had to admit, was a lady of more conspicuous talents than most. She had a mouth as satiny as the sky-blue sheets, and her slippery little tongue would go anywhere and do anything. She knew how to lead him to the brink of release and then hold him there for long, swollen minutes of exquisite torment.

Not that Walter didn't give as good as he got. The lady loved his massive, hairy body, and she loved to sit astride him, digging her heels into his flanks as though she were wearing silver spurs. When she came, it was with long, shuddering gasps that made it seem like her very life's breath was being torn out of her.

Now, she had just taken as much of him into her mouth as a mortal human could when the bedside telephone rang.

His whole body had begun to hum. His limbs were liquid and pinpoints of flame were dancing on the backs of his eyelids. It was a moment that all of the world's crises should not have been allowed to interrupt.

Nevertheless, out of habit he opened his eyes and looked over at the phone console. It indicated that the call was coming in on the line reserved for the most serious communications.

He sighed and gently disengaged the blonde lady from her creative oral coupling. She gave him a very disappointed look, but he held up an optimistic forefinger to indicate "one minute." Then he answered the phone.

The conversation lasted less than the promised minute. Nothing in Walter's end of it would have indicated to the lady what it was about, but by the time he'd finished, it was obvious that his thoughts were no longer with her.

He got out of bed and began getting his clothes together, telling her to do the same. Something important, he said, had come up.

The lady pouted and said, "More important than . . . ?"

"Yes," he said. "Even more important than that."

With genuine reluctance the lady pulled herself out of bed. It had to be something pretty damn important, she thought. But then, he *was* the Vice-President. Sometimes it was hard for her to remember that.

Walter selected his best, most conservative gray suit, a pastel blue shirt, muted tie and black wing-tips. Normally, he was much more casual, but he knew he had a strong first impression to make.

When he'd finished dressing and the lady of the moment had left, he went into the bathroom and opened the medicine cabinet. It was well stocked. He had lots of aches and pains, physical reminders of his playing days, as well as the odds and ends of habits accumulated over the years. He sorted through the brown plastic containers until he found what he was looking for. Today he was going to need all the extra energy he could come by.

He popped one of the amphetamines into his mouth

and washed it down. And he slipped a few extras into his jacket pocket. Just in case.

Brust reported first to his own office in the West Wing. He was nervous and wanted the most familiar surroundings as the day's events unfolded. Tom Read, whose office was adjacent, was waiting for him.

"What's the situation?" Brust asked after the two men had settled themselves in.

"Uncertain," the Chief of Staff said. "As I told you over the phone, the President's helicopter was fired on just after nine-thirty this morning. He escaped immediate harm, but because of the stress appears to have suffered a heart attack of unknown magnitude. He's at the Navy Med now, and there's a call in to you from there that I suggest you return. I believe it's from the First Lady. She was flown there immediately and she should be the most up-to-date on the President's condition."

"Yes, of course," Brust said, and he had his appointments secretary place a call to the medical center.

After a slight delay caused by the routine military screening of incoming calls, the soft Virginia accent of the First Lady came on the line. "Walter?"

"Yes, ma'am," Brust said. "I'm with Tom and he's filling me in. How're we doing out there?"

"Fine. The President's resting just now, but I think he's doing fine."

"Well, good. What do the doctors say?"

"Oh, you know doctors. They never tell you anything. But he's had an EKG and echo-cardiogram. It looks like a very mild heart attack. Nothing to worry about, but they want to keep him under observation, just to be sure there isn't something else coming. And they may want to do an angiogram, but not right away. He's on nitro and phenobarb at the moment. I talked to him before he went to sleep, and he said he's going to be up and around tomorrow. So keep the office tidy until then."

"I'll do my best, ma'am. Anything else we can do for him?"

"No," she said. "He said that you know what his policies are and not to do anything drastic without consulting him. You can call me in a real emergency and I'll see that he's made aware of the problem."

"All righty. You tell your husband to get well soon now, y'hear?"

Brust set the receiver carefully into its cradle. He found that he hadn't come away with a genuine sense of what was happening at the hospital. When he thought about it, he wasn't even sure what a heart attack was. He didn't know how one was treated, nor exactly how crippling a "mild" one might be. And he didn't have a clue as to how much was expected of him, or for how long.

"Good news?" Read asked him.

"Yeah," Brust said. "Back on his feet by tomorrow, he says. He's a tough old coot."

"He's more of a fighter than most men ever laced the gloves on. But nevertheless, we're gonna have to prepare for the worst."

"Okay, let's get to it. What do I need to know?"

Read silently prayed for the speediest recovery in the history of the human heart.

Out loud he said, "The most important thing right now is of course the terrorist situation. How extensive is your knowledge of what's going on?"

"I've got a pretty good idea," Brust said, "but maybe you better brief me anyway."

Yeah, maybe, Read thought, and he walked Brust through the events of the past eight days. When he'd finished, he was satisfied that the Vice-President had at least a superficial grasp of the facts and some appreciation for the seriousness of the situation.

Read took great care to stress that the major potential threat was of a sudden escalation of hostilities, so that the superpowers came into direct conflict. The President had been steering a tricky course with regard to Nicaragua, Cuba, and the Soviet Union. But the thrust of his policy was clear.

Brust could see all that, Read believed, but was the man capable of sure-handed decision-making? Inside, he shuddered at the thought of Walter trying to deal with the General Secretary.

"I think the best thing to do," the Chief of Staff said, "is simply hold the fort until the President can get back in harness. But you will have to get your own feel for how the anti-terrorist task force is proceeding. I scheduled a meeting in the Cabinet Room for half-past eleven.

After that you can set your own agenda. Other folks can brief you on other things."

"Okay," Brust said. "Thanks, Tom. I appreciate what you're doing for me."

"You'll have my best, Mr. Vice-President, you can count on that."

41

The staff had assumed their places around the Cabinet Room table much as they always did. Brust had been hesitant at first to take the presiding chair at table's head, but the others had convinced him that, under the circumstances, it was the proper thing to do.

He cleared his throat and tentatively called the meeting to order. Seven heads were turned in his direction, and each wore a different and distinctive look. Tension, expectancy, hesitation, hostility, caution, supportiveness—all were there in varying degrees.

"Well," he said, "I guess everyone knows the fix we're in by now. I was never expecting to be sitting in this chair." He smiled as he shifted his great bulk. "And I admit that it feels a little big for me. But I hope you all realize I'm depending on you for your help. I'm going to try and do some listening this morning. So what's new?"

"Well," National Security Adviser McBain said, "the President's position was that we'd negotiate on all points except the money, that we weren't going to pay it. That seemed to make the enemy angry. I think we may safely conclude that this morning's attack was his response."

Secretary of State Carini had been fidgeting in his chair, waving his hand in front of him to clear the air of the smoke from Gunther Schule's cigarettes that kept drifting in his direction.

"Mr. Vice-President," he said angrily, "how long are we going to wait? We lost the crew of a Cobra this morning. Seven civilians were killed on the ground. We came damn close to losing our president. I say it's way past time for us to hit back!"

Monty Banks, Chairman of the Joint Chiefs, said, "I'd have to second that. We're trying to bargain here without having put any of *our* chips on the table. That just doesn't make sense."

"And what do you suggest?" Brust asked.

"A preemptive strike on the Nicaraguan airfields," Banks said. "I speak for all the Joint Chiefs when I say that we feel that'll defuse the situation."

"If I may," Secretary of Defense Schule said softly. He laid his tortoiseshell cigarette holder on the lip of his ashtray. "General Banks's idea fails to take into account potential Soviet response to military action on our part. We could easily wind up confronting them directly."

"Well," Brust said, "how close are we to getting the missiles back, for goodness sake?"

"I'd say we've got a fair shot before they strike again," McBain said.

"Yeah," Attorney General Walker said, "give us a couple of days."

"What about the guy that was captured this morning?" Brust said. "Doesn't he know where they are?"

The Director cleared his throat and spoke. "He's in custody, sir. We thought it might be better if you didn't know exactly what was going on."

"What does that mean? What are you, torturing the guy?"

"He's being interrogated, Mr. Vice-President. Its—"

There was a discreet knock at the door. The naval officer attending scowled as he cracked it open, but his expression changed when he saw that it was the Situation Room's duty officer. He opened the door wider and admitted the man.

"I'm sorry, sir," the duty officer said to the Vice-President. "But the General Secretary is on the MosCom. He wanted to talk to the President, but . . ."

There was a pause, then Walter Brust said, "Very well. I'll speak with the General Secretary. The rest of you should come, too."

There was an almost audible sigh of relief, followed by the rustling of bodies lifting themselves from chairs and the low tones of quick, private conversations.

Amid the general shuffle Brust had the opportunity to transfer another pill from his jacket pocket to his mouth unobserved, then take a long swallow from his water glass.

Now he was ready for anything.

The area around the Situation Room was humming. The MosCom, a dedicated voice link with Moscow, had been installed by the incumbent. The President felt that the original "hot line"—which passed only printed messages—lacked the personal touch that might be needed during a real crisis. The link was tested daily, but no other use had yet been made of it. Thus there was a great deal of Sit Room speculation as to what the General Secretary now had on his devious mind.

Setting everything up took a few minutes, but soon the Vice-President and his staff were gathered in the austere, crowded room. The door was closed and the sign above it flashed on: MEETING IN PROGRESS. Some of those in the outer ring of offices busied themselves with the tasks necessary to maintaining a secure, bilingual, intercontinental communications hookup.

Inside, Brust said, "Greetings, Mr. General Secretary," to the air. The Situation Room was wired so that no actual phones cluttered the workspace.

In Moscow, the man to whom Brust spoke heard both his voice and the voice of a translator who was patched into the line from an adjacent office. The General Secretary's translator would supply his own Russian version as well. The Americans would then hear the General Secretary's response, as well as the Russian translator's rendering of the response into English and the American translator's interpretation. In addition, there were backup translators at either end who heard everything. Hopefully, the system was sufficiently redundant that nothing terrible would ever happen because of a translation error.

Brust pictured his caller in his mind, as he always did when he was on the phone. Unlike so many of his Politburo predecessors, the incumbent General Secretary's face was not at all unpleasant. It lacked that chronically dour Russian look of someone who knows that July and August are only times of preparation for another ten months of winter. In fact, the man had not only a rather cheerful face but, by Soviet standards, an almost sunny disposition to go with it.

Yet even Brust knew that the General Secretary had struggled to the top of a harsh and intrigue-ridden political system. One didn't accomplish such a feat without leaving a few stray bodies buried along the way.

The General Secretary returned the greeting, then said, "Let me also express our best wishes to the President and our hope for his most rapid recovery. We condemn international acts of terrorism, as you do, and you have my personal assurance that the Union of Soviet Socialist Republics is in no way connected with, nor in any way condones, this latest outrage."

"Thank you," Brust said. "I know the President appreciates your concern."

"We have other concerns, as well. We must also condemn the acts of aggression currently being perpetrated by the United States against the sovereign nation of Nicaragua."

"Well, I'd say they were committing a few against us, wouldn't you?"

"We are in communication with the incumbent government there, and I assure you that the terrorists are not representing that government's interests, nor are they receiving any measure of support from that quarter. They are being blackmailed equally as much as you are."

"We kind of see things a little different," Brust said.

"I hope that that is not so," the General Secretary said. "As you know, we have treaty agreements with Nicaragua. We fully intend to honor them."

"And what does that mean?"

"It means that we are bound to come to the defense of our ally in the event of acts of war. Mr. Vice-President, if American troops or aircraft were to carry out any operations within the boundaries or airspace of Nicaragua, then we would have to respond."

"I don't think we want to be shooting at each other, Mr. General Secretary."

"I don't, either. Our position should, however, be made clear, so that there might be no misunderstandings about this."

Brust looked around the room for help and General Banks mouthed some words that he repeated. "What level of response are you prepared to make, Mr. General Secretary?" he said.

Finally the reply came back. "The people of Cuba, in solidarity with their friends in Nicaragua, have volunteered to transfer a wing of MiG fighters to the mainland." He paused for dramatic effect, then continued, "If any attempt is made to interfere with Nicaraguan landing facilities, the Soviet Union is prepared to fly to Cuba, immediately, five Blackjack bombers."

Brust saw the stunned look on the faces of those around him.

McBain shook her head vigorously and Banks mouthed the single word, "Never."

"We would not permit that," Brust said.

"Then I would suggest the path of conciliation rather than confrontation," the General Secretary said. "Good day, Mr. Vice-President."

"Good day, Mr. General Secretary."

As soon as the Russian had rung off, the room exploded into a babble of hyper-excited voices that ended only when Brust slammed the palm of his oversized hand onto the table.

When some semblance of calm had returned, he said, "Now what does that mean in plain English?"

"We can't allow Blackjack bombers in Cuba," McBain said. "It's been the policy of every president since Kennedy that the introduction of long-range offensive weapons that close to the U.S. would constitute an act of war."

"They're that dangerous?" Brust said.

"They're that dangerous," McBain said. "Armed with cruise missiles, they could hit a dozen of our biggest cities before we had the time to take them out. It's unthinkable that we'd allow them ninety miles away."

"You can always trust a Communist . . ." Carini muttered, "to be a Communist."

"And if you don't mind my saying so, Diane," Banks put in, "it's also been policy since Reagan that no MiGs be allowed in Nicaragua."

"Right," McBain said. "The question, Mr. Vice-President, is whether the General Secretary is bluffing."

Brust turned to the duty officer and said, "Let's run a tape of that call again. And get me a map of this hemisphere in here."

A few moments later, the sound of the Vice-President saying "Greetings" came out of the room's speakers. The group listened as if it might have collectively misheard, but the conversation wasn't any more palatable the second time around.

"It's a bluff," Banks said.

The duty officer came back in. He set up a tripod with a large pull-down map on it. Then he receded into the background.

"Well, what about it, Monty?" Brust asked. "Could they get the bombers to Cuba?"

Banks got up and studied the map. Then, pointing with his forefinger, he said, "Yeah, I think they've just about got the range. They'd have to take off from Kamchatka here, and follow something like the course of KAL-007 when it got shot down. They'd end up cruising along just off our western coast, all the way to Nicaragua, which I think is the first country that'd permit them into its airspace. Then from there it's just a short hop to Cuba."

"That'd have to be it. Any other way and they'd have to figure out how to do some midair refueling. They'd be facing overflight problems as well."

Banks nodded and returned to his seat.

"They could make it," the Vice-President said, "unless . . . they were intercepted."

"Yes," McBain said. "We could take them out anywhere from Alaska on. But they'd be over the ocean, which is agreed-upon neutral territory. That's a first-strike act of war."

"And they would retaliate?" Brust said.

"They'd have to," McBain said.

"How?"

She just shrugged. Brust looked around the room, but no one had any better idea than she had. "All right," he said, "what do we do?"

Secretary of Defense Schule cleared his throat. "I think it's important to remember," he said, "that it's still the President's decision. And his feelings in this matter are clear."

"He's not aware of the latest developments," Carini said quickly.

"That's right, Mr. Secretary," Brust said. "And I'll be calling him as soon as we finish here."

"But if the President is incapacitated," Banks pointed out, "they're your decisions to make. We can't have a leadership vacuum around here while he's recovering. We've got a hell of a crisis on our hands."

"I know my responsibilities, General," Brust said. "All right, what about the guy we got this morning?"

The Director puffed on his pipe, then said, "I didn't want to involve you with this, Mr. Vice-President, because it's a little unorthodox. But the driver of the van from which this morning's missile was fired was apprehended very near Langley, and I ordered some officers to the scene right away. I also felt that our facilities were more conducive than the county jail to obtaining information from the man, so I had him brought to us."

He wasn't quite telling the truth. It was Smith who had monitored the car chase down the George Washington Parkway and who had given the order to take the terrorist into federal custody. But the story would hold. Smith had immediately told his boss what he had done, and the Director had concurred with the decision.

"We desperately need to know what he knows," he added.

"Who is he?" Brust asked.

"His name is Corrales," the DCI said. "We have a file on him. We believe that although he has been active in the Nicaraguan resistance, he is in reality an agent of the Sandinista government."

"Did he attack the President?"

"No, we think there was another man in the vehicle who actually fired the missile and escaped somewhere along the parkway. One of our primary initial objectives has been to learn the other man's identity, but we haven't yet succeeded."

"Do you think this Corrales knows where the Stingers are?"

"I don't know, Mr. Vice-President. All he'll say is that he wants a lawyer."

"How long can we hold him?" Brust asked.

The Director shrugged. "Some of the bleeding hearts might complain," he said, "but the President has a lot of leeway where the national interest is involved."

"It's involved here. I'll take responsibility for speaking for the President. Keep on questioning him. But I don't want torture, or anything like that."

The Director nodded and said, "The other thing is that it's important to put out a cover story about Corrales, preferably that he was killed resisting arrest. Identify him as some kind of shadowy international terrorist, show his picture on TV and all that. What we don't want is for the news media to mindlessly speculate about him and his friend. Give them a dead villain and maybe a heroic cop to play with instead."

Brust looked puzzled.

"An excellent suggestion," McBain said, and she turned to the Vice-President. "Corrales's accomplice is going to be missing him. If he thinks Corrales is still alive and that we have him, he'll be worried about what Corrales is telling us. He'll make himself very, very hard to find. But if the media plays up Corrales's death, the other guy will be lulled into a sense of false security and we may be able to get Corrales to lead us to him."

"Oh," Brust said, "I see. That's good thinking. Tom, can you handle that?"

"No sweat," Read said.

"If you don't mind, I'd like to send someone from the Bureau to the interrogation," Walker said. "We've got some people who've had experience dealing with terrorists. Maybe they could help."

"Of course," the Director said. "I'll see that they're expected."

"And a representative from the NSC?" McBain put in. "As an observer and liaison with the group here?"

The Director nodded.

"Damn good," Brust said. "I like to see the whole team pulling together. All righty, let's get to work."

Don Walker waited until he was back in his office in the Justice Department before unwiring himself.

It was an elementary surreptitious set up, with a mike masquerading as one of his shirt buttons and a voice-activated Viking microcassette recorder in his jacket pocket. He'd had no need for anything more sophisticated. No one who'd been in the Situation Room would have believed that the Attorney General of the United States was taping them without their permission.

Walker removed the cassette and swiveled in his chair for a moment, looking down at the tiny spool of tape with his one good eye, wondering what secrets it contained.

But there was nothing to know until he got a sample of Smoking Gun's voice for comparison.

*   *   *

General Montgomery Banks and Admiral Wesley Drake sat across from one another in a room on the second floor of the old Executive Office Building. Banks would have preferred meeting in the Pentagon, where he had greater control over the environment, but he hadn't wanted to leave the immediate vicinity of the White House. Too much was happening. The Vice-President might need a firm guiding hand at a critical moment. So the general had settled for the EOB, and had summoned Drake there for a very private conversation.

"Wes," he told his old friend, "we got ourselves one hell of a mess here."

And he laid out the details. When he was finished, Admiral Drake felt overwhelmed. He sighed heavily.

" 'Hell of a mess'," he said, "doesn't quite cover it."

"I know," Banks said. "How're the forces in the field? Ready?"

Drake nodded. "My commanders are on full alert. I've given them authority to respond in kind if attacked."

"Well, you know what we got to talk about."

Drake paused, then said carefully, "Yeah, I know. What if the President really is incapable of making a decision?"

"Even if we had him, I'm not sure he'd be able to see what the Russians are trying to pull here and how important it is to stand up to them."

"And Walter Brust?"

"Well," Banks said, "he showed a little more moxie today than I thought he would. But if the decision falls on him, I don't know if he'll be able to make it."

"My loyalty," Drake said firmly, "is to the Commander in Chief, I want to make that clear. It's his job to formulate policy, not ours."

"Of course. But we also need to consider what he would want if he was fully in control. We'd be derelict in our own duties if we didn't do that."

"And you can't be doing anything on your own, Monty. I won't back you up if you do."

"Don't worry, we're working together."

There was another long pause, then Drake said, "All right, let's keep a close watch on the situation."

"I'll be near the Vice-President all day," General Banks said.

42

Bruderdam was in his command center, pondering the latest turn of events.

He found that he wasn't all that concerned. True, Mosby had become a loose cannon, but the Nicaraguan's unilateral decisions hadn't been terrible so far. With the President on the sidelines, the desired result might even be achieved that much more quickly.

Still, the proper people must regain control of the operation.

Mosby had to go, first off. He'd served his purpose and, while he might successfully carry out his assignment, he couldn't be trusted. The missiles would have to remain at large, even if no more of them were used. At this point the threat was probably enough. The Vice-President had to be given a good kick in the butt, as soon as possible. And a few loose ends had to be tied up.

Bruderdam thought some more, then composed a series of messages to be fed into his electronic mail network.

Stonewall—Mosby must be removed from his position and associate dismissed. Merchandise should remain warehoused even if inoperative. All recovery personnel expendable as soon as Mosby located. Sherman.

Burnside—Ideal time to consolidate in absence of CEO. Make all effort to convert Acting CEO to our position and press for early decision. Supplementary action to convince him should take place ASAP. Sherman.

Mr. Grant—Mosby must go. Recovery team should be assisted as much as possible. Inventory control imperative until attainment of objective. Have instructed Burnside to relocate recovery team afterward, per your wishes. Sherman.

That about covered it, Bruderdam thought. Except . . . What the hell, it was worth a shot. He composed one more message.

Mosby—Excellent work. Expect action soonest from other side. Meantime, your situation precarious. Suggest return to home base ASAP. Will make usual arrangements directly I hear from you. Sherman.

Bruderdam sent the message with a prearranged code which instructed the recipient that it was to be relayed to the message drop he and Mosby had agreed upon. He had no idea if Mosby was even occasionally calling in to the drop anymore. But if he was . . . Well, snatching Mosby would be the ideal solution to all of the operation's problems.

Javier Vega had gone immediately to ground.

It was a fashionable condo facing onto the C & O canal, near Whitehurst Freeway. Colonel Salazar had purchased it several years earlier and maintained it as a safe house, keeping its existence secret from everyone but those of his associates who might someday need it.

The condo had a big color TV, from which Vega first learned that his Stinger hadn't hit Marine One but a Cobra gunship instead. He cursed violently until he heard that the President had suffered an apparent heart attack, then he chuckled contentedly to himself. That was just as good, maybe better. Now the bastards would be running around in the dark for a while, not knowing who was in charge.

There was nothing on the TV about the would-be assassins, outside of some vague speculation. They were presumed to be part of the terrorist group, of course. But they had vanished once again after the latest incident. The most massive manhunt in the city's history was underway.

Vega waited nervously for Corrales, who was one of the few with knowledge of the safe house, but Corrales never showed. Vega also called the phone drop several times. Corrales hadn't checked in there either.

Then, early in the afternoon, the story broke. The Arlington police called a press conference, jointly with representatives of the federal law enforcement agencies. Photos were shown of the van, Corrales, and the used Stinger launch tube found in the parking lot.

Corrales, identified as a well-known international assassin, with ties to Libya and the IRA, was dead. The high-speed car chase down the George Washington Parkway was described. When the van was finally cornered, Corrales had come out firing and had been killed by a rookie cop with a steady gun hand.

It was also revealed that Corrales's pistol was the same caliber weapon that had murdered an innocent bystander during the course of the morning attack on Marine One. Police were confident that a test firing would match up the slugs.

As far as Corrales's accomplice went, no one would admit to having any clues, but the search was continuing.

Vega felt little sense of loss; Corrales would have been dead soon in any case, from the ricin. And he had to laugh at the Americans' obsession with conspiracies. Corrales linked with Libya? The IRA? Very amusing.

No, all in all, things couldn't have turned out much better for Javier Vega. He was free, Corrales was dead, and the U.S. government was in turmoil.

Throughout the day Vega continued to call the phone drop. He expected that Salazar, or someone else in a position of authority, would make contact sooner or later. They'd have sense enough to stay away from the safe house.

But there was nothing on the message board that Vega wanted. What did show up, late in the afternoon, was an unexpected communication from Bruderdam. Or Sherman, as the idiot ridiculously insisted on calling himself.

Bruderdam wanted him to return to the island.

It almost made him laugh out loud. As if that splotch of sand was a safe haven for someone who'd just tried to kill the President of the United States. He shook his head at the balls of the man. The thing was an invitation to become shark food and he knew it.

Screw Bruderdam, he thought. Screw the whole rotten gringo connection. They'd served their purpose, they'd gotten the missiles into the hands of someone who knew what needed to be done and had the courage to do it. Now it was *his* mission to command.

He needed Bruderdam as much as he needed all those worthless exile military officers who'd lost sight of the true objective. Far too many of them were sitting on their butts, polishing their brass while they grew slowly fat in their adopted homeland.

He could do it absolutely alone if he had to.

Trying to pry open Corrales, Smith thought, was a bit like having been a general in Vietnam. He was allowed to question the man, then question him some more, but he had to stop short of using the techniques that would really get the job done.

The man was tough, Smith had to admit. And loyal. They weren't going to break him just by talking to him.

"My name is Corrales," the prisoner said, "and I demand to speak with an attorney."

Who was in the van with you?

"No one. I was alone."

You shot the man in the parking lot?

"What man? What parking lot?"

It isn't your pistol?

"I don't own a pistol."

Where did you get the van? (A registration check had indicated it was stolen.)

"It's not mine. I was running an errand for a friend."

What friend?

"A friend of a friend. I don't know his name. What about my attorney?"

And so on.

Smith had had a private go at Corrales when the man was first brought in, and he'd done his best. He'd offered immunity from prosecution, money, a new identity. Not a bad deal for someone who was facing trial for conspiracy to assassinate the president, a crime punishable by death. And all Corrales had to do in return was provide the answer to one simple question: where was Javier Vega?

"I've heard of him," Corrales had said, "but I never met him."

After that, Smith had turned the job over to a couple of professionals, with instructions not to leave any marks on him. They'd had a little quiet time with the man, but with no better results.

Then the circus had begun. People had arrived from the FBI and the White House, all demanding access to the terrorist. Smith was in no position to refuse. The order to cooperate had come straight from the DCI.

The problem with the influx of outsiders was that there was now no reasonable chance that Corrales would talk. Too many people with weak stomachs were watching for the finer arts of persuasion to be applied. Corrales's position was strengthened, and he'd know that.

Smith's only hope, a very faint one at best, was that Corrales would somehow change his mind and go for the deal.

Otherwise, Smith was going to have to come up with an alternative way of locating Vega.

43

March 22

Danilo Baez was more exhilarated than he had been in a long time.

At a little after one in the morning, the Honduran scuba diver was riding with "Joe," his contact with the Americans. Joe's car was a plain, four-wheel-drive Subaru station wagon, and it was back on Highway One, climbing from the coast up into the mountains, toward Tegucigalpa.

Baez was feeling good because he'd been handed one of the more difficult assignments of his career and had brought it off without a hitch. But professional pride was only the half of it. He was feeling especially good because the past few hours' work had earned him fifteen thousand American dollars.

As planned, he'd flown from La Ceiba, on the north coast, to Tegucigalpa, the capital city that lay at the mountainous heart of the poverty-stricken Central American nation. Joe had taken the same plane, but had shown no sign of knowing him. Later they'd met up and made the trip down to San Lorenzo in this same Subaru, arriving well after dark.

Just being in San Lorenzo made Baez a little nervous. It was Honduras's primary commercial Pacific port, but the number of soldiers in the streets suggested something more like a military base. For the town was on the Gulf of Fonseca, a relatively small body of water that was one of the most heavily patroled in the world. The reason was simple. The gulf bordered not only Honduras, but Nicaragua and El Salvador as well. And the two democracies kept a watchful eye on anything coming from their totalitarian neighbor to the south.

The American Navy, however, was allowed a lot of freedom in Salvadoran and Honduran waters. It had been using that privilege to anchor the frigate USS. *Studds* in San Lorenzo, while a team of specialists came down from California to make some repairs to the ship's computer that were beyond the expertise of anyone on board. The *Studds* was then scheduled to rejoin the carrier task force that was standing off Nicaragua, waiting for the resolution of the current political crisis.

Baez had felt that everyone in town was watching him, but no one had given him any trouble. Joe had dropped him off at the waterfront and he'd met his next contact, a man who ferried him in a small dinghy out to a yacht that was also moored in the harbor, about five hundred meters from the *Studds*.

The yacht was a seventy-two-foot sloop whose stern proclaimed it to be the SANGRE DE CRISTO, home port KEY WEST, FLA. It was the property of a Miami-based real estate corporation whose ownership could be traced, if one worked at it, to Enrique Salazar and Francisco Vega.

As Baez prepared for his dive, his nervousness faded. He was in his element now, doing what he did best. There'd be twenty feet of water separating him from the dangers at the surface.

He'd decided that twenty feet was deep enough that the faint green glow from his instruments couldn't possibly be seen, yet shallow enough that he'd run no risk of missing the frigate entirely.

As far as equipment was concerned, he'd elected to go with a shorty wetsuit top instead of the full Farmer John. The gulf's waters were warm enough, and not having his arms and legs encased in neoprene would give him a larger measure of flexibility. The wetsuit, along with his hood, tank, mask, fins, and hoses, were all black. The tank was a rebreathing model that left no telltale trail of bubbles.

That reduced the chances of detection, but it also meant that with each breath he was taking in a little more carbon dioxide. With a rebreather you slowed your rate of respiration as much as possible and you surfaced as soon as you could.

He carried the magnetic mine—also painted black—in a tough nylon mesh bag laced to his weight belt. He'd had a moment of hesitancy when he recognized the mine as Russian, but the moment passed. He was committed to the operation and had to assume that the others knew what they were doing.

Forty-five minutes after arriving on the *Sangre de Christo*, he slipped noiselessly into the water from the stern ladder. He was fully geared up and his nerves were rock-steady.

The plan was to stay on the surface as long as seemed safe. That turned out to be about half the distance to the *Studds*. Then he decided there was too great a risk of being seen and he submerged.

He dropped down to twenty feet, oriented himself with his compass, and activated his stopwatch. This would not only keep track of his bottom time, but would tell him how long it took to swim the final stretch to the frigate.

It was easy going—no strong currents to deal with— and he kept up a moderate, steady rhythm with his long, narrow power fins. Ten minutes later, something huge loomed across his path, showing just slightly darker than the surrounding water: the hull of the ship. He marked his time.

Carefully he followed the curve of the hull around and down, until he could make out the shadowy shape of a massive propeller, clinging to its shaft like a nightmare mutant starfish.

This was his one moment of deep, bowel-wrenching fear. If for some reason the ship started its engines, his body would be torn to pieces.

He went in and out quickly, taking time only to ease the mine onto the prop shaft so that it didn't make a loud metallic clang that might be heard inside the ship.

Then he checked his compass and timer and swam away. He kept to the twenty-foot depth, but moved faster on the return trip. Fifteen minutes out, he surfaced. He was only about a hundred meters from the *Sangre de Christo* and just a little to starboard. There were no other boats in the vicinity.

The rest had gone smoothly. He swam to the sloop, doffed his gear, and was ferried back to land, where Joe met him with the Subaru.

Now Baez was relaxing in his seat, enjoying his physical weariness and the anticipation of things to come. The Subaru climbed steadily upward into the inky night of a desolate mountain region beyond the reach of electricity.

It was such a small country, Baez thought, with so many millions of people, yet there was so much land where no one lived.

The road leveled out momentarily as it passed across a saddle between two peaks. There was even space for a turnout. And in the turnout a car was parked. A battered ten-year-old Chevrolet with its parking lights on.

Joe pulled the Subaru over next to the Chevy. "Change of cars," he said.

"Huh?" Baez said.

"You need to change cars. It's just a simple precaution, Danilo."

"I don't understand. Why?"

"We're afraid we may have been seen leaving Tegucigalpa. I'm going to decoy anyone waiting away from you. It's really for your own safety, my friend. Trust me. Go on."

Baez felt uneasy. But Joe had never lied to him before. "What about the money?" Baez asked.

"I don't have it with me, Danilo. Meet me in La Ceiba. Same place, six o'clock tonight. I'll have it for you then. Please, I've got to get going."

Reluctantly Baez opened the door and got out.

As soon as he did, the Subaru sped off into the night, and Baez knew that something was very wrong. Two men were getting out of the Chevy. He couldn't see their faces in just the glow from the parking lights, but by now he was sure that he didn't want to. He turned to run.

He'd taken only three steps when the first bullet hit him. It was a 9-mm slug and it knocked him flat on his face. With what seemed an extraordinary burst of energy, he pushed himself over onto his back. The lower half of his body was numb.

The two men were standing over him. They did not know what he had done, nor did they want to. He watched them bend, one at his hands and one at his feet, and pick him up like a steamer trunk.

And at that moment a profound change came over Danilo Baez. Suddenly his entire life made sense to him. Not in any way that could be put into words, but completely nevertheless. He felt a calm that he'd never known.

The two men carried him across the road. On the other side was an unprotected drop of five hundred feet to the floor of a canyon through which ran a small stream. No one lived this far up the canyon.

They swung him backward once, then forward, and they let go. Baez arced out into space. For an instant he was weightless, as he was when he dived. Then he began to fall, and the fall seemed to last forever. . . .

His body struck a ledge two hundred feet down, bounced off, then fell another hundred feet before tumbling the remainder of the way down the canyon slope and lodging at the base of a large boulder, where it would be discovered only by the carrion-eaters. A few loose rocks that had been dislodged by the falling object clattered for a while after it had finally come to rest.

The old Chevy growled away in first gear, and then there was only the unbroken silence of the mountains.

44

Kirk and Andino napped during the evening of the twenty-first, and by midnight they were up and ready to go. They dressed in dark, loose-fitting clothing, had some coffee, and armed themselves with a few carefully chosen things from Smith's bag of tricks, as well as a couple of specialty items they'd picked up on their own earlier in the day.

They arrived at Salazar's place off Broad Branch Road a little after one. Kirk parked the Eagle at the rear of the property, near the ivy-covered wall. The street was only moderately well lighted and very quiet.

Over the course of the afternoon they'd formulated their plan. It was of necessity a simple one, because it had to be flexible enough to deal with defensive measures that were of unknown size, strength, and configuration.

They'd settled on an elementary tactical diversion.

Their planning was based on a belief that no one like Colonel Salazar would live in a house that didn't have a perimeter security device. Since none was obvious to their trained eyes, the assumption had to be that he was using some sort of hair's-breadth tripwire or perhaps a seismic intrusion detector.

The former was more common, required less maintenance, and would be considerably cheaper for a parcel of this size. Therefore it was likelier that that's what they'd find. They had to determine for sure, however, which variety of defense they were up against, if that were possible, and to have contingency plans for both.

The two systems were equally effective. With either, someone trying to enter the property surreptitiously at night would trigger an alarm without realizing it. Which made it a certainty that the colonel would know in advance they were coming.

What would happen after the alarm went off was a question mark, but the range of possibilities wasn't infinite. Some combination of animal and/or human response could be expected. If the alarm also initiated an automatic call to the police, that would be bad, but Kirk doubted the colonel would have selected such an option. He'd want to know who his visitors were first.

Kirk and Andino wasted little time once they'd arrived at their destination. Shortly after parking, Kirk was hunched in the lee of the wall, while Andino waited in the car. The first step was to discover if seismic detectors were deployed on the property.

This was relatively easy to do. Kirk had brought with him a bag of large stones, which he proceeded to heave over the wall. One by one, they thudded to earth. If there were buried detectors, there'd be an alarm and someone from the house would respond.

Nothing happened.

Kirk allowed himself a slight sigh of relief. They could now proceed with the less complicated of their plans. He signaled for Andino to join him.

She watched as he went over the wall, marking precisely in her mind the path he took to the house. Then she left the scene, moving swiftly to a temporary place of concealment in Rock Creek Park, two blocks away.

Splitting up was risky, but it was a chance that had to be taken. Once Kirk was captured, the colonel would almost certainly have the immediate area searched to make sure the intruder had been acting alone.

Behind her, Kirk emerged from the trees and headed for the house's backyard patio. He knew that by that point he must have severed the tripwire. He hadn't felt a thing, though there was no reason why he should have. Trip*wire* was a bit of a misnomer. Trip*thread* would be more descriptive.

Tripwire was pretty efficient at staking out a piece of ground. It had been used extensively in Vietnam to secure encampments in the bush, especially at night, since there was very little chance you'd know when you broke one. The only way to defeat it was—as the Vietcong had learned to do—to crawl through the grass, literally inch by inch, until you touched it.

Kirk had been too young for the Vietnam War, but he

knew the ins and outs of tripwire. He *wanted* to break this one and as he cleared the trees, he realized that he had.

Nothing particularly dramatic happened. No floodlights, no sirens, no warning shots fired over his head.

Just a couple of low growls in the quiet night.

They were pit bulls, a pair of them. Both black, nearly invisible in the gloom. Ideal guard dogs, trained not to kill but to simply clamp the intruder in their powerful jaws and never, ever let go.

Kirk hadn't particularly figured on pit bulls. But he was prepared for whatever the first response was, as long as it was some living being.

He dropped to one knee, facing the charging dogs, and just as they reached striking distance, he stopped them dead in their tracks.

His weapon, which had been clipped to his belt, was the size of a pack of cigarettes. It was known as an IPG, or invisible pain-field generator, and it produced modulated ultrasonic sound of a frequency that caused intense pain in the creature toward which it was aimed.

The pit bulls, being more tenacious than most breeds, gave it a game try. After their initial disorientation they lunged for Kirk. But the closer they got to the IPG, the more unbearable the pain became.

Still they tried to get at the intruder. But with each attack they were further weakened by the pain until finally they lay writhing at the edge of the patio, unable to muster the energy to go on.

Kirk kept the unit trained on them until they finally lost consciousness from the pain. It took longer than he would have thought. They were tough animals. But once out, they wouldn't come to for an hour. That should be more than enough time.

When he was satisfied, he moved away from the neutralized guard dogs, keeping the IPG handy.

As he would have guessed, though, the human backup was not far behind. He hadn't gone more than a few steps when a man stepped from the cover of some evergreen shrubs, pointed a large-caliber handgun in his direction, and commanded him to drop his weapon, whatever it was.

Kirk thought for a moment that it might look better if

he put up at least some minimal resistance. But then he heard another hammer being cocked off to the right, out of his field of vision. It wouldn't do much good to get himself shot before he was captured. He dropped the IPG.

The two men converged on him. While one held a gun on him, the other gave him a rough search. Kirk noted with satisfaction that they were not as professional as they might have been. He could have taken them out with his hands and feet if he'd wanted to.

But he didn't. He let them confiscate all but the most well concealed of the items he'd brought with him. Then he allowed himself to be herded into the house.

Andino stayed well back in the cover provided by the park, but no one ventured that far from the house. This was the most difficult phase of the operation for her, huddling there doing nothing. She had no way of knowing how Kirk was being treated during this time.

They'd discussed who should play which part and, fortunately, there hadn't been much debate. Kirk, thinking it was the masculine thing to do, had volunteered for the more dangerous role of the captured intruder, and Andino had acceded to his wishes without argument.

Truth was, this was the only way she'd have allowed it to work out, and not because the rescuer role was more heroic. No, she'd been coldly objective in her analysis of the situation. This was the more professional way to do it.

Kirk, she'd decided, just didn't have a hard edge to him. He was extremely competent, a man whose technical skills you could trust completely. Yet he didn't have that ruthlessness, that feeling of *whatever*-must-be-done. He was far more a defensive weapon than an offensive one.

And in this case, they were definitely taking the offensive: attempting to kidnap a high-ranking Contra military officer.

That meant that the second person into the house had a succession of very serious responsibilities: release the other person; neutralize the opposition; assist in snatching Colonel Salazar. He or she might have to make some very quick decisions, quite possibly life-and-death ones.

Andino couldn't trust Kirk to make those decisions,

but she could trust herself. Salazar and his thugs were merely an obstacle to Kirk, people about whom he had no particularly strong feelings outside of the current crisis; they were sworn enemies. If she had no choice but to kill, she would kill.

She waited impatiently for fifteen minutes, as agreed upon. It was an arbitrary interval. They'd hoped it would be sufficient for any searchers to have gone back inside the house and the general alarm to have subsided, yet not be so long that Kirk was placed at serious risk.

When the time was up, Andino made her way back to the rear of the Salazar property. If she'd seen anyone at all, she would have assumed it was the enemy. But the streets were empty.

She went over the wall.

Their theory was that the colonel would wait until daylight before having the tripwire repaired. Thus, as long as she closely followed Kirk's earlier path to the house, she should pass over the already broken wire and be able to make her way undetected.

She moved smoothly, keeping low to the ground. It would have taken someone whose senses were highly alert to hear her coming or see the shadow moving among the trees, and the man posted at the back of the house was not that wide-awake. It was the middle of the night and he wanted to be in bed, yet he was stuck out here for God knew how long. Stupid, he thought, especially since they already had the intruder.

Andino crouched down, blending her shape with that of a small cedar. The man was sitting in a chair on the patio, smoking a cigarette, his whole front exposed to her. Two guard dogs were lying next to him, but they weren't stirring.

Distance to the target was less than ten meters. Well within range.

She took out her CO_2 pistol. It was already loaded with an automatic-injection hypodermic dart. The hypo was filled with a concentrated two-cc load of horse tranquilizer. Balancing her hand on an upraised knee, she aimed and fired.

The pistol was virtually silent. The man felt the dart hit him in the upper chest, of course, but one of the beauties of the weapon was that it caused little actual pain. It was no more irritating than a mosquito bite. Thus there was no initial impulse to cry out, and by the time the victim comprehended what was happening to him, it was too late.

The man in the chair slapped his chest, dislodging the dart that had already emptied its load into his body. It fell to the patio. The man grunted and leaned over, groping for whatever it was that had bitten him.

He never righted himself. All of a sudden the world had become a slow-motion place. He tried to clear his head by shaking it, but it barely turned on his neck. His hand seemed ten feet away from his eyes, down there trying to pick up something, he couldn't remember what. His mouth opened slightly, though no sound came out of it. Then the last of his muscles went slack and he toppled over and lay quietly on the flagstones.

Andino waited for a few moments to make sure no one else had been watching. She also reloaded the air pistol with another tranquilizer dart. Then she went to the fallen man. He was breathing, all right, but out cold, and would be for quite a while. Still, not wanting to take unnecessary chances, she stripped him of his gun and tossed it into the densely knit branches of the cedar tree.

Next she checked the two pit bulls. Kirk had done his job well with them. The dogs were satisfactorily comatose.

Then she scouted the immediate vicinity of the house. To her left, the lawn stretched away to the wall. She took a quick look around the corner. No one in sight. Nothing to see but the back of the garage. She retraced her steps.

Ornamental shrubs were planted along the west side of the house, and beyond them an extensive garden with hedges and flower beds. Very adequate cover. She made her way along the inside of the shrubbery until she could see around to the front, where she'd expected another guard to be posted.

But no one was there. A separate alarm system, she concluded. Better that than another person to take care of. Also a reminder not to get careless. If she lost the element of surprise, they were both in serious trouble.

Andino pressed her back to the wall of the house and took some deep breaths, focusing her energy for the task to come. This end of the house was dark, as were most of the above-ground rooms. She and Kirk had surmised that uninvited guests would probably be taken to the basement, and they'd apparently been right.

Directly above her, on the second floor, was a small casement window. Letting onto a bathroom, she hoped. They had decided that she should enter somewhere on the second floor—because of the lesser likelihood that the windows would be alarm-wired—and this was the point of entry she chose.

She pulled a small leather pouch from under her jacket and removed its contents: a set of claws and foot spikes she'd purchased at a martial arts supply store that afternoon. She unwrapped the cloth she'd used to keep them from clinking together when she walked. The items were lightweight aluminum, painted black, with the spikes curved slightly downward and sharpened to needle points.

Traditionally, the climbing aids were known as *shuko* and *ashiko*. She had never used them before today, but had practiced for half an hour—scarring up one of the interior walls of the house on Duddington Place—and felt proficient enough. She didn't have the slightest fear of heights. The devices fit her hands and feet as though they belonged there. And they adhered her to the surface like glue.

She laced them on and started up the east wall of Colonel Salazar's home.

It was a piece of cake. The claws gripped the stout board siding even better than they had the crumbly sheetrock she'd tested them on. The only thing that slowed her down was that she couldn't slap the points into the wood for fear of making a detectable noise. She had to press them in. Extracting them as she moved upward presented a similar problem.

Still, she took only a few minutes to reach the second-story window. It was an unlighted, empty bathroom. She could see to the hallway beyond and it, too, was dark.

She balanced on her feet and removed the hand-claws. From a jacket pocket she took a glass cutter and a suction cup at the end of a short stick. This was a crucial moment. She was going to have to make a little noise. If anyone was in an adjacent room, she'd be heard.

No point in thinking about it. She carefully scored a circle on the window, attached the cup, concentrated all of her energy into her fist and, holding onto the stick, delivered a precise, powerful blow to the scored area.

The circle of glass popped inward. She reached her other hand through the hole, slit the interior screen, and pushed the stick through the slit, finally dropping the glass and suction cup the last few inches to the thickly carpeted floor. Then she unlatched the window and cranked it open enough that she could crawl inside.

She crouched next to a marble pedestal wash basin, catching her breath, listening for the sound of someone coming.

No one came.

She listened more intently and heard something, right at the threshold of hearing. Human voices. But far away. In the basement perhaps.

It was time to move. She took a 9-mm Walther pistol from its holster and screwed the silencer to the barrel.

The bathroom let onto a long hall that encircled a wide, sweeping staircase to the first floor. A half a dozen bedrooms led off the hall. Four of them were open and dark. No light showed under the other two.

She thought for a moment, then decided. She had to start trading caution off against probability. She didn't want to take the time to inspect each room. True, someone might still be sleeping up here, but the odds were against it. Assume the second floor was as deserted as it seemed.

She crept to the head of the stairs. It curved down to a spacious parquet-floored foyer that was brightly lighted by a crystal chandelier. Several oil paintings hung on the wall along the staircase, a series of dark mustachioed men. The one at the top was dressed in the stiff uniform of the Nicaraguan military, and Andino recognized him. Enrique Salazar's father, colonel to the first Somoza.

The foyer was empty, but off it was one lighted room with an open door. Andino watched the room and listened intently, and soon heard a slight scraping sound that betrayed the presence of someone inside.

Otherwise there were no signs of life. A hall led off the foyer in one direction. On the other side of it was a pair of closed doors. She could hear the voices a trifle more clearly now, and they were definitely coming from the basement.

Make another assumption: everyone was down there except for the guard in the room off the foyer.

She went down the staircase fast, hugging the wall. The steps were heavily carpeted, so she made no sound. At the bottom she slipped off her running shoes. She couldn't chance them squeaking on the parquet.

Sticking close to the wall, she edged around the foyer to the open door. She held the pistol in both hands, snug to her right breast. Then she took a deep breath, let out half of it, and stepped quickly through the door.

In the first instant she scanned the entire room. It was small, with a desk and filing cabinets along the wall opposite her and a closed door to the left. At the long end of the room, to her right, was a large double window that overlooked the front of the property. A lone man was sitting in a chair next to the window.

By the time he had reacted to the intruder, Andino was in firing position, elbows locked, knees slightly flexed, pistol as steady as if it were on a tripod. There could be no doubt that the woman in black knew what she was doing and, at a range of less than ten feet, she couldn't possibly miss.

The man reached reflexively for his shoulder holster, but she merely shook her head once and he reconsidered.

"Not a word," she said. "Lie down on the floor, hands behind your head."

As the man complied, she walked over and knelt beside him. She pushed the tip of the silencer into the base of his skull.

"*Viva* Sandino," she said, invoking the name of the national hero for whom the Revolution had been named.

And the man thought he was going to die like a dog. He'd heard the stories of Sandinista agents coming into the U.S. to commit assassinations. But not someone like him. He was young, just an anonymous foot soldier pressed into service by his zealous parents. He barely remembered the homeland.

"No," he said softly. "Please."

"How many of you?" she said.

"Five."

"Including the colonel?"

"Yes."

"Where?"

"One in the back, the other two with him."

"In the basement?"

"Yes."

She had him go over the layout of the basement for her, then got back to her feet. He was just a boy. He'd probably told the truth. She got out the CO_2 pistol and put him quietly to sleep.

Confident now, she put her shoes back on and went to the door under the staircase that she'd been told led to the basement. She turned the knob and the door swung open noiselessly. Everything in the house was well oiled. The voices came up the stairwell, louder now but still unintelligible for the most part. She recognized the cadence of Kirk's speech.

These steps too were carpeted. She went down them, keeping her eye on the area to her left rear. She didn't expect that there would be a man posted outside the door, but that was where he'd be if there was.

A large, open recreation room lay at the foot of the stairs. There was a pool table, bar, and furniture grouping around a TV/VCR/Hi-Fi system.

The door back and to her left was slightly ajar. She could hear the voices clearly now. One was loud and insistent. That would be the colonel's. The other was Kirk's. It was softer but no less insistent, though it intermittently lapsed into a prolonged groan. From time to time a third voice cut in.

Kirk was obviously being questioned, and his questioner was becoming impatient. The lag time they'd agreed on had cut things a little close.

Andino pictured the room in her mind, as it had been described by the young man. Then she placed the people in the scene, figuring their positions from what she was hearing. She made an educated guess about the silent third man.

When she finally burst through the door, she found that she'd gotten it about right.

It was an exercise room, with weight benches, stationary bicycles, a Universal machine. Mats on the floor and mirrors on the walls.

Kirk was wrapped around a post in the middle of the room, facing the door, in a classic interrogation posture called the "Ghurka Scissor." He was sitting on the floor, with his hands bound behind his back. The pole was in the crook of his right knee. His left leg was bent over the right ankle, then to the rear of the pole, so that his left foot rested on his right thigh.

It looked something like a cross-legged meditation position, but it was hardly designed to induce clarity of mind. It was inescapable, embarrassing, and extremely painful in the knee and pelvis joints, though it caused no permanent injury.

The colonel was standing over Kirk, compounding his pain by using the IPG on him. The other two men flanked him, one standing, the other sitting on the edge of a weight bench. All three had their backs to the door.

The colonel's bodyguards reacted fast, but not fast enough. Andino froze them with a single warning shot that smashed one of the wall mirrors, sending shards of glass flying in every direction. After that, she kept her gun hand moving slowly and steadily, targeting first one of them and then the other. Like the young man upstairs, these two had a look at the enemy and decided against suicide.

Salazar hadn't budged, but now he turned so that he too was facing her. The hand that held the IPG hung limp at his side. Kirk gave her a weak smile.

The colonel nodded appreciatively. "Congratulations," he said. "You're very good, miss. What is it that you want?"

Andino pointed to the IPG and held out her hand. Salazar tossed it to her.

"Now let him up," she said.

The colonel knelt down and disentangled Kirk. Both men got to their feet, Kirk a little awkwardly. Salazar untied his former captive, and Kirk rubbed his wrists for a few moments.

Andino motioned to Kirk to take care of the two bodyguards. He frisked each of them in turn, removing their weapons, then had them lie facedown on the floor. Andino flipped him the air pistol and a pair of darts, and Kirk rendered the men unconscious.

"Now what, may I ask?" Salazar said.

"No, you may not," she said.

Kirk moved over to the colonel and searched him, but he was unarmed. Using the cord that had recently bound his own hands, Kirk tied Salazar's behind him. Andino then holstered her pistol. From one pocket she took strips of cloth and gagged the colonel. From the other she took a black hood and slipped it over his head, knotting it securely with a drawstring.

Then she whispered into his ear, "*Viva* Sandino. If I have to kill you, *Somocista*, it will be a pleasure."

Salazar nodded his understanding.

The rest was easy. They went out the back way, hoisted the colonel over the wall, forced him to lie down on the floor of the Eagle, and drove back to the house on Duddington Place. The street was completely deserted at that hour, and they hustled their hostage inside without being seen. They installed him in a small, windowless basement room that they'd cleared of everything but the four walls and the hard concrete floor.

"I'd suggest you get some sleep," Andino said, knowing how difficult that would be, and they locked Salazar in the room.

They'd decided that the best way to begin softening him up was to disorient him, keep him in a state of sensory deprivation for a while. That would also allow them a few hours of needed sleep.

Kirk set his watch alarm for seven in the morning, just a few hours hence.

45

The magnetic mine was remotely detonated from the *Sangre de Christo* at quarter past one in the morning, Eastern Standard Time. Everything on board the yacht that might be considered even slightly incriminating had long since been sent to the bottom of the harbor, against the possibility that civilian craft might eventually be searched. Immediately after the explosion the detonator was jettisoned, too.

The blast shattered the early morning quiet of the San Lorenzo waterfront. It also set in motion a sequence of phone calls. From the port city to the capital. From Tegucigalpa to Miami. And from Miami to Washington, D.C.

Initially there was a great deal of confusion. No one aboard the *Studds* knew what had happened, though everyone realized that something on or around the ship had blown up. The crew was rousted from its bunks and ordered on full battle alert until the incident could be sorted out.

When no further attack was forthcoming, bodies were counted and the frigate was inspected. No one had been injured, with the exception of one sailor who had been thrown to the deck and required six stitches to close a gash in his forehead. There was no discernible damage to the ship.

Only much later would it be discovered that the propellor had been blown off its shaft, leaving the *Studds* disabled for a long time to come.

In Washington, Smoking Gun had been waiting nervously by the outside phone for the call that finally came at one-thirty. The message was brief, its meaning unknown to the relay person in Miami: "Mission accomplished."

Perfect, he thought as he hung up and dialed the familiar number. They won't be able to ignore an act of war.

There was a risk involved in calling the reporter this quickly, but making the early edition of the *Post* was important. It was the one everyone read. Whatever it printed would set the course of events for the coming day.

This would be his last communication with the reporter, anyway. She'd been useful, but now, hopefully, she'd no longer be needed. And she was the kind of person, he was sure, who'd be easy to handle if anything ever did go wrong.

The phone rang six times before a sleepy voice answered. He put the expected rasp into his voice and said, "It's me."

Carla Stokes came instantly wide-awake. She reached over and flipped the bedside switch for the first time since Don Walker had installed the bug. The spools of the tape recorder, hidden in the desk drawer in the other room, began to turn.

"God," she said. "What time is it?"

"It doesn't matter," Smoking Gun said. "Something extremely important has happened. You'll beat everyone else with it."

Stokes glanced at the clock. She might be helping Walker, but she was also still a reporter. There was just time for a page one makeover if the story proved worth it.

"Go ahead," she said, "but make it brief."

"A mine exploded this morning on the frigate *USS Studds*, while it was temporarily docked at San Lorenzo, Honduras, in the Gulf of Fonseca. Evidence suggests that the mine may have been planted by a Nicaraguan frogman."

"Jesus Christ," Stokes said. "Are you sure about this?"

"Yes, positive. Have I ever led you astray?"

"No, of course not. But . . . is that all you have?"

"It's all at present. It only happened a short time ago."

"And just who am I supposed to attribute this to?"

"Say a 'highly placed Pentagon source.' That's close enough. The story's true, which is all your readers care about."

Smoking Gun hung up.

Stokes stared at the receiver for a moment, then switched the recorder off. They had him on tape now.

But first things first. She immediately called her editor and repeated what she'd been told. As concerned as she had been, he said he was going to have to clear something like that with the man upstairs. She said to remind the man that her source had a near perfect record. While he was at it, he might care to mention that she'd been promised they'd scoop everyone in the business.

After finishing with the editor, she called Walker. He sounded as groggy as she'd been earlier, but he perked up just as quickly when she told him what she had for him.

"Damn," he said, "we've got him. Good work, Carla."

As he said it, he discovered how much he'd dreaded this moment. What if the voice matched up with somebody on the Situation Room tape?

"I didn't do anything," she said, "except push a button."

"You did a lot more than that," he said. "Can I come over now and get it?"

"Come on, Don. I've got to get up soon enough as it is."

"Please. I want to hear that tape."

"Walker, no one is going to do you a voice analysis at two o'clock in the morning. Meet me here at seven. Okay?"

He sighed. "All right," he said. "But do me one favor, will you? Play it for me."

She thought about it, then said, "I'm sorry. I can't do that."

"What are you talking about?" he said icily.

"I'm talking about my job. At seven—"

"Your job?" he exploded. "What about the security of your goddamn country?"

"I'm sorry," she said firmly. "I've got to protect the story. At seven it'll be okay for you to hear it, but not now."

By then the paper would be on the streets.

Walker controlled his anger as best he could as he said, "What kind of story are we talking about here, Carla?"

"You can hear it when you pick up the tape."

"I can pick it up now. I can come there with a warrant for your goddamn arrest!"

"Please don't do that. I'll hide it, Don, I swear. You're not going to stop the story. I don't even think you'd want to."

Walker paused for a long moment. He knew that he could do all the things he'd threatened to. But he also knew the woman well enough now to gauge the strength of her will. He probably wouldn't be able to keep the story out of the paper, whatever it was. And the story wasn't the critical issue, he reminded himself. It was the voice.

"All right," he said wearily. "I surrender. How about just one little favor, though?"

"What?" she said.

"He must have said something at the beginning of the conversation that doesn't betray the story. Right? Would you at least play that part for me?"

"Okay," Stokes said. "Let me get it."

She trudged to her desk and returned with the portable recorder. "You still there?" she said into the phone, halfway expecting that he'd used the interval to start on his way to her apartment.

"Yeah, I'm here."

She rewound the tape and pressed the PLAY button, holding the receiver next to the speaker. She let the tape run up to the point where she'd been told she was going to beat everyone. Then she stopped it.

"How's that?" she asked. Silence. "Don?"

"That's fine," he said. "See you at seven, Carla."

And he broke the connection.

Stokes got off the bed and went to find a hiding place for the tape, just in case. Walker was a fine sweet lover and all that, and she trusted him, but . . . she was a journalist first and a friend of the federal government second.

At his end, Walker stared at the cradled phone. The man had done an excellent job of modifying his voice. There was no way Walker was going to quickly identify it, especially not from so few words.

Yet something about the cadence of the man's speech, the idiosyncrasies that are so difficult to disguise, that was familiar. Not enough for him to jump to a conclusion, but enough to set his mind roaming.

Who?

Slowly he began to think the unthinkable.

No, it wasn't possible . . . was it?

46

The Attorney General rang Carla Stokes's bell at twenty-five minutes to seven. She was up, as he knew she would be.

"Never trust a lover," she said wryly, but she handed the recorder over to him.

Walker didn't waste any time with social chitchat after that. He hurried down to Justice with his precious evidence. Though he was dying to listen to it, he had to wait. In order to get from Dupont Circle to Tenth and

Pennsylvania as quickly as possible he took the Metro, and he wasn't about to play the tape for the other passengers.

Once inside the great stone building, he went directly to his office, stopping for no one along the way. He removed the comparison tape from his safe. Then he walked across the street to the FBI offices and rode the elevator down to the forensic science area. He locked himself in one of the audio labs and ordered that he was not to be disturbed under any circumstances.

Finally he played Carla Stokes's tape. It was a shocking story, all right, and he grasped its implications immediately. His first reaction was to call the Vice-President straightaway, but then he realized that was pointless. The Washington *Post* would already be telling the world.

So he concentrated on the task at hand.

First he transferred Smoking Gun's words from the microcassette to a normal one, excising Carla's voice and the mining story itself.

Then he went to work on the other tape, the one he'd secretly recorded during the session in the Situation Room, to edit out anything that would tend to identify the speaker. He couldn't do a perfect job, of course. And the analyst might well recognize some of the voices of high-level administration officials. But as much as possible, he wanted to protect the innocent.

When he was finished he had a recording that contained snippets of conversation from people he identified as Speaker A, Speaker B, etc.

He turned the two tapes over to Christopher Holt, a young audio technician he trusted. Holt was instructed to make exhaustive comparison voice analyses, to the point of complete certainty, then to hand-carry the results to the Attorney General ASAP. He was warned to tell no one, either in the FBI or the Justice Department, what he was doing, nor to let anyone eavesdrop on his procedures. If Walker was not in his office when the job was finished, Holt was to babysit the tapes until his boss got back to him.

Walker's authoritative presence had Holt completely cowed by the time the instructions had been handed out. Christopher hadn't said "Yes, sir" so many times in succession in years.

Satisfied, Walker left the Bureau and returned to his office, where he locked the master tapes away. Then he headed up Pennsylvania Avenue.

By midmorning the White House was in an uproar.

There had been the usual delays in reporting the mine incident to Washington, so that Admiral Drake hadn't been awakened and notified until after four. He had then waited a couple of hours, maintaining contact with the carrier force off Nicaragua, to determine what kind of enemy attack was underway.

It was six before he convened the Joint Chiefs and almost seven-thirty by the time Vice-President Brust was informed.

By then, however, the Vice-President already knew. The first edition of the *Post* had printed the story. It was brief, but it was right there on the front page. Most maddening of all, the *Post* had quoted its "Pentagon sources" as saying that there was evidence the mine had been planted by a Nicaraguan diver.

"So what's the latest?" Seamus Croaghan asked Diane McBain.

The florid-faced NSC staffer had been called into the National Security Adviser's office for a private conversation. The missile crisis task force was taking a break after the first of what was bound to be a day full of highly charged meetings.

"Nothing much new," his boss said. "We did get the full damage report from the *Studds*. They lost a propellor and the hull sprung a couple of minor leaks, but that's about it. Whoever planted the mine just wanted to disable the ship, not kill anyone.

"But it's getting hot in there. I don't think it's going to be too long before some people start losing their tempers."

"No word yet on who did it?" Croaghan asked.

"Nothing solid. Round up the usual suspects."

"Meaning the Sandinistas."

"They are a popular choice. Method, motive, and opportunity."

"I don't know, Diane," Croaghan said. "I think there's a hell of a lot more going on here."

"Seamus, I don't want to hear about any plots within plots right now, okay? If there's something out there to find, then the people looking for the terrorists will find it. In the meantime, my job is simple. I tell the President what I think is best in terms of national security and I do what he tells me to do.

"Now, the reason I called you in here. I want you to keep an open line to the other members of the CAT. If we decide to go to an invasion—"

"You're talking about that?"

"It's an option we're considering," McBain said. "Of course."

"That's the last thing the President wants!"

"I know what the President's stated policy is, Seamus. But the President is in the hospital. And policies get modified if the events warrant it."

"Diane, this is crazy. The Russian subs. The MiGs. The Blackjack bombers, for Christ's sake! If the Soviets get sucked into this thing, we could be in a war before we can stop it."

McBain looked at her assistant coolly. "Don't you think we're aware of the risks?"

"I don't know what to think," he said.

"Well, think whatever you like. Just make sure you *do* what I tell you, which is to coordinate the CAT. I want everyone ready for anything." She glanced at her watch. "All right, I've got to go back. Get right on that, will you?"

Croaghan nodded, got up, and returned to his own office.

He was deeply troubled. Up to this point, cooler heads within the Administration—particularly the President's—had prevailed. Croaghan believed what the President believed, that regional conflicts must not be allowed to escalate into superpower confrontations.

But now Walter Brust was at the head of the table, at the mercy of those who would try to use the President's medical condition as an excuse to override his policy. Croaghan promised himself that he would do whatever he had to do to prevent that from happening.

It was no longer his job; it was his responsibility.

"It's an act of war," Montgomery Banks said. "Not just against us, but against Honduras, which has been a very good friend to us in Central America."

"I agree," Wesley Drake added. "It's a very serious international incident."

Walter Brust's brain was racing along in amphetamine overdrive. With all of the demands being made of him, he was just beginning to realize that he'd hardly ever said no to anyone his whole life. Even now, when he was clearly being called upon to take control. He'd agreed without hesitation, for example, when a private meeting was requested by General Banks, Chairman of the JCS, and Admiral Drake, the country's senior naval officer.

These boys were hard-liners. They had all the military and diplomatic facts and figures at their disposal—while he had almost none—and they made him feel unpatriotic if he raised the slightest question about their analysis of the situation.

"My understanding, gentlemen," the Vice-President replied, "is that there's still no hard evidence the Sandinistas were involved. Their ambassador phoned first thing this morning and stated their innocence quite strongly."

"What would you expect them to say?" Banks said. "That they rode the diver in on a fishing smack and then laughed their way back to Corinto?"

"I don't appreciate being patronized, General," Brust said, immediately flushing with pride. "Now, if you don't mind, would you try to explain why they would do something like this? It doesn't make sense to me."

"I can't claim to understand the Communist mind, sir," Banks said. "But tactically I'd say they're sending messages. Yesterday to the President, this morning to you. They want us to get on with the bargaining and they're confident enough of their position to attack any target they like."

"That's probably a fair assessment," Drake said. "They're saying they're not afraid to hit our military. Rigging the mine so that it only damaged the ship was by way of warning, I'd say. Next time I'd expect to lose some men."

"We can't afford for there to be a next time," Banks said firmly.

"Thank you, I appreciate getting your views, gentlemen." The Vice-President shrugged. "But it's really not my decision. It's the President's. I'll be briefing him as soon as I meet with the full task force again."

"If I may, Mr. Vice-President," General Banks said, "I think you need to consider the possibility that you may be the one forced to make the decision."

In the lengthy pause that followed, both of the military men watched Walter Brust closely for his reaction.

"Yes," Brust said finally, "I've thought of that. But last I heard, the President was quite conscious. So let's not get ahead of ourselves, shall we?"

Conversation in the Situation Room was loud and animated, but it dropped to a murmur when the Vice-President and Chairman of the Joint Chiefs walked in.

Brust squeezed his bulky frame into his chair and brought the meeting to some semblance of order. He laid his meaty hands in front of him, lacing the fingers together, and leaned onto forearms that were as big around as most people's calves.

"Folks," he said, waiting until the room was completely silent. "I guess I'm about as educated on this thing now as I'm ever gonna be. It feels like the whole world's waiting to see what we do next. So before I talk it over with the President, I wanted to get everybody's opinion on the record. Let's just go straight around the table here."

He gestured to Secretary of State Carini, seated directly to his left.

On that side of the table, opinions were firm. Carini and General Banks cast their votes for immediate military retaliation. Secretary of Defense Schule and Attorney General Walker spoke with equal conviction for ignoring the mine incident and proceeding with negotiations and a determined effort to recover the missiles.

With regard to the Russians' threats, the former two were convinced the Big Bears were bluffing, while the latter believed it insane to take the chance that they weren't.

The right-hand side of the table was more equivocal.

The Director of Central Intelligence, speaking first, admitted that the data collection effort during the whole crisis had been sub-par. He still couldn't say with certainty that the Sandinistas were involved, though it looked that way. However, he recommended that if military action was going to be taken, it would be imperative to do it in concert with a major subversion effort in Managua itself.

Diane McBain said that she favored caution as a general rule. But, if the mine should definitely be proven to have come from Nicaragua, then a military action was indicated. The limits of American tolerance must be defined, she argued.

Chief of Staff Tom Read spoke last. He agreed with McBain about defining limits, but proposed at least a twenty-four hour cooling-off period, during which a comprehensive set of responses could be worked out. In addition, he warned, everyone in the room must refrain from acting on their own. The President must agree to the implementation of *any* of their proposals.

"And if the war zone turns hot?" Carini asked.

"The President is still the Commander in Chief," Read said.

"The President is recovering from a heart attack," the Secretary of State said. "We may need a quicker reaction time than he is capable of."

There it was, out on the table. Carini looked around him, but no one wanted to touch it.

"Have the Soviets commented on the mine incident yet?" Brust asked instead.

"Nothing so far," McBain said. "If we don't hear, we ought to call them. We don't want them doing something because of what they *think* we're thinking."

Brust turned to General Banks. "When you talk about a military strike," he said, "what are you saying, basically? That you want to take out the airfields?"

"Minimum," Banks said. "At least if we do that we'll be negotiating from a position of strength. If we let them get MiGs into the country, they'd be close enough to hit the task force before we could get our planes into the air. Not to mention how much easier it'll make it when we *do* decide to restore democracy to the country."

"*If* we do," Gunther Schule said quietly.

The Chairman of the JCS glared at his civilian boss, but the Secretary ignored him.

"All right," the Vice-President said as he rolled his chair back from the table. "I'm going to speak with the President. We'll meet back here in an hour."

Brust wanted to be alone, so he walked back to his

own office to make the call. He was put through to the First Lady.

"Walter," the First Lady said, "the President is resting right now. He had kind of a rough night and he's in a lot of pain. He's weaker than he was. Is it important?"

"Yes, ma'am, I believe so," the Vice-President said.

"I just don't think he can talk very well. They've got an IV in him that's dripping Inderal and Demerol. He'd be pretty groggy even if we could get him awake. Is it about the crisis?"

"Yes. It's getting worse. There are a lot of people who think we have to respond in some way."

"You know the President's policy, Walter. Mandated defensive actions only. He asked me again this morning to make sure it's being followed."

"Well, we've got kind of an unusual situation here." Brust thought for a moment, then said, "Okay, don't wake him now. But if he does come around, have him call me right away, will you, please?"

"Yes, of course."

Ten minutes later, Brust was still at his desk, paralyzed by the twin fears of doing something and not doing anything, when General Banks and Admiral Drake burst into his office unannounced. The expressions on their faces were grim.

"What—" He cleared his throat. "What is it?" he asked with as much authority as he could muster.

"The MiGs are on their way," Banks said. "A flight of them just left Cuba, heading southwest. We picked off some radio transmissions."

The Vice-President just stared at them in disbelief.

"Come on, sir," Banks said urgently. "They'll be over Managua in an hour."

"The President is all doped up," was all Brust could think of to say.

"Then the decision's yours," Banks said, and Drake nodded in agreement.

Brust looked from one of them to the other.

"What should we do?" he asked.

"Get a dozen Tomcats into the air right away," Banks said. "We can intercept the MiGs before they get to the Atlantic coast. But only if we hurry."

The sweat had beaded up on Brust's brow and a couple

of drops were sliding down the side of his face, but he didn't notice.

"Please, Mr. Vice-President," Banks said. "We can't afford to wait until the President gets straight." He was barely hanging on to his self-control.

Inside Brust's head a little man was running around, screaming: I don't know what to do, I don't know what to do.

"Mr. Vice-President?" Drake said.

The admiral's deep, steady voice seemed to have a calming effect on Brust. The scenarios warring in his mind seemed suddenly to coalesce.

"All right," he said with more conviction than he felt. "Scramble the F-14s. Deny the MiGs landing, but don't engage them. Turn them back to Cuba."

"The airfields?" Banks said.

"Not yet."

"Yes, sir," Banks said stiffly.

"If we're fired upon . . ." Drake said.

"Then fight back, of course," Brust said. "And for Christ's sake, get somebody up there who speaks Spanish! I don't want any misunderstandings."

The two military men hurried back to the command center that surrounds the Situation Room. They were in direct satellite communication with the carrier's skipper and had in fact sent him an encoded message five minutes earlier in which he was ordered to start getting planes in the air. Now they tacked on the Vice-President's instructions.

Walter Brust hadn't moved from his desk. He found that he was unable to stop shaking.

47

The Vice-President was soon in contact with the General Secretary.

"We protest the introduction of Soviet combat aircraft into Central America," Brust said. "Our policy is the same as previous administrations. We will not permit this."

After the succession of translations and retranslations, the General Secretary's reply was, "The peace-loving peoples of Nicaragua have requested assistance from their Cuban allies, which is their right to do."

Brust had taken a mild tranquilizer to counteract the effect of the amphetamine in his system, and was feeling considerably calmer than when the news about the MiGs had first been broken to him. Upon reflection, it was obvious to him that the Russians didn't seriously expect the U.S. to allow the jets to land. The ploy was just a show of strength, to convince the enemy that the Soviets were, ultimately, quite serious about the situation.

Their real move—and God forbid it was the Blackjack bombers—would come later. So this time Brust had to face them down.

"Well, you can tell their Cuban allies what I told you," he said. "If the jets try to land, we'll blow them out of the air."

That felt good, he thought. Damn, but that felt good. Maybe he could get used to this chair after all.

Two thousand miles to the south, the aerial drama was playing itself out over the empty water. The twelve F-14Ds had gotten themselves into the air in plenty of time to intercept the MiGs. They circled a point a hundred miles off the east coast of Nicaragua.

Lieutenant Cliff Keker was looking at his aircraft's advanced imaging radar monitor and talking to his wingman. "Slipstream," he said, "this is Dead Head. You got the bogeys on your screen?"

"Shiiit," Slipstream said, "a bunch of fucking 21s, ain't that some trash? They can't be serious. Only way they sneak those crates past us is if all our radar broke at once."

"I make ten of them, Slip, fifty miles out, coming in at five hundred knots. They must be trying to squeeze the fuel."

"Roger. Hell, Dead, we could blow 'em from here."

"Negative, Slipstream. We give them a flyby, then show them the way home."

The Tomcats kept themselves five hundred feet above the deck being used by the MiG-21s. The MiGs weren't humping it, but they still closed the fifty miles in little more than five minutes.

"You got a visual, Slip?" Dead Head asked. "Give me a visual."

"One mile," Slipstream said, "a half. There they are!"

Everyone felt the rush of adrenaline as the MiGs sped by beneath them, flying in a tight formation that reeked of fear. The F-14s immediately banked and prepared to give chase.

"I made two external tanks," Dead Head said.

"Roger," Slipstream said. "Gives 'em less than a thousand-mile radius. They're gonna have to make their damn minds up in a hurry."

The chase was no contest. Within three minutes the Tomcats had the MiGs encircled. The venerable Soviet fighter/bombers were decent aircraft but slower, far less heavily armed, and carrying vastly inferior avionics. Still, they pushed doggedly ahead.

"What're those boys thinking?" Slipstream said. "Bluff?"

"Beats me," Dead Head said more calmly than he felt. "But I don't like it. And they aren't crossing the goddamn border. I'm going to missile lock."

"Roger. Eeee-*hah*."

By the time the planes were fifty miles from Nicaraguan landfall, all ten MiGs were under missile lock. And they knew it. Their own alarms would have been screeching in their ears.

"Sweat time, guys," Slipstream said.

"Six friendlies," Dead Head said. "Coming in from

the northwest. They're going to hit the bogeys square on the beam."

Six more missile locks.

They couldn't possibly risk it, Dead Head thought. Could they?

For a moment, as he watched the glowing screen, Dead Head could almost *see* the enemy aircraft hesitate. Then, slowly, the flight of MiGs began to turn. It curled off to the south, eventually settling into a broad, sweeping circle. The eighteen Tomcats remained in tight pursuit.

"E.T., phone home," Slipstream said.

Dead Head laughed. The present situation wasn't going to last long. If the MiGs wanted to make it back to Cuba, they couldn't afford to dawdle.

Five minutes later, the MiGs set course again. Northeast.

"Yeee-*hah*!" Slipstream yelled.

The F-14s stayed aloft, tracking the enemy for the next hundred miles to make sure the MiGs passed the point of no return. Then the Tomcats turned and headed back toward the carrier.

Word was quickly flashed to the White House command center, and spontaneous cheering erupted.

Having just learned what had happened, Seamus Croaghan wandered out of the Situation Room, looking for Diane McBain. He'd felt a flush, compounded of both pride and relief, at the news of the aerial victory.

It was a bluff, he thought. We called it and we backed them down, damn it.

Suddenly he stopped in his tracks.

He stood on the other side of a set of small cubicles that had been partitioned off with flimsy metal-and-fabric dividers. The cubicles were transient work spaces that hadn't been designed with any real notion of privacy in mind. They each contained a desk, telephone, computer, and printer, and their partitions only stretched partway to the ceiling. Many such fanned out from the Situation Room: places for checking data, retrieving a document, or having a quick chat.

The words Croaghan had overheard from the other side of the partition were: ". . . think that the Vice-President can be persuaded?" The voice belonged to Admiral Drake.

"Of course," another voice said. Montgomery Banks,

Chairman of the JCS. "His balls are going to be feeling big as eggs after making the Russians turn tail. Now's the time to do it."

"I'm not sure he'll go against the President," the first voice said.

"He will if we convince him he has to. Don't you believe it's in the national interest?"

"Getting the enemy out of there has always been in the national interest."

"Then all we have to do is make Brust see that. He's a weak man who's feeling strong for the moment. We can use that to give him a shove in the right direction."

"What if he calls the President?"

There was a pause, then the second voice said, "Then we convince him the President isn't capable of making an informed—"

A loud printer started up in the adjacent cubicle, and the rest of their words were lost to Croaghan. But he felt that he'd heard enough. He hurried out of the area.

His immediate intent was to find his boss and report what he'd heard. That impulse, however, faded fast. He knew what McBain would say to him. She'd tell him he didn't have the authority to interfere in decision-making at that high a level. She'd probably even go along if she thought it was the politically advantageous thing to do.

Gunther Schule? Surely he would be on the side of caution. But Croaghan didn't know the Secretary of Defense all that well, and had no clear idea of how much power he actually wielded.

Croaghan felt chilled to the core. The two military men hadn't said anything inconsistent with their beliefs. Yet, knowingly or not, they were about to try to make things go the terrorists' way. And they just might succeed.

The only person who could set things right was the President; there was no one else left to trust:

Croaghan knew that if he took the Metro, he could be at the Naval Medical Center in half an hour. He thought fleetingly that if he went out there by himself, he'd probably be throwing his career down the chute. But he never really wavered. His only concern was that he might not be able to get to the President before something irretrievable happened.

So he ran to the Metro. To other pedestrians he was a

comical figure, with his red face and baggy corduroy suit, jogging along in midtown D.C. Croaghan didn't care what he looked like. He hustled up 17th Street to Farragut Square and sprinted through the turnstile just in time to catch the Red Line heading north.

SHADY GROVE, the sign on the train said.

Shady Grove, my little love, I long for Shady Grove . . . The words to the old folk song ran disconnectedly through Croaghan's head, over and over.

When he got to Naval Med, he waved his credentials around, but couldn't get near the President. He did, however, finally persuade someone to put him on the phone with the First Lady. As soon as she heard the urgency in his voice, she came out to see him.

They huddled in a quiet corner of a small waiting area, near a pair of swinging doors guarded by four cold-eyed Secret Service men. Somewhere beyond those doors lay the President of the United States, hopefully recuperating.

Croaghan, as always, felt a little like a lout in the presence of the beautiful, patrician First Lady, with her gentle voice and gracious, Virginia hunt-country manners. But he pushed the feeling aside. He wasn't here to deal with the former debutante; he was speaking to the tough, intelligent woman he knew inhabited the same body.

He said immediately, "I think there are people plotting to make Walter Brust Acting President."

She visibly stiffened, and Croaghan could see the hard edge appear behind her hazel eyes. There was nothing, he knew, that she wouldn't do for her husband.

"Who?" she said.

Croaghan filled her in on everything that had happened that day, both at the White House and internationally. He included the overheard conversation and his own speculations.

"I see," she said when he'd laid it all out. "And you believe the ultimate goal is to persuade Walter that we have to invade Nicaragua."

"Yes, ma'am," Croaghan said. "I'm certain of it. And I think that'll be the easy part, once they get him convinced that the President is no longer competent and he has to take over. They're the two highest-ranking military officers in the country. He's bound to listen to them."

There was a pause, then he added, "If we go to war down there, it could escalate out of control before we could stop it."

"I know," the First Lady said: "It's the last thing the President wants."

"And I'm just afraid the only way to prevent it is for him to personally intervene. I'm sorry. I know the President is very ill. But I wouldn't be here if I wasn't sure we were on the brink of catastrophe. How . . . how bad is he?"

She fixed him with a stare and said, "Do you value your job, Mr. Croaghan?"

"Yes, of course. I . . . What are you getting at?"

"When the National Security Adviser finds out that you've done this, she'll fire you, you know."

"Maybe not. Diane and I are old friends."

"No, she'll have to and you know it. It took a lot of courage for you to come here."

He dismissed the thought with a wave of his hand. "Not really," he said. "My ultimate loyalty is to the President, and that's the way it should be."

"I agree," she said, "but in my experience most of a president's staffers' first loyalty is to themselves. I admire you."

"Thank you, but . . . ?"

"Yes, the President's condition. He's had a heart attack, Mr. Croaghan. Perhaps not a very serious one, but they won't be positive of what's happening until they run the angiogram, which they've been putting off until he feels a little better. This afternoon, we hope. Right now he's in a good deal of pain. He weakened considerably during the night and they're keeping him sedated."

She paused, then continued. "What is he capable of?" she said. "That's what you really want to know, isn't it? Can he exert his authority? Demonstrate that he's still the man in charge? I don't know the answer to those questions. But . . . well, I guess we're going to have to find out, aren't we?"

She rose abruptly, as if only at that moment coming to some decision. She offered him her hand.

"Let's go see the President," she said.

It wasn't quite so simple. She had first to convince a number of military officers and Secret Service agents of who Croaghan was, and that it was all right for an NSC staffer to be allowed in to see the President.

Croaghan had to submit to a thorough search.

And then the permission of the attending doctors had to be sought. They didn't have the power to keep out the President's wife but, technically, they could control whom she brought with her. It was agreed that a short visit wouldn't have a seriously adverse effect on the patient.

Finally the two of them were standing by the President's bedside. They were alone in the room, except for the naval duty officer who kept himself discreetly in the background.

Croaghan stared, pained by the difference a day could make.

The President was old, but he was a large man possessed of a vibrant, self-confident presence and the easy authority of the natural leader. Now all he looked was old, a formless lump under the starched hospital sheets. His skin was pale, his eyes and cheeks sunken, his mottled bald head like wrinkled parchment. A plastic identification tag, as if one were needed, was strapped to his wrist.

Nobody's shaved him, was one of the first thoughts to come into Croaghan's head.

The President's breathing was slow and labored. A cannula looped around his ears and delivered oxygen to his nose, while a half-full IV bag dripped the drugs into his vein. The vital signs monitor was on a mobile cart next to the other side of the bed. In the monitor's center a tiny, luminous dot glided across the CRT screen, pinging up into jagged peaks as the patient's wounded heart continued to beat.

The First Lady sat on one of the hard metal chairs next to the bed. She reached over and took her husband's hand. "Darling," she said softly.

Slowly the President's eyes opened. They appeared to have trouble focusing at first, but he gave a little smile when he recognized his wife.

This is not going to work, Croaghan thought. The man doesn't know where he is.

"Are you awake, dear?" she asked.

The President wet his lips with his tongue, then merely nodded.

She inclined her head toward the NSC man and said, "You remember Seamus Croaghan?"

The President nodded again.

"Walter Brust called earlier, and I didn't want to wake you, but now I feel that I should. I'm afraid Mr. Croaghan has some bad news for us."

As succinctly as possible, Croaghan outlined the day's events. The mining incident, the MiGs, Brust's handling of the American response, the Vice-President's conversation with the General Secretary. It was obvious that even through the Demerol haze, the President was being deeply affected.

Croaghan felt like he was on a tightrope. He was terrified of getting the President so agitated that another heart attack was the result. Yet he didn't want to play down the gravity of the situation. In the end, he simply stated his belief that the Vice-President—under strong pressure from the military, and contrary to Administration policy—was seriously considering an invasion. That was enough. There was no need to risk telling the President that there might also be an attempt made to declare him incompetent.

When Croaghan had finished, the President closed his eyes.

It didn't work, Croaghan thought. It took too long. I lost his attention.

He looked to the First Lady for guidance, but she was gazing steadily at her husband.

Then the President's eyes opened. He blinked a couple of times, as if to clear something away. There was a look of determination on his face. And, though it was obviously an effort, he spoke.

"Get ahold of Walter," he said to his wife.

She called the duty officer over, and five minutes later the Vice-President was on the line. The President reached for the phone next to his bed, which was usable, though the ringer had been disconnected so that he wouldn't be unnecessarily startled. "Walter, I understand you tried to call me earlier."

The effort that went into keeping his voice steady showed to those at his bedside. His wife beamed and raised her right thumb to him.

"Yes, sir," Brust said. "A lot of things have happened today. How are you feeling, Mr. President?"

"Better. Much better. Now look, Walter, I've been briefed on what's happened, and I just wanted to tell you I think you've handled the situation very well so far."

"Thank you, sir."

"I also wanted to make clear that no military action is to be taken without my specific approval. You know how much I support the resistance, but I will *not* send American boys into the fight. Our level of response so far has been entirely appropriate. The Russians know we're serious, and so do the Nicaraguans, and that's all we need. We can clear up this mine business at some later point. So don't let the Joint Chiefs talk you into anything. If any further retaliation is even *contemplated*, you get to the First Lady and she'll get to me. She has instructions to wake me any time you call, from now on."

"Of course, Mr. President. I'm doing my best to stick with policy."

"Excellent. You keep up the good work, Walter. I always knew you had it in you."

"Thank you again, sir."

The President handed the receiver to his wife, who hung it up for him. A moment later he'd closed his eyes and fallen once again into a deep sleep.

Croaghan stared down at the President's inert form, scarcely believing the man had been capable of what he'd just seen.

The First Lady reached out and cradled her husband's hand in hers. Her eyes had filled with tears that were just beginning to spill over.

PART VI

KIRK

They saw only the tracks of the deer, the tracks of the jaguar. The tracks weren't clear, nothing was clear. Where they began the tracks were merely those of animals. It was as if the tracks were there for the sole purpose of leading them astray. The way was not clear:

It would get cloudy.

It would get dark and rainy.

It would get muddy, too.

It would get misty and drizzly.

That was all the tribes could see in front of them, and their search would simply make them weary of heart.

—*The Popol Vuh*

48

The scene in the Situation Room was chaotic. Everyone wanted a piece of the Vice-President's attention. Everyone seemed to have the realistic analysis of the situation, as well as the only correct response.

For the first time in memory, even Gunther Schule and the DCI raised their voices.

Walter Brust listened as best he could to the various arguments that were being launched at him. He was still feeling a pleasant buzz from the way he'd handled the General Secretary and the praise the President had given him. After that, this was merely the cacophony of seven insects.

He was allowing the debate to proceed because he wanted to see who was on which side now.

Finally he'd had enough. He banged his oversized fist on the table, and quiet slowly came to the room.

To General Banks he said, "I take it you believe we need to make a pre-emptive strike."

"Of course," the general said. "If you don't mind my saying so, sir, there is no alternative. The enemy has shown his hand, and we should go in there and kick him out of Central America for good. At the absolute least, Mr. Vice-President, the airfields must be destroyed."

"But we turned the MiGs back, General," Brust said. "We can keep on doing that every time the Russians try to fly them in."

"Yes," Banks said, "but when the Soviets send the Blackjacks, it won't be a matter of turning them back, but keeping them out. And we can't stop them without attacking out over the ocean, in neutral airspace. If we take control of Nicaragua, though, then there's no way to get them to the Caribbean. There'd be no friendly country they can overfly."

"You really think they'll send Blackjacks?"

"Yes, sir. I'm certain that's the next thing they'll do. Unless they're absolutely convinced that the bombers will never make it to Cuba. And there's only one way to ensure that."

"Thank you. And who agrees with the general?"

Secretary of State Carini did so immediately and enthusiastically.

The choice was more difficult for the National Security Adviser. McBain wanted to believe that her people were closing in on a recovery of the missiles, yet she had no reason to believe that it was so. Lacking that, there was a real threat to her position within the administration if history later showed that she'd clung stubbornly to the wrong side.

As for the Director, he didn't have such confidence in the military that he wanted to commit his field officers to an operation on its behalf. At the same time, that was an integral part of what the intelligence agencies were for. Reluctance on his part could be the cause of a lot of future mistrust of the civilian sector by the military.

In the end, both McBain and the DCI played it as safe as they could. They crossed over the line to support the airfield strike, though neither would commit to an invasion. Unless warranted by subsequent events, of course.

Walker and Schule flat-out opposed, while Read, who was answerable only to the President, was a definite maybe.

When the votes had been cast, Walter Brust said, almost meekly, "I talked with the President this afternoon. He forbids any further military action." He shrugged.

There was an awkward silence, eventually broken by the Secretary of State.

"Well, I'm not going to pussy around with it," Carini said. "I don't believe the President is in any condition to appreciate what's going on here."

There the words were, finally spoken. Everyone knew what the Secretary meant. But the Chief of Staff decided he wanted it spelled out in plain English.

"What are you suggesting, Enzo?" Read said.

"Oh come on, Tom," Carini said. "I'm talking about the Twenty-Fifth Amendment and you know it."

"Now wait a minute," Secretary of Defense Schule said, "we don't have the right—"

"Yes, we do," Carini insisted.

"What is the law, Mr. Attorney General?" Diane McBain asked.

Walker quoted from memory the relevant portion of the Twenty-Fifth Amendment to the Constitution: "Whenever the Vice-President and a majority of either the principal officers of the executive departments or of such other body as Congress may by law provide, transmit to the President Pro Tempore of the Senate and the Speaker of the House of Representatives their written declaration that the President is unable to discharge the powers and duties of his office, the Vice-President shall immediately assume the powers and duties of the office as Acting President."

"We don't have the right," Schule said. "Without notifying Congress."

"It just says we have to provide a written declaration," Carini countered. "It doesn't say *when*."

"That's a *very* liberal interpretation," the Attorney General said. "Not to mention that no one has ever defined exactly what 'principal officers of the executive departments' really means."

"I don't think we're talking Constitutional fine points here," Brust said. "You want me to relieve the President."

"I think he's obviously temporarily incapacitated, sir," Carini said. "If he wasn't, he wouldn't be making that kind of decision." He looked at General Banks for support and the general nodded his agreement.

"The Joint Chiefs fully support military action?" Brust asked General Banks.

"Yes, sir," Banks said. "We believe it's crucial to the national security."

"You don't believe the Soviets will jump in?"

"No, sir."

"What about the Stingers?"

"We would hope that the terrorists would realize when they'd been whipped."

"You don't think they'd use the rest of them out of revenge."

"I trust they would see the hopelessness of their situation."

"Bullshit," Schule said, with an anger no one had ever

heard in his voice before. "Sheer bullshit. And that's all I have to say."

All eyes were on Brust now, and he felt every one of them boring into his flesh. He didn't want to be here. All he really wanted was to be out at Augusta, with no graver task than to propel a little white ball down the lush green fairways of Nicklaus's private preserve.

The effects of the various drugs he'd been taking were wearing off. He leaned back in his swivel chair, closed his eyes, and massaged his temples.

And he tried to remember. He replayed his favorite videotape over and over in his head, trying to recall the kind of person Brust the power forward had been, and where he'd found the determination that had enabled him to complete the play.

It was so long ago. The highly skilled athlete in the white uniform had been dead for so many years that his memory survived only in the minds of other people and on a skinny strip of plastic tape.

Dead.

Or was he?

Suddenly Brust felt once again the force of the impact— really *felt* it—as his shoulder crashed into the defender, knocking the two-hundred-and-forty-pound man flat on his back, as though he were as minor a hindrance as straw. The vibration of the rim as the ball slammed through thrummed again in his fingertips. There was the inevitable jolt as gravity sucked his feet back to the parquet hardwood floor, and the pressure on his eardrums from the roar of his partisans in the crowd.

It was the crowd that spoke to him then, and now. Out of all the hundreds of millions of Americans, the President had picked *him* to be here if this moment came.

He leaned forward in his chair. There was no hesitation in his voice as he said, "The President seemed quite possessed of his faculties to me. Until such time as I'm convinced otherwise, he is still Commander in Chief of this country, and what he says goes. I expect to be kept continually informed, but there will be no further military action at this time."

Gunther Schule slumped in his chair and began to breathe again. Don Walker smiled just a little.

There was a stunned silence among the others.

Then Enzo Carini shouted, "Mr. Vice-President!"

"This is a terrible mistake, Mr.—" General Banks began.

But Brust had already pushed his chair back from the table. He walked purposefully to the door, which the duty officer opened for him. As he was about to exit, he turned.

"General Banks," he said, "please be advised that the military is not to do anything foolish on its own. Should you disobey the orders of the President, I assure you that you will be court-martialed and sent to prison. Miss McBain, I'll be in my office. Please coordinate the flow of information to me."

With that, the Vice-President left.

Montgomery Banks watched him go with a cold, hard stare. The general's jaw was clenched so tight that the muscles stood out like chestnuts.

Croaghan was feeling pretty good about himself.

True, his tenure with the National Security Council was probably finished now that he'd gone over his boss's head. But he'd done a major service for the President of the United States and, incidentally, might just have helped stave off some catastrophic policy decisions.

Those were things a man in his position was supposed to do as a matter of course.

God, what a day it had been. He'd been so consumed by his concern for what he now thought of as the attempted White House coup that he'd neglected everything else. It was only when he was back in his office, alone, with the situation stabilized, that he was able to turn his attention to any other unfinished business.

One of the items, of course, was the information he'd promised to get Kirk.

That could be important.

Fortunately, the job was almost done. He hunched over his computer keyboard for half an hour, in order to confirm a couple of details, then collated his data and went outside to his favorite pay phone.

49

Kirk hadn't expected it to be easy, and he'd been right.

They'd kept Colonel Salazar in isolation well into the morning to let his apprehension build. The hood had been left on, and it would stay there. They wanted the colonel to be living in a dark, lonely place.

After what they thought was a suitable interval, his captors had gone to work on him with the classic good-cop/bad-cop technique. Andino played the villain, blistering Salazar with threats in rapid-fire Spanish. This alternated with Kirk as the colonel's friend, soothing him in English.

In both cases, they made clear that all they wanted was Javier Vega. Kirk reassured the prisoner that he'd be returned home just as soon as he revealed Vega's whereabouts; Andino warned him what would happen to him if he didn't.

They'd been at it for hours.

And they'd gotten precisely nothing.

Now, taking a break in the late afternoon, they brooded over coffee in the kitchen. Kirk was weary and frustrated. He'd had precious little sleep over the past few days. He could feel them closing in on the Stingers, yet the missiles continued to just elude their grasp.

"He's tough," he said.

She nodded. "It is as I expected," she said. "We have no respect for the enemy, but we do not underestimate them." She paused, then went on, "Kirk, I think that you should leave me alone with him."

Kirk knew what she was suggesting. They'd talked it out before starting in on the colonel, and Kirk had been emphatic about one thing. He would permit no physical torture, because there was no way for him to control what might happen. Salazar and Andino were mortal enemies.

He shook his head.

"I can break him," Andino said. "Without doing any permanent damage. There's no reason that you have to watch."

"No," Kirk said.

"Kirk, do not let your heart rule your head. We *need* Vega. Salazar knows where he is, I'm sure of it."

Kirk was sure of it, too. There was a feel to an interrogation; after a while, you could sense whether or not the subject was witholding the information you wanted. Yet he shook his head again.

"You are *so* wrong for this, Kirk. Colonel Salazar is in part responsible for the deaths of hundreds of your countrymen. Innocent people. Can you not take that into account? This man is not deserving of your mercy."

"I . . . I can't," he said. "Since Grenada . . ."

Since Grenada. Since the deaths of Susanna and Scottie. Since then . . . what? He tried to articulate the feeling, but couldn't.

Andino gazed steadily at him, but he avoided her eyes. Though the front he presented to her seemed impervious to her arguments, inside he was not nearly so assured that he was doing the right thing. He was grateful for an interruption like the ringing phone.

"Sorry it took so long," Seamus Croaghan said, "but I've got that list of properties you asked for. I wanted to make sure it was as complete as it could be. And then today has been a bitch and a half."

Croaghan gave him a capsule version of the crisis inside the White House.

"I think you did the right thing, Seamus," Kirk said when he'd finished.

"Yeah, I hope so," Croaghan said. "Anyway, here you go. Washington-area properties owned or controlled by Herrera, Salazar, and the Vegas, *pere et fils*. Turns out to be not so long a list. I guess most of the big-money stuff is in Florida."

Kirk got out a pencil and copied down the addresses as Croaghan read them off to him, along with any cross-directory phone numbers he'd been able to get and a brief description of what each property was, if that were known.

"You think you know who you're after?" Croaghan said.

"I know," Kirk said.

"Call me in when you nail him?"

"I'll try. In the meantime burn the list, will you, Seamus?"

"Sure."

Kirk took the list to the kitchen table, where he and Andino pored over it for a while, drawing black lines through the least likely candidates.

A number of the places were businesses, and those were rejected first. Some were addresses Andino recognized and checked off as unsuitable. Still others were eliminated for other reasons. Salazar's home, for example. Vega might have been the colonel's guest at one time, but it would have been a brief visit.

In the end, they narrowed the list to three, widely scattered around the city. One was owned by Salazar, one by Herrera, and one by the elder Vega. Any of them was a potential safe house.

"I think it's Salazar's," Kirk said. "I've got a feeling. It's more likely that Vega would hide there than somewhere owned by his father. Plus it's the only one of the three with a dummy up front, that humanitarian support fund the colonel controls."

"I agree," Andino said. "You want to try it on him and see what happens?"

Kirk nodded.

"Okay," Andino said. "But at least pretend that you're going to let me at him."

Kirk nodded again and they went down to the basement.

Salazar was where they had left him, tied and hooded. Andino walked over to him and stripped off the hood. Kirk stood in front of him. The colonel squinted in the sudden light.

"That's all the time we have, Colonel," Andino said.

She stepped behind the chair, took out her pistol and placed its muzzle against the base of Salazar's skull. Kirk moved toward her, but she cocked the hammer and shook her head.

"Don't," she said to Kirk. "This is between the two of us now. You don't come into it. I'm sorry."

Kirk stopped.

"Where is he?" Andino said to the colonel. "Three . . . two . . ."

"Wait!" Kirk shouted.

Salazar sat impassive.

"One." And she pulled the trigger. There was a click that seemed as loud as an actual gunshot.

"Oh, yes," Andino said, "the clip." Before Kirk could move, she pulled a cartridge clip from her pocket, rammed it into the butt of the pistol, and worked the slide.

"It's loaded *now*, Colonel," she said. "And you know I won't hesitate. If you're not going to tell us, you're as much use dead as alive. Three . . ."

Kirk could see that it was working. The colonel had wet his lips and his eyes were darting here and there; he just wasn't sure.

The trouble was, Kirk didn't know himself if she was acting. The dread that was showing on his own face, and that the colonel was obviously picking up on, was authentic.

"Two . . ."

Fortunately for Kirk, his response would be the same whatever Andino's true intent. He had to stop her or, if this was all fiction, at least convince the colonel that that was what he was trying to do. He raised both hands.

"No!" he yelled. "For God's sake, *don't*!" He paused for just an instant, then added as if it were a final, desperate plea, "We *know* he's at the Water Street condo! He *has* to be!"

The colonel looked sharply in Kirk's direction and, as their eyes met, Kirk knew he'd been right. Andino raised a questioning eyebrow and Kirk nodded.

"That's it," he said.

Andino relaxed the pistol's hammer, put up the safety, and slipped the weapon behind her belt. Rage leaked into Salazar's expression as he realized that he'd been outsmarted.

He directed his anger at Kirk. "You'll die for this," he said. "And your Sandinista whore too."

"Maybe," Kirk said. "But we'll get Vega first." He gestured to Andino and they left the colonel alone with his revenge fantasies.

The first thing Kirk did was call Smith to give him all of the addresses, minus one. Any of the places on it could be the hiding place for the Stingers, though Kirk strongly doubted it. He was beginning to think like Vega. The missiles would be elsewhere.

Still, he could be wrong, in which case it wouldn't hurt to have Smith send out search teams. Give the man something to do. Naturally, Kirk didn't mention the condo.

Just to be safe, Kirk then relayed to his father the same information he'd given Smith.

After the telephoning, Kirk and Andino sat down together. They talked until well after dark, discussing various strategies. When they'd finally agreed, they dipped back into Smith's goodie bag for the specialty items they needed, then headed for Water Street.

This time it would be Andino out walking point.

50

Smith was glad that he'd stayed late in his agency office, trying to sort through the bizarre twists and turns the affair was taking as this day crept towards its merciful end.

First Kirk had called, with a list of addresses he believed might be warehousing the missing Stingers.

Smith had no idea what the list represented, nor how Kirk had come by it, but he had great respect for his field man's abilities. He immediately began assembling a couple of search teams. With a little luck they could complete the job before the night was over.

But then had come the second call, from the officer watching Smith's detainee. The prisoner was becoming very, very ill. They were going to have to move him. Did Smith want to be there when it happened?

He did not hesitate. Of course he wanted to be there. Then he'd better get a move on, the officer said. The clearance-to-move orders had come from the very top. The chopper was already revving up.

Smith swore to himself. He really didn't want to lose control of Corrales. Not now. But there were limits to his power. He shelved his other effort for the moment and hurried down to the holding room.

The officer on duty opened the door for him immediately. "They're coming for him now," the officer said. "But he asked for you. Specifically."

Smith barged into the room. It was bare except for a small cot bolted to the floor. Corrales was supine on the cot. Next to him knelt a young man whom Smith recognized as a bright-eyed agency doctor who'd forsaken the higher salary he could have commanded on the outside in order to be close to what he still perceived as the glamorous world of espionage.

The young man looked up. "Mr. Smith," he said.

The body on the cot didn't stir, but its eyes opened at the mention of Smith's name.

"What in the hell's going on here?" Smith demanded. Corrales had been fine the last time Smith had seen him, six hours earlier. Now the man looked like a second helping of death.

"I don't know, sir," the young doctor said. "At first we just thought he was coming down with a late winter bug, but it's gotten so much worse so fast . . ." He raised his hands helplessly. "The only thing I can think of is Legionnaire's Disease."

The words hit Smith like the flat side of a shovel. Legionnaire's Disease—ricin poisoning. The two had identical symptoms.

Son of a bitch, Smith thought. Someone got to him. Even before we brought him here. Vega.

"I just hope we can get him to the hospital in time," the doctor added without real conviction.

It's already too late, Smith thought, and he said, "Move away for a minute, Doctor. The prisoner wants to speak to me."

The doctor looked from Smith to the man on the cot. It did seem like the man had something to say, but . . .

"I don't—"

"Now!" Smith said.

The doctor retreated and Smith knelt in his place.

"Corrales," he said gently, "I'm sorry, I didn't know. It wasn't us."

The enfeebled man nodded. "I know that," he said in a croak. "The *cabron* has poisoned me. I don't like you or your country, but I give him to you, Smith. I spit on his mother."

Corrales spat, or tried to. Then he rasped out an address over in the District. And then he closed both his eyes and his mouth.

Smith got to his feet and quickly left the room. As he was on his way out, two men pushing a gurney were on their way in.

The address, Smith noted, was not on the list Kirk had given him, whatever that meant. No matter, the thing to do was move fast. He still had a chance to be first on the scene.

He paused only long enough to locate his destination on a map and to recruit one other officer, someone tough who also knew how to drive fast and well.

The address was actually just off Water Street, between the C & O Canal and that stretch of Whitehurst Freeway which since Kirk's childhood had smelled like human waste.

Back in those days it had been an area of factories and warehouses facing on the Potomac. Now the old buildings had either been torn down or converted into condominiums and garden apartments that would be trendy by reason of proximity to the canal, if one could ignore the stench.

Kirk knew the area well enough but, to familiarize himself again and give Andino a look at it, he cruised once through the warren of narrow streets before parking on Wisconsin Avenue.

Then they explored the towpath, between Wisconsin and 34th Street.

The C & O canal, which runs along the southwestern edge of the city before emptying into Rock Creek, is a carefully preserved historical curiosity, left over from the days when it was important to have a calm stretch of waterway connecting Washington with western Maryland. It was designed for barges that were pulled along by mules tramping up and down the towpath, and it was heavily trafficked in its time.

No boats are to be found out on the canal now. Its locks are inoperable, its waters nearly stagnant. But the towpath beside it still sees a lot of use, mostly during the day, from hikers, joggers, and those just seeking an escape from the automobile-choked streets of the city.

Kirk and Andino walked the towpath, the canal on their left, a stone retaining wall on their right, the bare trees arching over their heads. The water was spanned by a series of steel trestle footbridges in addition to those heavier ones that carried vehicles. The path was dimly lighted and practically deserted at this hour.

The two rehashed their plan until they felt prepared for any contingency, even the appearance of a random mugger.

Finally, satisfied with their joint knowledge of the immediate vicinity, they parted. Kirk took up his predetermined position by the footbridge; Andino returned to the car. She parked it under the freeway, within sight of the condo, then stepped to a nearby pay phone and dialed the number Croaghan had given them along with the address.

Javier Vega, who'd been expecting a call all day, was startled when the phone finally rang. After taking a moment to calm his nerves, he answered.

Without waiting for him to speak, a woman's voice said in rapid-fire Spanish, "Vega, they've got Salazar and they're going to break him. The towpath, by the footbridge near Thirty-third. Ten minutes." And she hung up.

Vega dropped the receiver. He checked to be sure he had an extra clip for his pistol, then he was out the front door.

Cautiously.

The hall was empty. Vega took the fire stairs, two at a time, to the building's basement.

He had no way of knowing, of course, whether it had been friend or enemy on the line. But it didn't matter. Whoever they were, they knew where he was. That turned the condo into a potential death trap.

His best hope was to exit through the basement door, which he did. Again, very cautiously. He looked up and down the skinny street that ran between his condo and those under construction across the way. Nothing stirred but the mist that was drifting in from the nearby Potomac. In the background was the steady, rumbling sound of the traffic along Whitehurst Freeway.

Vega headed in that direction, away from the canal.

He had a brief debate with himself about whether or not to meet the woman. She could be from the U.S. government, or from Bruderdam and his people. Or she could be genuine, from his friends in the resistance.

Not the government, he thought. They weren't that casual. They would have sent in a squad of commandos from the Delta Force for someone as important as himself. He'd probably be dead by now.

And if she was one of Salazar's soldiers, fine. He might be in need of her help.

That left only Bruderdam. Vega just couldn't bring himself to conceive of the man as a threat. None of the good cards was in the American's hand. It might even be interesting to see what an emissary from Bruderdam had to say.

So he decided to meet the woman.

If possible, though, he wanted the element of surprise. He reasoned that she'd be expecting him from the south, the direction of the condo, or the east, along the towpath. Instead he'd circle way around and come at her from the direction of M Street, to the north.

As Vega turned the corner at the foot of Wisconsin Avenue, he still saw nothing suspicious. He pulled his hat down low on his forehead and walked briskly up to M Street, where he turned left and dawdled along the nightclub strip. There were a surprising number of pedestrians for a chilly March night, which suited him fine. Ten minutes after quitting the condo Vega turned left again, onto Thirty-third. Now he moved slowly and very, very carefully.

Back on Water Street, a black Ford with a turbocharged engine rolled to a stop after having spun through the complicated spaghetti loops at K Street and Interstate 66. Two men in dark overcoats got out and walked up a street lined with older row houses and illuminated by fake gas lamps atop squat, ornate iron posts.

Kirk crouched in the shadow of a dumpster on the south side of the canal, within ten yards of the footbridge. He held the silenced Smith & Wesson loosely in his hand. He badly wanted Vega alive, but was realistic enough to know that anything could happen. Even if they had the right address, and even if Vega did play into their hands, the man was still a fanatic and a cold-blooded killer. He might want to die rather than be taken.

Of course, it now seemed certain that Vega was the only one who knew where the Stingers were, so his death would not be entirely counterproductive. Within a fairly short time the missiles would harmlessly self-destruct. As long as no one stumbled across them before then, they'd do no further damage.

That'd be a satisfactory ending, except for one thing. Kirk had some questions he eventually wanted to ask Javier Vega.

He shifted his weight without moving too much. The position he'd taken was a good one. He had a clear view up and down the towpath, and back toward the condo. If Vega came out the front, Kirk was set to react, no matter what his quarry did.

The plan itself was a calculated risk. The more conventional approach would have been to storm the condo with as much backup as they could muster. They'd rejected that option as too likely to end with Vega dead, either as a result of the inevitable shootout or . . . Kirk simply couldn't shake the feeling that there were people who would rather see Vega killed than captured. If one of them were in the assault team, then there'd be no preventing an "accident."

A second possibility had been to attack the condo themselves, just the two of them, but that would have required either breaking in or trying to talk their way inside. No matter what, Vega would have held the high ground. It was too dangerous.

So they'd opted for luring him out and trying to take him on neutral territory.

The luring part would be no problem, Kirk had reasoned. Once Vega realized that someone knew where he was, he'd never stay in the condo. The question was, would he keep the meeting at the footbridge, where they had the best chance of pinching him between the two of them?

If he didn't, if he just ran, they'd still have a good shot

at nailing him. There were only two ways out of the building. Kirk had the front covered, though he strongly doubted Vega would choose that exit. Most likely, Andino would pick him up as he came out the back. She'd drawn that post because it was closest to the pay phone and she, with her superior Spanish, was going to have to make the call, then hurry to her position before Vega reacted.

Kirk stopped thinking as Andino began whispering in his ear.

She hadn't had to wait long.

She'd made the call and communicated to Kirk through the Ear Mic that someone in the apartment, presumably Vega, had taken it. Then she'd rushed back to the Eagle to watch the rear of the building from inside the car, where she'd be difficult to see.

Less than a minute later, Vega came out the door and started down the hill toward Water Street. He was fifty yards away, but there was no mistaking him. She was seeing with such clarity that it was almost like looking through binoculars.

As he came her way she squirmed deeper into the shadows and whispered to Kirk, "He's coming."

But why this way? What was he going to do?

Vega turned left on Water Street, then left again on Wisconsin Avenue. He moved with caution, but confidently. If he was headed for the footbridge, he was going in a roundabout way, which was fine. As soon as he disappeared around the corner, Andino slipped out of the Eagle and went after him.

She kept in steady contact with Kirk, detailing her movements and Vega's.

She tailed him up Wisconsin, then along M Street. He was taking his time. Obviously, he wasn't running away. It began to seem likely that the footbridge *was* his ultimate destination.

When he turned south on Thirty-third Street, that confirmed it. He was going to come at the bridge from above it and to the west. He was trying to keep his options open.

Andino was a block behind. She turned down Potomac Street, which parallels Thirty-third, and raced toward the canal.

"He's on his way to the footbridge," she whispered as she ran. "He'll be coming down from the Thirty-third Street side."

Vega stopped on the Thirty-third Street bridge and stood for a moment, looking down the canal to the east. It was a cold, clammy evening and no one was in sight, not even a hardcore after-dark jogger.

He was feeling more confident. If the Americans had been setting him up, they would have had the building surrounded and would surely have taken him long before now. So it was someone else, which tipped the balance toward keeping the meeting.

But where was the woman?

Inside the deep slash pocket of his coat, his fingers maintained a firm grip on the pistol. He'd wait for her, he decided. He walked back to the end of the bridge and descended the stairs to the towpath.

Kirk was so focused on what Andino was doing that he almost blew the surveillance.

He'd been looking back at the condo only sporadically since Vega had left it, and he might well have missed the two men in overcoats. But he didn't. He caught the movement out of the corner of his eye and checked it.

Two men, approaching the front entrance to the building. And . . . Kirk stared hard, trying to convince himself that he'd made a mistake.

He hadn't. One of the men was Smith. How in the hell . . . ?

Kirk immediately clamped off that line of thought. It didn't matter how Smith had found out. He had. And he was here.

The other man was bent over the front door of the building now, fiddling with the lock. Smith looked in Kirk's direction and Kirk pressed himself against the dumpster, trying to blend naturally with its shadow patterns.

Smith looked away as the other man pushed open the door. The two of them went inside.

"He's coming down off Thirty-third Street," the voice whispered in his ear. Andino was in place, concealed behind some trees on the far side of the footbridge. "He's on the towpath now, headed your way."

Kirk was worried. Whatever their plan, Smith and his companion were eventually going to discover an empty apartment. At that point they'd almost certainly call in some help and might begin a search of the immediate area. When that happened, the scene at the footbridge could go very bad very fast.

He thought of alerting Andino and decided against it. There was no telling how close her finger was to the trigger.

Nothing to do but sweat it out. Vega came within Kirk's field of vision as he edged closer to the footbridge. The Nicaraguan moved warily, but like a man in control of the situation. His ego must be sky-high, Kirk thought. He had the President of the United States paying rapt attention to his song.

Vega drew closer. He began shifting his attention from one side of the canal to the other. Searching for his contact, Kirk thought, wondering where she can be.

A solitary jogger came pounding down the misty towpath from the direction of Thirty-third Street. Vega spun around when he heard the man's footsteps, and automatically began pulling his gun hand from his coat pocket.

Kirk raised his own pistol. He wasn't going to let another innocent person die.

But the gray-haired jogger gave Vega a broad smile, shaking his head as if only a lunatic would be out on a night like this in shorts and a T-shirt. Vega apparently agreed that no one would come after him dressed like that. He let the jogger pass. The man clip-clopped along and was soon out of sight.

Vega passed under the footbridge and paused. He withdrew the hand from his pocket and let it hang loosely at his side. Kirk could clearly see the long, silenced pistol barrel. Then, after a last careful look around, Vega climbed the stairs to bridge level.

"He's coming up," Kirk whispered to his partner.

This was it. Andino had to make contact. She'd have maybe five seconds to convince Vega she was on his side, or else Kirk would have to break cover and hope for the best. At least no one else was around.

Vega took the steps one at a time, making no more

sound than a cat. When he reached the top, he stepped onto the footbridge, in Kirk's direction.

"Now," Kirk said over the Ear Mic to Andino. He raised his pistol and steadied it with both hands. The slightest wrong move on Vega's part and the terrorist was going to get shot.

Andino stepped out from behind the trees. "Vega," Kirk heard in his ear.

Vega turned sharply, bringing his gun hand up.

"I'm from Salazar," Kirk heard Andino say in Spanish. "You must—"

And then the man who'd been with Smith came out the front door of the condo. Without looking their way, he turned and began running down the hill toward Water Street. The sound of his footsteps was as intrusive as a marching band.

Vega reacted entirely on instinct. He spun around, saw the man running from his building, and decided in a flash that it had all been a trap. He whirled his body back around to face Andino, growling the single word, *"Puta!"* His pistol pointed at her chest.

Kirk knew what would happen next.

He fired, trying just to wound, aiming at a point low on the shoulder of Vega's gun arm. Vega pitched forward on his face.

Andino ran to him, turning him over and cradling his head in her arms.

The bullet had been off the mark and had done a lot of damage. Vega had a sucking chest wound. He was bleeding profusely and breathing only with great effort. He was dying.

Kirk, not knowing how badly Vega was hurt, emerged from behind the dumpster and vaulted up the stairs at the opposite end of the footbridge. The plan, he thought, was going to work.

"Javier," Andino said to Vega, her voice catching in a sob. "Javier." She stroked his head with one hand; with the other she snatched up his pistol, which lay where he had dropped it. "Why didn't you trust me?" she said softly.

"Who . . . are you?" Vega croaked.

Kirk sprinted down the footbridge and stood above them. Realizing immediately that Vega had received a mortal wound, he lowered his gun.

The two men gazed for a long moment into each other's eyes, then Kirk said, "It's over, Vega."

Andino looked up at him, her expression cold and hard. "Not quite, pig," she said.

She raised Vega's pistol. There was just time for the amazement to spread across Kirk's face before she shot him twice in the heart at point-blank range. The gun made as much noise as an apple falling on a pillow, but the force of the slugs' impact knocked Kirk flat on his back. He twitched a couple of times, then lay still.

Vega was staring at her, unsure of anything but his own mortality. She laid his head gently down and knelt beside him.

"There is no time," she said. "He was an American agent who infiltrated us. I was forced to bring him along. He was not supposed to . . . Javier, you're not going to make it. You must help us. It will be difficult without you and the colonel, but we can still be successful. You have to tell me where the missiles are."

Vega hesitated, holding on to the one thing he had.

Andino looked around. There was no one, but there soon would be.

"Please, Javier," she said urgently.

And, in words that escaped from him one by one, Vega told her where they were.

"Thank you," she said, and she began to get up.

"Wait," he said.

She stopped. Vega was a lean, muscular man, she knew. But now he looked frail and old, pitiable. He coughed, sending a fine mist of blood into the air. She leaned toward him to hear what he had to say.

Again the words came in a slow rasping procession, one at a time: "When . . . it's . . . over . . . go . . . to . . . Hammerhead . . . and . . . kill . . . the . . . bastard . . ."

Then he coughed again, this time more violently. Blood sprayed from his mouth and spurted from the chest wound. And he died.

"He's done," Andino said.

And Kirk came back to life.

He sat up, looking dazed. The Kevlar vest under his jacket had prevented the bullets from penetrating his body, but he'd received the equivalent of a half-dozen

Mike Tyson blows to the chest. The wind had been knocked completely out of him and it had taken a tremendous effort on his part to disguise the fact that he was gasping for breath.

"You were very convincing," he said to her.

"It was difficult," she said, glancing at the dead terrorist. "Having to touch him."

He nodded. "But you'd better get going. I can get it smoothed over as long as nobody finds you here." He paused. "And let us recover the Stingers."

She looked at him with disgust, started to say something, then turned and walked away.

"Wait," he said. She stopped. "Look, I'm sorry. It was a stupid thing to say after . . . I guess I'm still not thinking straight."

The remark about the Stingers had been an instinctive reaction to a situation in which he was at a distinct disadvantage. He had to let her go, while he stayed behind to mop up. It would take some time before he was able to mount the official recovery operation. In that time she could conceivably snatch the missiles herself if she wanted to.

"What are you going to do now?" he added.

She turned slowly to face him again. "The problem of educating your people continues," she said. "I have several more speaking engagements, which I will keep. As long as no one comes after me."

"They won't."

"Thank you. After that, in a couple of weeks, I'll be returning to my country, of course."

"Well . . . can I get ahold of you through the same number?"

"What for?"

"I don't know . . . I might . . ." He shrugged. "I don't know, I just have the feeling that it might not quite be over yet. I'd like to be able to . . . reach you. Despite what I said, I do trust you. Besides, you're one of the few competent people I know."

She nodded, with just a trace of a smile. "Yes," she said, "the same number. They'll be able to get a message to me."

There was a moment of silence as they took the measure of each other.

"Why?" she said. "Because of Hammerhead?"

"Partly," Kirk said. "Do you know what it means?"

"I have no idea."

"Me neither. But it's probably important. I want to keep close watch on what happens in the aftermath of this thing. There are still . . . personal questions for me."

"Your family." She nodded. "What I said about that stands. If you need me, I'll be around."

He felt rotten. "Thanks," was all he could think of to say. "For everything."

She nodded again, then turned, quickly climbed the hill behind the footbridge, and disappeared into the misty night.

51

Kirk pushed the button next to Salazar's apartment number. He hadn't seen anyone enter since the man had gone running down the street so, as far as he knew, Smith was alone inside.

The buzzer sounded, opening the door to the lobby, and Kirk felt pleased that he knew his man. Smith was there, all right, playing the game with his usual efficiency. He'd let in whoever buzzed, without speaking himself, as if the caller were expected. That way he had a good chance to entrap anyone who came looking for Vega.

Kirk went straight up and rapped on the door. He stood right in front of the peephole so that Smith could get a good look at him.

The door opened and Smith was standing there, still wearing his topcoat. He was so nondescript-looking that he could have walked down the street of any major city in the Western world and never attracted the slightest attention.

His bland moon face betrayed no emotion, but Kirk

could sense the choked-back anger when he said, "Kirk, what are you doing here?"

"Might be I could ask you the same, Smith," Kirk said. "This place wasn't on the list."

"I noticed." The sarcasm in his voice, though barely audible, was withering. "Corrales talked. And you?"

"Sorry. I got a late tip from Colonel Salazar and I wanted to move on it immediately. But we shouldn't waste too much time on the how and why, Smitty. Vega's on one of the footbridges over the canal. The one nearest to us. Up there."

He gestured vaguely to the northwest.

"What are you talking about?" Smith said, now openly angry.

"At least he should be," Kirk said innocently. "Unless someone's made off with the body."

Smith finally exploded. "You arrogant son of a *bitch*! If you've blown this operation, I'll—"

"You'll what?"

For a long moment the two held each other's eyes. All of the bitterness, past and present, flowed freely between them. They might have dropped off the edge of the earth that way, Kirk thought, and it would have been appropriate.

Then Smith turned and stalked to the phone. He made a couple of quick calls.

True to his profession, Kirk thought. The middle of an international crisis and he knows that the first imperative is still damage control.

When Smith returned he said, "My people will take care of the body. Now, how are we supposed to find out where the missiles are?"

"I know where they are," Kirk said.

"How?"

"I did try to take Señor Vega alive. Before he died, we had a heart-to-heart."

"And he told *you*? Why?"

"Look, Smitty, you've got your need-to-knows and I've got mine. Suppose we leave it at that."

Smith hesitated, then left it. "Where are they?"

"Uh-uh," Kirk said.

"I'm your control, Kirk."

"Which doesn't mean that I exactly trust you. I located them, so we do it my way."

Without waiting for any further discussion, he went to the phone and made his own mop-up calls. The first was to his father, to let him know in a general way what was happening, and as insurance that the word would be passed without delay up to the President as well as his stand-in.

The second call was to Croaghan to let the NSC man know when and where they should link up.

Then Kirk went to Smith and said, "If you feel you have to wait for the ghouls, you can. But I'm going to meet Croaghan."

Smith gritted his teeth and prepared to follow the man he was supposed to be leading.

It was an old, badly weathered frame house out in the Virginia countryside, near Centreville, with three or four wooded acres screening it from the road. The location was good, near Dulles Airport as well as Interstate 66, for quick access to the city, but secluded enough that a terrorist could come and go unobserved.

The address hadn't appeared on Croaghan's list. Vega would only have rented it, Kirk thought. Recently and under an assumed name. If he'd paid enough in advance, no one would have hounded him for references.

The house was dark and seemingly deserted when the five men approached it through the trees. Smith had insisted on having one of his agency colleagues along, while Croaghan had invited Colonel Webber, the military's liaison with the CAT. Kirk hadn't felt the need to bring anyone else. There were enough rivalries among the three organizations represented to ensure that the missiles would be properly handled.

Assembling the recovery team had taken less than thirty minutes. Once together, they'd driven out in Smith's car, left it down the road and covered the last quarter mile on foot. All were armed, Webber and Smith's man with machine pistols. No one assumed as yet that Vega had been working alone.

They also hadn't bothered with such legal niceties as search warrants, nor did they intend knocking politely on the front door. If Vega had lied with his dying breath, it was possible that an innocent Virginia homeowner was about to be unpleasantly surprised.

For about five minutes they huddled together and watched the place. There was no sign of anyone inside.

Then Kirk and Smith held a quick, whispered conversation. For the moment they tacitly agreed to put their animosities aside and work together like two professionals. Their consensus was that the house was as empty as it looked, and the others accepted their judgment.

Smith and his companion went in the front door while Kirk and Colonel Webber entered by the rear. Croaghan stood watch from the woods.

Once inside the house, the two pairs cautiously converged, flicking on lights as they came, checking at every step for tripwires and other booby traps.

There was nothing and no one.

Kirk's senses were finely pitched. He could feel the Stingers lying somewhere nearby. And Vega had been a rogue elephant—not at first perhaps, but at the end. Kirk was certain of it.

Nor were the missiles likely to be booby-trapped the way the warehouse had been. If the dying Vega had truly believed Andino to be on his side, and there was no reason to think otherwise, then he would have seen her as the fulfillment of his mission and warned her of any danger.

Kirk motioned the agency men upstairs; he and the colonel returned to the kitchen. A locked door there suggested it might lead to the basement. Webber splintered it open with a short burst from his machine pistol.

They found themselves looking down a flight of old, unfinished plank stairs. The musty smell of underground rose up to welcome them. Kirk flipped a light switch on the plaster wall and a bare bulb came on, illuminating the stairwell. Somewhere out of sight below, another light had come on as well.

There were no alarms, no explosions, no sounds at all.

Kirk went first, picking his way carefully down the stairs, setting his feet with unconscious caution on the outer edge of each step, balancing himself with one hand against the slightly clammy plaster.

The basement was small, unfinished—just the four block walls and the slab floor—but clean-swept and dry. Several adjustable steel posts were in place, helping prop up the first-floor joists. Pushed against two of the walls were long wooden benches that held hand tools, spools of wire, boxes of nuts and bolts, electronic components, a rusted water pump. Some of the tools had obviously lain there for a very long time, while others were shiny and new, brought in by the most recent occupant.

Another bright, bare bulb—this one inside a wire cage—cast garish shadows of the two men onto the concrete.

In the middle of the basement floor were the Stingers. The gleaming aluminum cylinders that had originally been packed three to a crate were now neatly stacked on a pallet.

Kirk and Webber stared at the weapons, then looked at each other as if to confirm what they were seeing.

Webber's face broke into a broad grin. "I believe this is what we're looking for," he said.

The colonel slung his machine pistol over his shoulder and knelt by the pallet of missiles to count them. Kirk went to the stairwell and hollered up for Smith to fetch Croaghan and come down into the basement.

When he returned, Webber was frowning. "You count 'em."

Kirk quickly did so. "Nineteen," he said.

Webber nodded. "That's what I got. We're one short."

Kirk ticked the known firings off in his head. Boston, Atlanta, Dulles, Marine One. Four out of twenty-four. There should be twenty left.

There weren't. One of the Stingers was still at large.

Why?

The other three men came hurrying down the stairs and nearly fell over one another when they caught sight of the tidy stack of man-portable surface-to-air missiles.

"They all there?" Smith asked immediately.

Kirk shook his head. "Nineteen," he said. "The other one wasn't in the van?"

"No," Smith said. "Nor in the condo."

"Maybe Vega left one at the next place he planned to hit," Croaghan said.

"Maybe," Smith said. "But it's still a loose end. I don't like it."

"I don't either," Kirk said, "but this is ninety-five percent of the threat right here. Let's get it back where it belongs. Colonel?"

"I believe that can be arranged," Webber said, and he went to call his superiors.

Two hours later, Kirk returned to the house on Duddington Place. He was gratified that most of the Stingers were safely back in custody, but he was bone-tired, and he still had to do something with Enrique Salazar.

"Vega's dead, Colonel," Kirk said to him. "We've got the missiles back."

"Vega was allowed to use my apartment whenever he pleased," Salazar replied. "I know nothing of his activities beyond that."

And so on. The interrogation was bound to be profitless, Kirk knew. Besides, he just didn't feel like he was operating at full strength without Andino in the room.

So he decided to give up. If Salazar were involved, that was for someone else to deal with. Kirk didn't really care what happened to the co-conspirators. He'd finished the job Smith had recruited him to do, and the time had arrived for some pay-back.

He fitted the hood over Colonel Salazar's head. He wasn't going to blow the safe house simply because he no longer cared about the agency.

Then, after stripping the house of anything he thought might be of future use, he drove Salazar home. He dragged the colonel out onto a sidewalk two blocks from his mansion, waiting until the last minute to cut the cords that bound him. Kirk's car was around a corner and gone before the surprised Salazar could disentangle himself from the hood.

After that, Kirk drove the Eagle to a downtown parking garage and left it. He could give the claim ticket to Smith when he saw him.

And he did intend to see the man again. But not now.

Since the Metro was closed for the night, he walked up to Massachusetts Avenue, where he checked himself into a hotel near Dupont Circle. Then, finally, he fell onto a bed and immediately into a long, dreamless sleep.

52

Walter Brust stared straight into the teleprompter, trying to look at least a little bit like a man in control of the situation.

"My fellow Americans," he said. "The President has asked me to speak to you on his behalf this morning. As I'm sure you all know, he'd be with you himself if he could. Even so, he wants you to know that his recovery is proceeding very rapidly and he's champing at the bit to be back at work."

The Vice-President had chosen the Oval Office as the setting for the telecast. It had a reassuring quality for most people, he thought. And for himself, it was a familiar place where he had expected to feel at ease.

He hadn't foreseen what it would be like to address the nation from behind the presidential desk. It was terrifying— more so even than going one-on-one with the General Secretary of the Soviet Union—yet, essentially, all he had to say was something positive, that the crisis was over.

Many people already knew that. The early papers had broken the official story: one terrorist dead from FBI bullets; his accomplice dying in the Naval Medical center, so close, ironically, to the President; and, most important, the missiles had been recovered.

Brust and the General Secretary had quickly patched up U.S.-Soviet relations. The Cubans had passed word that the MiG-21s on their soil would be undergoing "maintenance" for some time to come. The ground troops in Honduras and the task force off Nicaragua had been relaxed from Alert Condition Five to Three. And the domestic airlines' phones were in gridlock from the surge of reservations requests.

"It is my pleasure to report to you," Brust said, "that the antiaircraft missiles which had unfortunately fallen into terrorist hands have been recovered. Those responsible for the heinous crimes of the past week will, if they are still alive, be punished to the maximum. And a full investigation is underway within the military to see how we can more effectively safeguard our defensive weaponry.

"In the meantime, the gratitude of our nation goes out to the hundreds of members of our various law enforcement agencies who have been working around the clock on this threat to our security.

"The President and I wish also that we could thank each and every one of you, the American people, for your courage and forbearance in the face of this vicious terrorist activity inside our borders.

"God bless you and may our skies forever remain as friendly as they are, once again, today."

The little red light went out and Brust's massive frame slumped back into the chair. The cameraman gave him a thumb-and-forefinger circle. In a studio two hundred miles away, a smooth-voiced telenews commentator was translating the Vice-President's statement into English for the brain-stunned.

He was thankful for the coaching he'd received beforehand. The trick was to speak like Ronald Reagan—authoritatively, yet as though every viewer was a best buddy. And, especially today, it was very important from a political point of view to seem to have resolved something that one actually hadn't.

The speech had been tailored to that end, with the President's full approval. The affair's loose ends had to be summarily hidden from view, and the belief instilled that it hadn't been nearly as bad as everyone, in their heart of hearts, knew that it really had been. From Vietnam to Iran/Contra, this had become the final stage of crisis management.

It would work again, luckily. For the people, as every politico knew, were interested only in what directly affected them. In this instance, it was their safety as airline passengers. Once that feeling of confidence was restored, they wouldn't care a rat's ass that no one in the government could answer a fairly important question: who had masterminded the blackmail plot?

* * *

Christopher Holt had worked late into the night and then had returned to the lab long before the Vice-President made his morning address to the nation.

Contrary to popular opinion, voice analysis was not like a fingerprint comparison. True, each person's voice was distinctive. But there weren't those unique whorls and ridge patterns that you could match up and then declare with certainty that they were from the same person.

With voice, you had to carefully feel your way along. Success lay nearly as much with intuition as deduction, which was one of the things that had attracted Holt to the field. Yet the end result, it was always hoped, approached the accuracy of the most rigorous science.

Computers could do a lot of the detail work, but they could not be trusted to judge the guilt or innocence of a human being. Which is why most of Holt's long hours had been spent hunched over long sheets of paper covered with squiggly lines rather than seated in front of a glowing cathode-ray tube.

The process had begun with the spectograph, which converted the taped words into those printed lines, each one representing some aspect of the individual's speech apparatus, either from the vocal cavities (throat, nasal, and around the tongue) or the articulators (lips, teeth, soft palate, and tongue itself). No two people had quite the same combination of ingredients.

Holt had begun the process by taking the separate voices on Walker's tapes and converting them into spectograms. This step was repeated several times, in order to ensure that the result in each case was free of machine error.

Then he'd compared, line by line by line, the speech pattern of the voice on the first tape with those on the second. His job would have been a great deal easier if the voices were speaking the same sentences, but they weren't. So at best Holt was working with a few key words and phrases. Beyond that, the analyst used his experience and skill to create a general overall impression.

All in all, it was difficult, tedious work. Not until a full twenty-four hours later did he feel comfortable going to the Attorney General with his conclusions.

As instructed, he treated the matter as "A.G. Eyes

Only" and hand-carried the tapes, along with his analysis, to Walker's office. There he waited patiently an hour and a half for his boss to return from the White House.

"What've you got, Christopher?" Walker asked wearily when they were finally alone together. From his tone, it almost seemed to Holt that Walker didn't really want to know. But he handed over the tapes and his manila folder.

"Well, sir," Holt said, indicating the folder, "it's all in there. But to summarize, I believe that Voice 'C' on the second tape is identical with the voice on the first tape."

Walker looked at him critically, the weariness gone. "Are you sure?" he asked.

Holt nodded. "There's never a hundred percent certainty, as you know. But in this instance I would say we're in the ninety-nine plus range, Mr. Attorney General."

Walker looked at the other man for a long moment, then slowly shook his head.

"Jesus," he said.

As always, Walker disdained the chauffeured limousine service that was one of his prerogatives as attorney general. He preferred riding the Metro, with the people his office served. Not to mention that it was a faster, more efficient means of getting around the city.

He'd given a lot of thought to what young Holt had told him, and after weighing all considerations, he had decided that the only thing to do was speak directly to the President himself, sparing him nothing.

When he was finally shown in, after waiting an hour for the President to wake up, Walker was relieved. The President looked as if the worst were over.

"You the bearer of bad news, Don?" the President said.

Walker nodded. "I've been able to identify Smoking Gun," he said. "I put a tap on Carla Stokes's phone and she recorded his last message. Then I taped a task force meeting and had one of my best men run a comparison analysis."

"He's one of us," the President said, shaking his head.

"I'm afraid so, sir. It's the Chairman of the Joint Chiefs."

The President sighed. "Monty . . . Monty," he said. "Are you sure?"

"The voice prints are a close match," Walker said. "Considering that against the known level of the leaks, the probability of a mistake is less than one in a million."

"Monty . . ." The President looked his attorney general in the eye. "He did a lot for his country, Don."

"And a lot against it, Mr. President. Leaking highly sensitive information is bad enough, but . . . there's more."

"Dear God. What?"

"The timing, sir. The story about the mining incident was leaked so that it would make the first edition of the *Post*. But the people on board the *Studds* couldn't actually confirm that it *was* a mine until later that morning. There was a lot of initial confusion about what exactly had happened."

"You're saying that General Banks had prior knowledge of the incident?"

"It appears that way, yes sir."

"Then . . ." The President couldn't bring himself to say the words. They were talking about the military officer who ranked second only to the Commander in Chief.

"Then he was part of the plot," Walker said. "Probably from the beginning, though he may not have known what Vega intended to do with the missiles."

"You don't think he works for the Russians?"

"No, just the opposite. I think he believed so strongly that we should go in and oust the Sandinistas that he decided to take matters into his own hands. I doubt he thought the Soviets would respond the way they did."

The President shook his head again, then closed his eyes and said, "I've got to think about this."

He looks paler, Walker thought. God help me if I've overestimated his strength.

The President didn't say anything for some minutes, but he obviously hadn't gone to sleep. Walker waited. This was a critical moment, and he knew it.

Finally the President opened his eyes again and asked, "Who else knows?"

"No one," Walker said. "Unless my lab man guessed, but he won't talk. I brought it to you first."

"Good. We've got to put a clamp on it."

Walker was perplexed. "Sir," he said, "you're not going to let him get away with it?"

"Of course not, Don. He'll be relieved of command and tried for the leaks. He needs to do some jail time. But there's no point to dragging the whole story out into the open. We let him plea-bargain and wind the thing up as quickly as we can."

"Mr. President!" Walker said vehemently. "The son-of-a-bitch is guilty of *treason*! God damn it, you told me yourself, 'If treason is involved, throw the book at them'!"

"Please, calm down," the President said. "I know what I said, and I meant it at the time, but . . . let me ask you something: do you believe what Colonel North did was treason?"

"I don't see what—"

"Just answer me."

"You mean the missiles to Iran." The President nodded. "The first shipment, no. The second shipment, if President Reagan really didn't know, then yes. He took money, wherever it went, from one of our enemies in exchange for weapons."

"Fair enough. Now, do you recall anyone screaming that North be tried as a traitor?" Walker was silent. "No, no one did. The American people are happy when we catch a Navy clerk who's been selling documents to the Russians. But Oliver North or Monty Banks? No. Nobody *wants* to know what they did. It's too close to home. If our heroes are bad, then maybe we're all bad and we can't face that. Don't you understand?"

The tight-lipped attorney general hardly appeared as if he did.

"Look," the President tried, "General Banks will go to jail. His career's ruined. We can see that he never gets a decent job after they release him. I think that's about as much punishment as we can expect."

"Mr. President, I object! Banks may have been directly involved in the murder of his own countrymen! That's far worse than Ollie North and his stupid TOWs!"

"Is it? Suppose it was one of those TOWs that blew up Major Condon's car in Beirut?"

"This isn't about TOWs, anyway," Walker said defensively. "It's about Stingers."

"Yes, it is," the President said. "But you used the key

words yourself: 'may have.' The Chairman of the Joint Chiefs *may have* been somehow involved in the theft of the Stingers. Is there any hard evidence that he was?"

"He had prior knowledge of the mining."

"Which could simply mean that he decided to use the blackmail attempt for his own ends. That's reprehensible, and treasonous, but it isn't murder."

"On the other hand, he might have been involved from the start."

"He might have. But if he was, we'd have to prove it, and we're not going to be able to do that without a full-scale investigation that drags every bloody detail out into the light, with all of the attendant risks to national security. Is that really what we want?"

"I don't know what we want. I only know what I want."

"Justice?"

"Something like that. Why, is that too corny for you?"

The President sighed. "No," he said, "it's not corny. It's part of what I admire in you. But just what, exactly, would you have me do, Mr. Walker? Hand the entire wretched affair over to the six o'clock news? Shatter whatever little trust the American people still have in their government? Cripple this administration for the rest of its term?"

Walker shook his head. "I see," he said coolly. "We're talking about political expedience."

"Don, will you please remember who you're talking to?"

"My friend . . . I thought."

"Of course I'm your friend. I care about you very much. But I'm also the President of this country. Until you've seen the view from behind that desk in the Oval Office, I strongly suggest that you not rush to judgment."

Walker started to say something, then held his tongue.

The President's tone softened. "What we're talking about is not expedience, Don," he said. "It's sparing the nation unnecessary trauma.

"Listen to me: Vega's dead, the airways are safe again, that's what's important. So place Banks under arrest. Go on out and round up anyone else you think might have been involved. The guy who let the Stingers get away, some agency people, Nicaraguan exiles, whatever, those who've committed hard crimes. Find the lost missile if you can. Put people in jail without a lot of hoo-rah. And then let's get the damn thing behind us. That's what most of the country wants us to do, help them forget the nightmare. They'll thank you for it, believe me."

"What about the blackmailer?"

"You think it wasn't Vega?"

"Of course it wasn't Vega."

"Well," the President said, "find him if you can, but don't waste a lot of time. He has no leverage on us now. Like I said, I want the mess cleaned up quickly. Clear?"

Walker got up, the varied emotions still churning inside him. On the one hand, he couldn't believe this was the same man who'd been so irate at the possibility of one of his own people being involved. Yet, on the other, he was behaving exactly as presidents always did, maybe had to. Smooth the waters. Restore public confidence as quickly and painlessly as possible. It was all Walker could do to keep from throwing up.

"Yes, sir," Walker said in as controlled a tone as he could manage. "I'll do whatever you say. But I just want to get one thing on the record here. I believe the American people can stand a lot more than you give them credit for."

The President nodded and said, "Your objection is noted." He studied his attorney general's dark, angry face for a long moment, then added, "And Don, don't even consider going off half-cocked on your own about this. I may love you like a brother, but I'll have your ass if you do."

Walker inclined his head slightly, turned, and walked out of the hospital room. The athlete's physical grace was nearly lost in an unaccustomed stiffness.

53

"I'm so sorry, Steven," Smith said. He shrugged. "But you must know what it's been like. And you haven't exactly made yourself easy to find."

Kirk nodded. Three days had passed since Walter Brust had formally announced the recovery of the Stingers, and a lot had happened.

General Banks and Colonel Salazar had been arrested, although both men were quickly out on bail. Other U.S.-based members of the Contra hierarchy, including the elder Vega, were being questioned. Corrales had died of ricin poisoning—the fatal dose apparently administered by his late associate, Javier Vega—without revealing any further details of his involvement in the plot.

Within the Administration, the changes were still shaking themselves out: Seamus Croaghan had already been canned; other sacrificial lambs were sure to follow. The public needed reassurance that such horrors were unlikely to happen again.

There had also been a few muted reverberations within the agency, Kirk guessed. Smith probably had to spend some time seeing that his butt was properly covered.

In any case, Smith was right. Kirk *had* gone to ground. He had been so tired after the missiles were finally found that he'd spent most of the next day asleep. The day after that, as well, he'd kept his own company, and tried to take stock of his life. Then he'd gone after Smith, for the pay-back.

The man hadn't been that easy to get to. But now they were alone in the Watergate apartment, sitting in the sparsely furnished living room, sipping white wine as though they were the most congenial of neighbors. Miles Davis's *Sketches of Spain* played softly in the background.

Smith was dressed in his usual, unremarkable gray suit. His bland moon face registered about as much emotion as it ever did. It was possible that he had never been surprised by life since day one.

"Well, I'm here now," Kirk said. "I trust that my performance was . . . satisfactory."

"Exemplary," Smith said. "Of course. You know the regard I have for your abilities. I never doubted that you were the right man for the job. There'll be a presidential commendation if you care."

Kirk dismissed the prospect with a wave of his hand. "You know what I want."

"Yes, I do. Unfortunately—"

"Don't do this, Smitty. I kept my part of the bargain. I want to know about my family."

Smith pressed his hands together and tapped his forefingers against his lower lip. "All right," he said. "Let me be honest with you. I'll help you if I can. But right now I don't know much more than I did two weeks ago. I told you then that we have some evidence of involvement on the part of exiled PRG Grenadians, along with the far-left Sandinista fringe. I still believe that the answer may be there. But I've been jammed up night and day with the missing Stingers, which I thought had been hijacked by the same group. As you well know, I was mistaken. All I can promise is to keep working and give you whatever I find."

Kirk studied the other man's face, though he knew that was going to get him nowhere. To Smith, the difference between truth and falsehood was as meaningful as the distinction between half empty and half full. It was simply a matter of emphasis.

He decided to bide his time and see where the conversation went from here.

"Steven, look," Smith went on. "I know you don't like me, and I know you don't trust me, and I can understand why. But were the past two weeks so distasteful for you?"

Kirk felt as if his ears weren't working properly. "What's *that* supposed to mean?" he said.

"Only that you're very good at what you do," Smith said casually. "You have a lot more to give."

"Jesus, I don't believe this. This is a *recruitment* pitch?"

"We could use you."

"Smith, you're crazy. You're fucking nuts! What in God's name makes you think I'd want to work for you?"

"Not for me. With me. Tell me this, Steven, what are you going to do otherwise? Find another city to disappear into? Waste your life in some warehouse full of junk? What?"

Like it or not, Kirk had to admit that they were questions he'd also thought of.

The hand was being held out to him. *Where's the apple?*

"I don't know," he said. "Make me an offer."

The faintest trace of a smile flickered on Smith's face. *Here it comes. Take a bite.*

"Financial security," he said as though ticking off the company's high points at a quarterly board meeting. "Freedom to accept or reject an assignment, as you see fit. And a shot at finding the people you're looking for."

Stalemate, Kirk thought. Smith had snagged him two weeks earlier with the prospect of finding out who had killed Susanna and Scottie. Now, with the same bait, Smith was going to keep him on the line for as long as he could. Or until Kirk ceased to be useful, whichever came first.

Kirk knew that he would get nothing more without the appearance of acquiescence.

"All right," he said, his heart many degrees colder than his voice. "I'll think about it."

"Do that," Smith said. "These are good times, Steven. We haven't had so much free rein since Bill Casey died. You remember what Casey said?" His eyes unfocused a little as he quoted. " 'We have a chance to establish our own foreign policy. We're on the cutting edge. We are the action agency of the government.' " He returned his gaze to Kirk, a trace of enthusiasm still in his expression. "It was true then and it's just as true now. With people like you in the field, we can accomplish a great deal."

Kirk shrugged. "You want me?" he said. "Then tell me everything you know about the blackmail plot."

Smith paused, the momentary animation gone now. Kirk could almost see the agency man's mind at work, deciding what to reveal, what to protect.

"We screwed up," Smith said.

"No kidding."

"Say what you will about me, Steven, but I admit my mistakes. Basically, this was a logistical one, not a philosophical one. I still believe in bringing down the outlaw government, and I would willingly help arm the opposition any time.

"They need Stingers. Those missiles turned the tide in Afghanistan and they're the only defense our allies have against the FSLN's Soviet gunships. What with the new Sandinista offensive down there, that need became critical.

"Unfortunately, our friends on the Hill are in one of their short-sighted periods, so . . . we had to go black in order to get the resistance what it requires.

"I maintain complete deniability on this, you do understand that?"

Kirk nodded. "I'm interested only for my own purposes," he said. "Not the *Post*'s."

"Very well. We arranged for the diversion of eight pods that had been ticketed for Africa. Not a major shipment, but enough to signal the freedom fighters that we're still behind them despite congressional intransigence. And twenty-four choppers down is twenty-four fewer choppers.

"We did the switch in Norfolk, and Ruben Tellez was hired to drive the missiles to Corpus Christi. He was to leave them for a cutout named Vargas, who would get them onto a shrimper bound for Honduras. Somewhere in there Vega found out what was up."

"How?"

"We don't know for sure," Smith said. "But it wouldn't have been too difficult. Word could have spread through the exile community via either Vargas or Tellez. Vega had an elevated position in the hierarchy. He'd be expected to know when important things happened. And we trusted him in any case. He was devoted to the cause of retaking his country. We never thought he would have gone off on his own like this."

"So Vega killed Vargas and took his place."

"Yes."

"Who knew that?"

"No one. Tellez made a dead drop in order to blank the trail. And Vega was very clever. He let the Stingers go all the way to Honduras before he hijacked them. That way we didn't know anything had gone wrong until it was much too late, and our initial confusion was far greater than if he'd simply trucked them out of Corpus. We didn't know what to think at first, whether the missiles had been stolen or just lost. Vega bought himself some critical time by doing it the way he did."

"You think Vega was acting alone?" Kirk asked.

"Not entirely, of course. He had Corrales on his side, the guy he ended up feeding ricin to. Corrales was probably the one who met the SCOUT that Vega used to fly the Stingers back to this country, then dumped in a ravine in Texas. And then, there has to have been at least one other accomplice, the guy who made the phone calls to the President. But in the main, we think it was Vega's plan all along."

"With what motivation?"

"I believe he thought he could provoke us to military intervention in Nicaragua. If that didn't work, he stood to come out with a billion for the cause. Either way, he won. I expect he saw himself arriving in Managua to a hero's welcome."

Kirk shook his head sadly. "No matter what the price," he said. "What about the guy on the phone? Anything solid on him?"

"Negative. They set up their communications very well. We were never able to get a good trace. And I seriously doubt we'll be hearing from the 'Committee' again."

"How'd he get the President's number?"

Smith shrugged. "If he's one of the top Contras, he'd be likely to have it. Maybe it was Salazar. We're investigating."

"Where's Banks fit in?" Kirk asked.

"A loose cannon. There's nothing yet that connects him to the blackmail plot. He saw an opportunity and he tried to make use of it. The fact that his goals and the terrorists' were the same looks coincidental."

"So . . . the whole thing just dries up with Vega's death?"

"No one wants to prolong the agony, Steven."

"How about the missing Stinger?"

"It's troubling, but not that troubling. There's not much chance it'll be used before it self-destructs."

Smith's moon face was as remote and unruffled as the surface of its namesake.

"All right," Kirk said, "the sixty-four-dollar question: why did you think this might have something to do with Susanna and Scottie?"

"It's a guess," Smith said, "but an educated one. We know that there are exile Grenadians living in Nicaragua and we know that they hate you for what they think you did there. Our intelligence reports indicate that two of them may have been in the U.S. at the time of the car bombing. They seemed to be likely candidates. They still do.

"At the same time, we believe that these people are allied with a far-left faction within the Nicaraguan government which believes that the Sandinistas are not radical enough. Both groups harbor known terrorists. It was a natural assumption that it was they who had the missiles and that they were trying blackmail to bring about exactly what the 'Committee' was demanding, which would boost their own prestige as well. Not to mention that the money would have given the country's economy a massive shot in the arm.

"So I truly thought that when we recovered the missiles, we'd also get our hands on the ones who had set the car bomb. I was wrong. Believe me, Steven, I'm sorry."

Kirk finished the last of his wine and got up.

"When did you want a decision?" he said.

"Your choice."

"I'll call you."

When Kirk had gone, Smith made a brief phone call.

"I believe I can recruit Kirk," he said. "I think he enjoyed the action more than he'd like us to believe."

"Good," the voice at the other end said. "But if he doesn't go for it, I don't want anything to happen to him. Understood?"

"Yes, of course."

Then Smith went to the stereo and put on a timeworn copy of *Jazz Goes to College*. He got out his axe. This time he'd take it easy, play along with "Take the A Train."

The old Ellington piece started up, its signature opening phrase as familiar to a jazz buff as that of Beethoven's Fifth to a devotee of the classics or "Satisfaction" to a rock fan.

Smith wet his lips and prepared to accompany the incomparable Paul Desmond.

He had a feeling Steven Kirk was about to become a serious problem once again, and he wanted to completely forget about the young man for a while.

54

By the time Kirk left the Watergate and started up Virginia Avenue, he knew more or less what he was going to do next.

Smith's story had been plausible enough, but two things were wrong with it.

For one, he had said that Tellez dead-dropped the missiles in Corpus Christi, meaning that the deliveryman didn't stick around to see who picked them up.

Smith couldn't have known, of course, but that was directly contradicted by what Tellez had told Kirk and Andino on the last night of his life. Tellez had said that he put the van under surveillance, recognized Vega as the man who claimed it, and knew Vega but also knew that he was the wrong person. Furthermore, when Tellez had reported that to his Contra superiors, they had said it was okay and to come on home.

Someone wasn't telling the truth. Was it Smith, snug in his Watergate apartment? Or Tellez, terrified that a Sandinista woman was about to blow his head off?

The other issue was the money.

Smith had avoided talking about that, but a billion dollars was a hell of a lot of cash. One couldn't carry it around in a suitcase. Therefore, if the blackmailer was serious, he had to have some plan for processing the pay-out. And he'd indicated that a bank in the Bahamas was going to handle it.

It would require world-class clout to get a bank, even a Bahamian one, to broker a deal of that kind. Kirk had spent a good bit of time with the WALNUT dossiers on everyone whose name had surfaced so far, and he didn't believe that any of them had that degree of influence or, for that matter, enough of a Bahamian connection at all.

The inescapable implication was that the man on the phone wasn't a mere accomplice, but the person behind Vega. He'd be someone big. Someone not even necessarily a part of the Nicaraguan exile community. Someone with his own set of motivations, who had tried to use Vega and had gotten burned.

Someone whose code name was Hammerhead.

Find Hammerhead, Kirk thought, and a lot of things would come clear. He stepped into the Pan American building on Twenty-third Street, made a phone call, and two hours later was sitting down with Seamus Croaghan in the ex-NSC man's Foggy Bottom apartment near Washington Circle.

Croaghan's face was redder than usual, and it wasn't from alcohol. He had been angry for three days running. His rage rose up inside him like a cobra from a basket and, like the captive snake, remained poised there, not knowing where to strike.

He was angry over having lost his job, yes. Somehow he'd expected his friendship with Diane to count for more in the crunch.

What made him even more livid was the way the rest of the Stinger affair was being swept under the rug. Some token arrests made, personnel reshuffled, the CAT disbanded. And then the same hollow silence that comes down on you in the dead of a sleepless night.

It wasn't right. The crash victims deserved better, damn it.

Dermot deserved better. Croaghan's brother had died violently, and the ultimate responsibility for that death had yet to be decided. It could not be left that way. The long cultural history of his race whispered in Croaghan's ear, and it demanded vengeance.

So he had gone back over all of his notes, his files, things he'd lifted from WALNUT and Smith's database. He'd become convinced that the shadow government—the loose confederation of government officials, private-sector moneymen, and their international allies—was deeply involved in the recent blackmail scheme.

This President had been used by the shadow government. So had the CAT. And the agency. And crucial peripheral people like General Banks.

They were far from unique. For more than three decades, the shadow government had been out there, running a clandestine version of American foreign policy, financing it with profits from arms sales, drug smuggling, and other lucrative illegal activities.

Croaghan doubted there was any one leader of the shadow government. But each of its operations would have a nominal controlling figure, someone to formulate the plan and handle logistics. That was the man, or woman, Croaghan wanted, the one who'd specifically directed the Stinger affair, the person who must pay for Dermot's death.

Who? Croaghan stared at the glowing green CRT until his vision blurred, searching for the answer.

He walked himself through the major upheavals of his generation, and the people associated with them. He started with the Bay of Pigs and worked his way through the assassination of President Kennedy; Vietnam, which he suddenly realized had been as much about control of the Southeast Asian opium trade as anything else; the murders of Robert Kennedy and Martin Luther King; Watergate and peripheral scandals; Koreagate; the Australian Nugan Hand Bank that had laundered Golden Triangle heroin money; Iran, where fabulous profits had been turned arming the Shah; Chile; Ed Wilson and the C-4 *plastique* deal with Libya; Grenada; the southern African adventures; and finally the Central American mess, with a focus on the infamous Nicaraguan Contra/cocaine connection, which would have finally dragged the shadow government out into the public light of daytime TV if the joint investigative committee had had the courage to pursue it.

The story was alternately sickening and fascinating, and of astonishing breadth and complexity. But at its end Croaghan was still asking the same question: who had killed Dermot?

All he had was one tantalizing piece of evidence. The Provident National Bank on Grand Bahama, which was to have processed the blackmail money, had cropped up in SMITH. It had been used before. By the shadow government. Who had been on the receiving end remained obscure, but the bank was a point of entry. If nothing else appeared, Croaghan thought, he could go to Freeport and start leaning on people.

Then Kirk had called.

Within moments of their sitting down together, the two men knew that they had independently arrived at the same place. Both were convinced that, while Javier Vega had ended up being the central figure, the original controlling hand behind the blackmail plot had not been his. And both, for their individual reasons, wanted the scheme's mastermind.

Each of the two held keys that would help resolve the mystery. Croaghan knew where to look, Kirk what to look for.

Croaghan had now also been made aware of the existence of Piedad Andino, and of the details of how the search for the missiles had ended.

"Of course, we didn't expect Vega to get mortally wounded," Kirk said. "But when he did, the ruse worked perfectly. Andino pressed him to reveal the location of the missiles before he died, so that she could carry on, and he did.

"But those weren't his last words. The last thing he said to her was: 'Go to Hammerhead and kill the bastard.' I think it must be someone's code name. Whoever he is, Vega hated him and he expected Andino to as well. He's the one we want."

Croaghan leaned back in his chair and stared unseeingly at Kirk for a long moment, searching through the most complex database of all, his own photographic memory.

No question about it, the word had rung a bell.

Hammerhead.

Croaghan sat bolt upright. "It's not a person!" he said to Kirk, the enthusiasm spilling out of him like a millrace. "It's a place! You've got live-access codes for WALNUT, right?" Kirk nodded. "Let's use them from now on. Mine still work, but I may be getting flagged so they can track what I'm doing in there."

Kirk recited his father's codes. Quickly Croaghan booted up his personal computer and patched into WALNUT.

Three minutes later, the two were paging through the lengthy agency dossier on Henrik Bruderdam. President and Chairman of the Board of the Gustavia Brewing Company, among other highly successful business ventures. Owner and emperor of Hammerhead Cay, Bahamas, just west of Great Abaco. A man of clout, undoubtedly, with the Provident National Bank.

Bruderdam had a long association with the clandestine services. As a super-rich, prominent businessman who was welcome in nearly all of the world's countries, he was an invaluable gatherer of foreign intelligence. In addition, he'd occasionally served as secret emissary to governments that U.S. officials didn't want it known they were dealing with. And, with his international banking contacts, he'd been able to help with some delicate financial transactions.

"Look at this," Croaghan said excitedly. "The Imperial Bean Coffee Company, which Bruderdam owned, used to control thirty thousand acres of prime growing land in Nicaragua that was nationalized after the revolution in '79. And he never got it back. No wonder he's got a hard-on for the Sandinistas."

Kirk gazed at the screen and just said, "He's our man."

"He's got access to all the pipelines. He probably set up both the original missile deal and the hijacking. Hired Vega in order to ingratiate himself with the opposition leadership. Then if the Sandinistas do go down, he's a hero and maybe he gets his coffee plantation back. And if not, he disappears a whole stack of money through a Bahamian bank that's in his pocket. Either way, he wins. Except that Vega goes and crosses him up."

Croaghan shook his head. "And the sonofabitch is an American, too," he went on. "Killing his own people. God damn it, I want him, Kirk."

"Show me how to get into Smith's computer files," Kirk said. "I want to know how to do it, and I want to see what he's got on Bruderdam."

Croaghan thought about the risk of discovery, then decided this might be the last time he'd have to enter the database.

"Sure," he said, and led Kirk through the steps necessary to invade SMITH. "But if he has a file on Bruderdam, we're gonna have to work some to find it. Look . . ."

Croaghan showed him how the files were set up. All the material was there—events, dates, places, and incriminating personal data. All logically arranged and cross-referenced. It was a monumental compendium of greed and betrayal of the public trust.

But so many of the names were missing.

"He's got a code name for all the active ones," Croaghan said, "which in itself is an astonishing piece of work. And somewhere there's a key. But it isn't in here. I know; I've looked everywhere for it. Without that key we have to search for someone who sounds like Bruderdam. Even when we find him, there isn't likely to be anything to tie Smith directly into the Stinger affair. That's what you're after, isn't it?"

"Not really," Kirk said. "He admits he was involved in setting up the original delivery of the missiles. Which would mean that he must have had some contact with Bruderdam. But he denies knowing anything about the hijack and blackmail plots, which is possible. I'd just like to see what kind of stuff he keeps on Bruderdam. How about if we try keying in 'Hammerhead'?"

Croaghan shrugged. "Sure, why not?" He punched the word into a program he'd written to help him get around in SMITH. Then the men waited as the search was carried out. It took some time.

The program replied that there was one entry for that character string. A five-page document.

Croaghan asked for a display.

The two men watched quietly as the document scrolled past their eyes. The first page was a map of the Northern Bahamas, showing the geographic coordinates of Hammerhead Cay. The second was a nautical chart of the waters surrounding Hammerhead. The third was an aerial view of the island, with buildings and other prominent features located, and their functions noted. The fourth was a set of floor plans for the main residence. And the fifth was general information.

"Jesus," Croaghan said, "look at that. The sonofabitch has got a military five-meter dish with a satellite uplink. That's how he was able to make those untraceable phone calls."

But Kirk wasn't that interested in the communications technology.

"The place looks medieval," he said.

"Yeah," Croaghan said, "but we know what to expect. And we've got the element of surprise. Bruderdam thinks it's all over."

The two men looked at each other for the first time in a while.

Finally Croaghan said, "We're going after him, aren't we?"

"I don't know," Kirk said.

"Come on, Kirk," Croaghan said. "What're we going to do, tell the President? He and Bruderdam are probably buddies. He'll want some hard evidence and we don't have any. Nothing will happen."

"Maybe the agency?" It sounded lame even as Kirk said it.

"Sure. And how do we sort out the ones who are already on Bruderdam's payroll? Kirk, this guy has enormous resources. The shadow government he's part of has even more. The only way to get to him is with people he can't buy. That's you and me, my friend."

Kirk closed his eyes and massaged his temples with his left hand. Croaghan was right. And Bruderdam probably owned a share of the Bahamian government as well. He could sit in his island fortress and resist any challenge to his power.

With the possible exception of a carefully planned, perfectly executed physical assault.

And Kirk knew that he was most qualified to lead it. The weight of that knowledge sat on him like a block of marble. He felt tired, and the thought of further violence nauseated him.

Yet Bruderdam had to pay. And he might know . . . what?

He opened his eyes and looked at Croaghan. "What do you mean, 'you and me'?" he said.

"Don't give me that shit," Croaghan said angrily. "You're not going there without me."

"I don't know. . . ."

"Damn it, I was in the Army. I'm in shape. I can handle myself, okay?" He leveled a forefinger at Kirk. "You fuck me over on this and the first person I call is Smith. Then you can see if Bruderdam is waiting for you!"

"We're off to a great start, aren't we?"

Croaghan's expression softened. "All right," he said. "I'm sorry. But you can't leave me behind, Kirk. It's too important to me."

Kirk sighed. "Well, we can't do it alone," he said.

"The Nicaraguan woman. She's a professional, you trust her and she said she'd help you."

"I'd already figured her in. But I'd be a lot happier if we had at least four."

They thought about it.

Finally Croaghan said, "Don Walker."

"The Attorney General? On something like this?"

"I know him. He worked 'outside' the law when he was busting drug dealers. He has his own definitions, depending on the nature of the crime, and people are getting away with murder here.

"Listen, just before I was fired, Walker came to see me to thank me for what I did. And to say he was sorry about the way the mess was being cleaned up, but he was following the President's orders to sweep everything under the rug if need be.

"He was rip-shit, Kirk, I could tell. He wants all of the bastards strung up by their nuts and he won't be able to do it as A.G. He's going to quit his job, it's tearing him up so much, and then he'll be a pistol looking for a target.

"He'll go, I'm sure he will."

After a long pause Kirk said, "All right, I'll think about it. Now make some hard copies of the Hammerhead file, will you? We've got a lot of details to work out."

55

Diane McBain's heels clicked and echoed as she walked purposefully along the second-floor corridor of the Old Executive Office Building. She had her honey-blond hair tightly pinned back and was wearing a severe green wool suit. The laminated plastic White House ID card flapped from her jacket pocket.

The dust hadn't yet completely settled, of course, but it looked as though Seamus Croaghan was going to be the only NSC casualty of the Stinger affair. She'd regretted having to fire her old friend, but she was sure that he understood. There was no way she could tolerate her aides going over her head.

Then, too, there was the matter of the CAT. Croaghan should have done better, sniffed out the clandestine missile shipment in the first place and reported it immediately to her. That way they could at least have created a paper trail that showed their opposition to the illegal scheme, from the beginning. She might even have gained useful leverage on the agency, by threatening to tell the President what he wasn't supposed to know.

Whatever, Croaghan's loss was a small price to pay for keeping her authority intact and the National Security Council on an even keel. That was exactly what she intended to do during the difficult period that inevitably followed in the wake of a major crisis.

She turned in at the "sterile" conference room that was maintained in the building for the agency's convenience. The door was open and Smith was already there, looking serene in his dark blue suit, striped tie, and unfashionable plastic glasses.

He'd been vague about the reason for the meet, but

426

she felt little apprehension as she closed the door behind her, sealing the two of them away from the city of twitching noses. They could now say anything they wanted to.

McBain sat down and said, "What do you want, Smith?"

"I think you will agree that we are in a transition period, Miss McBain," Smith said. "Things are . . . unsettled. It is the Director's and my opinion that we should therefore settle them, as much as possible."

"I would agree."

" 'We' meaning our offices and those at the NSC. What with the unfortunate recent crisis and the President's health problems, it is entirely possible for this Administration's foreign policy to go dangerously adrift. We need to assume a position of leadership, to make sure that doesn't happen. Naturally, it would be best if we shared common goals."

God damn it, it was a set-up. What could the man have up his sleeve now? McBain's analytical mind paged quickly through the possibilities and failed to come up with anything.

"*I* make the NSC's policy recommendations," she said. "I'm certainly willing to consult with you. But if you're asking for a larger voice in our affairs, the answer is no."

"Not larger, Miss McBain. Just equal. So that we don't work at cross-purposes."

McBain felt a couple of drops of sweat begin to trickle from her smooth-shaven armpit down her right side.

"What are we talking about here, Mr. Smith?" she said.

"A working partnership," Smith said.

"With who calling the shots?"

Smith smiled, just a little. "Our common interest."

"You have something that makes you think I'd want to talk to you about this?"

"Yes. Perhaps you'd like to have a look at this Memcon."

Smith handed over the three-page memorandum of conversation. "*M* is yourself, *T* is Derek Trane and *S* is myself, of course."

McBain read the document through. It was dated March 18 and it was a death sentence.

"You sonofabitch," McBain said. "Croaghan fingering the Contras for the hijack and me suppressing an investigation of them because the President supported them? That's nonsense. I never did any such thing."

"Nevertheless," Smith said, "that is the recollection of both Mr. Trane and myself. And, of course, the Memcon is merely the hard-copy version of the tape."

"You can't have this on tape! I never said it!"

"I have the tape."

"Then it's a goddamn fabrication!"

"Miss McBain, please. We have a difference of opinion, but the position of Mr. Trane and myself is supported by a tape recording of your own voice. Think of how testy the President is about this whole subject just now. I don't believe he'd be appreciative if the Director played him a copy of this tape."

While Smith's demeanor hadn't changed in the slightest, McBain had slumped visibly in her chair. Smith was right. The President would quickly lop off the head of anyone he even suspected of having impeded the resolution of the Stinger crisis.

"You're a cold-blooded bastard," she said.

"I want what's best for the country," Smith said.

"Which is?"

"In this case, continuity. Stability. A foreign policy that serves its objectives."

"You mean your objectives."

"Our common objectives."

McBain sighed. "Be specific, Smith," she said.

"You will have to replace Mr. Croaghan," Smith said. "I would suggest bringing Derek Trane over from State. He could be a valuable liaison with that department, and he has our trust." With just the tiniest emphasis on the *our*.

McBain might have smiled at the incredible precision with which the man worked if his moves hadn't also been so cold and calculating. What an unmistakably Smith-like touch, using her own lover to spy on her. It had been a disaster to underestimate him.

"And Trane will represent your concerns to the NSC," she said.

"He will be in close communication with me, yes."

"I see," McBain said as she got up. "Is that it?"

"We'd like to move on this as soon as possible."

"I'd planned to announce my selection by tomorrow."

"That would be fine."

"Good day, Mr. Smith."

Smith tucked the Memcon back into his briefcase and watched Diane McBain walk from the room with as much dignity as she could muster. He had no idea of the effort required to keep her high heels from buckling under her.

56

March 30

Donald Walker pulled hard on his paddle, helping propel the small rubber boat across the shallow waters of Little Bahama Bank. The island was just a slight dark smudge against the star-strewn sky.

He still could hardly believe that he, the Attorney General of the United States, was here on the open ocean with Seamus Croaghan and two total strangers (including an agent of a foreign government), mounting an assault against one of the world's major arms traffickers. But it was unquestionably so. There was the steady, rhythmic *snick* of paddles entering water, the pungent salt smell in the air, the gentle up-and-down motion as they rode the light chop.

Of course, Walker wasn't going to be attorney general for long. Even now his resignation letter was sitting in Tom Read's in-basket. He knew he would eventually have quit in any case. He was tired of being hemmed in by the code of conduct demanded of the nation's chief law enforcement officer. And he just didn't want a damned desk job anymore.

But that wasn't why he'd used the power of his late office to set up this operation. It was because his emotions had finally gotten the best of him.

He'd been down, very down, as he alternated between

feelings of rage and the realization that he was helpless to act on them. Now he had something to believe in: if this venture were successful, it would force the details of the Stinger affair out into the open. People who ought to pay for the hideous crimes they'd committed would pay. And that, though the President would never forgive him, was what Walker wanted with a deadly passion.

Following Croaghan's initial call, which had inadvertently plugged right into Walker's need, things had happened very fast.

Walker had met the other three, examined their evidence, been easily persuaded that the U.S. government would take no official action, and decided to join them. They'd spent a long night working out strategy, and then Walker had put his clout to work.

First he'd requisitioned the necessary armaments. Next he'd arranged for the weapons to be shipped by boat to Abaco so that the group could travel clean. Finally he'd made arrangements with a Bahamian fisherman who was secretly on the DEA payroll.

They hadn't been easy things to do, especially not in an unobtrusive manner, but Walker had called in some favors, made a couple of veiled threats, and gotten them done.

The team had flown to Abaco. There they'd met the fisherman, who had transported the four of them and their gear to a point two miles southwest of Hammerhead Cay, where they'd been put over the side. The fishing boat had never stopped, so anyone watching from the island would merely have seen its lights glide on by.

The drop point had been selected to take advantage of the prevailing winds and currents. With four pairs of arms working, they figured on only about an hour to reach shore.

The team had studied all the waters around Hammerhead Cay until any of the four could have served as navigator. Still, their knowledge was only as good as their information, and few things are as inherently unreliable as a nautical chart. The sea changes things quickly and in unpredictable ways.

Navigating at night was also tricky, but they could hardly have mounted the operation in the daytime. So they'd selected what looked like the simplest plan of action: starting from the drop point, take a fix on the eastern tip of the island and head straight in. The target area was a short, narrow crescent of sand along Hammerhead's southeastern shore.

That would put them—the cay being shaped more or less like a left foot without toes—on the outer edge of the heel. From there, if they hiked northward, they would soon come upon the airstrip that ran down the center of the heel. And from there they could follow Hammerhead's single road to Bruderdam's compound, three miles west, at the top of the foot.

Walker pulled hard on his paddle, trying to keep from thinking about the precariousness of a rubber boat riding the swells of the sea. The streets of the city were his domain, not this.

To distract himself, he replayed his memory of the night they had nailed the Colombian drug lord. It had been in the heat and stink of Miami summer. They'd staked out the bastard's warehouse for two weeks, allowing business to proceed as usual, waiting patiently for the big man so they could legally tie him to the operation.

The boss had finally shown in the middle of the night, and Walker had only two agents to assist him in the critical moments before reinforcements could get there. Fearful of losing their quarry, they'd gone in anyway, up against half a dozen Colombians with machine pistols.

It was the first time Walker had ever used an Uzi in the field. The weapon worked well.

By the time police surrounded the warehouse, Walker was alone. Four of the Colombians were dead and the target himself lay dying at Walker's feet.

"We meet again, Mr. Walker," the man had said, his breath rattling around in his chest like tumbling dice.

"'It *was* your people who threw the grenade," Walker had said. He'd suspected, but not been positive.

"An eye for an eye." The man tried to laugh and coughed instead. "I should have listened to my uncle, no?"

"How so?"

" 'Guns,' my uncle said. 'Not drugs, guns. If it's drugs,

the Americans will kill you. But if it's guns, they'll help you.' "

And that was it. The Colombian had died where he lay, in the grime of the warehouse, with his bullet-perforated bags of cocaine spilling their crystalline contents out onto the floor.

Walker abruptly became aware of the sound of surf breaking on sand. The ghostly white of the beach was dead ahead.

They paddled even harder over the final quarter-mile, and then Kirk went over the side. He splashed through the last few feet of water and hauled the boat up onto the sand.

The group went into action with a minimum of wasted energy. The waterproof stuff sacks were opened. Gear and clothing were adjusted. Boxy Ingram machine pistols were slung from shoulder straps. Doubled-up thirty-shot magazines were rammed home. A few quick words were exchanged. Everyone knew his or her part.

In a few moments they were headed inland, with Kirk walking point. He remained the nominal leader of the operation, though any of the others could take over for him if need be.

They poked their way through the vegetation fringing the beach, mostly sea grape and tournefortia, and into the interior coppice, with its Bahama pine, silver and thatch palm, and occasional *lignum vitae*. The going was relatively easy. Hammerhead Cay received too little rain to develop a jungle undergrowth.

In ten minutes they reached the airstrip. It was dark, apparently deserted. An Aero-Commander was parked on the runway, a Huey helicopter just off it. Kirk and Andino checked out the single, small maintenance building and found it empty.

To the west, the single-lane, crushed coral road was a spectral strip of white in the starlight. It curved away into a palm thicket.

The intruders took a collective deep breath and started silently down the road.

The three-mile hike to the compound took a careful forty-five minutes. During that time no one in the group saw an animal larger than a bat.

At the entrance to the compound was an ornamental

archway. There was no door in it. The arch was surmounted by a gold scrollwork rendition of the famous Gustavia Brewing Co. logo: the G and B entwined around a royal scepter. One might be entering the British Embassy.

The only light in the compound came from the main residence, ahead and off to the right.

The group had decided back in Washington to split eventually into two buddy teams, with Kirk and Andino in one and Walker and Croaghan in the other. Just inside the arch they diverged for the first time.

Kirk and Andino checked the vehicle maintenance shed on the right-hand side of the road. The other two checked the two storage buildings to the left. All three structures were locked and quiet. A single Jeep could be seen through the front windows of the vehicle shed.

The two pairs converged after making their inspections. After carefully synchronizing their watches, they split up again. Walker and Croaghan headed off through the scrub to the left. Their objective was the staff quarters. Inside, they expected from Smith's files to find a groundskeeper, cook, pilot, and mechanic—all of whom were to be considered dangerous—as well as a couple of bodyguards.

They were to wait five minutes before going in. That would give the other team a chance to circle around to the right and check out the generator shed and desalination plant before gaining entry to the main residence.

If all went well, they had agreed that Bruderdam was Kirk's for the night, to be interrogated for whatever information Kirk could get.

Then, in the morning, Bruderdam would be kidnapped and flown back to the States, along with as much hard evidence as the group could come away with. His staff was to be spared, provided they offered no resistance.

Once they were safely home, Walker felt he had the leverage to get Bruderdam tried for murder and treason, at the least. The legal proceedings might take awhile—Walker had no illusions on that score—but eventually the man would pay. And with Bruderdam on ice, his assets confiscated, the conspiracy that Croaghan called the shadow government would suffer a serious setback.

Walker and Croaghan crouched behind a pair of mango trees and examined the building before them.

The long, two-story stucco structure resembled one of the mass-produced chain motels. All of the sleeping quarters were on the second floor. Each person's room let onto the open balcony, with no other exit. A light shone at either end of the building and one was lit inside, on the first floor. No one was stirring.

When the five minutes had passed, Walker and Croaghan went on the offensive.

First they swept silently through the downstairs. All of the rooms branched off a central hall. One of the team would cover while the other checked the room. Then they would switch positions. They worked their way quickly from end to end. A kitchen, a utility room, a lounge with a bar, two big bathrooms, and several others.

No one was up. A single light was on in the kitchen, but the room was empty.

They retraced their steps to the utility room, where Walker located the breaker box and cut the power to the building. The three lights went out and the electrical hums of the night subsided. Now the only illumination was from the stars and two lights on a pole in the driveway turnaround about thirty yards away.

Croaghan was already outside, covering the second-story balcony, when Walker came sprinting out of the building after having laid down half a dozen smoke grenades. He ran up the outside stairway and paused at one end of the balcony. Smoke billowed out the first-floor windows. When it had begun to be blown into the bedrooms, Walker ran down the line of doors, rapping on each one.

"Fire!" he called to whoever was within. "Fire!"

It certainly must have seemed like it to people who came awake in the smoky, unelectrified dark. They stumbled out of their rooms, coughing and rubbing their eyes. For a moment they milled around in confusion.

Then Walker stepped out of the storage closet at the far end of the balcony. Simultaneously Croaghan switched on the hand-held portable spot.

"Everyone down!" Walker commanded.

The blinded people looked to their left and discovered a living nightmare: a huge man with an eye patch throwing the bolt on a machine pistol. Down in the yard were who knew how many of his buddies. The people did as they were told. Walker counted five men and a woman. That would be right.

As the smoke began to dissipate, he said, "All right, now everyone move to the top of the stairs. On your stomachs. Hands on heads. Move!"

The people slithered on their bellies along the balcony, the spotlight following their progress. When they were clustered near the stairwell, Walker had them stop. Then he began checking the vacated rooms.

He could feel the extra surge of adrenaline. It was the most dangerous moment of the night. If someone had smelled the trap . . .

"Stay put!" Croaghan shouted to the knot of people, some of whom had begun stirring restlessly. The stirring ceased.

Walker worked methodically, reaching around the jamb of each door and triggering the flash cube. It was a small, simple, battery-powered device with a highly polished reflector. All it did was fire the four bulbs in the cube at once. The resultant light was intense enough to blind the retina for about a minute.

After firing the cube, Walker would scan the room with his own powerful flashlight, keeping low. Then he'd go in to check the closet. Closets were easy. He opened their doors, standing off to the side, and shined his light through the crack between door and jamb. No one can hide in a small closet.

No one was hiding anywhere.

When Walker had finished searching the rooms, he got the captives on their feet and down off the balcony. They were directed to lie prone in front of the building, while their captors stood over them.

Then, after restoring power, Croaghan and Walker settled in to wait. One watched the prisoners, while the other continually scanned the surrounding area. Since the latter was a more tiring job, they switched every fifteen minutes.

At the same time, Andino and Kirk had completed their sweep through the main residence. All she had discovered on the first floor was a slender man who wore steel-rimmed glasses and said his name was Thomkins, and two very young, very frightened girls who spoke only Spanish. Andino had done her best to pacify the girls.

Kirk, searching the second floor, had found more.

57

Only one of the rooms had a light on. The light spilled out into the darkened hallway through a door that was slightly ajar.

Kirk moved silently, checking the other rooms first, finding them all empty. It was a cursory search, but sufficient to assure him that his back wasn't completely uncovered. Then he returned to the one that showed light. His fingers tightened on the grip-stock of the gun in his hand, and he found that his tongue had involuntarily come out and wet his lips.

He was about to come face to face with Henrik Bruderdam, he could feel it.

Very cautiously he approached the door. His skin was tingling all over. Bruderdam was a very crafty, very dangerous man. He might have any number of defensive systems built into his room. Kirk peered through the space between the door and the jamb. No one was in sight. He noted the thick Persian carpet, a leather chair, and floor-to-ceiling bookcases. It was apparently a library of some kind.

Kirk took a deep breath, let it halfway out, and attacked the library. He pushed opened the door and stepped inside, pivoting on the ball of his right foot so that his eyes swept every inch of the room in a fraction of a second. The machine pistol was ready.

But it remained unfired.

There was one man in the room, sitting in a dark brown leather chair that matched the one Kirk had already seen. The man didn't budge. His face was placid, his gray Hong Kong suit was spotless, his wing-tips glowed. He glanced up as Kirk burst into the room, entirely unperturbed. In fact, he looked as though he might have been calmly waiting for just such a sudden appearance of a man with a gun.

Kirk froze, more startled than surprised. A long line of dominoes began falling, falling in his mind. His mouth opened slightly and a single word came out of it: "Smith."

Smith nodded. "Congratulations, Steven," he said. "I find it impossible to underestimate your abilities. How did you put it together?"

"Vega told me where to go before you arrived at the bridge. He died with the hope that we would take Bruderdam out."

"Touching. Greater love hath no man than that he risk his life for his enemy?"

"Under the circumstances, I don't exactly see Vega as my enemy."

Smith merely nodded. Oddly, Kirk found himself thinking that some old jazz record should be playing softly in the background. To keep his mind in focus, he began to talk.

"You planned the hijack," he said. "You and Bruderdam. You recruited Vega to do the actual work and you're the one who salted his WALNUT file to confuse me and anyone else who got onto him. And then what? Vega doublecrossed you?"

Smith didn't reply.

"Yeah, that's what happened. I know that Bruderdam was after his old coffee plantations. What about you, Smitty? What did you want?"

Smith shrugged. "It wouldn't do any good," he said.

"Try me."

"Steven, look, you're brilliant, tough, courageous, but you have a terrible Achilles heel. Your political judgments are emotionally clouded, ill-informed and much, much too short-sighted. You have no grasp of global geopolitics."

"Which requires killing planeloads of innocent people."

"I'm sorry about that, I truly am. For what it's worth, the plan that I agreed to was for the missiles to be taken and stored safely away. I felt that our objectives could be attained simply through the threat of their use. Unfortunately, Bruderdam and Vega had something different in mind. As soon as I realized what was happening, I helped you hunt them down, did I not?"

Reagan may have been Teflon-*coated*, Kirk thought, but this man was Teflon to the *core*. Like a master of *aikido* he never stopped an assault cold, he merely deflected it harmlessly away.

"Fuck it," Kirk said. "I know what you wanted out of this, and it makes me sick. Not money, not political changes in some third-rate country. It's all just a game to you, isn't it, Smitty? You do it to see if you can. When the tide shifts, you change sides, so that whatever happens you come out on top. I should kill you right now and make the world a better place."

"You won't kill me, Steven," Smith said, "because I'm a part of yourself."

Kirk's stomach churned as a wave of disgust swept through him. And he knew that the revulsion was directed not only at Smith himself but at the small kernel of truth in what Smith had said.

"You're right," Kirk said, "I won't kill you. But I promise you, I will take great pleasure in nailing your feet to the floor when we get home."

A ghostly, disconcerting half-smile passed across Smith's face. A few more layers to the onion remained, Kirk realized, and like it or not, he was going to have to peel them away. But not now.

"Where's Bruderdam?" he said.

"I would guess that he's in his office," Smith said. "He sleeps very little."

"Let's go."

Kirk motioned with his gun, then followed Smith at a wary distance until they found themselves in a spacious anteroom outside the second-floor entrance to the north wing. Andino was already there, with the two girls and the slender man. She gave Kirk a questioning look.

"He's part of it," Kirk said. "Shoot him if he looks at you funny. Who's this guy?"

"Thomkins," Andino said. "Works for Bruderdam."

"Bruderdam in there?" Kirk asked Thomkins.

"He may be," Thomkins said.

Andino and Kirk knew that that part of the house was one huge room containing the nerve center of Bruderdam's empire. Kirk went over and tried the heavy oak door to the room. It was locked.

He knocked on it. There was no answer.

Kirk gestured at the electronic keypad on the wall next to the door. "You have the combination?" he asked Thomkins.

"No, only Mr. Bruderdam knows the combination, and he changes it regularly. There is no other way in or out."

Kirk raised his machine pistol to fire at the door, but a disembodied voice said, "That won't do you any good. The door has a steel plate inside."

Kirk looked around. A fine-mesh grille was set high up in the wall in one corner of the anteroom. The TV camera would be behind that, Kirk thought, and it'd be trained on him. And what else might be trained on him?

He lowered his gun.

"That's better," Bruderdam said. "Good evening, Mr. Kirk, and welcome to Hammerhead Cay. Why am I not surprised to see you?"

Kirk paid better attention this time. The speaker was up there, too, behind the grille. He spoke to it.

"Our paths were bound to cross."

"Yes, I suppose so," Bruderdam said. "And this would be Miss Andino, wouldn't it? You are also welcome to my island, young lady, though quite lucky to be here. The late Señor Herrera was an excellent shot."

"Herrera was a pig," Andino said.

"Mmm-hmm," Bruderdam said. "But a useful man at times."

"So what do we do now, Bruderdam?" Kirk said.

"A good question," Bruderdam said. "I assume that you came to my home for some purpose."

"Yes."

"And I assume that you and Miss Andino are not alone. May I also assume that you have some colleagues who are at the moment detaining my staff?"

"Yes."

"Then we are stalemated, aren't we? Whatever it is you came for, I'm the one who has it, and there's no way for you to get to me before I call in my Bahamian friends, should I choose to. Trust me, this room is quite impenetrable, unless you blow it up. Which would kill me. That would subvert your purpose, would it not?"

"What do you suggest?" Kirk said.

"Why don't you come inside and we'll talk?"

"All right. Open the door."

"If my instructions are followed. You and Mr. Smith remain where you are. Miss Andino and the rest of you, over into the far corner."

Kirk nodded and Andino complied.

"Now, Kirk, slide the gun the other way, at least six feet from you, and strip to your underwear. Throw your clothes after the gun."

When Kirk glanced over at Smith, Bruderdam chuckled.

"The thought of Mr. Smith disrobing is an amusing one, isn't it? But there is no need. I'm quite sure he is unarmed."

Kirk did as he was told.

"Good," Bruderdam said. "Now roll your underpants down and turn around, slowly, all the way around." Kirk did. The girls gaped at his nakedness; Andino looked on neutrally. "Fine. You may roll your briefs back up. Now the two of you will please come in. And Miss Andino, do not try to follow them. Kirk will be dead before you take the first step."

There was a buzzing sound and Kirk was able to open the heavy door. It opened outward, so that the interior was out of the line of sight of Andino and the others.

Smith and Kirk stepped inside.

58

The door swung effortlessly shut with a solid-sounding *thunk*. Kirk had noted the relationship between the door and the overly thick wall it was set in. Undoubtedly concrete. He was enclosed in a very secure space.

He looked around the room and in a few moments had memorized all the important details. It was impressive: the computers and Fax machines and Telexes and laser printers, the video projection system, the large teak executive's desk on its dais. Kirk also noted the missile launcher, with its gripstock and headphones, sitting on a table shoved against one of the walls. The missing Stinger, he thought, number twenty-four. Bruderdam's souvenir.

The man behind the desk didn't get up. From what Kirk could see, Bruderdam was short and not in the best of shape. He was wearing a blue-and-yellow Hawaiian floral print shirt. His eczema-scarred arms rested on the desktop and in his right hand was a Beretta 9-mm semi-automatic pistol. He was smiling, his blue eyes sparkling at some private joke.

Kirk moved slowly toward the dais, with Smith following.

"Ah," Bruderdam said, "the mentor and the mentee. Together at last." He motioned with the pistol to a pair of chrome-and-leather chairs in front of his desk and added, "Please."

The two men sat down and Bruderdam gently set the Beretta on the desk in front of him.

"Mr. Kirk," Bruderdam said, "it's a pleasure. Your reputation precedes you. And as we can see, it was well founded." He paused, then continued, "You have cost me a great deal, Mr. Kirk—may I call you Steven? Tell me, who do you think I work for, the agency? Our unflappable Mr. Smith?"

"Sometimes," Kirk said. "Mostly I think you work for yourself."

"Very good. Look out the windows, will you? Well, figuratively anyway. If it was daytime, do you know what you'd see? A swimming pool, beautiful lawns. And most important, the *sea*, Steven. The sea is what defines Hammerhead Cay. The sea creates an area that is distinctly mine.

"I *own* this island, but it's not like owning a brick townhouse in Foggy Bottom, is it? This place is more than my home, it's my country. Nobody fucks with me here. I can do whatever I want, and the Bahamian government defends my right to.

"That, Steven, is the distinction between having money and having *money*, which is the sole meaningful distinction in the world."

Kirk had been listening with only partial attention. He continued to casually study the room, searching for anything that he might use to his advantage.

"Do you see what I mean?" Bruderdam went on. "I

have control over my environment. It's what other people lack. Including yourself. Or else you wouldn't have risked your life coming here. I obviously have something you want very badly, and I don't for a minute take you to be a super-patriot who's here to redeem the good name of the United States government. So what is it? What do you want, Steven?"

Kirk felt an almost physical sensation of a probe pricking his flesh. "More to the point," he said, "is why haven't you just blown me away? What do *you* want?"

"Fair enough. I want you."

"You knew I was coming here?"

"No. But now that you are, we may as well speak to our respective interests. As I said, your reputation is top-notch. And I admire the way you have tried to take my island. If some of my people had half your abilities . . . Never mind. I'd love to have you on our side, if you were interested."

"And what side is that? The brotherhood of international terrorists?"

"Don't be crude," Bruderdam said. "And don't close your mind until you hear everything. Our side is yours, the side of free enterprise and individual initiative and, yes, the American way of life. We don't condone terrorism. The recent fiasco just goes to show how an important and necessary task, undertaken with the best of intent, can be perverted by the whims of a single madman."

"The madman being Vega," Kirk said. "Not you."

"I'm not mad, Steven." Bruderdam gestured around him. "A madman is incapable of creating this."

Kirk kept a tight rein on his temper. "Maybe," he said.

"God," Bruderdam said, "you don't think we *planned* to have Vega going around shooting down commercial airliners, do you?"

"I don't know what you planned."

"He wasn't actually supposed to do it. He was just supposed to threaten it. We presumed that that would be enough. Enlighten him please, Mr. Smith."

Smith merely nodded.

"Enough for what?" Kirk asked.

Bruderdam sighed. "To persuade the government to

do the right thing in Nicaragua," he said as if flogging the obvious.

"To get you your coffee plantations back, you mean."

"A fringe benefit. I don't really need them."

"How about the billion dollars. You need that?"

"The money was incidental. We threw the demand in to have something we could bargain away. Getting rid of the Communists was the first, last, and only objective."

Kirk bit down hard on his anger. Bruderdam was lying out his ass. He had to have been the one who overrode the HBO signal and broadcast the video of the 747 going down. That was not the conduct of a man who was surprised by Vega's actions. Kirk wondered if Bruderdam actually expected to be believed. Or whether he was taunting Kirk with his naked, shameless lie. Or whether the man was just loon-crazy, unable to distinguish fact and fiction.

"Sure. No one ever does anything wrong," Kirk muttered. "Who was the last? Kennedy with the Bay of Pigs? That was a long time ago."

"Don't be too quick to judge, Steven," Bruderdam said. "Our motives were not ill-taken. You probably haven't seen any intelligence reports in the past, ah, couple of years. And the news isn't good. The Soviets are making some major moves in Nicaragua."

"Come on, Bruderdam. I heard the same line about Grenada. That was bullshit and this probably is, too."

"Yes, I know of your unfortunate Grenadian experience. But I must say, I'm surprised to find you such a Sandinista apologist. Under the circumstances."

Kirk's muscles tightened involuntarily. "What's that supposed to mean?" he said.

Bruderdam shrugged. "Think about it," he said. "Something'll come to you. In the meantime, let's consider our mutual friend. Why do you think he's here?"

Kirk glanced over at Smith, but the agency man's expression was unchanged. "I suppose he's running salvage," Kirk said.

"Precisely," Bruderdam said. "Or so he would have us believe. The tying up of loose ends, the kind of thing he prefers not to entrust to electronic mail. All very logical, of course. But, as is generally the case with Mr. Smith, appearances are not to be relied upon. Actually, he came here to kill me."

Again Kirk looked at Smith, and again the man showed no outward indication that they weren't discussing the weather.

"And to destroy my files, of course," Bruderdam continued. "It's the only form of damage control that makes any sense. He did know enough to realize that he had to come alone, and unarmed, which makes me wonder how he intends to do it."

Bruderdam looked expectantly at Smith, and when there was no response forthcoming, said, "Well, no matter. He's not going to kill me. In fact, once my Bahamian friends remove the two of you from my island, neither of you shall have the opportunity to threaten me again. But he has been an entertaining guest, not to mention informative.

"Smith screwed up the whole operation, as I'm sure you've guessed. Vega was his man, and Vega was a very bad choice. Worse still, our friend made a unilateral decision that the operation wasn't going to fly after Vega turned into a loose cannon. So he went for coverage of his own butt instead of continuing to pursue our mutual objectives."

"Hardly surprising," Kirk said.

"Granted," Bruderdam said with a smile. "It's a shame the fellow is so damned well placed, isn't it? But frankly, right now I don't care whether he lives or dies. I'm inclined to just let nature take its course. If you'll excuse me, I'm going to go for my Bahamian friends. Whatever you choose to do to each other . . ."

A chill seeped into Kirk's bones. "What do you mean?" he said.

"Oh, come on, Steven," Bruderdam said. "Any small trust you may have had in this man, he betrayed it right from the beginning. Surely you care." Bruderdam paused, and when Kirk didn't say anything, continued. "Well then, what on earth do you think he meant to do with you?"

"Just what he did. Use me."

"Exactly. Use you, because of your particular skills, as a trump card for whatever unforeseen difficulties might arise. Get it? What that job turned out to be, after Vega doublecrossed us, was to find Vega and the missiles. And then what? You must realize that Smith wanted Vega dead and the Stingers back under his control. Which makes you a major liability, no?"

There was truth in Bruderdam's words. Yes, Smith might even have carefully planned Kirk's death. Strangely, though, Kirk couldn't generate any real passion about it. It was part of the game. If Bruderdam thought it was going to turn Kirk homicidal, he was mistaken. There had to be more. *Under the circumstances . . . Think about it . . . Something will come . . .*

"Say what you have to say, Bruderdam."

"All right. I figure there are two main reasons why you're here. First, you wanted to know what really happened in this unfortunate recent mess. For whatever purpose.

"Well, now you know. Our aim was action in Central America, and we had everything behind us: a president who basically agreed with us, the weight of public opinion, key people in the military and private sector, other government officials, some very ready and willing fighters, Nicaraguan and Cuban. We've even got supporters in place in the Sandinista Directorate itself, just waiting for us to commit.

"All the Stingers were supposed to provide was a little push. *Without* innocent people being killed. We didn't want what happened, the airliners, the Russian threats, none of it. Hell, if I wanted a global war, I could cause it with my satellite dish a lot faster and more certainly.

"One simple goal, Steven, and we would have achieved it if only Vega had kept himself under control."

Kirk nodded. None of this was news. "What's the second reason, Bruderdam?" he said.

"Ah, yes. The second reason you have come—and the more important one, I think—is this: I believe that you are seeking information about your family, and you thought that I might have some—"

Kirk bolted up out of the chair, but almost before he reached his feet the Beretta was back in Bruderdam's hand. It was pointed steadily at Kirk's heart and Kirk felt instinctively that Bruderdam's aim would be true.

"I would love to have you on our side, Steven," Bruderdam said. "But I have no disincentive to kill you."

Kirk stood there, willing the anger back, stilling the trembling. Bruderdam picked an infrared remote control unit off the desk with his other hand. Then he too got up. The pistol never wavered.

"Steven," Bruderdam said, shaking his head. "Steven, Steven. And you don't even know half the story yet. I would suggest that you consult with Mr. Smith. Then see what you feel like doing to him."

Bruderdam pressed one of the buttons on the remote, and a small section of wall behind the filing cabinets turned on hidden hinges, revealing the rungs of a ladder set into the concrete.

As he walked to the wall, Bruderdam said, "Enjoy yourselves, gentlemen. I'm sure you have a lot to talk about." He chuckled. "I wonder what we shall find when we open this room tomorrow."

He slipped behind the cabinets and started down the ladder to the basement. As he descended, the section of wall closed seamlessly shut. He took the remote control device with him.

59

Bruderdam avoided the road. Instead he took the footpath that ran along the north coast of the island. He was familiar enough with the way that he didn't need a light.

What a strange and interesting turn of events, he thought. Steven Kirk was a very capable man, no doubt about it. It was truly going to be amusing to see what he did to Smith. A real shame that his personal vision was so limited. But . . . there was no one who couldn't be made to see, eventually.

Or was there?

For a moment anger bubbled up inside him. How dare Kirk and his hired help insult him by thinking they could just waltz in and take over his island? As for Smith, he loathed the smug agency bastard. Bruderdam's hand trembled at the thought that he could have simply pulled the trigger and killed them both then and there. They'd cost him so much. The sight of their blood—blood that he'd personally spilled, not left to some hired hand—would have been so satisfying.

Reluctantly he forced the image from his mind. No, too messy. The logical thing to do was fly to Freeport, return the following day with a few official friends, and get the lot of them off Hammerhead as efficiently as possible. In the meantime he was going to enjoy the night on Grand Bahama. He knew a couple of girls from Nevis. . . .

He emerged from the scrub at the west end of the landing strip. As he had surmised, there was no one around the aircraft. Kirk would have come in with a small, well-disciplined group. Maybe two others besides himself and the woman. And both of them would have been needed in the pacification of staff quarters.

It had been ages since Bruderdam had flown the Huey—that's what he paid his pilot for—but once upon a time he'd learned. One never knew.

He got a flashlight and a couple of tools from the maintenance shed, then walked over to the chopper. Should be a piece of cake, he thought. Just a light breeze. No moon, but clear skies and all those glittering stars. And Grand Bahama was such a nice, well-lighted place.

Bruderdam worked quickly. First he released the tie-down ropes, checking the tail rotor at the same time. Then he did a cursory preflight inspection, as best he could from memory. He crawled under the belly of the Huey, pushed the fuel-drain valve, and let a few ounces of fuel spill out onto the concrete. Just to get any water condensation out.

After that, he climbed up the side of the aircraft, using the foot holes just behind the pilot's door. He walked around the Huey's flat roof deck, giving a cursory check to the rotor hub, mast, transmission mounts, and control rods. Finally he examined the Jesus nut at the top of the mast, the thing that kept the whole business aloft.

Satisfied, he climbed back down into the cockpit and sat in the left-hand seat, the position he preferred. The Huey's instrument panel was truncated on the left side so that the person in that seat could peer down through the plastic bubble at his feet. It was a little harder to see the gauges to the right, but Bruderdam liked to know what was going on below.

For a moment he just sat there, one hand on each of the control sticks, his feet on the pedals, remembering what everything did. Flying a helicopter was a lot more difficult than piloting a small plane.

His left hand was on the collective stick, which controlled motion in the vertical plane. Pulling or pushing on this increased or decreased the pitch of both main rotor blades concurrently, thus causing the chopper to either rise or fall. The throttle twist-grip in the handle of the collective stick must be worked in sync with the pitch changes. More throttle as he raised the collective, less as he lowered it.

The cyclic stick that rose from the floor between his legs controlled movement in the horizontal plane, and his right hand rested on that. Moving the cyclic left or right caused the blades to increase their pitch and move higher on one half of their cycle while feathering on the other half. This made the craft lean one way or the other.

Underneath, the two foot pedals operated the tail rotor, an anti-torque device. Because the main rotor turned clockwise, the fuselage wanted to turn in the opposite direction. The spinning tail rotor stabilized it by setting up a counter-force. This rotor could also be used to turn the aircraft on its axis, allowing its nose to shift left or right without any horizontal movement.

Keeping a chopper in the air required the pilot to fiddle with all of these controls, all of the time.

After sitting quietly for a few moments, Bruderdam switched on the cockpit lights. He leaned forward and ran his hand over the glowing instrument console to determine that all of the switches and circuit breakers were in their correct positions. It was a doublecheck by feel against what he could see. Then he pulled on his helmet and strapped himself in.

He twisted the throttle to the starting position click-stop and pressed the starter switch on his collective stick.

There was a shrill, whining sound as the electric motor began to turn the heavy rotors. Very slowly the blades began to accelerate, flipping past his field of vision. The fire caught in the turbine with a loud hiss.

The exhaust-gas temperature gauge flipped up into the red zone as the rotors spun to a blur, then it subsided back into the green. All of the other gauges looked normal. The Huey was ready to go.

Contrary to popular opinion, a helicopter does not lift straight up into the air. When Bruderdam opened the throttle to operating position and pulled back on the collective, the chopper's nose came up first, to be followed a moment later by the tail as he eased off. He hovered, stabilizing the craft, getting a feel for its tendency to drift and other idiosyncrasies.

When he was confident he could fly it, he turned it on its axis and aimed it toward the compound. Just a little look from above, to see what was happening, he told himself, and then on to Freeport. He nudged cyclic and collective, and the Huey rose some more and skimmed off to the west.

Kirk and Smith had stared at each other for what seemed a very long time.

Kill him, Kirk thought to himself. He deserves it. Kill him and get it over with. But he knew, even as he thought it, that Smith would have a small, concealed lethal weapon, something. He wouldn't go down easily, if he went down at all.

And then a tiny, nagging voice inside told him he didn't really know the whole story yet. If he killed Smith, how would he ever learn about his family . . .?

"Before you do anything rash, Steven," Smith said finally, "please consider something."

Here it comes, Kirk thought. It wasn't going to be a concealed weapon after all. As usual, Smith's protection would be his stock in trade: information.

"Right now," Smith said, "you probably think I masterminded the whole operation, and I wouldn't blame you." When Kirk didn't respond, Smith continued. "But think more carefully, Steven. You know me. I'm not a mastermind, I'm a facilitator. I'm a field man. I turn other people's dreams into reality."

"And in this case?" Kirk said.

"Every operation requires that someone supply the seed concept, and that others implement it."

"Spare me, Smitty. You're trying to convince me that Bruderdam ran the show?"

Smith dismissed the notion with an idle wave of his hand. "Bruderdam is a fool," he said. "Useful at times, but a man of too many bizarre personal tastes. An untrustworthy man, and a traitor. He's right, I did come here to kill him, and would have if you hadn't arrived. Now I fear he'll fly his helicopter to Freeport and we'll be left to deal with the Bahamians tomorrow."

"Not you. Not Bruderdam. Then who?"

Smith gazed steadily but neutrally into the younger man's eyes. Kirk closed to within arm's reach of Smith.

"The truth, Smitty." Kirk's voice had an unmistakably hard edge. "I won't kill you, but I can still cause you a lot of pain."

Smith's answer, when it came, caught Kirk completely off-guard. "Javier Vega and Eden Cabrera Cruz," he said. "I have the photos."

At first, the words meant nothing to Kirk. Yet they had hammered his head like sand-filled gloves. What . . .? Then, slowly, comprehension came to him.

"At the time," Smith said, "you didn't want me to know you were investigating the Contras. I believe your words were: 'Don't tell anyone about this. Especially not my control.' Is that about right?"

"My . . . father?" was all that Kirk could say. Even those words came only with great difficulty.

Smith nodded. "He's not the only member of the President's Foreign Intelligence Advisory Board who shares our interests. But in this instance he was more or less the controlling factor. Charles is a great man, Steven. And . . . much more of a father than you give him credit for."

Kirk felt physically ill. Conflicting emotions passed over him like clouds obscuring the sun. Before he'd even made up his mind what to do, his right arm lashed out in a blur and he struck Smith on the side of the neck with a hard sword-hand blow. He unconsciously pulled the punch enough to avoid rupturing the trachea, but Smith still fell like a stone.

Kirk stared down at the unconscious form for only a moment, feeling nothing. Then he knew he had to get moving. He might still have time to intercept Bruderdam.

He went over to the door and tried it. Locked. There

was no indication of how to open it. Somewhere there must be a button.

He raced back behind the desk. Now he could see the anteroom on one of Bruderdam's monitors. Andino was waiting patiently. The two girls still looked scared, Thomkins bored. Kirk searched for anything that might control the door. Negative. The remote control unit that Bruderdam took with him was probably the only device.

He examined the phone console until he figured out how to use the intercom and opened the line. "Piedad," he said.

He saw her look sharply toward the speaker. "Kirk," she said. "What's going on in there?"

"Smith's out cold, but Bruderdam's gone. There's a concealed exit in this room. He didn't show up out there?"

"No."

"All right, you walk those three out to the other house and warn Don and Seamus. You can leave Thomkins and the girls with them. Then come back in here. I'm going to try to find a way out, and I may need your help."

"Right," she said.

For the next few minutes Kirk thought about his predicament. He was in his underwear, locked inside a room with concrete walls about a foot thick, unbreakable plastic windows, a steel-core door, and an emergency exit that was undoubtedly protected with steel as well. He looked at the section of wall that hid the exit. Probably also controlled only by the missing remote. And possibly booby-trapped against being forced.

"I'm back."

He glanced up and saw Andino in the anteroom, alone.

"Don't happen to know the combination, do you?" he said.

"Walker's okay," she said, "but Croaghan's getting a little jittery. No sign of Bruderdam out there. You make any progress?"

"I don't know. . . . Wait a minute."

Asking about the combination had triggered an idea. There was an electronic keypad next to the outside of the door, but none on the inside. Of course. The room was designed to be difficult to break *into*. Bruderdam wouldn't have expected that someone might need to break *out* of it.

What did that mean? It meant that opening the door from this side would be a matter of triggering a solenoid that released the lock. It also meant that all the wiring was likely to be inside the interior wall.

Assume that the electronics were somewhere near the door. There would still have to be a power source. . . .

"I think I can get the door open," Kirk said. "Don't go away."

He walked over to the door. It was hinged on the left. He examined the wall adjacent to the right jamb: sheetrock. He rapped on it, moving his hand slowly from left to right.

Hollow . . . hollow . . . solid . . . hollow.

He envisioned what lay just out of sight. Furring strips would be attached to the concrete, with the sheetrock nailed to those strips, which were probably 2 x 2's. The room's wiring would be in the space created by the studs, between the sheetrock and the concrete.

He looked around for a suitable tool.

The missing Stinger caught his eye. Not the missile itself, but the solid-looking wooden table it rested on.

Kirk went over to it, lifted the Stinger components off and set them on the floor. Then he turned the table end-wise and jammed it against the wall.

He took in a deep breath and coiled his body, pulling his right thigh in close to his belly. He held the posture for a moment, then violently expelled the held breath. At the same time he lashed out with his foot, putting all the power of the thigh muscle behind it. The side of his heel struck the table leg about six inches from the floor, snapping it off in a crunch of splintering wood.

Kirk hefted the table leg. It was a serviceable sledge.

Back he went to the door. The wire he wanted would enter the door somewhere below the latching mechanism, he reasoned. He rapped the wall again, to make sure he was between furring strips, then smashed at the sheetrock with his makeshift hammer.

Within a few moments he had opened a fist-sized hole in the sheetrock. He reached into it and groped around. There were several wires inside.

He attacked the sheetrock again, slashing at it, pulling away chunks with his hands. The air filled with a choking dust, but he ignored it. The hole grew larger.

Finally he could trace the path of the wires. One of them came up from below and ran off to the right. Another came in from the right and angled upward. A third disappeared into a steel box adjacent to the door.

That would be the one. The locking mechanism would be inside that box.

Next he needed something sharp. He looked around, settled on the clock behind Bruderdam's desk. He went over to it and shattered its face with his club.

Taking some shards of glass, he returned to his hole in the wall. He pulled out a section of cable. It was standard Romex, two individually sheathed heavy copper wires, with a cased ground wire between them. There was no reason it should be hot, but Kirk still felt a twinge of nervousness as he began to saw away at it.

The gray plastic sheathing was tough. Kirk found that he made better progress if he just tried to slice away one small piece at a time. Slowly, steadily, he gouged out a shallow U-shaped cut in the plastic. He hit the black inner sheathing, slit that, and laid bare a short section of copper. Then he went to work on the other side, digging through the plastic and the white inner sleeve until copper showed there as well.

Now he needed a live wire.

Bruderdam had a brass lamp on his desk. Kirk unplugged it, then yanked the cord from its base, exposing the two small multi-stranded wires. He ripped the plastic groove down the middle and stripped back a couple of inches on either side with his teeth. He twisted the individual strands into two tight braids.

Then he returned for the last time to the hole in the wall.

"Piedad," he called. "I think I'm ready. I'm going to try to hot-wire the door lock. Put your hand on the knob, and if you hear the buzzer, open the door."

"Okay," she said. "I'm there."

Kirk, who had a healthy respect for electricity, didn't like what he had to do next, but he had no choice. He held the lamp cord in one hand, making sure the two wires were well apart from each other; an accidental short circuit would negate his efforts. Then, with the other hand, he plugged the cord into an outlet.

The wires were now hot. Cautiously he maneuvered

them around the edges of the exposed Romex cable and simultaneously touched all four copper surfaces together.

The solenoid activated and the buzzer sounded. Andino pushed the door open.

"Don't let it close," Kirk said.

With his foot he jerked the lamp cord's plug from the socket. He tossed the cord away and chocked the door open with the table leg; he wanted to be able to get at Smith without having to fight through the door from the outside. Then he stepped out into the anteroom and pulled on his clothes.

Hurriedly the two discussed alternatives. If Bruderdam was still in the building, then this would be a good place for one person to stay. But should someone search the house alone? Should one of them remain in the house and the other head for the airstrip? How about relief for Walker and Croaghan?

The discussion was only a few moments old when they heard the steady *whumping* of chopper blades.

Bruderdam eased the Huey down and buzzed low over the compound. He was running without any exterior lights.

Looking down through the plastic bubble at his feet, he saw immediately what had happened. There were two others, besides Kirk and the woman, and they were holding his staff at gunpoint. His people were lying facedown on the ground.

The chopper skimmed past at an altitude of forty feet. As it did, the noise and the prop wash agitated the scene below. Some of Bruderdam's people jumped to their feet. Don Walker stitched the ground next to them with a burst of gunfire.

"Nobody move!" he yelled. "Nobody fucking move!"

The tableau froze in place. Walker was tense. He didn't want to kill any of these people, but he had to maintain control of the situation. Who in the hell was up there in the chopper, Bruderdam? What the fuck was he doing? Andino should have briefed them better. She'd been in such a hurry.

If the damn thing buzzed them again, Walker thought, he might have to shoot at it and to hell with who was inside. Assume the enemy.

Croaghan was nervous. Something had gone wrong. His finger tightened on the trigger of his machine pistol. If anyone stepped out of line, even a little . . .

Bruderdam headed due west, across the lawn and out over Abaco Sound. He'd intended just to make for Freeport, of course, but now he began to reconsider.

Kirk and Smith were safely locked up. The other two were out there in the open, and the woman would probably be coming out of the house after hearing the sound of the chopper. If he returned, he might be able to nail the three of them, or at least provide enough covering fire for his own people to get into the action. He might well be able to reassert control, and have Smith and Kirk all to himself.

Why not? And besides . . . He felt a warmth spreading out from his belly. He'd never flown the Huey in assault mode before. It would be an added pleasure.

He eased the aircraft into a broad turn. It looped around to the south and came straight back at Hammerhead Cay, flying low and slow. When it crossed the bluff at the end of the island, he flipped a toggle switch on the side of the collective stick. Twin six-million-candlepower searchlights slung under the chopper's nose flashed on, and the dark land below was illuminated like a carnival midway.

The light was utterly blinding, a merciless glare that seemed to have weight and substance. Everyone on the ground was pinned down like a jacklit deer.

Bruderdam leaned the craft to the right and swept across the compound from main house to staff quarters. His fingers tightened on the cyclic stick and his right thumb poised itself over the firing button. He could see Kirk and the woman emerging from the house.

Kirk? he thought. What in the hell . . .?

Then he cursed himself for the moment's delay. His thumb tightened on the button, and the .30-caliber machine guns began to chatter like disembodied teeth.

Two lines of bullets raked across the compound. Kirk and Andino dived for cover behind a marble wall. The stone exploded inches above their heads.

The chopper continued on toward the staff building. One of Kirk's men—Bruderdam could see that it was a black man—was returning fire as he sprinted in the direction of his prisoners. Bruderdam adjusted the pitch of the Huey's blades slightly.

The helicopter's flight path now took it straight across the courtyard in front of the building. Bruderdam's people were scrambling to their feet, but they were right in the line of fire, and his thumb was glued to the button. There was no will in him to ease off.

The black man stopped in front of the two young girls, shielding them as best he could. He continued to fire at the chopper until the moment the death stream hit him, almost slicing him in two.

The others caught fire as well. Their bodies whirled and spun as the bullets hit them, six men and a woman jerking about madly in a grotesque parody of a disco dance floor.

Croaghan stared, unable to move a muscle, as the lines of bullets whined past him, barely missing, and lashed into the building behind him, smashing windows and shredding stucco. The cacophony was deafening.

Only then did he begin to scream.

As soon as the chopper had overflown them, Kirk and Andino were on their feet.

"See what you can do over there!" Kirk shouted.

Andino nodded and ran toward the awful carnage off to her right. The guns had stopped and the noise of the rotors was receding, leaving just the moans of the wounded and one high-pitched wail that seemed only half human.

Kirk heard it at the edge of his awareness and ignored it. He rushed back into the main house and across the second floor to the north wing.

Come back, Kirk thought to himself. Come back, you bastard.

Bruderdam made a tighter turn this time. He was determined to get the rest of them. Then he could land and hunt down whoever remained. He'd instilled fear in them now and they'd be no match for him. They would pay for the accidental deaths of his people.

He opened fire earlier, spraying the area around his house before sweeping across the open ground to the staff quarters.

Kirk exited the house on the west side, to the rear of the helicopter. He sprinted past the pool and out onto the broad lawn that led to the bluff. The satellite dish was a vague shadow to his right.

Out there in the open he jammed the earphones over his head, attached the grip stock, braced his feet, and slung the launch tube up onto his shoulder.

The chopper noise was receding again, to the southwest. He could follow it by its searchlights for a moment, then they went off.

He couldn't wait. He had no way of telling if Bruderdam intended to make another pass. It had to be now.

Kirk flipped the switch that released the argon coolant and activated the seeker. No tone came through the phones. He had forty-five seconds before the seeker was rendered useless. Find the chopper.

He peered through the gunsight. Systematically he scanned the night sky, searching for a small dark spot where there were no stars.

Fifteen seconds. Twenty. Thirty.

Sweat ran down his face. Where was the sonofabitch? If Bruderdam didn't turn, the chopper's profile would be very narrow and very hard to locate.

Kirk moved the sight in a careful, tight spiral, outward from the brightest star he could find.

Thirty-five seconds. Forty.

The tone shrilled in his ear like a siren. *Lock-on.* Kirk waited two more seconds just to be certain, then pulled the trigger.

Die, you murdering sonofabitch.

The twenty-fourth Stinger popped out of its tube. A moment later, the rocket motor ignited in a sudden flash of light and the missile was gone.

Bruderdam was one hundred feet over Abaco Sound and three-quarters of a mile off Hammerhead Cay. His back was to the island, so he never saw what was coming.

The missile crossed the intervening space in two and a half seconds. Point of impact was low on the chopper's tail. When the warhead exploded, it sheared off the tail rotor and ruptured critical hydraulics. The aircraft immediately began to pitch and yaw, turning wildly on its axis now that the anti-torquing rotor was gone.

Bruderdam, taken by surprise, didn't realize what had happened. Disoriented by the erratic motion of the chopper, he frantically manipulated his sticks, stomped at foot pedals that no longer did anything, began to make mistakes. He fought to regain control, but it was a losing battle.

The Huey plummeted from the sky, slammed into the sea, and quickly plunged beneath the surface. As it sank, it stirred up the bioluminescent plankton, which marked its passage with brief sparkling pinpoints of light before the waters turned black again.

PART VII

SMITH

Lord, why is your heart not good? I will
bring up now the drum from the under-
world, land of the dead; I will bring up
the beater from the mouth of darkness.

—*Gilgamesh*, XII-i

60

"I just wish I could have gotten at Bruderdam's computer files," Croaghan was saying. "God, I'll bet there's some stuff in there."

"We had no choice," Kirk said.

"I know," Croaghan muttered, feeling a little guilty that he was having these thoughts when lives had been at stake. "But there's more. So much more."

Andino laid a hand on his arm. "You've done everything you could possibly do," she said. "Your brother is at peace."

"Hell, my brother was always at peace; who if not him? I don't know, maybe what I'm doing is for me, not Dermot."

The three of them were in Kirk's room at the Freeport Holiday Inn, drinking cold drinks and enjoying the sudden pleasure of freedom after three days in jail.

Negotiations for their release had taken awhile, even though they had behaved admirably. They'd quickly evacuated the island by forcing Bruderdam's pilot, who'd been only slightly injured during the chopper attack, to fly the Aero-Commander to Grand Bahama. And they'd willingly turned themselves in.

Two of the more seriously wounded—one of the young girls and Bruderdam's assistant, Thomkins—survived due to their prompt action. The household's cook, the other girl, and the pilot had also made it. The rest were dead.

The local government had been perplexed at first. Then, as talks with Washington became more specific, it began to realize what had happened. An international terrorist ring had been operating out of one of the Bahamas, and these people had smashed it. No Bahamian nationals had been visibly involved. It was surely best to leave it that way.

Nevertheless, officials in Freeport had to express their disapproval of paramilitary activities in some way, and foot-dragging was it. By the time terms were agreed to, it was late at night, and the detainees were turned loose to sleep over in the posh hotel, courtesy of a U.S. government that had decided it would be quietly grateful for what they had done.

In the morning, Kirk and Croaghan would fly back to Washington, while Andino would be prepared for deportation to Managua. She'd be met in Miami by federal agents and escorted to the flight to Honduras. There was no way she'd be permitted to remain on U.S. soil.

Since she wasn't American, there'd even been a half-hearted attempt to keep her in jail overnight, but Kirk had raised such a stink it'd been deemed easier to let her out. She wasn't going to cause any more trouble in the Bahamas.

Smith, of course, was already long gone. He'd been freed two days earlier, after making a couple of carefully worded phone calls.

"You want them, then keep after them," Kirk said.

Croaghan chuckled. "You think I'll get my old job back, now I'm a hero?" he said.

"You can come at them from the outside," Kirk said. "And you do still have some contacts who might be willing to work with you."

"Ah, I don't know," Croaghan said. "Now that I think about it, maybe I'm more beat than I thought. The damn shadow government's like poison ivy. You wipe it out in one place and it just pops up in another. Pretty soon you go crazy with the herbicide bottle and end up killing all the good plants along with the bad."

"The price of freedom is vigilance," Andino said. "One of your own presidents said that. We recognize that the Revolution is not an end result, it's a process. If we don't keep correcting its faults, it will fail."

Croaghan started to take issue, then thought better of it. The woman was a decent person, a fighter, and far braver than he. It would serve no purpose to argue politics with her.

Instead he said, "Well, I don't know about you guys,

but I'm done in. I think I better get some sleep. Who knows what kind of ordeal they're going to put us through tomorrow."

He nodded to the other two, who wished him good night, and left the room.

When he'd gone, Kirk and Andino sat in silence for a few moments. Kirk had a thought he hadn't had in what seemed like a long time, that Piedad really *did* remind him of Susanna. Physically, for certain. And they shared something of the same spirit. Andino, of course, was far more serious about her life. She had to be.

Susanna had been so . . . young.

"I've wanted some time alone with you," he said.

She looked him in the eye and he knew he had her undivided attention.

He sighed. "Bruderdam talked to me."

"I assumed so."

"I didn't say anything before because of Seamus. I don't want him in this until after I finish what I have to do. Others were involved besides Smith and Bruderdam. I . . . I know some of them."

She nodded.

"But there's more. You've done everything you said you'd do for me, and then some. I owe you. So . . . I don't know whether this is something you really want to hear, but I wouldn't feel right holding back on you."

He took a deep breath and let it out. "It was a large-scale conspiracy," he said. "Americans in and out of government. Contras. And . . . people on the ground in Nicaragua. Bruderdam said that at least one member of the Directorate was in his pocket. I don't know who. But that person, along with others in Managua, was going to support the invasion from inside. I've got no reason to doubt that it's the truth. I'm sorry."

There was a pause, then she said, "Thank you for telling me. I'm not surprised. What I said about vigilance, I believe. We will find the traitor." Another pause. "And what will you do now, Kirk? Did you find out about your family?"

"No. But I think I know who does know."

"Will you kill him, if he had something to do with their deaths?"

Would he? Kill his own father?

Then he wondered why he'd even had the thought. Charles may have been involved in the blackmail plot, but there was nothing to suggest that that had anything to do with the deaths of his son's wife and child. Smith, on the other hand . . .

"'I don't know. I might."

"You are a strange man, Kirk, not like the others. You have your own code, and it touches that of your countrymen only here and there." She smiled. "I believe that you would make a good revolutionary."

He laughed. "I'd be sent for reeducation so often," he said, "you'd have to keep the room made up for me."

"No, I don't think you know what I mean," she said. "What you have flows in your blood. No amount of education could instill it in you, and no amount of pain can drive it out of you."

He flushed, at first with embarrassment, and then . . .

Neither would have been able to say who was the initiator, unless it was Andino with her words, but there was a mutual assent as they came together, wrapped arms around each other, felt the warmth that had been dammed up by too many cold and calculating days finally spill over.

For a long time they just held each other, enjoying the close fit of their bodies, letting the tensions that had driven their relationship drain away. She was as he'd imagined, Kirk thought. Soft, pliant, and yet solid as hard-packed earth. He breathed deeply, drawing in the scent of her. And abruptly began to laugh.

She looked questioningly up at him.

"Don't worry," he said. "It's just that, I don't think either of us has had a shower in days and, well, I believe we could probably use one."

She smiled too, then.

They spent a long time at it, drawing down the Holiday Inn's hot water supply, soaping and rinsing and exploring with none of the usual awkwardness of strangers. It was almost as if he had seen her nude before, her small breasts and narrow waist and sturdy hips and beautiful, muscular legs. He savored the Indian in her, the coppery skin, the wispy underarm hair, the stout nipples with their nearly black areolas.

And yet . . .

After they had toweled off, she pulled him close to her and said, "It is your wife, isn't it?"

Hearing the words brought it all home to him. As much as he was drawn to his naked companion, the surge of sexual desire hadn't come. It *was* Susanna. And Scottie, too. And Charles. But mostly it was the lost partner of whom this woman reminded him so much.

That part wasn't over yet. Until it was . . . He marveled at Andino's insight and felt a rush of affection for her.

He nodded. "Think we'll ever have our moment?" he asked.

"You never know." She shrugged.

"Maybe by then sex won't be counterrevolutionary."

She laughed, and then he laughed with her. They laughed and laughed as neither had, perhaps, for years, until the tears slicked their faces.

And Kirk, for a long pleasant moment, stopped thinking about what he still had to do.

61

Kirk and Croaghan flew home together on a plane that also carried Don Walker's body. He was going to get a state funeral. The Vice-President was scheduled to speak.

After deplaning in Washington, they parted with a quick handshake. Croaghan was going to hole up with his computers, to try and put together a chronicle of the shadow government's activities over the previous thirty years. After which . . . After which, he didn't know what. Kirk wished him luck.

Then Kirk had taken a long walk, steeling himself for what he had to do in spite of the sense of dread that clung to him like a damp spiderweb. It was a dread as yet unfocused, which made it all the worse.

He had never felt so alone. He longed to just take the

expense money and disappear again. Perhaps to some off-the-track Caribbean island like Dominica or Montserrat. Make a living in the tourist trade. Marry someone local who didn't know where Pennsylvania Avenue was. Raise a family.

It was a warm and simple dream, and it was within reach. But not yet.

In the end, he did the only thing possible. He headed for the Metro.

As Kirk rode out to Friendship Heights, he found that scenes from his life flicked past his interior eye like the lights of the subway tunnel. Invariably, there would come a freeze-frame on himself as a boy, squatting cross-legged on the mat, the sweat dripping from his chin, telling his *sensei* in all earnestness that the reason he was studying martial arts was to learn how to kill his father with his bare hands.

He had meant it then, but time and physical separation had blunted the feelings. Though he was still stiff and awkward with Charles, the fact remained that it was Charles he'd gone to when he wanted someone he thought he could trust.

And he'd been betrayed once again.

Or had he? His emotions, after all, were inflamed because of what *Smith* had said. The same Smith who made no distinction between lies and truth, who thought nothing of sacrificing innocent lives in pursuit of his political—or were they merely personal?—ends.

Yet Smith's words had jangled a bell inside him, a bell that rang true. An obscure connection existed between the Stinger affair and the fate of his family, he still felt that. It went back to Smith's original recruitment pitch, the promise of revelations about Susanna and Scottie. Smith wouldn't have dangled that particular carrot without having something, no matter how small, to deliver if need be. He just didn't work that way. He never made a move unless *all* his bases were covered. But it would be hopeless to try to pry information out of him; he never gave up anything he didn't want to.

However, Kirk now knew that Charles had been involved with Smith all along. So there was a good possibility that whatever Smith knew, Charles knew. In addition, if those who had taken the lives of his wife and child *had* come from Central America, that was all the more reason for Charles to have known.

If he did, then Kirk could not avoid a final confrontation. It wasn't just that his father was bound to be an easier source of information than Smith. Charles was the *proper* person to hear the whole story from. He must be made to answer the inevitable, consequential question: why hadn't he told his son what he knew?

Those were the important things. Kirk found that he couldn't care less that a highly placed agency man and an influential PFIAB member might be traitors. The underbelly of the country was full of such people, ready to trade their country in a heartbeat for a dollar or a yen; America would survive if she deserved to. At least these two weren't primarily motivated by profit.

Focus on Susanna and Scottie. Fuck the rest.

The mind-images flickered, and the picture of the young martial artist was replaced by a snapshot of Kirk's own six-month-old son, clutching daddy's shirtfront with tiny hands, and Kirk being flooded with feelings of love, the only love he could remember knowing and maybe the only real love life has to offer, that of parent for child, the sole love that is absolute and unconditional.

Had Charles ever felt that way about the infant Steven? Had he held the baby at all? There were so many of his generation who had not, and it was obvious from the way they had chosen to run the world.

The train pulled into the station, and Kirk was once again aware of the anxiety that had dogged him from the moment Smith had spoken the names of the two Nicaraguan exiles.

The dread enclosed him as he came up from underground and made his way through the concrete-and-steel maze of Friendship Heights. It slowed his step as he walked into Kenwood, feeling as always like he was entering alien territory even though the magnificent cherries were now in full bloom. It had turned his feet to cement by the time he stood among a few fallen blossoms, gazing up at the house on the knoll.

The house's grim facade—its fieldstone, slate, and heavy exposed timbers—stood in stark contrast to the splendor of the flowering trees surrounding it.

For several long minutes Kirk just stood there, breathing the sweetly scented air, unable to will his legs to motion. Thoughts of the peaceful, remote Caribbean island passed through his mind again. He could turn around; he could walk out of this life and into another, and no harm would be done; he didn't need to know everything. Whatever happened here wasn't going to bring Susanna and Scottie back to life.

But when he tried to force his body to turn, it refused. In the end, when his muscles finally did respond, they would propel him in only one direction, forward.

Esperanza answered the door. She seemed genuinely glad to see him. For the first time, he felt a surge of affection for the diminutive Salvadoran woman—she'd been through a lot, and he'd always failed to credit her strength—and he hugged her. Though astonished, she hugged him back.

She knew, though, that he had not come to see her. She motioned him toward Charles's study and disappeared.

Charles wasn't diddling with his computer this time, he was just waiting, as though specifically for his son. Kirk looked at the frail figure with the sunken blue eyes and close-cropped silver hair. Charles looked very . . . old. A lot older than he had just a few weeks earlier.

Kirk wondered if this was how that first sweet rush of parental love always ended up, with two grown men who neither understood nor trusted each other, at opposite ends of a room that might as well be an unbridgeable chasm. Was it different for other people?

"Sit down, Steven," Charles said. There was a weariness in his voice that seemed almost absolute.

Steven walked to the mahogany desk and sat down heavily, across from his father. The weariness was a contagious disease.

"Congratulations," Charles said. "Henrik Bruderdam was tough. I wouldn't have thought you could take him so easily."

"It wasn't easy," Steven said. "Five people died. Not counting Bruderdam."

"You've talked with Mr. Smith, I take it."

"Yes."

"And you know?"

"Not the whole story. Smith wouldn't. I decided it would be better to ask you."

"I see. You want to know everything?"

Kirk nodded. "Start with Susanna and Scottie," he said. "End with today."

"It will make you hate me—"

"I'll take that risk."

"—hate me even more. But . . . at least you will understand me. That has been a long time in coming."

"Just tell me."

Charles reached over and grasped the head of the cane that leaned against the desk next to him. He turned it beneath his hand as he spoke, rotating it back and forth. The tip of the cane twirling in the rug made a small sound reminiscent of a distant scythe, cutting grain.

"Smith told you about the exile Grenadians living in Managua?" Charles said.

"Yes," Steven said.

"They hate you. They believe you subverted the People's Revolutionary Government, thereby causing the extremist takeover and the subsequent American invasion."

"Not any more. There's someone down there right now, setting the record straight."

"Well, they *did* believe it, that's the important thing. They've been looking for you ever since they fled their country, and last summer they finally located you. When they did, they set out to kill you. You and your entire family. Which is when we grabbed them." He looked over at his son. "Smith explained who *we* are?"

"He said there were others on the PFIAB." Steven shook his head. "White-haired terrorists. I don't need to know their names."

Charles nodded. "I expect that you wouldn't approve," he said, "but we feel we're doing the only thing. There are times when the constraints of political consideration—"

"You can skip the self-justification."

Charles paused then continued, his tone softer, more resigned. "All right, the original warning came through the agency. I was informed at once, of course, and we were able to get to the assassination team just after they entered the country. Unfortunately, there were five of them in the hit team and we only got two. That's when we had to . . . begin to negotiate."

Steven felt the rage welling up in him. "God damn you, Charles, you better not be saying—"

Charles held up his hand, and there was such sorrow in his face that Steven was brought up short.

"It's not what you think," Charles said. "Two of the remaining three went to ground while the other opened communications with me. If we could have nailed all five, that might have been the end of it, but we couldn't. So we tried to deal. When we didn't get anywhere, they . . . kidnapped Esperanza."

The old man's face clearly showed what that had meant.

Charles paused for a moment, then continued. "We had to let the other two go," he said. "I got Esperanza back and a promise that they wouldn't kill you or my grandson. My part of the bargain was that . . . that I wouldn't tell you what had happened." Charles's head dropped and he stared down at his lap. The cane slipped to the floor. "God help me."

The revelation triggered waves of nausea, which Steven struggled to control.

When he could finally speak, he said hoarsely, "The car bomb was never meant for me."

Charles shook his head. "No."

"And Scottie? *What about Scottie?*"

Charles looked up. There were tears trickling down the furrows in his face.

"An accident," Charles said. "A terrible accident . . . When I heard what they'd done, we went after them with every resource we had. But we never found them."

Steven sat motionless, consumed by the horror. In his mind he saw Esperanza's words, written in blood: *It is rarely wise to unbury the dead.*

"Steven," Charles said, "you must understand. I had no choice. I believed I had *saved* Scottie."

"Susanna . . . forgive me . . ."

"I know it won't replace your family, but Christ I've tried to make it up to you, Steven," Charles pleaded. "Can't you see that?"

Oh no, Steven thought. *Oh God. Please, no.* "What do you mean?" he managed.

"The Stingers, Steven. The Stingers."

"The Stingers? That was for *me?*"

"For you. For Susanna and Scottie. For the country, too. We *needed* to convince the President to commit troops. Once the Communists were defeated, and our allies took control of Nicaragua, we could walk in and grab the people who wired the car bomb. They'd be war criminals. I would have turned them over to *you* if I could."

His expression begged for some sign of forgiveness.

"I don't believe this!" Steven said, his voice rising in pitch to a near shriek. "You caused the deaths of hundreds of innocent people! You almost started World War III out of some crazy notion of . . . of . . ,"

Of what? Steven couldn't put a word to it. The combination of twisted logic, false patriotism, and thirst for vengeance didn't have a name.

"And you thought I'd *thank* you?" Steven's tone was shrill, unfamiliar even to himself.

He jerked himself to his feet, pitching the chair backward onto the carpet, and glared down at Charles. His own wild mix of emotions was something else he couldn't put a name to. He only knew that he had to get out before he was suffocated by the foul air in this room.

Abruptly, Steven did an about-face and started for the door.

"Steven," Charles called after him. "Steven . . ."

Steven stopped, then turned slowly to face the other man.

"Father," he said, nearly choking on the word that he hadn't been able to speak in years. "You have no wife. And no grandchild." He paused. "And no son."

He felt an overwhelming urge to leave some sort of mark on this room that he would never visit again, yet he knew that any gesture he made would be as hollow as his heart.

So he simply walked away. Out of the stone house, and into the pink-and-white glow of the famed Kenwood cherry blossoms. He didn't look back.

62

"You know, Smith," Kirk said, "I was thinking on the way over here that the real criminal class in this country has moved inside the government, where there's so much more protection than there is on the street. So we get people like Liddy and North and all the rest, who commit their crimes and then go on to become very wealthy folk heroes. And you. Is that what you want too?"

Kirk had come directly from the turbulent meeting with his father and Smith, like Charles, had almost seemed to be expecting him.

His opening words were time-wasters. It had only been by a tremendous effort of will that Kirk had managed to bring himself under control, and keep his outward appearance calm. That was essential, because a small, insistent inner voice nagged at him, saying: It was too easy to get in to see him. He's prepared. Be careful.

"An interesting analysis, Steven," Smith said, "though flawed. We're not criminals. We're an integral *part* of contemporary government; it couldn't function without us.

"Just think of the presidents of your lifetime. Carter and Kennedy, a couple of intellectuals who couldn't get along with anyone. Stumbling mediocrities like Bush and Johnson and Ford. Eisenhower and Reagan, old men who were too dim to be capable of dealing with anything more complex than whether or not to salt their eggs. Our incumbent, who isn't much better. And Nixon, who was interested only in Nixon.

"Given leadership like that, we're a *necessity*. And don't think they didn't know about us. Some of them didn't like us, but they all realized that we need to be."

Smith paused, then added, "But no, I'm not Gordon Liddy. I like my job. I don't crave notoriety."

"Yeah," Kirk said. "I'll bet you don't. Never the light of day, eh?" He paused, then added, "What was it you told me? 'I'm a facilitator,' wasn't it? 'I'm not a master-mind.' Uh-huh."

"I was hoping you'd come here a little less combative," Smith said.

"But you knew I'd come."

Smith shrugged. "It seemed likely. On the one hand, there was always the chance that you'd finally understand why we—and I stress the *we*—had to do what we did, and accept it, and that you'd recognize your natural place among us. The alternative was that you'd return here to kill me. It would appear to me that it's the latter."

Smith's poise was eerie. What did he know? Kirk wondered. What *could* he know that would compare with the horrors already revealed?

The inescapable conclusion for Kirk, after he'd left the house in Kenwood, was that Smith's fingerprints were all over everything in sight. Charles may have proposed the Stinger operation, but Smith had unquestionably run it. More important now, it was a virtual certainty that he'd also orchestrated the deal that had ended with the deaths of Susanna and Scottie.

Kirk felt as if he'd been unlayering an onion and was approaching its center. Charles didn't have the nerveless-ness needed to negotiate with terrorists. Smith did. Smith would have been the one the old man turned to.

"You don't seem concerned," Kirk said.

"I'm concerned," Smith said. "Matters of life and death concern me. But I know you well, Steven, far better than you think I do. For you to kill me would be a highly irrational act, and you are not an irrational man."

Smith was sitting in his chair, facing Kirk, who sat on the couch only a few feet away. Kirk could be on him long before he could react. Why?

"What happened to my family?" Kirk said.

"I would have thought your father had told you," Smith said.

"I want to hear it from you."

"We agreed to release our hostages in exchange for theirs, and a few other considerations, such as your life. Charles only wanted you to live, Steven. And Esperanza, of course."

A few other . . . And suddenly, Kirk knew it all.

"You bastard," he said, his voice little more than a feral snarl. "It wasn't just not telling me. You actually traded away Susanna's life, didn't you?"

The room was silent as a churchyard. There was no jazz on the stereo, this time.

"Didn't you?"

Smith's moon face was emotionless. "The child wasn't supposed to be there," he said. "No one, especially not your father, would have—"

Kirk lunged at him, delivering a forearm blow that flattened Smith's nose against his face and sent his glasses skittering off across the floor. The two men tumbled backward over the chair as the blood flowed onto Smith's spotless shirt front. He held up his arms to ward off any further punches, but Kirk slipped a right hand through that smashed his cheekbone.

"Steven," he burbled, "stop. Listen to me, you don't know everything. Please. *Stop* it."

Kirk's hand hung in midair for a moment, then it went inside his jacket and emerged with his gun. He snapped back the slide, chambering a round.

"Yeah," he said, "what's the point?" He jammed the muzzle of the silencer against Smith's forehead and flicked off the safety. "For Susanna, Smitty. And—"

Smith looked him right in the eyes and said calmly, "If you pull the trigger, Steven, you'll never see your son alive again."

The sound of a gale force wind whistled in Kirk's ears. His finger reflexively tightened on the trigger and the weapon fired. Kirk never heard the paltry noise it made.

A minute passed. Two minutes. Kirk was frozen where he knelt over Smith's supine body. He didn't want to know. He'd thought he'd known it *all*, but there was more, there was always more, and he didn't want to know what it was. He wanted to turn away from it, and it wouldn't let him.

The horror pulled at him, tried to force him into that dark place that was empty of everything except his deepest fear.

Kirk stared at the spot where the slug had burrowed into the floor, inches from Smith's head. Then he looked at the man beneath him. Nothing made sense any more. Nothing related to anything else.

"Please let me up," Smith said.

Mechanically, Kirk complied. Smith got to his feet and brushed at his suit, although he could not whisk away the blood. He took out a handkerchief and crimped it under his nose as he went to his desk.

Kirk stood where he was, rooted to the spot, with the dread still wrapped tight around him and the floor threatening to give way under his feet.

Smith returned with a photograph. When Kirk made no move to take it, Smith pulled up his arm and shoved it into his hand. Kirk's head moved as if it belonged to someone else. Without willful effort, he found himself looking down at a picture of his dead son.

Only this wasn't the charred corpse of a six-month-old. It was a seemingly healthy infant. Half a year older. Very much alive.

It couldn't be Scottie. But it was. Kirk knew, with the certainty of a parent, that he was staring at his own child.

"We couldn't trust the terrorists," Smith said. "So we monitored the entire operation. Susanna left the baby in the car in the parking lot, while she went into the store, and we switched them. Susanna never suffered. She never had time to realize her son was gone."

"*Switched* them! Switched *who*?" Kirk's voice was a screech, and he was hyperventilating.

"Please, Steven. The other baby was already dead, but close enough in appearance. My God, you don't think we would have sacrificed a living child. . . ."

No. It didn't make any sense. Smith couldn't possibly have been so prepared at the moment the assassins planted the bomb. Unless . . .

Kirk knew that he had finally arrived at the center of the onion.

The hairs stood up all over his body and he realized that he had never before understood the derivation of the expression "to see red." It had nothing to do with waving a flag in front of a bull. It referred to the way the world looked when the blood of utmost rage boiled behind one's eyes.

"*You* killed her!" Kirk screamed. "Not the Grenadians! That was your *deal*! *That's* the only way it *could* have been!"

Kirk raised the pistol again and aimed it at Smith's

head. His gun hand trembled, and he braced it with his other.

"Don't, Steven," Smith said. "Scottie is alive. But if anything happens to me, the people who are holding him have their orders."

For a moment, Kirk was prepared to pull the trigger anyway. For a horrifying moment, even poor little Scottie's life didn't stack up against ridding the world of this man.

But then, slowly, Kirk lowered his arm. The fire that had been roaring inside him subsided into a small, steady flame. There would be a way. He would have Scottie back, and Smith would pay. With his life. However long it took, Kirk would not rest until he found the way.

As if detached from his body, Kirk watched the scene play itself out.

"What do you want?" he asked.

"Simple," Smith said. "As I said once before, I want you to work with us. You're a valuable man, and I think in time you'll come to agree with what we do. When that happens, your son will be returned to you."

The room seemed empty of everything but anticipation. There was silence. Then, from some far-off place, came the sound of a novice practicing the trumpet.

Kirk nodded.

EPILOGUE

Seamus Croaghan was working like a man possessed. He worked without regard to time, and it was night when his doorbell rang. Croaghan went to the door carrying the small .38-caliber pistol he'd recently bought.

He kept it always within reach these days. He'd learned too much about the shadow government to feel secure.

The anxiety faded when he peered through the peephole and saw Steven Kirk. He opened up.

"Jesus, Kirk," he said, feeling an unexpected rush of affection. "You look like five acres of hell. Come on in."

Kirk walked into the apartment. He'd come to Croaghan from the Watergate, the cold fire burning within him, the fire that he knew would never go out until Smith was finally defeated.

When they'd settled themselves over a cup of coffee laced with rum, Kirk said, "Smith was behind it. The whole thing."

Croaghan nodded. "I know," he said.

"But there's more."

And Kirk told him the whole story.

When he'd finished, Croaghan just shook his head and said, "The evil bastard. I don't know how you kept yourself from pulling the trigger."

"I nearly couldn't. But I want Scottie back, Seamus. There's a way to get to him, and I want to find it. There has to be a clue in Smith's files. That's the one advantage we have. He doesn't know that we know how to get in there." He paused, then added, "You're my best hope of finding what I want. I need your help."

"You don't even have to ask," Croaghan said.

"You'll be risking your life."

"I'm already doing that. Just from what I've put together so far, I can ruin about four dozen very influential people. This scandal reaches from the foot soldiers right into the Oval Office. My life isn't worth diddley-shit.

"We'll find your son, and the pope can kiss my ass if we don't rescue him, and then I will personally hold Smith down while you rip his throat out."

Kirk studied his companion, a wild-eyed, florid-faced man in a rumpled brown corduroy suit worn over a T-shirt printed with the message: I ♡ Washington.

"Why?" Kirk said. "Why, Seamus?"

"You know," Croaghan said, "I've thought about that. A lot. And what it is, I guess I just came to the end of my rope. It might sound corny, but I believe in this country. I believe it ought to be as good as it *can* be. I believe that the Constitution is more than an antiquated scrap of paper that's lost its relevancy.

"The past thirty years, we've just gone along, getting fed one shit sandwich after another, until we *almost* can't tell what we're eating any more. Penny-ante crooks somehow get transformed into heroes, the people tolerate all kinds of crimes being committed in their name, even presidents have to get pardoned.

"The bastards have got to be stopped, Kirk, and I think they will, because this time they went a little too far. When they start murdering their own people, no one will be able to look the other way. It's only gonna take one person to say, 'Enough. God damn it, we've had enough. We're Americans, and by Christ we don't do this kind of thing.' One person to say it, and say it so loud that everyone can hear."

Croaghan paused, then smiled. "Ah, hell, Kirk," he said. "I talk a good speech, don't I? You want to know the simple truth? I loved my brother."

"I guess that makes us about the same," Kirk said. "I love my son." *And you too, buddy. You, too.*

"Well, let's find him, then."

"Yeah, let's do that," Kirk said.

AUTHOR'S NOTE

This novel is, in part, about the functioning of a computer-age Presidential Administration during a major, unanticipated crisis. To the best of the author's ability, all weapons, aircraft, computer systems, and other hardware have been accurately depicted. Fidelity has also been maintained to other impersonal details, such as physical aspects of the White House, its routines, and the normal interrelationships of staff advisers.

During the course of the story, certain real persons are named, and matters of actual historical record are referred to. However, all characters herein are entirely the product of the author's imagination and are not intended to bear any resemblance to their real-life counterparts, either past or present. The events portrayed, while hopefully realistic, are likewise completely fictitious. Nor is the author suggesting a connection between any real persons, named or unnamed, and the kinds of illegal activities described in the book.

There is, of course, considerable evidence that the "shadow government" does in fact exist, and that it has done so since at least the early 1960s. If so, the extent of the damage it has done to American democracy remains to be seen.

ABOUT THE AUTHOR

Doug Hornig's *Foul Shot* was nominated for the Edgar Award for Best First Novel of 1984. His other novels include *Hardball*, *The Dark Side*, *Deep Dive* and *Waterman*. A former federal government employee, he now lives in Virginia.